THE RESET

JACK MOORE

First edition 2022
Ebook: 978-1-7367398-8-4
Soft cover: 978-1-7367398-2-2

twitter.com/theresetnovel

This book is dedicated to whoever makes it to the other side.

"Intersubjective entities depend on communication among many humans rather than on the beliefs and feelings of individual humans. Many of the most important agents in history are intersubjective. Money, for example, has no objective value. You cannot eat, drink or wear a dollar bill. Yet as long as billions of people believe in its value, you can use it to buy food, beverages and clothing. If the baker suddenly loses his faith in the dollar bill and refuses to give me a loaf of bread for this green piece of paper, it doesn't matter much. I can just go down a few blocks to the nearby supermarket. However, if the supermarket cashiers also refuse to accept this piece of paper, along with the hawkers in the market and the salespeople in the mall, then the dollar will lose its value. The green pieces of paper will go on existing, of course, but they will be worthless."

Yuval Hariri, *Homo Deus*

"The U.S. government has a technology, called a printing press (or, today, its electronic equivalent), that allows it to produce as many U.S. dollars as it wishes at essentially no cost. By increasing the number of U.S. dollars in circulation, or even by credibly threatening to do so, the U.S. government can also reduce the value of a dollar in terms of goods and services, which is equivalent to raising the prices in dollars of those goods and services."

Former Fed Chairman Ben Bernanke

PROLOGUE

11 DAYS AFTER THE RESET — NORTHERN ONTARIO, CANADA

THE NIGHT AIR is damp and cold. Zero light pollution. I sit in silence with Alison by a fire outside a small, isolated cottage on a lake near Huntsville, Ontario, Canada. The fire burns hot and orange. It crackles. Alison curls into herself, shivering as I grab another brick of US $100 bills and slide it into the glowing oven of embers. I stare as the bundle's bill strap burns off and I watch an image of Ben Franklin slowly curl, blacken and disappear. We are burning money to stay warm.

"This is fucking insane, Charlie."

I'm too tired to respond verbally so I offer a half smile and drop back into the janky lawn chair; it sags under my weight. Heat turns a tiny pocket of sap inside a log into vapor and an ember pops. Sparks firework. Alison turns and vomits into the grass beside her chair. I see ribs through her thin sweater as she buckles forward.

"Sorry," she spits.

"Don't be sorry."

Things have stopped getting worse, but it will be a long time before they get better.

There is the issue of Alison and I: broken up but still together. And there is the matter of the plus on the stick. And 500 miles south-east of here, America has finally snapped. New York City is burning. Coming apart at the seams.

In the Fall of 2008, Ben Bernanke jammed a needle full of monetary heroin directly into the heart of the financial system and the US economy snapped back to life. But the system never returned to full health. Instead, for years it stumbled forward, undead like Frankenstein's monster, pumped full of methamphetamine. Every time Ben or Janet or Jay or whoever tried to wean the market off the drugs, the economy got the flu.

This is the story of what happens when a society refuses to take the pain of withdrawal. This is the story of how trees do not grow to the sky. This is the story of how capitalism committed suicide.

PART ONE

COUNTDOWN

TRADING IS AN ART.

A science.

A drug.

An addiction.

A passion.

An action and a reaction.

Rhythm, timing and mojo.

Man vs. computer.

An organic ecosystem, infested with bots.

The ultimate puzzle.

Unsolvable.

Today is Thursday. I strap on my Nintendo CeeMee goggs and open ↑Marketz!↓ with a haptic wave. The German NeueMark (NDM) rips higher as investors flock to the safe haven currencies. Ever since Black Sunday (the night Italy pulled out of the euro, triggering a global liquidity crisis and flash crashes in the euro, crypto, and global bond markets), people have rushed into Swiss and German assets and out of everything else. Everyone wants the hell out of Dodge. And DOGE. The NeueMark is up again, almost 2% higher than yesterday's close.

I sense that the rally is overdone, but any attempt to top tick a market like this is suicide, so I scale in. I sell 50 million NDM/USD at first, to test the waters. Over the next few minutes, I slowly scale the position up to 500 million. There is no shortage of buyers. I started selling at 1.8500. I added at 1.8600. 1.8650 trading now. If it goes above 1.8750, I'm pretty much screwed. My position is too big but it is too late and there is no CTRL-Z in trading. I get excited sometimes and put on positions that are way too big.

I have great instincts and terrible discipline.

The market rallies to 1.8680. 1.8690 paid. The price is still rising but the pace of the rally slows; this is a good sign. Gut feel is all about the second derivative. 1.8700 trades. Gah. Sphincter tight. Knuckles white.

I know this is the right trade but the reality is that I always know it's the right trade, even when I'm wrong. *Roll over, man. Roll over.* It won't back off. 1.8720 trades. I need to buy the whole position back if 1.8750 breaks. I am dying for a cigarette. Always jonesing for a cig-o.

1.8740 trades. I grip the haptic, ready to buy if 1.8750 triggers.

Then, an urgent beep. A red light flashes on the peripheral horizon. NEWS ALERT. NEWS ALERT.

*GERMAN BUNDESBANK CUTS DEPOSIT RATE 100 BASIS POINTS TO CURB SOARING NEUEMARK

Fuck a robot. I'm saved.

This is a total surprise. Not priced in. The first print after the headline is a full four neuemarks lower at 1.8350. This is a get out of jail free card and I'm gonna cash it in. My hands make smooth coordinated movements, sending a series of limit orders to the currency market. By the time 1.8000 trades a few minutes later, I am out of the position. I've made a profit of nearly 2.1 million dollars. My payout is 10%, so that's $210,000 for me today, before tax. Not bad for 45 minutes' work.

You might say I was lucky on this trade and I won't disagree. But there's no such thing as luck in the long run.

I pull off my trading gear, set it down on the desk and pull out a pack of Marlboro Gold cigarettes. I flick my scratched up retro Super Mario Bros. Zippo and fire up the smoke. The apartment is a mess. Two half-filled ashtrays and twenty or so empty beer bottles sit atop my coffee table.

My mind is still hazy from last night. My skull is filled with smoke and I need to get some sleep because tonight is a huge night out: Night One of flatland @ Meat Packing. And I plan to completely destroy myself.

Because that's what I do.

I press my half-smoked cigarette into a pile of dead ash, close the blinds and get into bed for an all-day supernap.

■ ■ ■

It's midnight and I am still in my apartment. Woke up around 10:00 PM, showered and sat down for a couple of solo drinks. I've got a nice buzz going. Nights out with flatland at the helm of the starship start late, so there's no rush.

I drip two drops of Sight onto each eyeball and tilt my head back. The cold liquid blankets each cornea and vision instantly swirls. Each Sight trip is unique—that's one of the drug's unique selling features. Not only is the drug itself new but it has a built-in novelty as no trip is exactly like the last. My favorite effect: random onset synesthesia.

On a good Sight trip, the color red might make you feel cold. The letter B might give you an erection. The sound of an ambulance might trigger the sight of colorful fireworks that fade when the sound of the ambulance fades. You can see how the recreational features of the drug go way beyond the club scene, right? You can drop five mills of Sight and sit at the train station or watch the sunrise from a graveyard and have a time and a half.

I walk out of my apartment and head for the club. I know everyone in the scene so it's fine to go out like this by myself. Not weird at all. Totally normal.

There's nothing wrong with me.

I step outside my apartment and the New York air smells sweet, like honey covered almonds. Like the whiff circle that surrounds a Nuts 4 Nuts cart. Steam vapor billows up from a huge orange and white striped plastic tube, like something out of a Dr. Seuss book. Neon lights bounce at the edge of my peripheral vision. My cigarette tastes like caramel. Honking horns trigger waves of goosebumps across my back. All the humans I see look gigantic.

I enter the club.

The DJ tonight is a mad professor; a musical mastermind with maniacal mathematical methodology dropping sonic ecstasy directly into the collective consciousness of the gyrating horde. The reigning ruler of Robo. The DJ tonight looks out and sees 1,000 streams of consciousness in the warehouse—she tweaks her musical output until those streams start to join together and eventually the whole room is a single organism vibrating as one, responding only to her inputs. The DJ tonight delivers a sermon on the mount via audible ones and zeroes. It is not quite music but not quite noise. She brings the worshippers to the edge of emotional ejaculation but not yet. Not yet.

The DJ tonight is called flatland.

OONTZ OONTZ OONTZ. Time dilates. It's 1:19 AM. It's 2:44 AM. It's 2:45 AM. It's 2:46 AM. It's 3:44 AM. Time is normally an endless series of identically-sized cubes stretching from now into the infinite distance. But tonight, those cubes are made of Jell-O.

And flatland shakes them around in a bowl.

New York Times music critic Ron Cheney described Robo this way: "Close your eyes and imagine an armada of alien ships coming over the night horizon. As they get closer, you see that they have no weapons on their spacecraft, only massive speakers on each side. Suddenly, they attack, firing electronic sensory overload and pulsing beats directly into your mind, bypassing your ears completely. A cocktail of serotonin and dopamine showers your brain and you convulse involuntarily. You cannot not move with the music. There may be no beat. There may be no rhythm. But the result is perfect magical chaos."

I climb into the DJ booth with flatland and tell her that I am in awe of what she has delivered tonight. I kiss her on the cheek and see guys wondering: flatland's taken? She's not. I duck down and drop two more mills of Sight. It's almost 4:30AM. I wander the venue and take in sights and sounds. Faces. Some rando gives me a red pill. I swallow it with some warm bottled tap water.

So. Much. Fun.

My brain clicks and pops as I slam a tequila shot then suck the lemon. MDMA, Sight and crystal meth surge through my blood-stream. I am exploding with positive energy and maybe 65 percent insane. I see bubbles around my thoughts as I think them and then the thought of the thought bubbles is its own thought bubble.

The thought bubbles start to have thoughts of their own: why am I here? What does salami taste like? The kind of stuff you would expect thought bubbles to think.

The music is a eurythmic pulse. Sonic Froot Loops. flatland paints the air with audio graffiti. The sound system is modern and expensive. A particular bass riff makes my hair vibrate in a way that gives me a weird spinal chill. This rhythmic bassbuzz chill passes through me at intervals as I walk around the room and soak in the crowd. Beautiful happy freaks, everywhere. No idea where my friends are but it doesn't really matter.

I see that guy Blaise I've talked to a million times. A regular here. Cool guy. Nice guy. A Cheshire Cat smile extends wide off each side of his face as he breakdances super old school like he should have a flattened cardboard box under his feet and a Vision Streetwear jacket on his back. Ones and zeroes pulse from the computer beneath flatland's fingers, through unseen wires and out of speakers that loom overhead. The binary data flies through the air, orbiting in waves, ricocheting off pillars and walls like billions of miniature, invisible audio frisbees. The data pour into my my my my my ears and wash over my brain, bathing it in dopamine.

A girl, super cute (I think?) with giant anime eyes stares at (or maybe through) me for 10 or 2000 seconds and I smell cigarette smoke and then a waft of citrus and coriander as the cartoon girl walks toward me like disco lemonade. I see the individual frames of her cartoon walk and then imagine a guy in a blue Mohawk sitting in an animation studio at a drafting table. He draws the still images of this girl and now these still images become animated frame by frame as she walks up to me and says:

"Hi."

Her voice comes from far away. A distant land. She is massively right in front of me and occupying my entire field of vision, but her voice is tiny like a Whoville Who's.

I want to yell something like "Hey! What's your name?" or "You're cute!" or something or anything but the motor skill that allows for speech is apparently not functional. This is not the first time I have been unable to talk while on Sight but it's a tad alarming nevertheless. Kind of like when you are in a dream and you can't scream. But I can deal.

I fall into the space between two thoughts for many, many evers.

The smell of citrus brings me back; it is so strong it makes my eyes burn and actual tears form and roll down my cheeks as I stand there dumb, still staring at anime girl. Her eyes grow and create black pulsating vortex pools. She gets the gist of how fucked I am and turns to her just-magically-appeared friend and says:

"This kid is tripping balls! Stick a Chupa Chup in his mouth!"

The friend sticks a Chupa Chup in my mouth and sourtacular swirls explode off every taste bud and send red pink and orange dopamine showering over my brain.

Thought bubble: If I can't talk right now I am definitely nearing maximum buzz. Must make the best use of this mind-state. I head to the dance floor and take in the show.

Neon green Cheerios fly at me, growing as they pass over the dance floor. They become large circles of light that pass around over and through me. Now pink neon Cheerios. Now orange neon Cheerios. The music comes at me in layers. A car horn minus the treble. A vocodered bird noise. A clicking metronome.

flatland controls visuals from a second laptop. On the walls, via projection, she constructs a museum of unreality where, for example, images of crystals collapsing in on themselves appear and disappear, visible not to the eye but to the mind. Images flash and leave a mental imprint despite disappearing before the conscious mind can see or process them. Flashes from 1950's black-and-white films. Ants marching. Close ups of soapy water flowing into a sewer. A North Korean military parade. Surreal visual side orders to accompany the musical main course.

DJ flatland you fucking genius I love you. I love this. She layers in some other sounds (a waterfall, an electronic siren of some sort, a spaceship landing?) and they all build in this layered and perfectly logical and inevitable way. African drums, hissing, and the ding of subway doors come in on top and it builds and it builds and gets louder and builds and this girl beside me is dancing and sweating like an athlete and our eyes meet and I yell:

"This is fucking galactic!!"

Apparently, I can talk again. That's good. The girl smiles and the music builds and builds and the tension is sexual as the crepuscular crowd heaves as one to the buildup. Awaiting the drop... flatland

14

slows things all the way down to 5 bpm and then back up to 120. Roller coaster.

The music builds and gets louder. Drums and trumpets and lasers and all kinds of shit overlap and weave in and out and it can't possibly build anymore... Delicious musical skittles. I hear telephone buttons pushed randomly coming from another dimension. Crinkly paper. Sound of water rushing whooosshhhhhh. Sound of air hissing fssshhhhh. Everything builds to a mind-rinsing crescendo. And the girl beside me yells:

"I think I'm gonna come!!!!"

And then. The drop.

The greatest drop of all time (ever, I swear to God) and now the crowd mentally orgasms together and everyone dances, free and happy and in love like no one is watching and they have never been hurt and there is no hunger and no hatred. No pain, no loneliness. And just for this moment, there is no outside world. And there is no such thing as time. There is just right now. ::::::::::::This perfect, infinite right now.

I don't ever want this to end.

flatland closes with a track she produced herself called MY WORK HERE IS DONE. It is a banging collection of bees buzzing, French horns and old movie audio of some random action hero saying: "My work here is done". Cheesy but delicious. The crowd is fully robotic, moving as one under the dual influences of the music and the drugs. Loss of muscular control. Kaleidoscopic vision.

Thoughts become scrambled. Lights in the club come on. My face is ghastly and translucent in the streaked bathroom mirror. I think I kissed a girl earlier. My right palm is dyed purple but I don't know why.

I stumble out of the club.

I am inundated by artificial light and information. I stare a bit too long at a neon sign and it burns tracers in my vision and this reminds me of when I spun sparklers with my little sisters on the Fourth of July. *RIP my small friends.*

I cannot let my thoughts go there.

Wave of sadness, be gone.

I wander Manhattan for an hour or more with a completely empty brain. Too tired to sleep.

It is dawn. My thoughts unscramble and I drag myself up onto a small island of lucidity. A moment of clarity longer than a flash but shorter than the space between two heartbeats. I want to stay in it. I see the beauty of Everything for a picosecond. Wrappers float. Pigeons hop. Every building is perfect, like it was 3D printed. Beautiful black garbage bags pile by the curb.

Raw data pours out of every object, person and building. I am firehosed by information. There is a maple tree and I see a flipbook mindsequence as it changes from helicoptering seed pod to sprout to sapling to tree (now) and then death, snag and stump.

It is full on daylight and the sun is unrealistically bright and it pours through my strrrrrrrrretched pupils and burns the backs of the insides of my eyes. Pinks blast and orange hurts and where the fuck are my sunglasses here they are oh thank god I need a hot dog or something and how the hell am I going to get home with four dollars left I can't walk for 45 minutes feeling like this I think I am floating...............

■ ■ ■

1 YEAR AND 247 DAYS BEFORE THE RESET

Let me explain a few things.

A couple of years ago, Nintendo was flailing as game consoles went obsolete—the advent of streaming, full VR and unlimited mobile computing power meant there was no point to consoles anymore. Kids can stream any game, any time, on any platform. But Nintendo has been around since 1889; they know how to adapt.

From somewhere deep in the mind of a Nintendo game designer in Tokyo came the genius idea: release a real-time financial markets video game. Gamify the stock market. He saw that financial markets were already the world's largest massive multiplayer online game and dollars were how people kept score. Robinhood was the start, not the end of gamification.

The Nintendo game, called ↑Marketz!↓, lets gamers play the global capital markets the way they play vids. Like every good game, there is much pattern recognition. Streaming, real-time financial data displayed via augmented reality lets me play with the big boys in the global casino.

Initially, the game was meant to be virtual. Trades done were not executed for real. But over time Nintendo executives and Merik Capital, the hedge fund that consulted on the creation of the game, noticed something interesting. There was a small, but consistent group of players that steadily outperformed the market. In fact, the best traders outperformed just about every hedge fund in the world. Consistently.

Over time, gamers' success or failure in this virtual trading simulator allowed Merik to sort the players into buckets by success rate. Those players whose success was demonstrated statistically to be nonrandom were then plugged directly into Merik's live trading engine so that each time gamers bought or sold in what they believed to be a virtual world, their trades were executed in real life.

Eventually, word of this setup leaked and there was an outcry as the parents of the profitable gamers felt they should be compensated. Some old school critics also argued that this venture was not an appropriate use of US financial markets; but given the ups and downs since the late 1990s and the rapidly diminishing holding period of the average investor, it was widely acknowledged that the original purpose of capital markets had been jettisoned long ago.

In other words, the markets had already become a video game, and the Nintendo/Merik partnership was new only in terms of its interface, not the substance of the human / market interaction. Anyway, I am one of the best ↑Marketz!↓ players in the world and it is making me rich AF.

It is 6:45 PM. I get out of bed after another wonderful daylong nap, check the market, and order some food. I sit down and flick on the baseball game. Little League World Series. Tokyo Kitasuna are up 4-3 against the 12-year-olds from Pennsylvania. My heart beats a bit faster than normal as I remember something: Last night, while some-what rekt, I bet $30,000 on a parlay. If Tokyo wins and the total score is under 8 runs, I win $105,000.

Thing is, though, I meant to bet $3,000. (And yes, I acknowledge that betting on the Little League World Series is pretty degenerate). Squishy from the drinking and the Sight, I typed an extra zero on my phone by accident and my vision was blurry enough I didn't even notice until this morning. It's the biggest bet I have ever made.

It is the bottom of the final inning, runners on second and third. Two outs. De'Shaquan Milller is on the mound—the best closer in Little League according to the guys on ESPN. Full count on the batter. All I need is one more strike and I win $105,000. De'Shaquan turns, steps and fires to the plate. A laser beam on the outside corner. A strike!!! No. Ball four!?

I leap out of my chair instinctively, ready to yell at the umpire. But that is an anachronistic reflex, I know. Umpires no longer call the balls and strikes with their eyes. Instead, they rely on PitchFX: a system of 33 cameras mounted throughout the stadium in Williamsport. A computer triangulates, then measures, the speed, location and trajectory of the ball once it leaves the pitcher's hand.

The system simultaneously establishes the exact dimensions and location of the batter in 3D space. It then cross-references the batter's strike zone and the location of the ball as it crosses the plate and makes a 100% accurate determination whether or not the pitch was a ball or a strike. The PitchFX system then instantly relays the call to a special watch-like device on the umpire's wrist and the umpire calls out the balls and strikes in the old school way.

That was ball four. Bases loaded. I still just need one more out to win. My heart rate is elevated.

The phone rings.

"Yo," I answer.

"Yo, it's flat," that's short for flatland, the famous DJ and producer and light show freak and current ruler of Robo and Kalei-doscope. Also, my best friend since Grade 9. She is a girl who likes girls so our friendship is not complicated. "Time to go pistachios again tonight, suckah. You coming by?"

"Yeah, I'll be there."

My vision flicks back to the TV. The game is already over. The kids from Tokyo are running off the field. Dude from Pennsylvania flew out. I win $105,000. Sweet.

"I'll be there, flat. But just FYI. Technically pistachios are not nuts. They're drupes. So, I agree with you conceptually… I'm ready to get acorns. I'm ready to go hazelnuts. But I am not ready to go pistachios. Pistachios aren't nuts."

"Dude. You need professional help."

"Agree."

I feel kind of weird about the $105,000 I just won on a total fluke. Like… I don't deserve it or something. Without another thought I tell flatland:

"So that money you were trying to raise for St. Mike's?"

"Yes guy! You plan on parting with some of those ill-gotten gains from the capitalist casino?"

"Ha. What was the fundraising goal again?"

I know the answer.

"One hundred thousand."

I doge $100,000 from one of my accounts direct to St. Mike's, which is still in my phone because I donated $500 to them last Christmas. flatland is gonna be stoked. And while technically I have just been charitable, I never deserved that money anyway. Probably better to put it to good use rather than let it sit in my SportzBetz account where it will eventually be spunked away via losing wagers on meaningless sporting events.

"Right, OK. Just curious. Laterz."

"Brother. Before you go. You have enough Sight to share tonight?" flatland asks.

"I got 50 mills."

"Nice. OK. I need 20. Is that cool?"

She won't touch booze or drugs but she doesn't preach either; she's just scoring for friends.

"Yeah man. 20 is fine. You got 20," I reply.

"Dude. Don't call me man."

"Sorry man," I reply.

"Har. Har. See you soon."

Click. She hangs up. I shower. Blast music to get pumped. Get dressed. Light a smoke. The first cig of the night always tastes incredible. I open the window and let in the fresh New York air; it smells like optimism. I look outside at the shimmering city and take it in. This is one of those amazing Manhattan nights, pregnant with possibility.

Sight is the street name for Xylanyx, a product originally developed for eye injuries or something like that. Pharmacological entrepreneurs recently discovered that if you cook Xylanyx down into a very pure form, mix it with contact lens solution and then drop it in your eyes, it can have some rather interesting effects: Kaleidoscopic tracer vision. Loss of muscular control. Synesthesia. Time dilation. Frenzied rushes of energy.

Reports have surfaced recently that on higher doses of Sight, users are seeing a color previously unseen by humans. The nth color. The holy grail of the Sight experience. I haven't seen it yet despite consuming my share of Sight over the past year or so.

SouthLine Beckham Pharmaceuticals, the manufacturer of Xylanyx, pretends to have no idea why off-label prescriptions have skyrocketed, attributing the spike in sales to "a patient-centric focus, closed loop marketing, enhanced sales force effectiveness efforts and a subsequent 37.6% increase in reported year-over-year brand affinity."

■   ■   ■

1 YEAR AND 246 DAYS BEFORE THE RESET

It's 1:00 PM on the day after flatland Night Two. My brain floats in toxic chemical brine and I drift in and out of consciousness. Last night's electronic audio still Pongs around in my skull and I am fully dressed, on top of the covers. Occasional wafts of stale ashtray drift in from the living room, and I remember coming home in the daylight with such a buzz there was no chance of sleep. I watched some 3D natureflicks and smoked about 2,000 cigarettes and jerked off (twice?) until I was finally exhausted enough as the last calorie in my body burnt off and I collapsed onto my bed and into the black.

At 3:04 PM I wake up with a jolt. I am suddenly aware that it is Friday and I have a big position in the Australian dollar. I would prefer not to keep it over the weekend. Currency markets close at 5:00 PM Friday and then reopen at 1:00 PM on Sunday afternoon (i.e., 7:00 AM in Wellington, New Zealand) and if any news comes out over the weekend you can get hurt by a gap in the price. Example: the weekend in 2003 that Saddam Hussein was captured, the dollar gapped two percent higher on the open Sunday. Traders went bankrupt on that move.

I flip on ↑Marketz!↓ and check my status. The Australian dollar is up about half of a percent so I show a profit of $465,280 right now. Not bad considering I was either flying, or fast asleep for most of the past 48 hours. I make a few sharp hand motions and close out my position.

I fall back into bed. Beyond exhausted. Seventeen nights in a row I have consumed alcohol or done drugs. I am wearing thin. Need to stop.

Must. Get. Normal.

■　■　■

1 YEAR AND 244 DAYS BEFORE THE RESET — WESTPORT, CONNECTICUT

It is 5:15 AM. Alison is awake in bed. She hears Dad leave downstairs.

Quiet the mind. Stick to the plan.

She tosses. Turns. Falls into short bursts of dreamless sleep. Adrenaline outmaneuvers melatonin. Feels like she's hardly slept.

7:10 AM. The sun peeks through the blinds but it's still crazy early. Alison has been up for 15 minutes. She jams stuff into her backpack. It all feels like the teenage runaway stories she wrote as a child or 'A House Without Windows' or something. Dreamlike.

She gathers essentials. Sleeping t-shirts, a brush, her old diary with lock (to be burned ASAP, obv), some notebooks, 12 benzodiazepines, 11 Ritalin, two thirds of a 15ml bottle of Sight, a pack of Camels containing seven cigarettes, some disposable contact lenses, two bottles of Grey Goose she stole from downstairs… And $150,000 in cash, mostly hundreds.

Mom's still deep asleep and Dad is long gone to work. She walks out of the Westport mansion, into cool morning. Hops in a waiting Lyft to the train station.

The loaded Metro-North train rattles toward New York City. Alison sits next to a short, weathered construction worker of (maybe) Italian descent. He's got worn steel-toed boots and she's got Sharpie-marked Nikes. A couple of teenagers sit directly across from them. The train slows almost to a stop for no reason (as Metro-North trains tend to do).

The boy looks out the window; the girl's head rests on his shoulder. She's asleep. They both hold half-empty water bottles without caps. Alison stares out the window at a pile of used tires.

BAM! A small bird (maybe a chickadee?) crashes into the train window and falls straight down, leaving a tiny oiled imprint of its last moment on the glass. The boy looks at his girlfriend but she is still asleep on his shoulder and so he looks over at Alison and they share a non-verbal "What the fuck was that?" and then Alison quickly goes back to phonethumbing.

Everything on her phone is boring so she sleeps it and pockets it. She fingers a text tattoo on her left forearm and runs her index finger back and forth over three small cutting scars just below.

Despite a birth date well after Kurt Cobain's suicide (she's 19 years old), Alison is obsessed with music from the 1990s. She is imbued with that particular brand of teenage angst that connects to the visceral self-hatred and wailing perfected by Kurt et al. Wicked poetry plus he's got, like, vocal chords of razor wire and soul dangled over the abyss, hanging by a thread.

And then down, down he fell.

Just like me.

Oh, don't be so melodramatic.

Oh, fuck you, other self.

She has various 1990's song lyrics tattooed on various body parts.

All in black, 10 and 12-point Helvetica, mostly. Nirvana, Radiohead and Pearl Jam lyrics, paraphrased.

I love you. I will not schism.

I'm a geek. I'm an oddball. Purpose unknown.

Do not refer to me as daughter. Photos serve as mental fodder.

Some other tiny images. A mosquito. And a beetle.

She's always looking for new ideas. But it has to make sense. Has to mean something.

Most recently she got just **?** in 6-point Helvetica behind her left ear. As in: don't believe everything you hear, I guess?

The only color tattoo is an orange small daisy (just below her right armpit).

Her brain is empty but she is not asleep. When the Manhattan skyline comes into view, she feels wide awake for the first time in ages. The instant you make visual contact with Manhattan, a pulse of electricity crackles into and through you. As if invisible threads of energy flash out from the city and not-so-gently pass through you for just a moment. The one and only greatest city in the world. For all the fake-itude and selfish agenda and bullshit the city represents, she cannot ignore that it is the only place she has ever felt alive.

She smiles and sings softly to herself.

Stepping out of Penn Station, Alison realizes she has never slept alone in a strange place before. She doesn't know where to go, but the SoHo Grand is safe for one night; she'll find something more semi-permanent tomorrow. *Might as well run up Dad's cards before he figures out I'm not coming back.*

On the way to the hotel, she passes a rando tattoo shop and gets new ink in 10-point Helvetica on the inside of her left leg.

Daddy's little girl: No longer a girl.

"I'll take a large suite, something with multiple rooms, please."

"Right away, Ms. Leary. If I could just see a credit card for authorization, please."

Alison plunks a Black AMEX onto the white marble counter. It's in her name, but Dad pays the bill, obv. The transaction is complete and she holds her phone up to a scanner to load her room key onto her smartphone.

She enters the room, drops her shit on the floor and falls backwards onto the bed. Lies in upward-facing starfish pose. As she lies there, she smells hotel soap and a slightly sour right armpit. She is exhausted but will not waste tonight.

My first night away from Westpo. Let my real life begin.

Well, let it begin a bit later, I am fucking exhausted.

Sleeps for hours. Wakes up. Briefly disoriented.

Where the hell am I? Oh yea. Shit.

Or maybe: 'Yay'?

She smokes the best cigarette of her life and cracks two 187ml bottles of Cabernet from the mini-bar. Chugs one; eats a bag of chips. Eats a Kit Kat. Notices the "Non-smoking room, $250 cleaning charge" sign. *Oh well.* Sips the next mini bottle of Cab. Pulls out her phone. By the time she puts it down, she's invited seven friends to join her in the suite. It's 8:00 PM.

Arrivals:

8:25 PM: Chantal. She lives at N. Moore and Hudson. Dad's an architect from Canada. She is stick bug skinny and wears a shirt that says (in tiny 8-point font, off center, just above belly button level): SKINNY FEELS BETTER THAN FRENCH FRIES TASTE. She is masculine, almost pretty, with eyes the color of lime Life Savers. She has those skinny, low-contrast "I have no lips" lips that detract from otherwise attractive features. She brings drugs.

8:40 PM: Jesse. Student. Starfucker. Jesse is big into Robo and blatantly stans for the big DJs. Arrives straight from the NYU library where he was researching a paper. He is handsome but bald as cheese. He brings a cigar box full of drugs.

8:55 PM: Tommy and Israel show up. They own a clothing shop in SoHo. Their four mofo successful parents financed it. It's doing well. Israel is almost a model but not quite and he can't figure out why. Fact is, though, his skin is a bit off, like 1% jaundiced or something and his lips are too skin-colored and these subtly wrong features give him this weird alien / doll-like appearance that makes you feel uncomfortable. And his voice is so twee it's like, ridic.

9:20 PM: DJ Sakra. He's a biggish (popularity-wise) DJ from Santa Monica. Alison has never met him before but Jesse texted him and he shows up. He brings this cool flip-out DJ in a box thing called JACK. It is a miniature DJ set up, about the size of a tablet computer, with two flaps that flip out and deliver ridiculously crisp sound. On the screen are tools to mix and remix music. It is very fucking cool. Jesse raves about it like a poser.

Poseur?

Whatever. Sakra has a cool haircut and no drugs.

9:55 PM: Hotel Security (not invited). Paul Blart Guy asks everyone to keep the noise down. Alison says "But of course".

Fucking millennials.

10:15 PM: Chloe, Hugh and Emma. Three of Alison's best friends from high school; they all go to Columbia now. They have zero cash or drugs between them but the vibe is communal and sharey. Chloe has turned a tad sketchy over the past year. Ripped clothes and a Hitler hairdo. The Sight is getting to her. She steals. She misses school. Unexplained bruising. Hugh and Emma are fine.

The cheap coffee table is covered with empties and ash flick dust and greebles of coke and now it's midnight. Sakra manipulates JACK and Alison tips out a pile of white rocks from a small baggie. She crushes them into a fine, white powder using a miniature mortar and pestle on her keychain and dumps the fine talc onto the desk in the corner. Repurposing the Black AMEX, she strokes out eight parallel perfect lines of speedy Peruvian cocaine. Lock and load.

1:30AM or so. The whole group of them rides the NRW to a pop-up party in Murray Hill. These pop-ups fall somewhere between "large house party" and "very small rave". The vibe is amazing because of the format.

First, the organizer invites seven people via the SuperPops app.

When they accept the invitation, those seven are allowed to invite two more people each. The capacity of the party is predetermined and when the number of acceptances reaches the party maximum, no more invites can be sent out. Security scans your phone at the entrance to keep out crashers. Hot pop-ups with good DJs can fill up in minutes. The DJ at the pop-up gets some invites himself and in this case Sakra has extended his eight invites to Alison and the others. They open the app and sign up using their phones.

...

I am on a lame Tinder date with a girl that was super cute in the photo but doesn't seem all that super cute in real life and there is a risk that I may be a little buzzed at this point (three Asahi + one gin and tonic) and I don't want to be an asshole or anything but I currently find myself in a bathroom stall tipping blow onto the tank cover of the toilet. I have zero interest in this date at all. What's my exit strategy?

My phone buzzes. A text from Danny. A link to click on.

YOU ARE INVITED TO SEE DJ SAKRA at a SuperPops event. Tap YES to accept. Invitation expires in 10 minutes.

I tap YES, of course, and send an invitation to flatland. I have another invitation but I definitely don't want to invite this girl and I see flatland hit ACCEPT right away because she was sitting at home probably making music or whatever or reading or meditating and now I'm excited to see DJ Sakra because he is getting a lot of hype and I've never heard him live and so...

"Something came up. I'm really sorry. I have to bolt," I tell the girl at the table.

"Oh. Umm. Ok..." she is surprised and/or offended. Some combination of the two.

"I'll pay, obviously. I'm really sorry."

I drop a hundred-dollar bill on the table and turn to head out before she can suggest I call her or text her or something but before I can get clear of the table, she says:

"So, like, you want to text me and we can try again?"

And I am buzzing a bit and maybe smalls wired so forgive me for just saying:

"Nah, I'm good."

Which isn't very nice but anyway the DJ Sakra popup event thing is amazeballs as one might expect and flatland and I spend most of the midnight to 3:00 AM period in one corner discussing important and intelligent and world-changing matters like why organized religion does more harm than good and how technology will take us all to the promised land despite universal vexation and how some sort of post-capitalist world might emerge one day and the have nots will have but the haves will have even more and it's win win win and words words words words words words more words more words and words words words words words.

An incredibly cute girl bounces over to us. She has choppy green hair, some freckles, dope artsy clothing. Kind of edgy but in the best way and some text tattooed on her arm but I can't quite read it.

"Are you flatland?" she asks.

"Yeah. I am. This is Charlie. How's it going?"

"Good... I'm good. I'm Alison... I'm drunk..."

I tingle. I feel something. Something real for the first time in a while. Not synthetic. She is stunning in the literal sense. Like, the first sight of her and: TASER. I cannot speak for a moment. She scratches behind her left ear nervously. The word "coquettish" pops into my head and drifts away.

"You look interesting," she says to me. Slurring. She is wasted.

"Ummm, thanks?"

"I mean you look like an interesting person."

I smile. Want to say something witty but instead just say:

"Thanks."

Attractive girl with whom I feel an electrical connection is dragged away by a friend.

I like you. Goodbye sweet girl. You are the most beautiful thing in the world.

"Man. She's cute," says flatland.

"Um. Yes," I agree.

My brain is steeped in chemicals and the popup starts to wind down and so we circle up a few randos and head back to my apartment to extend and pretend.

...

As is common, the post 4:00 AM conversation has turned to super big picture topics like the ridiculous fact that all this All exists thanks to a chain of events that started with the explosion of something one billionth the size of a grain of sand which is still expanding into larger sizes of infinity and we somehow occupy a massive but also irrelevantly minute nearly-spherical ovoid where amoebas turned to fish and then at some arbitrary moment decided to walk out of water and now suddenly we are just years away (an infinitesimally small measure of time in all this) from making the leap from organic to purely technological beings as our minds and memories look destined to find eternal life on hard drives or in the cloud or something as we abort this slow and gradual, 4.4 billion year process of species to species evolution and make a complete phase shift and evolve into some new inorganic nonspecies of post-singularity mind-machines. *Fuck.*

"OK now just think about this, dude: right now we could be breathing the same molecules of air that Jesus breathed."

"Whoa."

"Truth."

"Mind. Blown."

Juvenile philosophy. Fun. We carry on like a bunch of Kants. The conversation is engaging and I pipe and chime here and there but now we just took a wrong turn somehow (and plus I'm starting to feel the kind of heavy tired that can't be cured by any amount of powder) and Jeremy's going on one of his idiotic rants about religion. His mom is / was hardcore Catholic and he's busy making the case, high school debate, "let it be resolved" style, that the entire Old and New Testament are meant to be taken not literally, but as huge, epic metaphors. To me this is so self-evident that it's not even worth discussing, like starting an argument about whether clouds are wet, and you would think everyone would collectively shrug but some of the others in the room actually find this swill interesting and so the discussion catches fire and burns and burns while I slowly fade back and tune out.

You know those conversations where it's just the drugs talking but everyone is super into it and so they take on this tone of great solemn intellectual seriousness as though they're the first ones to think these thoughts and, like, really dig deep into the meaning of it all? When you are in that zone it's fantastic and mental engines rev and spark and new ground breaks and doors open that sometimes never close again but right now I'm on the outside looking in and it all seems juvenile, worn out territory and I wish I could get into it but I can't.

I am high as fuck so I can't quite figure out what my problem is and there was a time when I would absolutely angle into this convo but right now all I'm feeling is a bit of the old been there done that. There's only so many times you can cover Catholic guilt or the near future or deep future or past relationships or drugs themselves before the topics grow moldy and everything tastes stale. And what's this craptastic music we're listening to, anyway?

Or maybe it's just me? Am I just being a total buzzkill here? I can't tell. My thoughts skitter. *It is important that people like me.* My lip hurts from the biting it so much. Stop being boring and go have fun!

I get up and circulate. Pour myself another gin and tonic. Three girls are playing cards in the kitchen and maybe this is more the type of mindless activity I'm looking for so I sit down and tip some coke out on the kitchen table and cut a red plastic straw into thirds and pass each girl one to snort with. I am in that state I tend to hit lately where I need a line every 15 or 20 minutes or I completely run out of gas. Diminishing returns.

My throat is dry and scorched from sucking Marlboros all night. I roll up a one-hundred-dollar bill, stick it in my right nostril, lean down and Dyson two huge lines. The powder is clumpy and tastes sour like crabapples and it burns the back of my throat which is already sore and wickedly parched. I imagine my trachea to be the red, cracked clay of a dried-up lake. Half the blow falls back out of my dried-up nasal passages and onto the table. The girls may or may not notice; I can't tell but also don't really care at this point. I drag my card along the table, slide the remaining crumbs of coke into a line, lick my finger tip, dab up the coke and rub it on my gums.

I pour three drinks for the girls (still a great host! That Charlie guy is *so nice)* but they barely acknowledge the effort and I must say at this point in the night I'm pretty fucked up and coked to the gills and so it was, indeed, quite an effort to pour three drinks without spilling or getting confused or falling over for that matter and so a bit of appreciation would be appreciated but is not forthcoming. Jaw grinds and post-nasal drip drops down my narrowing throat.

These girls are too young and too dumb and there is no flow to the card game because they keep stopping to talk about handbags (yes handbags, I swear) and that new club on 14th and I can't shake this feeling that I want everyone to leave so I can go to bed but I don't want to be a downer. Without a word, I get up and head to my bedroom. I walk into the bathroom and brush my teeth.

The brushing of the teeth takes extra effort as I first spread cortisone cream onto my toothbrush in error and so have to engage in some extreme rinsing of the bristles before finally cleaning my teeth for real. I look in the mirror and see a pasty beige face and huge black pupils and feel something like sadness, but not that exactly. More like shame. There is a tiny paper cut on the edge of my left nostril and it stings.

An accusation runs through my mind:

Cokehead.

There will be no sleep for many hours. My coke was cut with way too much speed and so I lie here now for painfully long, stretched minutes and hours. Listening to everyone laugh and snort and talk and listen to tunes in my apartment and now it's 5:06 AM and 5:54 AM and I can't stop myself from looking at the clock over and over 6:03 / 6:42 / 7:09 / 7:55. Every sound rattles me like Lego, poured. Shut up, heart. Quiet, clock! Brain: go to sleep. Thump thump.

Thump thump. Thump thump. My heart bangs around in my chest like David Foster Wallace's shoe in a dryer.

I'm about to fall asleep (maybe?). Drifting. Hopeful.

Connor rips open my bedroom door.

"Charlie, you seen my phone?"

"No dude. No idea. Sorry."

Peace shattered. Heart pounds. Fully awake again. All signs of the chemical buzz have disappeared and in its place, only its absence. My mind is in a state of extreme awake which I have no idea what to do with. Frustrated. Why didn't I just take a Benadryl? Too late now. Sun pours in from cracks in the curtains. Blinding shards of hideous daylight slice through my pupils like throwing stars through rice paper. Even when the apartment is quiet, my heart beats loud enough to keep me from drifting off but then finally, finally... Is this it? Can I be both asleep and wishing to fall asleep at the same time? This is weird. The first few frames of a dream flicker across my mindscreen:

Walking through Future Tokyo, lost. Tripping on some sort of potion; an empty brown apothecary vial in my hand. Urge to vomit. I bend over and heave. A thousand blue butterflies come out of my mouth and disperse into the windless, neon-lit darkness.

IRL, a door slams. I'm wide awake again. Thump thump. Thump thump. Thumpity thump. Shit. 8:37 AM / 9:05 AM. Gahhhhh. I need to sleep. I am going mildly insane now and have I slept at all? I hear more people leave my apartment and it's quiet now and way too much sunlight is coming in but I'm tired, really tired and drifting into more asleep than awake. It's a continuum. Awake is awake and asleep is asleep but there are is an incredibly wide chasm in between and though we usually hyperspace across that landscape I am floating slowly across it again now. Slowly. More awake than asleep. More awake than asleep. More asleep than awake. Asleep.

Super happy birds chirp outside. Tweet chirp TWEET chirp TWEET. And the city wakes up and fire trucks wail / cars honk ::::::::::::::::::::: idiots yell. The construction site across the street is fully operational and jackhammers hammer and pile drivers drive directly into my mind.

Now it's 10:15AM and I'm guessing I got an aggregate total of 15 minutes of sleep in three-minute increments over the past five hours but I'm too sketched out to stay in bed and I haven't heard any noise from the living in room in ages so maybe everyone is gone and so I get up to survey the damage.

Full ashtrays, empty bottles; half full bottles used as ashtrays. Spillage and coke crumbs and empty plastic baggies and sticks picked from a bag of weed. A Doritos bag disgorges orange triangles onto my white rug. The 5-inch wide vanilla candle that nobody thought to blow out has melted into a supercool puddle of hardened waxy liquid that hangs down one side of the wooden crate table. It looks kind of Dali / suspended animation-ish and I See the Beauty of it for a flash and then I picture the table up in flames and the apartment engulfed and I cannot unpack any feeling about it or if I would actually care even if I was asleep and engulfed in flames when it happened.

Nah, I would care. I don't want to burn to death. I feel pretty sure about that. I like living.

I go into the bathroom and blow my nose. The Kleenex is soaked, bright red. I will pretend that did not just happen. On a related note, someone spilled a red drink on my foosball table and made no effort to clean it up and now it is hardening into a semi-circle of gooey gel.

There is a somewhat catalog attractive girl, maybe 22, with short brown hair and expensive pre-ripped jeans asleep on my couch. flat-land is asleep on the floor right below her. I recognize her but cannot summon her name from its tickly mindspot. Not Alison, the cute girl from the popup. She was so cute. Crazy attractive. Obviously smart, even while drunk.

I don't want to be rude and start cleaning. I'm too sketched out to reason. Too tired to read. Too awake to nap. I consider a beer and a line but I'm in too much pain from last night for canine fur. My thoughts go to trading but the market's not open.

I put on my goggs and enter the Virtual Utopia Project. It's a newish game. Another one of those fully-immersive open world crowdsourced metaverse sims. Massive and trippy. Virtual surreality.

I wander the Utopasphere, plucking bilgeberries to boost my HP. Wander aimlessly across the (literally) infinite pink sand desert zone. It's very peaceful and meditative here. And quiet. I summon a rake and groom the sand, zen garden style. Relaxing. Green Twirlybirds whirr by like frisbees overhead.

I can't keep getting drunk and high like this three or four (or seven) times a week. Too damaging. I feel too sketched out all the time and the simple fact is that it's just not very fun anymore. I'm not even sober yet and the guilt has kicked in. The huge nights out to see flatland and all that are still well worth the damage done but it's these random no reason apartment get togethers and the mid-week chopfests and solo club wandering that need to stop. I am not proud of who I have become.

Addict. Degenerate.

The tricky part about not having a real job is that it's too easy to live a life without discipline. Up all night / sleep all day. My trading has suffered and my soul is wearing thin. A few months ago, I signed up for a 9:00 AM yoga class, three days a week, just to give myself a reason to wake up in the morning and thus perhaps stay clean the night before.

I've missed 8 of the first 10 classes on account of being violently hungover or drunk or messed up or still awake from the night before when 9:00 AM rolls around. The instructor texts me on a regular basis to ask me where I am and when will I see her next. She is like 50 years old and super leathery but one of the most interesting people I've met in ages. So calm and smart. Fleeting thought of committing a Harold and Maude. Blech.

A group of five blue vampire Rabbidogs runs by and I follow them. My hit points are low and the Rabbidogs will lead me to more bilgeberries.

The girl on my couch IRL opens her eyes then bolts upright. She looks at me, completely lost, surveys the room and asks:

"Jesus Christ. What happened?"

■ ■ ■

@realdemocracy tweeted
"capitalism is the astounding belief that the most wickedest of
men will do the most wickedest of things for the greatest good
of everyone."
john maynard keynes

■ ■ ■

9 YEARS BEFORE THE RESET – MIDTOWN MANHATTAN

I had the book and street smarts for investment banking and with
my dad in the biz theˆre were obvious nepotistic opportunities and
so I did some shadowing and interviewing at a few Wall Street firms.
My first impression was that most of the traders I sat down with
were not as smart as I would have expected. As in: borderline
retarded.

Trader is an anagram of retard.

How they got their MBAs or whatever degrees was unclear but
the topics on the trading floor were not quantitative finance or
behavioral economics or monetary policy or even which way the
market was going. Instead it was mostly talk of Fantasy Football,
Michelin-starred restaurants, where to send the analyst for lunch and
the odd freshmanic and factually incorrect discussion about politics
or global affairs or celebrity infidelity. It seemed knowledge of
upscale restaurants and professional sports were valued way above
math, trading or problem solving skills.

In my junior year, before I got kicked out of Brown, I had the
chance to do a few Super Days at major Wall Street firms. My dad
told me that the one thing everyone on Wall Street loves to talk about
is himself. So at the end of the interview when they ask: "Do you
have any questions?" don't ask something about the firm or about
finance or about the job. Ask the interviewer a question that will put
him in a position to talk about himself...

"Yes. Thank you very much, I do have a question."

The interviewer is 42. Wearing a dark blue, pin-striped Brooks
Brothers suit with a rumpled Boss shirt and a $175 Thomas Pink tie.

The type of guy who bought the suit on sale for $775 last year at the end of the season but when another trader asks the price of it he says it cost $1800. His face is ruddy and freckled and square and probably helped him get laid a lot in college. His hair is dark brown. Or you can call his hair red if you want a punch in the fucking face, asshole.

It's just me and this guy talking but the room is one of those massive 30-person conference rooms with a 25-foot table in the middle and Herman Miller chairs all around. On Super Day, they need every available office as 50 candidates are interviewed 7 times each and that's a lot of meetings. There are three Polycom SoundStation triangular videoconferencing units equally spaced on the table and a big projection screen at the end broadcasting nothing but a live unchanging stream of someone's Windows desktop. Off to the side is a small table with those midget bottles of Poland Spring water, a few mini-bar sized Cokes and a small plate of surprisingly delicious-looking chocolate chip cookies.

"My question is: what is the best trade you've ever done?"

"You mean besides getting divorced and trading up to a younger wife?"

The guy laughs at his own joke and doesn't care or notice if I laugh (I don't). Then the laugh recedes into a smirk and he shifts into a more comfortable position in the way someone might when they know they're about to tell a long story.

"So yeah, best trade of all time? Easy. September, 2001. The first plane just hit the building but the market wasn't freaking out yet. Everyone thought it was an accident. I'm always looking for an edge and so while everyone else was glued to the TV I was thinking 'What if this isn't an accident? What will the market do?'

I called a good buddy of mine, a fraternity brother, a commercial pilot at Delta. He says 'No fucking way it's an accident' and before he can finish his sentence I hang up on him and start hitting bids in the futures. I sold 3,000 S&Ps and a shitload of single names. Hit three banks for 300 USD/JPY each. Went to more than five times my aggregate position limit but I knew nobody was going to be paying attention to limits when a plane had just crashed into the World Trade Center. When that second plane hit, I knew I was fucking golden. I added to my short, just fucking piled it on like a pig. I mean I know it was a terrible tragedy... of course but I mean... What a fucking trade. 40 sticks in a week. That's 40 million dollars. Average payout here is 10% so you can do the math."

I sat there mute for probably 30 seconds. Finally, I just said:

"Thank you for your time."

I had three more interviews scheduled after that but I just went straight to the elevator and walked out.

■ ■ ■

@realdemocracy tweeted
"give me control of a nation's money and i care not who makes the laws."
amschel rothschild

■ ■ ■

5 YEARS BEFORE THE RESET

Unlike Alan (no middle name) Greenspan, who quickly fell into disrepute after his easy money policies caused the 2008 Mortgage Melt, Ben Bernanke's halo remained long after his departure from public office. The nation is forever in his debt for his role as leader of the Committee to Save the World II. He was the Fire Chief, hosing a torrent of easy money all over the burning financial system and saving Main Street from Wall Street moral hazard and a second Great Depression. Without Ben Shalom Bernanke's repeated doses of turbo quantitative easing, who knows what might have happened. If only he had done more, eh Krugman?

The Ben Bernanke thru-way (South Carolina Interstate 385 near Greenville) was the first public show of respect and dedication but now the Bearded One's visage appears in plaque, bust and decorative bush form (respectively) at: Ben Bernanke International Airport (Wilmington), the Ben S. Bernanke Building (Manhattan), Shalom

Gardens (Brooklyn) and of course, the still-popular-after-all-these-years "Ben Bernanke's Head" Piggy Bank. Available for $17 plus shipping on Amazon.

The most ambitious of the dedications is the 39-foot statue of the Esteemed Chairman rolling into Zucotti Park right now with full police escort on the back of a huge flatbed usually used for transporting mobile homes (marked WIDE LOAD, obviously).

A few protesters have gathered but there is zero threat. The only way to gain access to the Zucotti environs (i.e., within two square blocks) is to wear a wristband which can only be obtained after you show a valid driver's license or other government ID to an officer at one of various control points around Maiden Lane, Fulton and Rector Streets. The wristbands are neon yellow, similar to something you might wear at an all-inclusive (e.g., Beaches, Turks & Caicos) and contain an embedded RFID chip cross-referenced to your ID.

360-degree video is captured by police-emblazoned mini-towers in plain sight at each intersection. Software tracks the wristband-wearing public and pre-reacts to potential threats by detecting aggressive facial geometry, rigidity of gait, abnormal arm movements and the like. Anything that implies the potential for harm, something other than normal walking, talking or non-threatening consumption of halal or falafel sold by Middle Eastern dudes out of the repurposed metal coffee carts will trigger a security response.

The sizzling chicken has been sitting on that steaming, hot, flat brown grill all day but man does it smell good! A Croatian guy sells fruit from a table. No abnormal facial geometry or aggressive body language detected.

"C'mon over and get a Falafel, man! Six dollars!"

A single chain is wrapped around the Esteemed Chairman's arm and a medium-sized Terex crane slowly and carefully pulls the bronze statue up. It finally stands fully erect atop a huge 7X7 foot cube of granite. Inscription:

We, the American people, celebrate the tenacity, single-mindedness and courage of our Esteemed Chairman who brought the US Financial System back from the brink of the 2008 Global Financial Crisis.

Statue and installation paid for by the Frito-Lay Company (NYSE: FLC).

■ ■ ■

AUGUST 2007 — MANHATTAN

Tuesday morning risk meeting at the investment bank affectionately known as Organ Manly. The room was full and all the main risk-takers were there, including Todd. His coffee was half full but getting cold. His suit was kind of rumpled. With each passing day, he slipped one nanometer further away from Super-Engaged-Loves-Trading-Guy towards something more fraudulent. Imposter syndrome. Some days his suit felt like a costume, like he was dressed up for Halloween as Mr. Wall Street Trader. He wasn't any good at trading anymore. What was he good at?

You are good at sleeping.

His mind slipped to existential back and forths.

Why am I still doing this job? You don't need the money. But what else am I going to do? Just quit and figure it out after.

He saw a greeting card once at Whole Foods that said: Jump and the net will appear. He liked that, found it clever.

Do they know I just really don't give a shit anymore? Can they tell by my voice?

Is this all punishment for that time I killed the bird?

"Todd, you hear me? Answer the question."

"Yeah… Yes, the CDO risk is well-hedged. We're short a ton of ABX against it and long a plenty of S&P vega."

Why is Risk so worried these days? Didn't they hear? Subprime is contained. Bernanke said it himself. The Fed's got my back. If this shit turns sour, there is ZERO chance they let housing go tits up. What are they going to do? Let Organ Manly fail? No freaking chance. Exactly zero chance.

Todd's mortgage was paid off. He wanted to get out of the business; he realized that more every day. At some point the whole thing was no longer macroeconomic analysis or even puzzle solving but just numbers vibrating on a screen. Charts unfurling randomly. A job where you guess whether a semi-random number on a computer screen will go up or down. When you guess "up" and it goes up you feel temporarily happy. But if you guess "up" and it goes down, you feel really depressed for a few days.

What Todd felt was the exact opposite of burn out. More of a gradual fade away type of thing as the passion dripped out bit by bit with each passing day. Each argument with a salesperson, hedge fund drive-by, 60-mile commute, morning without breakfast, client night out, bottle of red wine, stale bagel, summer subway sauna ride, 6:30 PM gin and tonic and so on. It wore him out.

It wore him out.

Last week, he bought a bunch of New Zealand government bonds on a whim, one of those stupid pointless trades you know are dumb the second you put them on. Then twelve hours later a headline comes across the wire:

*MAGNITUDE 7.2 EARTHQUAKE HITS NEAR WELLINGTON, NZ. INJURIES REPORTED.

And his first instinct was to pump his fist and think "YES!" because the disaster was good for his bond position.

Then, he realized what he had thought and hated himself for thinking it, even as a reflex. *Who am I? That first voice that cheers the earthquake news? Or the second voice that reprimands the first? Or some third voice?* When two voices in your head have differing interpretations of events: who is you? This was the sort of recursive thought pattern that went on and on in his head, all the time. One brain vs. the other vs. quieter third, fourth, fifth and other selves. Cacophony.

Todd was always a nice guy, a good person. A pleaser. He was the kind of guy that said "thank you" to the grumpy sandwich artist at Subway, even when he (Todd) was in a bad mood himself. But he found as time passed his niceness felt more strategic than real. *Be nice to the Platinum Client's personal assistant because you know she will tell her boss what a nice person you are and that will make you look good and get you more business.*

After so many years he could no longer separate whether he was actually a nice person or, was he just *being nice*? When he spoke he often heard his own voice and it had a robotic, fraudulent quality. Brain 2 would hear Brain 1 talking and yell "Fraud!".

Work felt more and more vapid. A part of Todd had become morally opposed to the whole financialization of America and his own (admittedly minute) participation in the process. But then again he's just a guy doing his job, right? Trying to pay the bills, etc. Doing the best he can. He went through the motions. He had above average smarts (street and book) and he'd been doing the job for years so he could fake it as and when necessary.

Back when he had the fire in the belly, he had a dream. Trade like a rock star, run a desk. Get rich. And now, he had done all those things. Dream come true! But after you achieve the dream, it's like an ejaculation; all the excitement drains out and this deeply disappointing and dark "what now?" feeling fills up the space left by the realized ambition.

Now he has no ambition other than to scale another day and continue to receive a pay check. Possibly nail one more huge bonus on the back of a massive coin flip wager. Sleepwalk through, collect direct deposits that are subsequently transferred to: landscaper, swimming pool company, handyman, Amazon, Williams Sonoma, private school, sports camp, Crate and Barrel, local government, state government, federal government, Tiffany & Co., Mercedes-Benz of Fairfield, Whole Foods, Starbucks, etc. etc. etc.

No matter how much money he made in each of the past ten years, expenses were somehow always 1.03 times income. In fact, Todd never felt richer than all those years ago when he earned $60,000 in one year, at age 23. In 2007 he made more than forty times that sixty grand and still he felt like he was barely getting by. Back in the day he knew exactly how to go after his dreams of more, more, more. The tricky bit with dreams is that once they come true, they're gone.

The dog chases the bus but has no clue what to do when he catches it.

Now Todd had too much and it was not enough and he had no idea how to strive for less. At first these thoughts of "I want out" were easily batted away but now they cling and multiply, invasive and overwhelming, like zebra mussels.

The ambition to aspire to less is not something society teaches. American homes have tripled in size but storage facility business is booming. MOAR MOAR MOAR MOAR. Once you learn that he who dies with the most toys does not win, you want to divest yourself of all these possessions which are not assets, but shackles. But nobody ever told you how to do that. Buy, add, grow, increase. Those are the keywords in the lexicon of debt-fueled capitalism. Less, give, relax, decrease are all anathema. Embarrassing to think these thoughts, nevermind say them out loud. I WANT LESS! It might be true but it makes no sense when you hear it out loud. It runs too abruptly against the narrative.

Consumption maximization has been confused with utility maximization.

Todd reasoned that the only way to get less was to get more first. Then he could hit his eff-you number and quit outright with no mortgage, private school or future college costs to worry about. You only have to get rich once.

Anyway, his plan was to take one last shot. Double down on all the putrid collateralized debt obligations (CDOs) he held in inventory and wait for the Fed to bail him out as they cut rates all the way to zero. The fecal securities would turn to gold; he'd get paid five million dollars or so and then quit. And if he blew up, he blew up. It's not like they would take back his previous bonuses. He gets fired and takes a few years off. Decide what's what.

"Todd! You hear me? Any other risk factors?"

"Um. Sorry. No. We're really well-hedged. We ran three different stress models and even under the most adverse scenario, we're still in a strong position. In fact, the profit on the hedges exceeds the losses on the underlying in two of three stress tests."

The Risk Guy turned to talk to someone else. Todd checked his phone. An e-mail from his son Charlie. The kid won $400 playing online poker. Good job.

In a recent survey only 26% of those who work on Wall Street said they would recommend a job in finance to their children. The lowest percentage of any profession.

How many smart, creative people has Wall Street hooked with financial lures, yanking them away from useful, creative pursuits? How many carpenters, writers, sculptors and entrepreneurs sit in Manhattan offices playing glorified video games for money, instead of producing something useful?

Just one more year and I'm out. No matter what. For sure this time.

How many songs unwritten, sculptures uncarved, inventions uninvented? How many father-to-son conversations never held as instead Dad gets a pinched nerve in his neck trying to sleep on the delayed Metro-North train while Mom puts the kids to bed alone? A shitload, that's how many.

But it pays so well.

Hard to get in. Impossible to get out.

■ ■ ■

flatland's frame is as minimal as her philosophy and the only things dramatic about her are her afro and her musical genius. she inhabits a white apartment without any real furniture or appliances. one wall is covered with books stacked on raw oak beams she mounted like stripes and painted white. another wall has sound equipment and computers on tables. there is a lime green rotary phone on the wall. it's the only item of color besides flatland herself. on the wall is a clock with no hands and the word "now" centered in black three-inch times roman.

food comes delivered. a singular plastic mug hangs from a hook on the wall in the area where there once was a kitchen but now, post-renovation, only a sink remains. not a great place to visit when you're feeling snacky.

some people think flatland is aloof, maybe a tad stupid. she is neither. she does not engage in a lot of chitter chatter / small talk. likes to keep things minimal. does not deal in snark or irony or sarcasm but also not antisocial. not type a or type b. a rare type c personality. she has finally killed off her ego and banished fraudulent thoughts. totally committed to unconditional happiness. idolizes jesus (the man not the myth).

in theory you could probably label her some kind of minimalist nerdy chic but if she occupies that slice of the societal venn it is purely due to labels applied to her by others. her thoughts are clean and she does not question how others see her. it's not a facade. cucumber sandwich on whole wheat with vegannaise for lunch just about every single day. has a tattoo of mr. rogers on her foot.

she truly cares about only three things: music, democracy and friends. her musical tastes run through almost every genre and cover every decade from the 50s to now. she can get into 1950's rockabilly or 1980's country music just as easily as she can recite guns 'n roses or duran duran lyrics or natalie merchant or arcade fire. her tastes are not hipster or snobby. she appreciates miley cyrus as well as lorde and fleetwood mac. there's this one cyndi lauper song that gives her goosebumps. her musical knowledge is wikipedic.

she is politically active. her interest in politics comes from the frustrated observation that most americans still believe that the united states is a capitalist, democratic republic when it is in fact a corporate oligarchy where a tiny elite holds all power. the united states is a new brand of capitalism: winner take all.

she started @realdemocracy to get the message out and her political relevance has grown exponentially. 2.1 million followers on twitter. she sees herself as a rage against the machine type of influence, bringing politics to a new, younger audience. thing is, her followers run from edm junkies all the way up to nyt intellectuals. she strikes the right balance between passionate / fiery and lucid / well-reasoned common sense.

flatland's dj career has gone vertical in the last 18 months with the boom in robohouse. @flatland = 3.4 million followers. right place at the right time but also crazy talented so really it's more about skill than luck. she has made more money than she knows what to do with and she just logged into her bank account and the balance is well into seven figures so she's on the phone to charlie, asking for some financial advice.

"so what's my finance guru saying? what do i do with all this scrill?" flatland asks.

"i'm more of a short-term guy, flat. i trade, i don't invest. but in the long run this is a greater fool market."

"no comprende."

"it means that for stocks to keep going up you need to have greater and greater fools buying from the previous fools who bought. so yea, you could buy now and hope to sell to a greater fool down the road, but i say we've come a long way. too far too fast. and we're gonna run out of fools sooner rather than later. the disconnect between prices and fundamentals is so wide... trees don't grow to the sky, if you know what i mean."

flatland tunes charlie out pretty quick. she doesn't care much about money. you could say she doesn't believe in money. she thinks pretty much everyone is missing the point on the topic. it's a measuring system for potential future consumption, not some score in the top right corner that shows who's winning or losing the videogame. and there's really nothing flatland needs to pay for beyond food and rent (which are easily covered). incremental money is like having twenty or fifty or even a million jelly donuts on the counter instead of two. if you can only eat two donuts, the rest of the donuts don't really change anything. more money means nada to flat.

"but not even cash is safe now. the fed is intentionally letting inflation go. gold, silver and german equities are the optimal portfolio. a third, a third, a third. i can help you out if you want. not a lot of diversification but there aren't exactly a lot of safe assets in a world where the supply of money is exploding and central bank balance sheets balloon. my dad called it 'the reset portfolio'. the only assets that you want to own when the whole shebang comes crumbling down. each central bank victory is only temporary."

"dude. enough. this is so boring. i get it. fiat money is bullshit. i'll give you my account info and passwords and you just take care of it, okay? leave me 25k spending cash in there."

"ok flat. i'll do my best. goodnight. i love you."

flatland responds sincerely even though she knows charlie is attempting to be ironic with his earnestness.

"i love you too, charlie. goodnight."

flatland hangs up and heads for her computer.

■ ■ ■

@realdemocracy tweeted
"the united states can pay any debt it has because we can always print money to do that.
so there is zero probability of default."
alan greenspan

■ ■ ■

1 YEAR AND 237 DAYS BEFORE THE RESET

Regional shortages of bread, rice and water are more common. New York City is immune to the shortages so far but the news from around the country is very gradually getting worse. I log into ↑Marketz!↓

The dollar has dropped another one percent overnight and my positions are all deep in the money. The question is whether to take profit and relax or press the advantage. I'm up $255,000 overnight so that's about $25,000 for me if I just cash out here and take the money.

There is an expression in trading: "You can't go broke taking profit". It is total bullshit. There is another saying: "Cut your losses and let your profits run". The two expressions are obviously contradictory but that doesn't stop the financial entertainment industry from regularly trotting out both. Bulls and bears get rich and pigs get slaughtered. The trend is your friend. Don't try to catch a falling knife. Buy the rumor / sell the fact. There must be 100 financial market clichés but unlike real world clichés, most of them are not true.

The dollar trades oddly well. It should be down more than two percent given the Midwest food riots making headline news. And there is growing likelihood of yet another round of GDP-targeting bond buys from the Fed. The money printers' mantra is: if it doesn't work, do more! But the dollar is down less than one percent. My gut says it's going to rally from here so I am in the very uncomfortable and illogical position of bullish and short the dollar at the same time. I will buy the next dip.

USDJPY is 55.70. The plan is to cover my short position at 55.10 and then go long at 55.00. There is a US inflation data release at 8:30 AM today and I am almost 100 percent sure that the inflation numbers will be worse than expected. The market will sell dollars on a high CPI print and that will give me one last chance to get out. Unlike the good old days when strong inflation was good for the dollar, high CPI now means sell bonds, sell dollars. Higher inflation is unambiguously bad.

No matter how bad the number is, I will buy back my USD. No matter how bad the number; I will buy back my dollars. Say it again. *No matter how bad the number; I will buy back my dollars.*

CPI comes out at 8:30 and the market expects something around 12%. Right now it's 8:28:33 and I'm nervous. My guts start to churn. Butterflies. This is typical right before a major data release. Economic data is a psychosomatic laxative. i.e., I have to take a shit.

Obviously I can't go right now so I clench my sphincter and await the data release.

8:29:30

8:29:40

8:29:55....56.....57......58.....59.....

16.5 percent!!!!!

This is a godsend, the absolute end of the dollar as we know it. My previous plan is out the window and instead of buying USD, I add to my short. I sell 100 million more USD and then another 100 million, increasing my position from 50 million to a big short of 250 million. I sell at 54.90 and keep hitting it all the way down to 54.70. In less than 30 seconds it trades below 54.50. I pull up a daily chart and I see no support until at least 53.00.

The dollar lurches lower again, to 54.10. I am up 50 pips on 250 million USD which is a quick $2.3 million dollars of P&L. I know I said I was going to buy back my USD no matter what the number, but I have changed my mind. I'm going to wait til 53.10 and extract a bit more from this move. Then I'll square up and have my big daysleep. USDJPY drops to 53.30.

The currency pair drifts for a bit, trading either side of 53.50. An angry buyer then rips it back up to 53.90. The air leaks out of my P&L. Suddenly, a massive MASSIVE buyer comes in. 54.50 bid. 54.90 bid. 55.40 bid!! USDJPY erases all the day's losses in seven seconds and my huge profit is now a big ass loss. My brain screams at me to square up and get out, but my body won't respond. Every ganglion in my cerebellum screams COVER THE POSITION but it is like that nightmare where no matter how hard you try, you cannot move. 56.10 bid.

Thirty percent of my trading account just disappeared in less than one minute. *You idiot. You were bullish. It's going up. And you're losing money. You suck.*

Finally, I regain motor control, spam some buttons and I'm out. I have just lost an unbelievable amount of money, almost half my account. My brain detaches from the organism that is the market and begins to cool. I have lost money before. Everything will be fine. Nobody died. I can recover. Everything will be fine. Everything will be fine.

■   ■   ■

1 YEAR AND 179 DAYS BEFORE THE RESET

I haven't had a serious girlfriend in more than two years and as I move from 20ish to almost 30 years old I really don't care much about it anymore. It's not that I'm not interested in women, it's more that I've been alone long enough to see that it's fine. There were plenty of times with my ex-girlfriend that I felt lonely when I wasn't alone. Alone and lonely, while sharing a common root, are not the same thing. I'm not even sure if they correlate, to be honest. So I've embraced the idea that I will never have another girlfriend and if that is true it's fine and if it's not true, that's also fine. Maybe I'm deluding myself but I think I have fully accepted the idea of me, single. Forever. It's fine. I use the word solo as a substitute for alone because I think it sounds more positive and less depressing. Less likely to be conflated with lonely.

Anyway, I tend to swipe left, not right. I have spent most of the past six or seven years chasing the night and getting high and trading and so there has never been a strong desire or much time or need for a girlfriend. Too much other stuff to do I guess. The relationships I have been in have been like when you're flipping through radio stations in a rental car in some random city and you keep hearing stuff that maybe sounds good for a second but meh, nope. Not good enough to really stop and listen for real. On to the next station.

I have lost a lot but I still have plenty. I try to be grateful. My mom told me that there are mermaids that wish they could be little girls and little girls that wish they could be mermaids and little kids that wish they could fly and probably birds that wish they could be little kids. I hear my mom's voice, like an echo:

"Don't be one of those. Just thank God for what you are. For what you have. For who you are."

I try to be thankful every day. I'm not always good at it. But I do try.

I miss you, Mom.

■ ■ ■

Alison has a thing for math. She's good at it and she likes it a lot. Symmetry and fractals and especially everything at the intersection of art and numbers. Pi and phi and Escher and Hypatia and Gauss and imaginary numbers and factorials and all of it. She's down with GEB. Her first tatt was a Möbius strip on the inside of her left forearm. As a kid she would giggle inwardly as she wrote four factorial, hearing "four!" In her head. When someone asks her "how was your day?" she might respond: "Oh, pretty good... 33 out of 37".

Alison is 19 years old but looks >=22.

She tends to dream about numbers and still often flashes back to a dream she had at age 10 where the air was a thick fog of tiny swirling numbers and she could only see two feet in front because of this flowing numberswarm. Airborne digits swirled like a Moscow blizzard.

Alison likes to change up the standard order of adjectives just to fuck with you. This reversal of adjective order induces in her a weird vertigo-like feeling in the pit of her stomach. She likes that feeling, the way you like how it feels when you poke the hole from a recently extracted tooth with your tongue. Bad and good at the same time.

"The green big dragon flew across the blue bright sky" she might write, for example. The adjective order thing is so arbitrary and we don't even get taught it so is it really a rule or just, like, another societal convention we sheeple don't bother questioning?

"You're weird, Alison."

"Shut it ya fat big turd."

Or whatever.

People that don't know her very well think she is well-adjusted. Very smart and polite.

Her laugh is like the sound you hear when you pass a schoolyard. Light and truly happy and full of real joy. It is the sound of the little girl trapped inside who comes out for a moment to smell the fresh air and have a look around. But just for a second. The girl gets scared. She feels too exposed. It's too risky and so Happy / Free Alison always retreats quickly back into her cage. Her mind tends to pace around and around like a lynx in a financially strapped, family-owned roadside zoo.

Her face is biracial. Mexican / Mestizo genes from mom and European / Irish American from dad. Hair cut short and croppy, dyed a different color or colors depending on the week. She has excellent facial symmetry with the exception of one crooked fang rotated maybe 20 degrees off line which adds significantly to her "cute" score but detracts modestly from her "beautiful" score while leaving her "sexy" score unchanged. Freckles in a vaguely butterfly-like formation on her nose and cheeks. Mexican-Irish. Rare. Stunning.

She saw the freckles as bad, like typos. Dad tried to tell her they were cute:

"Don't be like that Tigger. They're just beauty marks."

And she tried to believe him but she wasn't too sure.

She got the pet name Tigger at age six. Dad brought home a jumbo stuffed Bengal tiger from FAO Schwartz. One of those toys only super rich kids get. Alison already had a small stuffed Tigger doll and so she and Dad would play together sometimes in the upstairs playroom. Dad was the Bengal tiger and she was Tigger and Dad would move the big tiger around and growl and she would giggle and squeak and it was nice.

Alison's voice has small, endearing cracks. Like the squeak from a chord change on an acoustic guitar or the static clicks of an LP. Additive imperfections at conversational inflection points.

Cool as Banksy most of the time and nails the whole fashion thing without appearing to try. Mix and match style, e.g., cheap vintage boots paired with a highbrow t-shirt, jeans dotted with paint splotches, barely any makeup and a $700 pair of sunglasses. Lowbrow meets highbrow is her style though it isn't a conscious choice but more wicked fashion sense paired with a subconscious need to reject anything that betrays her membership in the one percent of the one percent.

She is rich but she hates rich people.

She kissed a girl once in the back of the movie theatre in Norwalk (and she liked it). She has had sex with zero females and three males: 1) a red headed boy named Andy Jaffers in freshman year. 2) Evan Williamson, high school lacrosse captain. And 3) her dad.

■　■　■

1999 was the peak for America and the beginning of the end of the good times for Mike and Claudia. It was the climax of the NASDAQ / internet bubble and the apex of US optimism and self-confidence and the pinnacle of foreign respect and admiration for the US of A. Capitalism had won the ideological war and there were no enemy survivors.

All you needed was a Dell desktop, an AOL dial-up connection, Netscape 1.0 on a floppy plus a cool idea and you were an instant millionaire. IPOs flew off the shelf like e-toys, POS B2B stocks got upgraded to Strong Buy with a $1,000 price target, and Americans downloaded Fatboy Slim, Smash Mouth, Sugar Ray and Limp Bizkit off Napster, pirating without consequence. The internet made promises it wouldn't keep until more than ten years later. Everyone partied like it was 1999.

Nerdy and cool also completed their merger around this time. Every subculture became mainstream, leaving nothing cool in the sense things were cool pre-internet. Nothing can remain underground because the internet offers instant global exposure to anything fantastic. Anything great is instantly and fully revealed and exploited. The instant it becomes cool, it is lit by a beaming spotlight and then raped by the marketing machines and twisted and perverted into a lame facsimile of itself. Skateboarding was the first example but dance floor culture and LBGTQ followed. The era of subcultures and cult followings and underground is over. Everything is mainstream.

Mike and Claudia were freshly married. He was still the funny, overconfident fraternity smartass, the kind of guy that frequently used "motorboat" as a verb. The kind of guy that teaches you, the hard way, the difference between college drinking buddies and real friends. And she was not yet "The Wife" but still Claudia, the rocked-up half-Mexican hotty with a porn star hardbody and nothing but upside. Closer in looks and attitude to the high school cheerleader of years past than the empty-behind-the-eyes, botoxified, fake-titted angry robot cunt she'd become. She was fun, athletic and dumb once but now she is broken and severe and OCD and pissed off, with a continuous migraine, scanning the house for something to get mad about.

They met at a frat party in college. Technically Mike's buddy Pat had called dibs but with an eminently fuckable package like Claudia, all the rules went out the window and point was you gotta do what you gotta do, right? Mike had plenty of friends anyway so fuck Pat and his dibs even though Mike sure as shit would have lost his mind if the tables were turned.

1999 was an awesome time to be rich. Make money and be proud. Go on CNBC and tout. Henry Blodget and Maria Bartiromo and Alan Greenspan were rock stars. Stocks with five-billion-dollar market caps jumped 5% or 10% on a random mention by Joe Kernan. A few grizzled curmudgeons yelled at clouds and called poppycock and balderdash from the sidelines but overall the mood was wildly optimistic as the United States knew it was the best and so did everybody else.

America, fuck yeah!

Mike was in his early 30s at the time, trading mortgages for Swiss Bank. He and Claudia had plenty of time and cash to travel and go wild. Mike made good money and Claudia came from a rocked-up Greenwich, CT family with a 7,700 square foot home and a 4,000 square foot beach house on Shelter Island. They took weekend trips to Vegas or South Africa or Parrot Cay or Spain. When he went to London and Tokyo for work, she tagged along, shopping all day for Prada and LV and Coach while he traded mortgages exclusively from the long side, mostly unhedged.

Life could not be better. They were self-centered and narcissistic, but in love. They had all the money they needed, all the friends they could hope for and all the drugs they could drop, chop, smoke or snort. They got high and stayed out til sun-up, listening to cheesy vocal house. They hit Ultra in Miami three years in a row, did Art Basel and had regular tables at Balthazar, Felix, Babbo and Au Bar.

If the continuum of drug use runs from experimental to recreational to hardcore to addict, Mike and Claudia's drug use in the late 90s could be classified as aggressively recreational. They got high on a regular basis but ringfenced the activity, keeping it to mostly appropriate times. Friday to Sunday was a parabola as they got sky high and then crashed, but they always managed to get their shit together by Monday. Mike was a great trader. Managing Director at 32.

This unstable equilibrium was not meant to last forever and their relationship and happiness peaked on just about the same day as the

United States, right around New Year's Day, Y2K. Not long after the turn of the millennium, Claudia peed on a stick and saw a plus. Mike wanted an abortion; but Claudia wanted the kid.

Chumbawumba was big in those days so Mike would sing:

"I get knocked up. But I get an abor-shee-un. We ain't ever gonna keep the girl. I get knocked up. But I get an abor-shee-un! We ain't ever gonna keep the girl..."

Mike would laugh afterwards but Claudia did not laugh much anymore. Mike thought it was cool that he got to bang a preggo chick but otherwise didn't see much upside to the whole baby sitch. He never forgave The Wife for winning that argument or himself for losing it. Two thousand zero zero, party over. Oops, out of time.

The baby's name was Alison.

■　■　■

Alison walks past the marble big lions guarding the New York Public Library and into the impressive stone building. She makes her way past reception and up to a large bank of public computers. Desktops, remember those? Whirring, ventilated metal contraptions parked inside beige veneer cabinetry. She brings up a bank website and clicks on "No-fee credit cards! Apply now!"

Even after more than four decades of manic debt-fueled consumption there is no new way. The remaining banks still lure undereducated consumers into "cheap" credit cards then pray those consumers get far enough into debt that they can never get out—but not so far into debt that they stop paying. FICO scores and prior history help the banks set credit limits at optimal levels so that consumers will max out quickly but still survive to pay monthly interest charges. Optimal for the bank. Perfectly suboptimal for the consumer.

The setup is structured to serve pathological corporations and their singular focus on profitability. The entire legislative and political process has been completely hijacked by corporations so the singular goal of the nation and its institutions is to maximize consumption and corporate profits. Alison fills forms with false names and false claims.

Occupation: Corporate Law. Annual Income: $375,000. Etcetera. The cards will be sent to a post office box in Albany, New York.

■ ■ ■

1 YEAR AND 172 DAYS BEFORE THE RESET

I get bored a lot at night, especially during the week. Today is Wednesday. It's 7:07 PM. My thoughts skip around a flowchart of options: Bet on baseball? Get some groceries? Work out? Jerk off? But the mental marble rolls around and finds the deepest neural canals which all lead to thoughts of a 12-pack and a 2-gram baggie of coke. And so the battle begins. Like the dieter and her donuts, I engage in a heated, schizophrenic argument.

C'mon! You have nothing going on tomorrow anyway. Don't waste a whole night doing nothing! Stimulate yourself! Have fun!

I really don't want to be sleeping in until 2:00 PM again tomorrow. I need to get up, eat some real food, go for a run...

Go for a run? Ha! Not going to happen. Stay home, get high and bet on baseball—that's what I'm talkin' about! Baseball! Baseball! Get high! Baseball!

I need to stop doing this. It's wearing me out, hurting my trading, ruining my focus. Not gonna call Danny.

You're right, you DO need to stop. But not today. How about one more night with me then you can stop? Sound good?

Addiction has an amazing ability to create intricate internal monologues featuring highly convincing personalities. The conversation always leads to the same conclusion. The chutes and ladders of my brain all lead to the same square. Like an itch that attracts more and more of your attention until you finally have to scratch it. *Don't call Danny. Don't call Danny. Think of something else to do tonight.* It is a conversation abruptly cut short as the automated subcortical motor program takes control and executes the predetermined outcome.

I grab the phone and call Danny. I ride the elevator down to the ground and go out behind my apartment building. The New York air

smells like wet and I pick up the sour balsamic scent of a trickle of
garbage juice leaking into a small stream out of the bottom of a
dumpster by the wall.

Danny rolls up in a black Acura with tinted windows and I hop
in the back. He's wearing a two-piece burgundy Adidas track suit.
Straight up old school. We exchange a few words.

"Hey man," I say.

"Hey."

"How's things?"

"Yeah good. One Special?"

"Yep..."

"You got it."

Once we are driving slowly along the street, he pulls out a small
cellophane package and passes it back to me. One Special, i.e., five
grams of blow wrapped up in one of those impossible to open and
close origami mini paper envelopes. I pass him fifteen twenties. We
drive back around to the pickup spot and I get out. I like Danny's
professionalism. $300 for one Special is a bit rich but maybe inflation
impacts the price of cocaine too? Heart rate gaps higher in anticipation. I head back into my building.

I smile at an elderly lady on the elevator. I wonder if she ever
dabbled in recreational pharmaceuticals back in the day.

■ ■ ■

Danny hears voices. Police sirens. Wolves. Full paranoia mode. He
drops Charlie off and drives away. At the first red light, he snorts
some perfect, uncut coke from his plastic bullet and puts it back in
the hidden pocket sewn into his jacket. *I can't keep doing this. I am
drowning.* His consumption exceeds net profit now so what the hell is
the point. A living cliché, high on his own supply.

Tony Montana seemed so cool back in the day.

Danny needs to get back to Illinois and start over. He imagines
Mom in the kitchen back home, making those cookies you buy pre-
made in a tube. She cuts the cookie tube of cold raw dough into

slices while his dad does the *New York Times* crossword and drinks a coffee.

How the fuck did I get here?

Yes, he is a drug dealer but he also recycles and holds the door for women at Dunkin' Donuts. Not a bad person. Most drug dealers are, in fact, good people that just stumbled by fluke or necessity into a banned line of work. Good entrepreneurs with no outlet. And it pays so well. Hard to get in. Only three ways out. Dead, OD or jail.

Bzzzzt. Bzzzzt. NEW TEXT MESSAGE. Another delivery.

■ ■ ■

@realdemocracy tweeted
fiat (noun): an arbitrary order.

■ ■ ■

I wander the UtopiaSphere aimlessly in an attempt to distract from the late stages of a medium-large hangover. Four full hours of last night are completely absent from my memory. Hippocampal area CA1 is bruised. My brain feels, like, offal. When I woke up this afternoon I nervously checked for rogue texts or ↑Marketz!↓ trades as I have this nasty habit of trading while hammered and/or sending cryptic and/or nonsensical texts to Tinder acquaintances.

No rogue texts and no rogue trades this morning and I see the markets are not doing much because tomorrow is Thanksgiving so I am looking for bilgeberries and killing time. I'm too hungover to do anything productive but I slept from 3:00 AM to 3:00 PM and so I'm not tired and I'm not meeting flatland until eight. We're going to hang out at her place and make sounds.

My ↑Marketz!↓ alerts are running in the background in case anything interesting or tradable happens but at 3:00 PM on the Wednesday before Thanksgiving I wouldn't expect anything.

I would be wrong.

An alert pops up and I and toggle over to ↑Marketz!↓ I look left and see the currency heatmap looks pretty ordinary but when I look right at the cubes representing the daily change in each S&P 500 component I immediately notice that two of the 500 S&P components have moved very, very aggressively lower while the other 498 are vibrating close to unchanged. MSFT and SBUX are down almost 10% in a dull market; it makes no sense. Given the two companies are in uncorrelated businesses, I know it's not an industry-specific headline driving it so there can only be one reason this is happening.

I only have a few seconds before things mean revert, so I move my hands in a series of quick and precise command moves, sending a flurry of orders to buy MSFT and SBUX and sell S&P futures to hedge. I recognize what's going on right away because this is now the third time it has happened in the past month. Russian or Chinese hackers send worms to infiltrate an investment bank, ECN or exchange computer and trigger an avalanche of rogue orders in a group of stocks—just for fun. Financial vandalism. Sabotage, possibly funded by governments.

Random market crashes are more and more endemic. There used to be less than one per year. The Flash Crash in 2010, the yield crash in 2014, the cable flash crash in 2015, etc. Now we get maybe 75 to 100 different mini crashes of some sort in various markets each year. It might be coffee futures one week and then MSFT the next and 2-year German bonds Schatzing the bed the next but the regulators have pretty much concluded that these waterfall moves are an inevitable result of computers trading against computers. Sometimes crazy shit happens when there are no adults in the room.

It is way too impractical to undo trades in the age of algorithms, so the old concept of unwinding "clearly erroneous" trades no longer applies. All trades are irreversible no matter how egregious the rate so if you can identify one of these dislocations in real time and take the other side, it's almost free money.

In this case, two minutes after I buy MSFT and SBUX there is a red headline.

*HACKER FINWORM CITED AS CAUSE OF RAPID DROPS IN SBUX, MSFT

This confirmation brings in a tsunami of buying and the stocks reverse quickly into the green. I hit some bids and unwind the S&P hedge for a total profit of $128,000. That's $12,800 for me. I just made enough money to cover Christmas shopping and December rent. Zinger. It's nice to make this sort of free money but these mini-crashes are also a disturbing warning sign of fragility. A canary in the coal mine. They boost my confidence that The Reset is coming.

The Reset is the day sometime soon when inflation will explode, paper money will become worthless, US stock markets will go to zero, food and water will become scarce, and the United States financial system will burn to the ground to be reborn in a new form that serves not just the financial elite and the venal corporatocracy but the entire population. All debts will be expunged and prior contracts void. The vacuum will be filled, at first, by chaos.

Over time, real democracy will emerge from the ashes of a broken system. Moral capitalism will replace a system built on bulimic binge and purge debt cycles. There will be no more singular focus on quarterly profit to the exclusion of common sense morality and responsibility to external stakeholders. The government will represent the American People, not sociopathic corporations and corrupt donors. As paper money becomes worthless, Americans will hoard physical assets such as gold, silver, land, diamonds, non-perishable food and so on. New decentralized global currencies will emerge.

The Reset will come slowly. And then all at once. Wild and unpredictable.

When the final wave curls up out of the financial sea and comes crashing down through Manhattan, across the United States and over the world, it will be too late to hedge. Too late to convert from electronic and paper money into real assets. Too late to buy real estate in Canada or Iceland or wherever. The shared illusion that allows standardized circular pieces of metal and printed rectangular sheets of paper money to be exchanged for goods and services will evaporate.

A lot of people planned for The Reset in 2008 and ended up looking like kooks and/or idiots. But this time actually *is* different. The capitalist system of debt and spending fueled by yet more debt and spending is bloated and obese. Monty Python's Mr. Creosote is about to explode; beware the wafer-thin mint. Too much money has been printed and it is finally about to unleash an unstoppable wave of inflationary hell. The Holy Church of Credit will burn down and we will start again. Unicorns will die.

Forests need fire to clear the undergrowth and trigger the release of new seeds and new growth. At the start of the 1900s, the US Forest Service embarked on a new and complex strategy to aggressively reduce the number of forest fires in the United States. The policy worked very well at first but over time, there were fewer fires and so undergrowth built up and dry dead branches accumulated, providing more and more potential fuel for future fires. Meanwhile, the seeds for future trees remained trapped in their pods as small fires failed to trigger pyriscence.

While the Forest Service snuffed out most of the small fires, they weakened the forest infrastructure and laid the groundwork for the megablaze of the future. Unintended consequences. When humans intervene (always with the best intentions) to prevent forest fires, the tinder builds up year after year until finally, a monstrous, out of control superfire erupts, burning up the soil and sending waves of flaming hell through, then beyond the forest.

Starting with Alan Greenspan, the central banks have been terrified of the business cycle, refusing to allow even the smallest of fires in the system. Every time a tiny spark was lit (Asia, LTCM, Greece, China, Italy, Brexit, whatever) the central banks rushed in and extinguished it in a panic. Periodic recessions used to be the price to pay for a long-term healthy economy. Not anymore.

Too low for way too fucking long.

As Kondratieff winter ends, the fire erupts. All to ash. Then finally, the inferno will burn itself out, leaving only scorched earth. Creative destruction. From that blackened ground real green shoots will emerge and something new, something better will grow. A new system will emerge. Sustainable, democratic and just.

But not everyone will survive the transition.

The last bit of my veisalgia is gone and the adrenaline from these bang bang MSFT and SBUX trades has me back up and running. I head to the kitchen to grab a beer and as I walk past the coffee table I hear two lines of coke left over from last night calling my name.

Charlie… Charlie…

No thanks, guys.

I'm tempted to wipe it all up with a wet paper towel but that seems like such a waste of good blow. This batch of coke is wholesale; big rocks, not powder. Definitely passes the sniff test. I cannot toss it; especially when it's been so hard to find decent chop these days. Half the stuff Danny gets is that Mexican yeyo that tastes so much like gasoline it gives me flashbacks to helping my dad fill up the Volvo at the Mobil station when I was a kid.

I don't like thinking about Dad; it just gets me all sad and that's not the way I want to feel right now. *I miss you Dad.* There. Now move on. I shake my head a few times to get the thoughts of Dad out. I do some jumping jacks to get the blood flowing. Three thoughts fly by like airplane banner ads: *I'm sorry I didn't go to your funeral. That was wrong. I was just a kid.*

I shake my head again to get rid of the bad thoughts.

There's still two hours before I meet up with flatland so if I rail the lines now I should be fine to eat by the time we meet up for dinner. I don't like to snort coke before dinner because my throat closes up and then it's impossible to eat but in this case it's such a tiny amount I might as well just get rid of it and clean up and move on with life. I pull a 50 from my wallet, roll it up, snort the powder and clean up the table.

The blow has a wicked laxative effect and my gut cramps and then I'm pushing out unrealistic amounts of Korean Barbecue from last night and then wow now I feel way better. Emptied. Ready to go for the night. Game on.

@realdemocracy tweeted
"it is well enough that people of the nation do not understand our banking and monetary system, for if they did, i believe there would be a revolution before morning."
henry ford

* * *

1 YEAR AND 168 DAYS BEFORE THE RESET

There are periods in trading where I am so in the zone I detach from normal consciousness and become one with the mind of the market. Like TRON, I go from playing the video game to living inside it. The only thoughts that invade from the external world are thoughts like "I really have to pee" and "Who keeps texting me?".

Physical awareness recedes and it is a purely mental journey through the aggregate price action. I fly, arms outstretched, over a numerical landscape. I swoop, turn and dive through flocks of variables. Hands move automatically to buy and sell, possessed by the subconscious mind, in perfect synch with the market. Sometimes this can go on for 10 or 15 minutes and when I finally emerge from the fog I become aware of what a ridiculous amount of money I've just made.

As the years wear on, the flow of dopamine to my brain is solely determined by my P&L and biochemical and pharmacorecreational pursuits of happiness. All the other ups and downs of life are inconsequential. Traders are generally predisposed to hard partying as the night tries to compete with the bipolar euphoria / disappointment of the day just done. Only by chasing the night right through to the chirping birds can the trader keep from crashing off the day's highs. Looking for higher highs. But hitting lower lows.

* * *

11 YEARS BEFORE THE RESET – WESTPORT, CONNECTICUT

Mike is in bed with The Wife. Their relationship has gone from chilly fall day in New York to Ozark January morning to Antarctic midnight in the past couple of years. They sort of tried the hopeless roller coaster that is marriage counseling for about two years but found it just gave them something new to argue about. Plus: Expensive and time consuming. Now they are locked into a stable equilibrium of mutual stonewalling. They have not touched each other in months. He sees her as you might a shuttered, rundown mini putt. It used to be so much fun but now it just kind of makes you sad when you look at it.

Mike slides a foot over and puts it against hers, just like he used to all the time when they started dating. Not because he loves her anymore but because he's horny. She used to say how good it felt when he touched his feet to hers. Now, she moves her foot away.

"Don't," she says. Voice of ice.

His feet were warm and comforting for a long time. Years. They slotted against hers like a missing piece. Then she became indifferent to them for a while. Now they are scaly, scratchy, clammy, repulsive. Disgusting. But nothing about his feet has actually changed. He should probably feel like crying but crying is so fucking gay.

He murmurs: "Fuck, whatever," under his breath and flips over to face away. He falls asleep in 40 seconds. She tosses and turns, thinking about how she does not like this man she married and wishes he was not in her bed. His escalating microaggressions torment her. She just wants him to go away.

She used to try to turn towards him.

"That was a really good movie," she might say.

And even though he had really liked the movie, it caused him physical discomfort to agree with her so he would say something like:

"Well, yeah, I guess, but not best of all time or anything."

Or through the pain she might manage to get out something like:

"I still love you, you know…"

And Mike would respond by rolling over and flicking off his light.

But if she left, where would she go? It might be worse. And what would happen to Alison? Poor, sweet Alison. *I'm sorry, Tigger. I'm trying. I really am. But it's just so hard. Everything is just so hard.* She finally falls asleep just after 1:00AM.

THE RESET

As The Wife falls asleep, Mike is deep in that recurring dream where he's at Peter Luger's Steak House. He is sitting by himself at a circular table for 10. Scraps and crumbs everywhere. Dirty plates and bread crumbs spread all over and emptied cracked up lobster claws in a silver metal bowl and fatty bits of uneaten bacon. Red wine and grease stains dot and streak the white tablecloth like a Jackson Pollock. Mike is out of breath; he's been gorging for hours. He forks the last bit of red meat and swirls it around in the puddle of blood on his plate. He bites the meat and chews it. Enjoys its mouthfeel. The waiter scurries over in a dirty and blood-spattered apron and asks:

"Did you enjoy the placenta, sir?"

■ ■ ■

Mike today is not too different from College Mike.

College Mike was a LAX bro before LAX bros were a thing. Captain of Harvard Lacrosse and spent twelve hours a week lifting. To avoid lifting around the (bigger, stronger) guys from the football team, Mike avoided the varsity training facility and lifted instead in a secondary weight room.

It was a long, thin basement room with exposed pipes, dripping water and peeling paint. It was ghetto and thus barely used. The few regulars nicknamed it "The Dungeon". The room was usually empty and so Mike frequently went in there and benched two and a half plates without a spotter, or squatted three plates/side, solo. Super fucking dangerous but he knew he could handle it. *Work those fucking pecs! Work the glutes, motherfucker! Work them! YEAHHHH!*

He would yell and grunt and push the bar up, his primal rage echoing loudly around the 40 X 10 room:

"C'mon you fucking fucker! Push! Push! Don't be a pussy! Arrrrrr!!!!!"

And once the bar was fully up, he would hold it there and try to hold it long enough to hear three drips of water from the irregular drips dripping into the room via various cracks and fissures. Plink. Plonk. Plink. And then "CLANK" he would drop the bar aggressively back down onto the stand. Just like they tell you not to do.

63

Then maybe 20 reps on each bicep with the 50 pounder. Incline, decline. He would pull the rowing attachment and thrust his pelvis forward, smiling at himself in the mirror as he recalled finger-banging that sloppy-drunk New Haven chick at Dan's party. He carried a tiny notebook and pen from station to station and dutifully tracked his progress. Disciplined like a machine. Intense like a Nazi military parade.

Brett, the emaciated 130-pound attendant, sat outside the room at a desk. He made three bucks an hour checking student IDs. He hated the carnivorous, acne-backed meatheads that cycled through the place but needed the job to pay the rent and buy weed since he dropped out and Mom and Dad cut him off.

Brett had three responsibilities: sign people in and out (students and faculty only), wipe down the equipment twice a day, and mop up the puddles so nobody slips. He got in and out of the room as quickly as possible as the place reeked of hot testosterone or sweaty balls or whatever. He literally gagged in there at least once a day. The rest of the time he was free to sit at the table in the silence of the hallway reading Camus or Dostoevsky or Sartre. Real heavy existential shit.

College Mike was jacked. Ripped like Jean-Claude van Damme. Two rows of perfectly aligned Chiclets. He was in the right frat and wore all the right preppie gear. He shaved his chest every Sunday night and also reshaved before any night out where there was even a small chance he might pick up. Girls approached him with the transparent desperation of Caribbean craft market vendors. He was a big swinging dick on campus before he became a Big Swinging Dick on Wall Street. And no idiot, either.

He perfectly understood the Game of College and used optimal strategy to maximize his GPA. He knew he needed a top-decile GPA to get the good jobs. He wasn't going to be some bitch analyst working 100 hours a week at Salomon or Bear. Only a trading job straight out of college would do. Classes that could be skipped, he skipped and bought the notes. Classes where participation counted towards your grade, he sat front row center, hand pushed high like morning wood. He bought essays and cheated when he could. He was a fantastic regurgitator. The Scantron King.

His brother's girlfriend bought him *Liar's Poker* for Christmas when he was 15, and by page 20, he knew he had to be a trader. A real fucking trader, not some equities in Dallas shitface. He stayed up until 5:00 AM that Christmas night, reading *Liar's Poker* cover to cover in one shot. Could not put it down. He wanted a job on Wall Street more than any of these other fucking pussies. And he was gonna get one. No matter what. He was a lifting, fucking, drinking and test taking machine. Unstoppable. Invincible.

■ ■ ■

14 YEARS BEFORE THE RESET – MANHATTAN

The city is dark. A relentless late winter rainstorm punishes Battery Park. Swirling winds. Nearly frozen raindrops fall diagonally in sheets. Mike walks out of the gleaming headquarters of SquidCo, the most respected and feared investment bank in the world. He exits into the goddamned rain and pops open his Maglia Francesco umbrella. A solitary cold raindrop hits the bald spot from which dark reddish-brown hair recedes orbitally. His hair has thinned enough that he feels the coldness of the raindrop as it hits then trickles an inch or so across his scalp. He is pissed off about tonight. He is pissed off about work. He is pissed off about losing his hair.

Fuck the world.

A black Escalade with bitching chrome rims is parked directly in front, waiting for Mike. The driver hops out quickly to open the door as Mike approaches. Investment banksters exit HQ, duck under umbrellas held by drivers and into waiting SUVs. On their way to client dinners, round tables, drinks and later: New York Dolls.

Mike notices a good-looking professional woman, maybe 28 years old. He tries to get a look down her shirt to catch the outline of her tits. They are like globes ready to burst out of the taut, bulging fabric of her silky blouse. They push against the shirt buttons like Greek anti-austerity protesters on a police barricade.

Beautiful orbs. Reveal yourselves to me.

The beautiful tits are a waste though, paired up with such an ugly face. Like a monkey with beautiful eyes.

His driver speaks:

"Good evening, Mr. Leary, another rainy one."

"Yeah, Taj. I need to get to the school ASAP. I'm late. The Wife is going to be livid."

Taj closes the door behind Mike and hurries to the driver's seat. Mike checks the market on his Blackberry then goes straight to e-mail as they drive off. The e-mails come in endless waves, like enemy soldiers in a bad dream. He picks them off one by one but can never stop the tide. Always falling farther behind.

Mike's phone rings. It's The Wife.

"Yep. Ok. Yep. No. Listen, I'll be there as fast as I can. No. There is nothing I can do at this point. I know. I know. No. Listen. I'm hurrying. Yep. Best school in Connecticut. Yep. I know that. OK. Yeah. Bye Honey."

Mike has got a few other more pressing things to deal with than choosing a school for his daughter right now. Public school sure as hell was good enough for Mike. He's gone from lower middle-class son of a Michigan mailman to Global Head of Fixed Income Trading at the biggest investment bank in the world. Public school works plenty fucking good enough. Now he's about to cough up fifty thousand after-tax dollars to send his pampered little snowflake off to a glorified daycare with a bunch of entitled 4-year-olds parented by helicoptering tiger moms? He shivers.

Alison recently completed the PRE exam, which is an IQ and problem-solving test for kids under 5 years old. The SAT for toddlers. The good schools use it to filter out the quality from the retards. Anything below 95 and you can forget about getting into Beardsley or Spence. Under 90 and you are talking Williamson or Cordoba, bottom of the barrel private schools but still private school at least. God forbid your toddler scores below 85—then it's off to public.

There, you mix with the gun-toting, underfed foodstampers in overcrowded classrooms led by rubber-room-quality teachers. Free milk though, at least. Meanwhile, the elites roll in Escalades and Land Rovers to 50k/year facilities to learn Mandarin and swim in Olympic-sized pools after eating a lunch of pulled pork and biscuits paired with butternut squash soup. Yum! The chefs at the good private schools have amazing blogs, too.

Mike flicks away e-mails and checks the market on his Blackberry. Thinks about buying a newer 911. Flexes the place where his six-pack used to be. Drifts off for maybe 20 minutes and dreams of banging the coffee cart lady at work until she bleeds. She is black, fat, hideous. Precious, but dumber.

A normal mind runs this sort of program.

```
10    LET X = NEW THOUGHT OR ACTION
20    IF X < > LEGAL GOTO 90
30    IF X < > MORAL GOTO 90
40    IF X < > ETHICAL GOTO 90
50    IF UTILITY(X) > 0 GOTO 70
60    IF UTILITY(X) < 0 GOTO 90
70    DO X
80    GOTO 10
90    STOP
100   GOTO 10
```

Mike's program is missing lines 20, 30 and 40.

Taj finally pulls up outside the school and Mike sees The Wife standing there, arms crossed and face tight with impatience. She got here by taxi 40 minutes ago. Mike is not in the mood. He wants to fast forward and get this over with but he has to do the monkey dance and pretend to be interested. He checks the market on his Blackberry then gets out of the car. Mike and The Wife barely acknowledge each other as they enter the school side-by-side.

A short, wiry Vietnamese woman with supernormal, hard, spherical breasts stands at reception next to a possibly gay 50-year-old man in a $4,000 grey suit with pink pocket square. The man's skin is too white and too soft, like mozzarella di bufala. Mike ponders the woman's boobs. He finds them interesting but asexual, the way one might find someone's giant and perfectly shaped nose interesting.

They shake hands with the admissions officer and president of the school. *Admissions Officer? Really? These kids are four years old.* Mike wants to punch the fag in the throat though he can't deny that's a quality suit. Brioni, maybe? The Wife apologizes profusely to the admissions lady; they are 25 minutes late.

Admissions Lady starts her pre-packaged spiel and Mike can't concentrate as he pictures her with a leather strap around her head and an orange ball in her mouth. He imagines her bone-dry snatch. As he pictures it, four or five cockroaches scurry out between her scaly, dry vagina lips. The vomitous chemical odor of perfume fills Mike's mouth and nostrils like napalm.

The questioning continues and Mike keeps mostly quiet. He stares past Admissions Lady at a school photo that shows an incredibly diverse set of young kids, lined up perfectly in rows. Mike is impressed by the transparently deliberate heterogeneity.

Slope, check. Paki, check. Niglet, check. Diversity quota met.

The Wife volleys each question deftly with a pre-packaged response. She's done hours of practice interviews with the top preschool admissions consultant in Fairfield County and so she knows exactly what to expect and what to say.

Of course the Admissions Officer knows these pre-packaged answers too well and doubts The Wife's sincerity or intelligence. Like a good professor, she can detect The Wife's plagiarism. *Obviously coached.* Mike is thinking that he needs to sell some bonds. And there's layoffs coming... He needs to knife 20 direct reports by next week. *Fuck. Forgot about that.* He could use a cigarette. Mike sneaks a check of the markets on his Blackberry and The Wife sees him do it and so she huffs audibly.

Vietnamese tits on a stick goes on and on about the outstanding (buzzword) of the school and how it excels at (buzzword) and has a unique ability to (buzzword) and deliver (buzzword). The Wife sticks to the script but Mike finally elects a different strategy, more out of boredom than any need to get his daughter admitted.

"Let me assure you, Mrs. ..."

"Miss Vuong," is the Admissions Lady's name. Mike notes she has a bad case of resting bitch face.

"My daughter has a 96 PRE. She's plenty smart enough for this school. I averaged $7.7 million dollars a year total comp over the past five years. If Alison is admitted, I will be a platinum donor from day one. I guarantee it."

"I see," says Miss Vuong.

The Wife shrinks to half her normal size and experiences a terrible episode of tunnel vision.

"I'm sorry, Miss Vuong," she begins, but Miss Vuong does not respond. Instead, she gathers the papers in front of her and turns to the school president. He shifts uncomfortably in his chair and looks down at his left shoe. He has a date later with some rando friend of a friend and he's kinda dreading it so he is not really present the way his Kundalini meditation coach has guided him to be.

"Our process is quite involved, as I am sure you both know," starts Miss Vuong. "We generally take two to three weeks to make our determinations and our selections go out by mail after that. So you should hear within a month."

Some more paper shuffling and then: exeunt.

On the short ride home, there is mostly silence. The Wife is near tears.

"I can't believe you ruined this for me," she sputters. Mike checks the market on his Blackberry.

"It'll be fine," he mutters. He thumbs his phone again. Gold is up 8 bucks. S&P's are down 22. Oil unch.

Three days later, they get a call from the school. Alison got in.

■ ■ ■

1 YEAR AND 162 DAYS BEFORE THE RESET

Alison walks into the Port Authority bus terminal in Times Square and buys a one-way ticket to Albany. The bus is disgusting, packed with vile fellow passengers. She is locked in a wheeled fuselage that smells of diesel, piss, bathroom disinfectant and sadness. People who get in the car or on an airplane for a trip are full of excitement .... anticipation. In contrast, people take buses to run away from home, to commit suicide Up North, to get to the nearest town after prison release or to visit their insane sister in Chappaqua, NY. Alison tosses around marketing ideas.

Greyhound: Sadness on Wheels.

Greyhound: The opposite of joy.

Greyhound: You probably won't die.

Greyhound: Eaperchay. Owerslay. Elliersmay.

Greyhound: Almost free! (For good reason).

The four-hour trip up I87 and I84 is predictably boring and Alison sits near the back and reads a book made of paper to pass the time. A youngish (17?) skater-douche hits on her and she politely turns him down. He goes and jerks off in the bus bathroom and she can faintly hear slapping and panting, she thinks.

The PO Box location is a 10-minute walk from the bus station and she arrives 15 minutes before closing time. Her heart speeds a bit as she pulls out the mailbox key. A few weeks ago, she applied for 25 different credit cards online. Visa, MasterCard and AMEX supposedly have sophisticated fraud screening, so she figures the box might contain four or five cards. Maybe seven, max. Sure, she knows the obvious tricks, avoids the blatant red flags, uses the correct self-checking digits and such, but the fraud detection business is pretty tight. Not much chance more than 7 or 8 cards got approved.

She opens the mailbox and...

25 envelopes spill out.

In a nearby park she shits herself with excitement (not literally) as she rips open envelope after envelope and pulls out brand new card after brand new card. CHASE NEW YORK. LIMIT 7,000. CITIBANK. LIMIT 11,000. CHINA COMMERCIAL BANK NEW YORK. LIMIT 17,000. 22 envelopes contain credit cards. 3 contain rejections. So much potential spending energy. Holy mama. Almost two hundred thousand dollars in available credit. It will take her weeks to use it all.

Most 20-year-olds would have no idea how to spend this much "money" but Alison already knows how she will spend every virtual dime. Silver and gold. That's it. She will buy as much as she can find on eBay and other sites without raising the tentacles of the fraud-bots.

For Alison, money means one thing: freedom.

She does the circuit between the library, the bus station, cheap motels and various post office boxes for about three weeks and manages to collect every Johnson-Matthey one-ounce gold bar and Canadian Gold Maple Leaf she can. In total she purchases more than 150 silver and gold coins and bars of various denominations. Two hundred grand in gold and silver coins is heavy, if you're wondering.

Finally, duffle bag in hand, she boards another bus and heads even further north.

@realdemocracy tweeted
"in the human brain, monetary gain stimulates the same reward circuitry as cocaine – in both cases, dopamine is released into the nucleus accumbens, reinforcing the behavior. in the case of cocaine, we call this addiction. in the case of monetary gain, we call this capitalism."
andrew w. lo, professor of finance at the mit sloan school of management

■ ■ ■

1 YEAR AND 157 DAYS BEFORE THE RESET

Another Wednesday night. The fog of the weekend's excess has cleared from my mind and I'm trying not to think about... *Sight*. There it is. The silent voice that whispers in the back of my subconscious.

Sight.

A recent bad habit: I've taken to doing a gram and a half of coke and a few mills of Sight by myself on random weeknights. Need to stop that. Not good. Flip on the TV. Nothing much to watch but I throw something on. *Sight*. The voicenoise in my brain gets a bit louder. Heated discussions between pro and anti-drug coalitions. Battles erupt between dozens of tiny brains inside my head.

Eventually, there is a conscious conversation inside my head discussing pros and cons. From a logical point of view, the cons have it every time but the pros are tenacious and defy reason. The last thing I need is another sequence of chemical blows to the head. Really gotta do some serious trading tomorrow, with full concentration. But there's nothing else to do right now. Kinda bored. I can work through the hangover. The TV is an unbearable racket so I turn it off. Is there any beer in the fridge? My stomach churns. Too much recreational pharmaceutical action does nasty things to one's intestinal constitution. The contents of my intestines are a liquid of yellow brown.

Don't think of a cold beer. Don't think of a white bear. Don't think of a white bear.

Beer is a terrible idea. Destroyer of willpower. Alcohol. The ultimate and only true gateway drug. I pick up a book and read a bit but the war in my head breaks out again. *Sight. Maybe just a few lines of blow and in bed by 2AM?* My brain pleads. Begs. *Can I? Can I? Please??? Cmon!* I shut it out. Read a bit more. It's only 8:15 PM. Need to go for a walk. *It's freezing outside.* You're right. I won't be tired until at least midnight. Maybe a beer will quiet things down in my head.

Thank God I don't have any blow handy or I would have spilled it out onto the coffee table and chopped it into powdery smithereens by now. My hand is shaking a bit, I think. Nah. I go into the bathroom and hold up my hand / look in the mirror. It's not shaking. I look straight into the mirror and see the twitchy, judging eyes of a jonesing, sketched-out cokehead. Is that me in there?

Neck and cheek stubble indicate a decline in personal grooming habits. I need a haircut. I should really just go to bed. Get up early tomorrow and go for a run, maybe. Choose life. I scan the apartment and see my electric cigarette on the counter. Can't resist. I light it up and suck in the nicotine-rich water molecules. Ahhh, that's better. I relax. Thoughts follow the well-worn path from nicotine to alcohol to Sight to blow and round and round.

I pull out my Gretsch guitar and strum for a bit but I'm kind of bored of guitar in general and I really should take some more lessons. The F chord is causing me all sorts of problems and I can't play half these tabs without an F chord. I lean the guitar against the fuzzy purple recliner I bought for $40 at Goodwill in the days before I had cash.

Maybe just one beer. Take the edge off.

Three beers empty and there is no more war in my head. The bad guys won as they always do. Idle hands. I call Danny and he's here and gone in less than half an hour. I rail half a gram of blow right away. The strategy is to frontload. The more I do now / early, the less I'll have left later.

Done early is always best so you start with big lines and chase it with as much booze as possible. In the early days I use to do blow to keep from getting tired after too much beer but now I drink beer to keep from getting wired after too much blow. Lately I'm spending too much time rolling around in bed listening to my heart hammer jackrabbit style and the noise of cars driving by outside—cars slash across the wet road and make a sound like paper ripping.

And then usually a benzodiazepine or two to drop into full black sleep after two hours plus of rolling around thinking it'll be fine and I'll fall asleep eventually.

Two more beers go bottle to stomach. The coke tastes like gasoline. Shitty Mexican stuff again. Supplies of good blow have been few and far between lately with all the border enforcement stepped up and full out narco civil war raging across Mexico and half of South America. Dirty high too. Sketchy like a train station bathroom, not altogether enjoyable. Note to self: when you know the different types of blow and can identify their provenance like a drug somme-lier, you just *might* have a drug problem.

I need some Sight to even things out. I find a bottle in my top dresser drawer. Lay flat on my back on the couch and pull the lower eyelid out a bit for optimal delivery. I drip a viscous drop into the pocket of my lower left lid. Same again on the right. I lie there staring at the ceiling and let the tide roll in. It doesn't take long.

Time wrinkles then rips. I focus on my favorite part of the ritual. The numbs. I shake my head and feel my eyeballs knock around in my skull, wobbling loose in their sockets. Thoughts go from analog to digital. 5/20 vision.

Minute hand rotates visibly around clock face. Unable to calcu-late quantity of time passing. Aware that time is a human construct.

Intermittent feelings of acceleration like I'm driving through my living room and everything is fractal:::::::::::::::::::computerized animation::::::::::::::::::::flying by. Back to normal speed. Drips from the ceiling. I touch my arm and it feels like sandpaper as I rub it back and forth. I hear distant bells. Cars rip the water on the road like paper. FSHHHHT. FSHHHHT. Honking? More lines but it truly tastes superbad, like actual powdered gasoline. I carefully pour the rest of the two grams of cocaine out of the tiny Ziploc baggie and onto a spoon. I flick my Zippo open and hold it to the bottom of the spoon. The janky blow melts. I reholster my Zippo and watch the melted narcotics cool to a semi-liquid crystalline state. I dab the hot end of a lit cigarette in there and smoke it like crack. Cocoa puff.

Intense acceleration. Not super fun. More like: alarming, a Mario Kart-style tunnel vision nightmare. I cannot regulate this trip.

Even when I shut my eyes I'm flying forward at seventy or a hundred thousand miles an hour. Sort of like the spins but moving straight ahead and not around and around. I struggle to stand up. It's difficult to walk but I make it to bed. Mind briefly goes to static and then back to the acceleration feeling. I close my eyes and start to slow down. Stop. Then accelerating slowly but backwards. Then flying backwards. Fuck. I need something to put me to sleep so I get up and head for the kitchen. I wash two benzodiazepines down with a three ounce pour of Canadian Club Whisky. Back into the living room and then I trip over my guitar and stumble. Crack my head on the side of the bookcase.

CUT TO: Black.

BEEP BEEP BEEP. 6:30 AM. Need to start trading. My brain is catatonic and uncooperative. What was last night? Oh yeah. Remembering. I step over the blood on the carpet, walk into the kitchen and make a cup of coffee slowly and deliberately. Incredibly focused pain behind my right eye halfway between eyebrow and temple. Like a hammer has hit that part of my skull, but from the inside. My right cheek is numb. My breath tastes like black death.

You must have to be pretty sick to die.

I wake up my CPU and logon to ↑Marketz!↓ The neuemark has appreciated a bit overnight but nothing too exciting going on. Some idiot is on CNBC bitching about the Citigroup/JPMorgan merger but you can't stop progress. Gold has dropped every day this week and nobody knows why.

I flip through a few charts and notice that the divergence between gold and S&P is as big as it's been in weeks, maybe months. I do some work and confirm my suspicion. Gold is three standard deviations cheap to the S&P so I put on the relative value trade and buy S&P / sell gold. If the Great Inflation is here (and CNBC and Zerohedge seem to think it is) then S&P and gold should both be going straight up. When one lags you buy it. BTFD: buy the fucking dip.

My gut says this is one to be careful with because a lot of really messed up shit has been happening in the market lately. I allocate $400,000 of capital to the long gold / short S&P trade and then the raging pain behind my right eye boils up again so I head to the bedroom to lie down. There are dried cokesmears all over the coffee table. A spattering of blood across the carpet. What is wrong with me?

There is something wrong with you, Charlie.

I get into bed, shaking a bit from low blood glucose levels. My comforter is low quality and crumpled. Somewhat yellowed. It needs to be washed. My eyes pop open against my will as I lie here and try to rest. I'm sketched out from last night's dabbling. I get back out of bed, put my goggs back on and check the market. Gold is 4 bucks lower and I'm already down $25k but I don't really care. This is a 2-week trade. I'll ignore the random jiggles. Focus on signal not noise.

I'm tempted to drop some Sight just to let this day fly by but I've made a pact with myself: no blow and no Sight before 7:00 PM. I can feel that I'm starting to tip slighhhhhhhtly over the edge here with the midweek chopfests and I need some rules.

That was a favorite expression of my dad's. "Make your own rules. But then stick to them." Dad got zero advice his entire life from his angry alcoholic father and so I think he overcompensated by dispensing copious advice to me all the time. Some of it stuck. He had so many awesomely trite sayings. He called me Charlie Brown.

"You're a good man, Charlie Brown," was as close as he ever got to saying "I love you."

I never told him either. I told him a few times diagonally via Fathers' Day poems or whatever but I never wrote or said those exact words to him. As years passed, it was like this huge elephant in the room. I know he was dying to say it to me just like I was to him but we just couldn't. There were times that were clearly obvious "I love you" moments and yet we had gone so many years and been mute through so many of those moments that it eventually got to a point where I think we feared that if we did say it, we would trigger some sort of nuclear explosion or something. A glitch in the matrix. Or like: don't be so gay; we both know we love each other. Or something. So we both just assumed that the other knew he was loved and left it at that. I wish I'd had just blurted it out at some point. I almost did a few times. Like at Mom's funeral.

I did finally whisper "I love you" to him once at the cemetery. Maybe he heard me.

I try not to think about Dad. I know you're supposed to revel in the life that was lived and all that but I always end up thinking about The End. Even when I'm thinking about the good times my memory inevitably fast forwards to The End. Was it on purpose? An accident? Unclear. Truthfully, I don't really care as much what the answer is… I just want to know either way so I can stop wondering. Did he kill himself on purpose? Yes, or no? It's the not knowing that sucks.

HEY! YOU THINK SAVING IS DUMB, RIGHT!? WRONG! CALL BROOKLYNCAP TODAY TO FIND OUT WHY!

An ad for BrooklynCap just popped up in my goggs. MeggaHD right in my face. These things still scare the crap out of me. You can get free access to the goggnet but you have to deal with one of these full facial 3D popup ads once an hour. This one is for Brooklyn Capital, the biggest name brand in retail hedge funds.

Since hedgie advertising has been fully deregulated in the interests of greater transparency and superior liquidity, Brooklyn Capital has rapidly taken over as the number one hedge fund in the world. They were the first to realize that every hedge fund was essentially pursuing a combination of just three or four basic and highly-similar strategies and so with more and more hedge funds doing the same thing and Sharpe ratios dropping steadily year after year, the real edge in the hedge fund business would come from marketing, not trading. Fundraising, not speculation. Advertising, not analysis.

So they created a strategy to mirror the performance of the leading hedge funds (not difficult) then absolutely blew everyone's head off with a marketing budget over 10X the runner up. They quickly learned that investors are a lot more interested in investing in something cool than trying to figure out what hedge fund is going to outperform this year or next. So as long as you're in the ballpark on performance—it's all about the brand. And even the smart investors have been fooled by randomness enough to know that chasing the best-performing funds is an absolute waste of time—like betting red on a roulette wheel because it just came up red seven times in a row.

BrooklynCap has parlayed a sexy spokesavatar, inner-city guerilla marketing and all kinds of innovative, outside-the-cube thinking to capture a ridonkulous 22.4% of the retail hedge fund market. Their closing jingle capitalizes on recent cultural trendspikes in musical haiku and the defunct BASIC programming language from the 1980s.

Music

(erotic female robot voice)

Hey! Don't let your money nap!

Zero rates are total crap.

GOTO: BrooklynCap

Music ends

I take off my goggs and go back to bed. Soon, I'm in the gap between conscious thought and dreamscape.

■ ■ ■

1 YEAR AND 152 DAYS BEFORE THE RESET

I walk into Whole Foods and head straight for the fruit. Need to get healthier. My body needs nutritional resuscitation. Retro dubstep plays on the overhead sound system. I pull two brand name apples from the ridiculously risky fruit pyramid and four more tumble out of the display and bounce like years-old tennis balls at my feet. One of them hits the side of my foot and rolls off, escaping frantically west. I make a quick move to capture it and bump into a worn formerly white sneaker covered in scribbled black Sharpie. I see the word YES written in black on the white sneaker toe before I stand and look up to face the wearer. It's Alison, the girl from the popup the other night. Still super cute. I feel flutterbies.

"Unnecessarily precarious fruit displays," I say.

Alison smiles, picks up the fugitive produce and holds it out to me. Three straight-line scars mark the back of her hand like the

Adidas logo. They look fresh. She makes really solid eye contact when she speaks.

"We met at the popup the other night, right?" she asks.

Alison is the rare combination of cute, beautiful and sexy. The elusive Holy Trinity. This is not a misogynist statement or objectification of females. Cuteness, for example, goes far beyond external veneer and radiates via personality, self-deprecation and sense of humor. Sexy is confidence and chutzpah. Intelligence multiplies beauty. You get the idea. Her apparent failure to recognize just how awesome she is (meek gait, quiet demeanor, self-disfigurement via text tattoos all over her arms) adds another layer of attractive.

"Yep, that's right," I reply.

"You don't seem like a grocery shopping kind of guy," she says.

Is that a mild insult? *Don't overanalyze it.*

"I'm a bodega guy trying to be a grocery store guy. A 6:00 AM guy trying to be a 1:00 AM guy. You know."

What the actual fuck am I talking about?

"Yeah. Fitter. Happier. I get it. Umm. So... I'm off to get the rest of my food I guess. See you, Charlie."

"See you."

She glides away. Remember that feeling in, like, 6th or 7th grade when the cute girl knows your name and you are surprised because you thought you were a nobody but obviously if she knows your name then that proves that you actually exist? I have that exact feeling right now. Floating. And BTW, her bum in a pair of Lulu pants is suitable for calibrating protractors.

■ ■ ▩

Soylent hit the market around 2015 but it's taken until now for the meal replacement category to truly take off. I'm standing in the meal replacement aisle now, still thinking about Alison and how I should have asked her out then and there because I don't even know her number or where she lives or who she hangs with or what she does or anything. She is the most beautiful thing in the world.

I'm looking for strawberry banana Nootch. It's a scientifically formulated meal replacement tailored to bodyweight and physical activity levels to optimize caloric intake and match energy expenditure. I pick up a six-pack (male, 160 to 180 pounds, moderately active) and put it in my cart.

I scan the barcode of the Nootch with my smartphone to do a quick price check with the Vortex app. Whole Foods (NASDAQ: AMZN) knows I'm going to do this so the pricing is probably competitive, but it never hurts to check. The price is fine but as I go to swipe the app away, my phone bricks.

I hear frustrated yelps and cursing from various locations in the store and I know this is another cell failure. Rolling internet and cellular brownouts are common now as hackers and international pains in the ass have figured out that you can cause a lot of havoc with a little effort by blacking out cell towers and glitching the net. The brownouts hurt economic activity and freeze up traffic.

Good times.

■ ■ ■

APRIL 2004

The 5:30 AM New York air is damp and smells metallic and vaguely soapy, like the inside of an empty washing machine. Todd walks out of the Dorchester Building and steps out towards Broadway. The Upper West Side is quiet and dark; he can see a few sets of headlights as he looks north toward 72nd Street. The light fog in the air is to the light fog in his head as water is to vodka after an unnecessary night out with co-workers last night. He walks to the bus shelter and waits for the bus. Yes. The bus.

Don't tell anyone he takes the bus, it's kind of mortifying, but also by far the most efficient way to get from 68th/Broadway to Times Square at 5:30 AM in the morning. Sure, he could take a taxi but that's 8 bucks times 200 trading days per year and you don't get rich spending it, right?

Bagel, coffee and up to the trading floor. The lights don't come on until 6:30 AM but today is payrolls day so he's in early. A few other traders and research assistants are around but the trading floor is pretty much silent. CNBC is on most of the TVs, muted. Todd is a prop trader so he sits in a glassed-in room called the Fish Bowl with five other guys from the prop group. His job is to take risk in any product he wants and make as much money as possible. He gets paid 10% of his P&L. If he loses money for more than 18 months or so, he loses his job. Decent gig. Reasonable comp.

His grande Pike Place from Starbucks is leaking driplets of coffee onto his desk at very slow intervals and there is a drip of coffee on the white French cuff of his Charles Tyrwhitt shirt already. Can they make a coffee cup lid that doesn't drip? Geez.

He checks the P&L. Up 400k overnight on some random drift in the bond market. Not much is going on. Other traders trickle in one by one but he barely notices. By 8:00 AM everyone has arrived but he's got his head down. Not much conversation. Tippity tap tippity tap tippity tapping of sales and traders chatting electronically with friends, business acquaintances and oft-hated but necessary clients. Regular moments of no voice conversation at all. 200+ in sales and trading all just: tippity tap tippity tap tippity tap. Bonds are up a few ticks, drifting on nothing.

It's 8:27 AM and nonfarm payrolls, the biggest economic release of the month, is released at 8:30 AM. As the seconds peel off, he feels the nervous anticipation. Guts start to heave like a mosh pit. Todd gets the butterflies. Also known as the shits. As in, he needs to take a shit. But he can't because the biggest economic number of the month is coming out in two minutes. He pings his buddy Jose on Bloomberg:

TODD BLOOM: 8:28:15: GOTTA SHIT. FKG TYPICAL.

JOSE PERRERAS: 8:28:29: Nervous poo. Thanks for the heads up, amigo. GL with the #.

Last night was another lost night—out with brokers. Six vodka tonics, three bottles of Cakebread split four ways at Smith & Wollensky and things kept going until around 2:00 AM. Seemed like the brokers were doing blow given the number of trips they took to the men's but that was never Todd's thing. Bullshit, market-related conversation all night as if talking finance from 7am to 6pm wasn't enough. He hasn't seen his son Charlie in three nights. Exhausted.

Nobody cares how tired you are.

And he needs to shit. But needs more badly to get ready to sell as many bond futures as possible if this number is strong. His whole book is positioned aggressively for a weak number. All long duration and spread tightening stuff so he's praying for major weakness in the data. Essentially hoping that as many people as possible lost their jobs last month so that he can make a profit on his positions and then get paid 10% of that profit next February (60/40 cash/stock split with the stock vested a third a third a third over three years).

He doesn't think about it in that way, of course. There is a built-in defense mechanism if you work on Wall Street where the obviously disturbing existential ethical questions are taboo. As a market maker, you can't think about what it actually means when you profit off, say, a university endowment or a pension fund when they come in to execute a trade.

"I just made $400,000 off the teacher's pension fund!"

"Nice trade, Bobby! Long-term greedy!"

Bleh.

US 10-year bond futures trade around 115^00. The jobs number is expected to come out at +120,000. A number under +80,000 is a home run for Todd. Above +200,000 is a problem. Above +250,000 is a total disaster.

Number's out in 5 seconds. 4, 3, 2, 1...

OH. MY. GOD.

+308,000.

Bedlam. Bedlam on the trading floor and bedlam in Todd's bowels. His mind stops and his heart beats at 140bpm. He needs to sell a shitload of bond futures here, stat. His brain leaps into a state of heightened awareness and everything slows down around him, like the time stop feature in a video game. He reaches for the keypad to sell 5,000 TY bond contracts and presses:

BUY

5,000

ENTER

Blam. He buys the whole lot instantly at 114^20 and it is immediately lower. 114^10. 114^01.

Wait. His mind goes black. *Did I just BUY? Oh shit.* He needed to sell.

This has never happened to Todd before. It's the trader's worst nightmare, the ultimate mindfart. He dealt backwards. He looks up nervously but nobody pays attention to him. There is carnage on the flow desk as an avalanche of selling storms in from hedge funds, real money, corporates and hedgers. Screams of abject terror.

His P&L has gone from green to red and now he's down more than $3,000,000. Bad but not devastating. His year-to-date is around $25 million which is a fantastic result for early Q2. If he just shut down now, he could cruise for the rest of the year and pocket a $2.5 million bonus. But he doesn't think that way. It's not really about the money. It's more like you're playing Pac-Man and you've already got the high score and it's not even really all that fun anymore but it seems lame to just walk away from the game before the end. Wall Street attracts the naturally competitive. $25 million minus $3 million is still $22 million. A minor flesh wound.

One of the first lessons any young trader learns on Wall Street, besides how to get coffee and lunch, is that you always cut your mistakes right away. Don't try to trade your way out of a mistake or rationalize the position or make excuses. Get flat and reassess.

Before Todd has another thought, though, he watches himself buy another 5,000 TY at 114^01. Almost a full point lower than his first purchase. Weeks later, thinking back, he has no idea why he did it. Just an impulse to double down emanating from some deep, panicked part of his brain.

The price continues to buckle under the weight of the relentless selling. 113^20. 113^10. 113^05. Bonds are down almost two full points and still heavy as balls. Clowns on CNBC freak out. Todd is down $10 million. $15 million. $18 million. The screen updates in real time. His mind goes numb. Vertigo. His whole year is almost gone.

Now he is a gambler on tilt. *If I buy another 5,000 down here and it bounces, my average will be OK and I can get out with a small loss.*

Completely robotic and impulsive, he buys another 5,000. Then he goes to buy another 5,000 but he fat fingers the key—and buys 50,000 instead. *Oh stupid god damn dog shit mother—*. It's a gargantuan position. A monster bet, for no reason. Offside and out of control. Every tick is a million dollars now and the futures are jumping around in 5 and 10 tick bursts.

Bonds drop another 9 ticks then a huge round of stop loss sell orders trigger. Bonds gap down to 112^10. 112^05 trades. Low of day. Every human being on the trading floor gasps at the ferocity and impulsiveness of the move down. Bonds are down nearly three full points on the day now, a seven standard deviation move. A fat tail. One of the largest one-day bond market moves ever. Todd pants in short dog-like breaths. Full panic attack. His P&L is minus $48 million; double his entire year's trading profits have just been obliterated in less than 15 minutes. He is going to get fired. He might go to jail.

He falls, falls, falls, falls down a sinkhole. Cold drops of sweat form on his temples. His face is red, flushed and hot. His back is soaked with freezing cold sweat. The much-needed shit churns like molten green bowel stew. He wants to fart but if he does, there is a 100% chance he will shit his pants.

Todd checks the P&L monitor. Minus $48.2 million. Long 65,000 bond futures at an average rate of 112^29. You might be surprised to learn that investment bank risk management systems in 2004 only measured risk at the end of each day. No intraday risk monitoring whatsoever. Todd knows this.

When in trouble... Double.

He buys 50,000 contracts at 112^07 and his mind begins to flash _____like_____near-death experience type of stuff. A slideshow of memories flash, like: playing catch with Dad, circa 1970-something. The phone call from Charlie the day Jessica died on the sledding hill. A random and meaningless girlfriend from college, crying. His daughters dying, pinned against the tree.

As a kid: running through long grass, chased and stung by hornets. Angry buzzing. The smell of dust and flowers and wild grass. He dives into the lake. Underwater, there is no buzzing. It is safe. *I can't hold my breath forever...*

There is a scream of "Oh my God, you guys see this headline?" from a female salesperson on the other side of the floor and Todd looks up to see two red headlines on Bloomberg:

*BLS SAYS PAYROLLS DISTORTED BY WEATHER EFFECTS AND DELAYED AUTO FACTORY SHUTDOWNS

*BLS SAYS DISTORTIONS ADDED 140,000 TO HEADLINE FIGURE

Oh. My. God. Part. Deux. Insane roller coaster. The payrolls number was not as strong as the market thought. It was distorted by one-off factors. The selling in bonds will reverse.

Bonds spike higher by a half point and trade 112^21 before Todd can process. His hands shake so violently he fears he can't hit the right buttons. He watches his P&L spin higher, cartoonishly fast, like a pinball machine score on fast-forward. Mind still a void, he presses whatever buttons he can, selling 20,000 contracts at a time. His hands float to the buttons without conscious thought. His position shrinks. 115,000, 95,000, 75,000...

His P&L is now green, +$5.5 million. Unreal. It is still a fast market. His hands shake like he has Parkinson's. He feels like puking and shitting his pants simultaneously. He can't hold the colonic storms back any longer.

He sells the last of the futures contracts. Bang. Done. Out. Flat. Total P&L +$4.7 million.

Thank you, Jesus.

He sprints for the can. He runs right by his boss and a sales guy and down the hall, into the bathroom.

"Todd, you alright?"

He runs through bathroom door, scans for an empty stall. GAHHH!!! Every stall is occupied. Runs, sphincter clenched, up two flights of stairs. Storms past reception, down the hall towards the management bathrooms and into the unoccupied bathroom stall...

... And ...

Release.

■ ■ ■

1 YEAR AND 149 DAYS BEFORE THE RESET

I stand, waiting for the elevator to my empty apartment. I feel lonely today. Not sure why. My guts are rotten from too much MDMA and cheap Thai curry. The elevator doors open and an electric shock passes through me as the most sensational beautiful black woman walks on. I avert my eyes much too quickly and she smiles a shy girl smile. My heart pumps noisily in my ears and sexual tension crackles through the elevator. I flex my core to ensure there is no question of my superior fitness level as she most certainly makes her assessment of me as a potential future mate. Slight tingling in my nether regions. A quick check of the ring finger indicates zero hardware.

If this were a book or a movie, I would do a James Dean type of cool, classy come on and be having dinner with her by 7. Naked by 9.

Instead, the flexing of my core makes me fart and possibly shit (slightly) in my pants. Funny story for later maybe but also: what is wrong with me? MDMA is rotting my guts and turning my insides to liquid. I need to get healthy. No reaction from the woman.

Hopeful internal monologue: *Maybe she didn't hear?*

I get off the elevator at my floor.

As soon as I get inside, I check: yes, there is a small Hershey's kiss in my underwear. *What is wrong with you, dude?* I really need to get my shit together. Ha ha.

■ ■ ■

1 YEAR AND 146 DAYS BEFORE THE RESET – TORONTO, CANADA

Wet snow falls and passenger breath fogs the windows so Alison cannot see anything outside other than the kaleidoscopic starring of street lights. The Greyhound bus turns left on Bay Street just before the Eaton Centre and pulls into the Toronto Coach Terminal bus station. Alison is obviously worried about her duffel bag and the safety of its contents (gold and silver) so she rushes off and collects it from the underbelly of the bus, intact.

She double checks the address of the hotel. Only a few blocks. She estimates 80 seconds per block times three blocks = 4-minute walk plus 25% premium for slushy sidewalks = 5 minutes. She plods through wet slush. The bag weighs fifty pounds and her feet drag uncooperatively through soggy grey snow. A businessman wants to help but he looks a bit like her dad and from his cheesy demeanor she thinks he might be coming on to her.

"I'm OK, thanks."

"You sure? I'm happy to give you a hand."

"Listen, buddy. Fuck off, OK? You get me?"

He fucks off. That was probably a bit harsh, she realizes.

Sorry, eh?

This is Alison's third trip to Toronto (or Tronno, as the locals pronounce it). She is intrigued by the sameness yet dissimilarity of the city compared to NYC. "Toronto is like New York, but without all the stuff" is how Steve Martin put it. The people are tamer, like puppies, apologizing when you bump into them on the sidewalk. The bars show seven different hockey games on seven TVs and curling on the eighth instead of New York baseball, hoops or Sports-center. The natives wear Jays hats atop unusually large foreheads, partially revealing neomullets. Leafs jerseys drape frumpy torsos.

They use washrooms not bathrooms and wear toques instead of ski hats as they sip Tim Horton's double-doubles instead of Grande Soy Macchiatos. They go on road trips to Mun-treal and pound Molson Export as "Wheat Kings" by The Hip plays in the back-ground. They dream a bit smaller and settle for less but seem genuinely happy about it as Americans scratch and claw for that incremental dollar which delivers zero or negative marginal utility.

Alison has an ongoing interest in the relationship between money and happiness as her parents provide a strong counterfactual to any suggestion of positive correlation. Below subsistence levels the posi-tive correlation between money and happiness is obvious but above average working wage, she thinks the correlation drops to zero then goes negative. The curve is positively sloped up to $150k/year and then flatlines. It inverts around $400k.

And then there is the second level rich person problem where if you are loaded but not happy it's a double whammy because a) you are not happy and b) despite having what advertising and society told you will make you happy (the Maui Jims, the black M5, the holidays in Grand Cayman and so on) you still cannot find satisfaction. But you're rich! You have no excuse for being unhappy. Can't blame circumstance; so what do you blame?

What is wrong with me that I have such a pretty house and such a pretty garden and yet still I am sad and alone? I was happier before I had all this! What the heck? The spiritually lost and beleaguered rich seek therapy to solve these existential quandaries. But the highly paid therapists are trapped in the same confusing inversion where the more they accumulate, the less they feel. So the therapists read the same self-help books they've prescribed to their patients and there is a whole lot of faking it but not much making it. Meanwhile, couples come out of therapy and soon find themselves in a meta clusterfuck as they argue now not just about the old pre-therapy stuff but also the new stuff that has emerged in therapy.

Alison is aware of the kinked / inversion point on the happiness vs. material wealth curve and so her goal here is to get enough money to be free and then pursue something meaningful like math or art or zen or something, who knows what.

But what she really wants and needs is mental peace.

She is only faintly aware of this need on a conscious level but it is her main underlying motivation most of the time. In the short term, she has no idea how to find peace for real so she pursues temporary fixes. Booze, drugs, TV, online math, yoga classes. She has the faint knowledge back there somewhere deep in her brain that she will need to, at some point, find a more permanent solution to exile the demonic bats that swarm in great clouds around her mindspace; but for now she self-medicates and uses that slick new meditation app Winnie told her about last Christmas.

Longer term the plan is simple: buy a cabin in Canada, leave everything behind and never, ever come back.

She tried therapy a few times but found it lacking. Therapists are ill-equipped to handle her unique and exceptional issues. Her demons are special. She is also aware of the therapist's duty to report child sexual abuse and who knows what squalid details of her life she might blurt out in the depths of therapy? The last thing she needs is cops crawling around the house. If Dad went to jail, who would pay the bills? Mom??? Ha.

Canadians are so cute and cuddly! She passes bundled up Torontonians walking north on Dundas towards the Eaton Centre. She honestly has no idea whether she envies or pities them. Both? Can one feel simultaneous envy and pity for a single subject? She feels a surprising burst of sonder as the pedestrians passing her suddenly blaze with fictional complexity.

Alison enters the hotel and checks in with the help of the most polite woman in the world.

The next day, sunny and cold. Two Celsius and windy.

In small handfuls, she brings the silver and gold to various banks and small retail metal dealers and exchanges it for that funny, multi-colored Canadian money she saw a few times as a kid. The fives smell like maple syrup! How the hell is that possible? Despite its multicoloration, Canadian currency is in heavy demand as US dollars slowly devalue and non-US citizens see greenbacks more and more as monochromatic Monopoly money.

Over the course of 12 hours she converts the entire contents of the duffle bag into cold Canadian cash. Mission accomplished; now she has two days to kill before she meets the real estate agent.

The itinerary was airtight and jammed, right down to the optimized route she took to the various silver dealers and commercial banks. But now she has two free days and nothing on the agenda. She brought Ayn Rand's *Atlas Shrugged* and read a chunk of it on the bus north but found it retardedly simplistic and also childishly fundamentalist and completely lacking any value whatsoever and so her simple plan (to read for two days) was spoiled. Suddenly, it hits her and she is jonesing like a bulimic in line at Magnolia Bakery. Needs a drink or maybe something more psychoactive. She checks her phone to see if any decent music is in town.

flatland. Tonight. @ Guverment 2.0. Doors open at 9PM.

Fuckin' eh!

Shocked and stoked. Her favorite DJ at the world-famous Guverment 2.0 warehouse club. Unreal. She quickly scans her mind for any drug connections in the Great White North but comes up empty. Canada is still pretty lax on Molly enforcement so she knows she can score at the club. The benefits of the Holy Trinity. Easy to score drugs at a club. Time for a nap.

Too excited to sleep. Too excited to sleep. Exhausted. She can't fall asleep and then an inhalation of slightly moldy hotel smell triggers an olfactory memory of her father especially drunk one time on a family trip in Barbados. Her mom had gone out for a walk and didn't come back for two hours. She remembers lying there, praying for her mom to come back. To walk into the hotel room and see what was going on. And save her. But she didn't. She never did.

Alison gets out of bed. Wants a cigarette. It's a non-smoking hotel. Like every other hotel. She knocks her hand around inside the minibar and pulls out a Molson Export. No bottle opener in sight but her 10th grade boyfriend showed her the trick where you perch the very edge of the bottle cap on the edge of the dresser and hit down hard with an open palm. Pshhht. The cap flies a few feet up and then down to the ground and there is a healthy chunk out of the dresser (oops).

She tilts back and drinks almost a third of the beer in one swill. Tart, full taste. Not pissy like American beer. Beer with balls. She lets it pour slowly over the back of her tongue and feels the individual bubbles roll down her throat. Fizzing. Aggressively carbonated and fucking cold. O! Canada. May I have another? Two beers clear her mind of the ghastly Dad memories and she's asleep and dreaming ten minutes later.

She wakes up at exactly 12:00 midnight and so her brain is confused into thinking the clock is broken. *The clock worked fine when*

I fell asleep. I remember it was 9:15 PM. Weird. Before she can think it through anymore, the clock turns to 12:01.

She bought a ticket for flatland on her phone earlier but it's only good for guaranteed entry 'til 1AM and after that she'll have to line up like everyone else and since flatland is now on the Top 100 DJ's in the world list it'll be pretty much impossible to get in at that point and plus she straddles two genres (Robo and Kaleidoscope) and so her fan base is absolutely huge. It's snowing big wet happy snowflakes outside. She bangs on some clothes and rushes out of the hotel room.

Toronto is not New York when it comes to Lyft penetration and in fact some people still call a taxi in Toronto and so needless to say when it's snowing on a weekend it's basically impossible to get anywhere. Lyft is in rare "No cars available" mode and so she waits 20 minutes by the hotel entrance, hitting refresh on the app before, what luck, a taxi pulls up and drops off and a couple gets out and makes fresh prints in the snow, and she climbs in.

"Guvernment 2.0, please."

■ ■ ■

I come out of the bathroom and see that I have mustard on my pants. The street meat in this city is completely off the charts, no prissy food cart bullshit; just Arabs selling puffy, volcanically-hot $4 mouth pleasers and I had two before I got to the club because I slept all day and didn't have time for dinner. flatland threw up in her mouth as she watched me take the first bite and juice and ketchup and mustard and relish all squirted every which way and I thought I jumped out of the way of the condiment waterfall but I guess some caught my pant cuff and there it is. Yellow like Charlie Brown's shirt. Dry like paint. Beautiful / ugly.

My thoughts are failing to properly sequitur as the Sight kicks in. Time for a shot of tequila. I came up to Toronto with flatland and now I'm running solo as she's backstage getting ready. I like these solo trips. I'm not overly bovered with finding or meeting up with anyone.

flatland wanted someone to fly up here with and the promoter gave her an extra airline ticket if she wanted it so here I am. The opening DJ was pretty good but kept things moderate in order to pay proper respect to flatland and not get the crowd overly hyped before the main act. I'm set to peak at exactly the right time. I have this down to a science now and so I mixed the Molly and the Sight in the hotel room and then tipped one drop of Sight around 9:00 PM and then the full Sight dosage at 11:00 PM and now I'm starting to zoom::::::::::

The bathrooms here are perfect for dropping. Individual stalls with proper floor-to-ceiling doors. Silver ledges for proper crushing and snorting of whatever powdered recreationals. Plenty of loud noises and activity in the main part of the bathroom to obscure any loud sniffing or sounds of liquid being shaken before use. And no bathroom attendant slinging dental floss or Dior Sauvage or Acqua de Gio or whatever. Perfect.

flatland has launched into some Kaleidoscope pretty early on and the vibe is pretty chill and so I just walk around, looking at smiling faces. Girls, boys. Everyone is beautiful. Everyone looks way smaller than usual. Tiny, cute girls. Small, handsome boys. Crisp baseball caps and huge dumb smiles. Nicely dressed. Happy. flatland is up in the booth, up in her own personal heaven, smiling down on the peeps below and it's a peaceful vibe. I remember the AM radio news was on in the cab on the way here (more riots in Boston) and try to shut those thoughts out of my mind. Buzzkill.

The riots and the protests seem like some hideous parallel universe that can't even be the same planet as the one I'm gliding over right now. Pitch-shifted snippets of broken glass sent down a metal slide in Classic Park, Riverside, Manhattan. flatland's microwave beep, sped up. Slowed down. Sped up. Slowed down. Every sound is bottled fresh. Every sound is bottled fresh. Every sound is bottled fresh. I hear my own voice saying it. Over and over. *Every sound is bottled fresh. Every sound is bottled fresh.* What the hell? Is it me or the music saying it? The drugs are passing whispers of my own voice through my mind? Then I remember saying that once and flatland recorded it.

Maybe three weeks ago. And now it's part of her mix. Holy shit; this is amazing.

Every sound is bottled fresh. Every sound is bottled fresh.

"Whisper it," says flatland into the mic.

And the crowd whispers it.

Every sound is bottled fresh. Every sound is bottled fresh.

In the background she raises up other sounds. Water gushing from a tap. Reverbed train horn. Mechanical chattering eaglet chirps. The beeping of a truck backing up, sped up to 140bpm. Rhubarb clicking as it grows.

Every sound is bottled fresh. Every sound is bottled fresh.

Everyone whispers in unison and their voices around me and my own coming out of the speaker make me feel like I am levitating slightly off the ground or maybe I just can't feel my feet and the sounds all mix together and strobes and lasers pulsate and I hear water gushing, air releasing, hand dryer at max, and every sound is bottled fresh and every sound is bottled fresh.

And then the bass drops.

OONTZ. OONTZ. OONTZ.

The Robo drops over the kaleidoscopic soundbites and the crowd turns into an ecstatic, pulsing horde all smiles so big they hurt the cheeks and feet moving with no conscious input from the mind and arms flailing with zero self-consciousness and everyone is secure and everyone is present and everyone is in love and everyone is sweating and thirsty and full and ready to erupt.

"Charlie?"

I snap out of it. There is a floating face beside me. Pink hair. Pale face. Freaky glow-in-the-dark eyes.

"Charlie is that you?"

Her hand is on my arm and I feel energy passing from her entity to mine.

"Alison?"

"Yeah. Holy shit!?"

She's jumping up and down. Excited. Like a little kid.

"We keep bumping into each other," I say. "What does it mean?"

"I know crazy right? Must mean something?"

The night boots off as I share my Sight and Molly with this incredibly cool girl and she is doing Special K off the back of my hand at one point (where did I get the Special K? That skinny Filipino kid with the backwards Hanshin Tigers baseball hat in the bathroom, I think) and we are both completely off the rails fucked up and time extends and rips and folds like we're inside the underside of Stephen Hawking's mind and my motor skills are in steep decline and we dance for a while then hang out by the bar and talk about (what?) and it's fantastic and I know I can love her or I am already in love or something with this girl. She is so cool and I just have this instant and crazy connection.

We exchange numbers and my thoughts drift to maybe we'll end up having sex back at a hotel or something but then at some point I go for a piss and lose my bearings and when I come back out of the can and I look everywhere for her but I'm lost in the funhouse now and the square room seems to have five corners and there are new rooms where there were no rooms before and my facial recognition software has broken down and everyone looks the same and all the faces look borderline maniacal. Strobes flash out of synch with the music. No matter how hard I look, I cannot find her. The square room seems to have five corners and there are new rooms where there were no rooms before and my facial recognition software has broken down and everyone looks the same and all the faces look borderline maniacal. Strobes flash out of synch with the music. No matter how hard I look, I cannot find her. The square room seems to have five corners and there are new rooms where there were no rooms before and my facial recognition software has broken down and everyone looks the same and all the faces look borderline maniacal. Strobes flash out of synch with the music. No matter how hard I look, I cannot find her. The square room seems to have five corners and there are new rooms where there were no rooms before and my facial recognition software has broken down and everyone looks the same and all the faces look borderline maniacal. Strobes flash out of synch with the music. No matter how hard I look, I cannot find her.

Faces are hard to distinguish and mildly demented like scary clowns. Laughing. Unsettling overstimulation as my sensory focus and filtration capabilities have broken down. All information comes in and it is too much to process. Slight slipperiness to the floor. Lights. A salty sensation in the front right corner of my tongue. Bitter in the back. There are three numbers on this painted support pole. How has that cotton lace woven itself into my shoe? Who are all these people? Itch on left ear. My hearing flub a lubs like someone left one window open in the car.

I am on a crazy bad trip buzzkill type of thing for maybe an hour and then I give up, tell flatland I'm out and somehow weeble back to the hotel.

■ ■ ■

@realdemocracy tweeted
"i am a most unhappy man. i have unwittingly ruined my country. a great industrial nation is controlled by its system of credit. our system of credit is concentrated. the growth of the nation, therefore, and all our activities are in the hands of a few men."
president woodrow wilson (regretting signing into law the federal reserve act)

■ ■ ■

3 YEARS BEFORE THE RESET

Marc Guilford is 33. He is a clean cut, intrepid journalist. Fit, mostly from tennis. It is early morning and he just put a pot of coffee on. He hears some sort of commotion outside his house and so he puts down the *Saturday Times* and walks to the front door. A full-sized dump truck is backing up half onto his driveway and half on his lawn in Ridgewood, New Jersey. The dump bed starts to tip backward.

"Whoa! Whoa! What are you doing?" Guilford yells.

"Just doing my job man. Following instructions," responds the driver. He's doing the textbook 'driver backing up a truck with head partly out the window' thing, trying to stay off Guilford's lawn.

Guilford's daughter and wife come outside to see what is happening.

"What's all that paper, Daddy?"

"I think there's been a mistake, honey. Let's see."

His wife stares, mute and confused.

Twelve cubic yards (over 200,000 pages) of meeting notes, e-mails, correspondence and the like slide out of the dump truck and pile up on the flat driveway. The lightest of winds barely rustles the enormous stack. A few pages float around, but not many. This is the government's latest attempt to circumvent the Access to Information request Mr. Guilford submitted almost two years ago.

Mark Guilford is the most-respected reporter at Bloomberg. His objective is to get access to the notes from the secret Black Room Fed Meetings. For years, these meetings were just a harebrained Zero-head conspiracy but Guilford found out through a whistleblowing source that these Black Room meetings were in fact real and were held in parallel to the normal Fed meetings during the Global Financial Crisis in 2008. Attendance was limited to Ben Bernanke, Hank Paulson (and later Tim Geithner) and an unknown third amigo.

The Black Room authorized secret stock market interventions which conspiracy nuts called "The Force" due to their all-powerful impact on markets. Originally born as the President's Working Group on Capital Markets after the Crash of 1987, The Force is also sometimes called the Plunge Protection Team or PPT. But that is a misnomer. The Force is accused of buying in all kinds of markets, not just plunging ones. Nobody really knows if The Force is a real thing or just another stupid conspiracy theory. Maybe just sour grapes from gored bears.

Guilford's theory was that much as the NSA suffered from mission creep and drifted substantially off its original intended purpose following 9/11, the Fed viewed the Global Financial Crisis (GFC) as a wakeup call, justification for a "whatever it takes" approach to protect the financial system.

Guilford was not wrong. While various illegal and gray area

activities were carried out by the Black Room Committee, the primary and most interesting actions were its Price Keeping Operations (PKOs).

PKOs were introduced early on in the Financial Crisis and gave the Fed Chairman immediate and direct access to stock markets via a numbered Federal Reserve entity posing as a hedge fund based in Grand Cayman. This hedge fund had unlimited access to the Fed's Balance Sheet and operated via stealth, executing orders through various investment banks, primarily SquidCo.

Not even the SquidCo partners had any idea of the fund's connections, though after a few trades, their client-tracking software quickly informed the key risk takers that the relatively new and unknown "Inflection Point Capital" had a nearly 100% hit ratio on its trades over a 24-hour time horizon. Best to go with the flow when Inflection Point comes in, they soon learned. Piggyback like crazy. Wrap that blood funnel around the face of anything that smells like money.

There is a market cliché: "Nobody's bigger than the market."

Wrong.

The chink in the confidentiality armor was the execution trader who sat in Grand Cayman and did most of the trades. Even with their incredible academic, banking and policymaking resumes, Paulson and Bernanke did not have the trading chops to press the buttons when it came time for the Fed to intervene in S&P futures. A few years after the fact, the execution trader saw the moral hazard and ethical issues of what he had been a party to and placed the surreptitious whistleblowing call to Mark Guilford in an effort to clear his conscience. This was almost two years ago.

Now Guilford has obviously (finally) struck pay dirt. The only problem is that the answers are buried in this mountain of words and paper. The bad news is this ridiculous Everest of documents, but the good news is that there would be no reason for such needle/haystack style obfuscation from the Fed if the information request had been off-target. Guilford gaps from annoyed straight to laughter.

The Fed has a sense of humor still, at least.

They always kept their sense of humor, even in the darkest days of the Global Financial Crisis. Guilford's favorite excerpt from a Fed meeting transcript was one from January 27, 2009, when the stock market was at the lows and panic rampaged through the financial system.

Donald Kohn: It is a pleasure and an honor to recommend Ben Bernanke to be Chairman of this Committee. I am not sure what sins you committed in an earlier life, but I sure hope you had fun. [LAUGHTER]

Guilford finishes his coffee and decides at that moment that he *will* find those Black Room transcripts in this pile, no matter how long it takes and no matter the cost. The dump truck driver never gets out of his seat through the whole procedure. He pulls away, leaving a trail of documents all over the road as he raises the dump bed back to horizontal. Guilford stands and watches as the truck turns left and disappears around the corner. As Guilford turns to go into his two-car garage to get a broom and a wheelbarrow, another full dump truck turns the corner and heads towards him. Then another. Then another. Four dump truck loads of paper.

Our Father. Who art in heaven. Hallowed be thy name.

■ ■ ■

10 YEARS BEFORE THE RESET – WESTPORT, CONNECTICUT

It's 2:30 AM. Mike is drunk and high in the back seat of an Escalade on the way home from a client dinner in the city. He is horny as hell but The Wife stopped fucking him years ago. He's been too busy to jerk off and now his balls hang heavy against his thighs like overripe late-summer tomatoes in a thin plastic produce bag. He contemplates jerking off right here in the back of the SUV but he's not sure where the final product might land. He's been drinking heavily all night and snorting coke and managed to ingest some MDMA too, for good measure.

It is not practical to get a hotel room and a pro right now and he is way too tired to organize all that anyway—but man, his ballbag is full and needs emptying. He needs an outlet. His mind is so off the rails drunk and high he spends 30 or maybe 45 seconds contemplating whether or not it might somehow be possible to fuck himself up the ass.

He would fuck a squirrel right now if he could hold its head still.

Mike stumbles into the house, desperately trying not to set off the alarm or wake anyone up. He is flying. Way too high to go to bed. But gotta be at work tomorrow so might as well try. He climbs awkwardly out of his clothes and drops them in a heap in the laundry room. Walks naked down the hall. Bumps into a wall in the dark. Heads for his bedroom. Passes Alison's bedroom. The door is closed.

BAM: Out of nowhere. A revelation. There is a simple solution to his problem. Right in his own home.

His daughter's naked 9-year-old body appears in his mind like an apparition. Decision made. He opens Alison's door and walks in to get from her what he can no longer get from The Wife.

This coin has two sides for Alison. On the one hand is the hellacious warmth of her father's body up against her and inside her maybe once a week from that night on. On the other hand is a new relationship, totally out of the blue.

Part of the unspoken arrangement, she realized after a while, was that Daddy would pretty much say "yes" to whatever idea she could come up with after that. Six Flags? Sure. A new phone? Sure. Another new phone because the other one I bought three months ago is out of date? Sure. She found that as long as she didn't say "no" at night, he would not say "no" during the day.

It was not all hell, all the time. Day time was mostly fine. They exchanged plenty of normal daylit father/daughter moments. In fact, Alison had a better relationship with her dad than her mom.

She (her Mom) was tired and breaking down and hypochondriac for most of Alison's life and thus seemed more robot than human. With Dad, at least there were ups and downs. Mom was a flatline.

Alison and Mike had a tradition which she loved. About a week after Christmas, Dad would take the Christmas tree out of the living room once the assistants had undecorated it. He would drag the tree out back as The Wife screamed "Watch the vase! Careful for the plant! We need to vacuum these needles, Mike! We need to vacuum these needles!" and so on. Once outside, Alison would buzz around in her pink snowsuit and bunny rabbit ski hat while Mike chopped up the tree with a hand saw. They worked together after, dragging the pieces into the forest. This continued right up until she was 15 (sans bunny rabbit ski hat by that point, obv). The smell of sap still reminds her of those days.

Close your eyes and the monster will go away. Close your eyes and the monster will go away. She closed her eyes so tight she thought they might pop backwards into her skull. But the monster never went away.

They did other fun stuff too. He took her ice skating. Helped her pick out a graduation dress in 8th grade. Bought her chocolates on Valentine's. Picked her up from school sometimes. One Saturday, she convinced him to help her bake cookies with Winnie. He occasionally took her to her golf or tennis or swimming lessons at the club.

Hell came only in the dark.

As she got older and thus better understood what was going on, her asks got more aggressive. A new car. $1,000 cash.

"What do you need that for, Tigger?"

He still called her Tigger sometimes, even when she was in high school.

"Don't worry about it, Dad."

Shrug.

Last year he bought her a $2,200 dress for the Spring Dance. Everyone at school was envious of Alison's immaculate perfection. *She's the coolest!* Smart, funny, well-dressed, hot. She has an incredible ability to convince people she's a happy and well-adjusted teen. Darkness obscured by blinding light.

Mike came by Alison's room more and more often. He preferred her natural teen odor and unperfumed armpits to the oversweet bubblegum and perfume smell of the strippers he still banged here and there.

Where was Alison's mother through all those years? Surely she knew what was going on after a while, right? She was the same place as every other mother in stories like this. Out of earshot.

The confusing thing for Alison (still) is that her dad is the only person that ever showed her any kind of real love. And so she still loves him. Her memories of the good times with Dad are full of paralyzing cognitive dissonance and so she shuts them out as much as possible. But there are still good memories.

At least the bad memories are straightforward and unambiguous.

After a while, Mike felt like Alison was using him just like he was using her and so he got bolder as she got older. Quid pro quo. He got bored of the normal routine and introduced belts and slapping and other variations. As things got nastier, she could no longer deal and an escape plan emerged. She stopped asking for anything other than cash.

Mike earned north of $7,000,000 that year and had completely lost all understanding of what money means. His humble lower middle-class Michigan back story was just a bunch of dusty, distant memories that seemed more like a book he read once, not moments actually lived. Money was in infinite supply now: just numbers on a screen. Printed rectangular slices of cotton/linen/paper available in unlimited quantities on demand from machines on every street corner. When you manage billions and get paid millions, the thousands start to look tiny and meaningless. Completely abstract.

Alison built her escape account judiciously. She stopped spending almost completely. Her contribution to US GDP collapsed. Younger girls at school noticed her increasingly tattered look and tried to emulate it.

Hilarious.

Unlike Dad, Alison had a very concrete idea of what money meant. Money was freedom. Money was escape. She figured $150,000 would be enough to leave and never, ever come back. She planned to steal a few choice tchotchkes on the way out and boost her net worth to over $200k. She knew $150k wasn't a reasonable ask in a short period no matter how pretty and naked she was at night, so she decided at age sixteen that her 18th birthday would be the target exit date.

She divided her number by 104 weeks and figured a bit less than $2k/week. It seemed reasonable. Too risky to keep a bank account (Dad might track it down somehow after she leaves) so she squirreled the money away; it was well-hidden deep in her locked closet where nobody ever went, not even Francisca and Rosa, the cleaners. All cash.

$150k in one hundred dollar bills isn't that big. It weighs about three pounds.

■ ■ ■

1 YEAR AND 111 DAYS BEFORE THE RESET

So I got this text from a number not in my contacts this morning that starts off: "Wanna play Scrabble?" and I wasn't sure who it was so I had to ask 'who this?' and it was Alison. I'm obviously intrigued and frantically Google to see if "play Scrabble" is a euphemism or slang for something sexual but it doesn't seem to be. Not to be insecure, but this girl is younger than me and cool as Mr. Orange so maybe she has access to a whole 'nother slang dictionary I do not.

Today is Wednesday and I have no plans for tonight other than to try not to drink and try not to do drugs for one night and so playing Scrabble would possibly help me achieve these goals and so I text "How about tonight?" and she replies "Sure."

On the way there I refrain from smoking so that I don't reek when I get to her place and then it's the opposite because I catch the sweet perfume smell of flowers as I pass a bodega so why not pick up something and be a gentleman? I grab six beers too just in case the flowers make me look weak. I think this huge bouquet of tiger lilies (which I repeat, smell amazing) and the six pack of beer presents just the right combo of manly and sensitive.

I also might be overthinking this.

So now I am at her apartment which is actually her friend's apartment where she is crashing for now she says but her friend (who is in social marketing) is gone to San Fran for the week and so...

I sit down on a worn leather couch in the somewhat typical cluttered 900 sq. ft. 1BR NYC apartment. It smells vaguely of dust or fresh kitty litter and there a few of those ultra-cliché vintage posters from France and Switzerland (Folie-Bergeres, Chamonix, Mont Blanc) and we exchange pleasantries and drink two beers each (a little too quickly) as we show evidence of nerves but it's mostly butterflies not anxiety and soon we are sitting on a rug in the main room on either side of a rotating Scrabble board and I am warning her:

"Just FYI: I'm pretty good at Scrabble."

"Not worried," she says, fully taking the bait.

"Care to make a wager then?"

"Loser buys dinner."

"Winner chooses the restaurant?"

"Done."

She tucks her hair behind her right ear and smiles. We each grab seven letters from the Crown Royal bag. We play. The game is back and forth until she drops a beastly trifecta of ZYGOTE (55), QAT (32), and FAQIR (44, using the Q from QAT, obv) and suddenly I am down 315 to 219 before I know what happened.

"Nice word. Fuck-ear."

Not super funny. Kind of awkward, like a poorly chosen simile. Maybe rude? I could really use a cigarette but I don't want to be yuck so I don't say anything.

"What's that outside?" I point in slightly exaggerated fashion at the main window that faces the darkening cityscape. Alison turns and I quickly snag the Z tile off the board and put it onto my tilesofa.

"What's what? What are you talking about?" she asks.

"Oh weird, nothing. Maybe it was a bird or something."

With an exaggerated lack of chalance, I play the word ZEBRA on a double word score and earn a quick 52 points. I quickly update the scoresheet. Anyone who has ever played Scrabble knows there is only one Z in the game and so Alison is quickly confused and then bemused and then amused.

"What the fuck, cheater?"

"Are you saying I consume large orange gourds?"

She reaches to take the Z from zebra and put it back on zygote and I try to grab it from her hand and she laughs. As we fakewrestle I notice her breath smells like purple Jolly Ranchers (my favorite) and I am halfway on top of her and it's a bit awkward but she seems into it and then it's all happening and we are making out kind of high school style on the floor which leads to a bit of dry humping after a bit and then I scrabble unsuccessfully at her zipper and then she rolls out from under me and says:

"I don't want to have sex with you. I'm sorry."

"Sure of course. No problem. Sorry, I wasn't planning that; it just kind of happened."

"Yeah it's fine. I just think I might actually... Like you... Or something, so I want to wait OK?"

"Sure... Of course."

It sounds uncomfortable but it is kind of a nice moment especially for me to hear that for some reason she likes me. No idea why, but anyhoo. The rest of the night is one of those perfect nights when you first meet someone and you think you might be instantly in love and you share life stories and hopes and dreams and all that and the entire outside world dissolves into nothingness and you lie together intertwined and your skin normalizes at the exact same temperature and two people are briefly one and the distance between you shrinks to exactly 0.

My life story: smart kid loses entire family, comes out OK. So far.

"You don't seem very sad, considering everything that has happened. You have a super positive energy."

"Yeah, as long as I don't think about stuff too much, I'm pretty happy. You know about baseline happiness?"

"Hmm, not sure."

"It's the idea that everyone has a baseline level of happiness and no matter what happens, we just revert back to that level of happiness, roughly. There's been research on people who get paralyzed in accidents or win massive lotto jackpots and within a year, both groups are back to feeling about how they felt before the traumatic or euphoric event. So my baseline happiness is, like, an 8. And no matter what happens, I'm back to 8 again pretty fast."

I don't spend a ton of time thinking about what I've lost. My sisters. My mom. My dad. It's not like I'm ignoring the holes, they're just part of the landscape. The way the Grand Canyon is part of the United States. I figure you can focus on what you've got or dwell on what you've lost and I would rather keep moving. When I do just sit and try to process the sadness, it quickly morphs into this crazy unmanageable heavy feeling of worthlessness.

I am an infinitesimally small white dot on an infinite white landscape that is expanding in every direction at light speed. Without a family it really makes zero difference whether I live or die or win or lose or make money or blow up or whatever.

This existential hot potato burns and must be tossed ASAP. And anyway, things could be worse. I'm still alive, right? What's the point of me being the last Bloom, only to bitch about it and go all "woe is me"? Better to move on and try to enjoy. Friends can be surrogate family. At least friends you get to choose. Instead of getting stuck with a selfish dad, for example. *Sorry for thinking that, Dad.* These thoughts of family drag me underwater like rocks in Virginia Woolf's pocket. I try my best to ignore the thoughts or just let them flow through the mindsieve. Move on. Keep moving...

I am reminded of Dad the most. News stories reference the financial crisis. The Mets lose in extra innings. That sort of stuff. Which is the worst because he is the one it hurts most to remember. The twins barely ever pop into my mind, which makes sense since I was only 8 when they died. I just have this one string of consecutive flashbulb memories that lights up whenever I catch a whiff of wet, late-October leaves. Olfactory memory trigger:

I'm bouncing on the trampoline by myself. It's full of leaves because Dad set it up right under a huge maple tree (which Mom told him was dumb). The sun is almost down. It's sneaky cold outside but I'm sweating from bouncing on the trampoline and bored because Mom is inside getting my sisters into their Halloween costumes. Finally, the girls are ready and we head down the dark gravel lane.

The bang of the car against the tree. Mom freaking out. The girls' final, simultaneous scream.

"What happened? What happened?" I yell. But nobody hears me.

Frogs croak at the edge of a distant stream.

Dad stands, white-faced, shaking, mouth open a bit. He just stands there, doing nothing. And the girls in their matching pink Halloween costumes. Both pinned between the bumper of the car and the huge pin oak. Bodies buckled and broken. Eyes closed. Already dead.

Steam hisses out from under the car's hood. The smell of maple cookies.

Her life story: entitled Connecticut existence with exorbitant privilege. Nothing special to report.

"C'mon. Nothing? You had a normal childhood?"

"Yep," she responds, "Pretty basic stuff except we never had to worry about money, I guess."

Through high school her self-image was that of a dorky math nerd, very insecure. Outwardly she was popular and ran with the cool kids. Quick and sarcastic and smart.

"Most boys were scared of me because I wasn't an idiot."

"I'm not scared of you."

(Alison bares fangs)
(Charlie recoils in fear)

Lips meet, hearts beat, tongues touch.

■ ■ ■

1 YEAR AND 97 DAYS BEFORE THE RESET

Alison is at a party, getting drunk and a bit high out of boredom. Jax's parents are away again and the Upper West Side brownstone is full of 18 to 22-year-olds and the air is full of perfume and cigarette smoke and girl sweat. Jax took all the vases and other 4-figure tchotchkes and numbered them with masking tape and put them away and now the shelves and tables of the apartment are filled with little numbered squares of masking tape marking the locations of the objects so they can be replaced correctly when the party's over and the cleanup is complete tomorrow afternoon.

Thing is, the parents know about the parties (from the neighbors) and honestly zero shits are given so long as there are is no damage and no cops. But Jax doesn't know this and so keeps up the good boy routine and the parents don't mention they know he's high all the time and failing school. They figure it's a phase. He'll figure things out. Plus, they have bigger things to worry about with the foundation and two types of therapy and all that.

It is a lame party, immature. There's a kid standing in the kitchen, eyeballing vodka. His friends think he's cool. Alison is giddy with thoughts of this new thing with Charlie and really doesn't want to be here now but she promised Jax a few weeks ago and so here she is but she can't get into it.

I am getting too old for this shit.

Jax is high, wired on coke (already) and he is in this annoying mode, unable to recognize negative emotions in others. He traps her in conversation and won't go away no matter how clipped her responses to his prodding.

"So, what's the new guy like?" Jax asks.

"Fine. He's cool," Alison says. She picks at a bit of loose cuticle on her left pinkie.

"You like him?" Jax sniffs then wipes his nose with the back of his wrist. Sniffs again.

"Yeah, I guess. Yeah."

"Do you LOVE him?"

"HA HA."

"You guys all, like, boyfriend girlfriend now?"

"Stop! He's not my boyfriend, Jax. We hung out a couple of times. Four or five times I guess. Anyway, who knows. He's a good guy; I like him. I think."

"But you hate your dad. You hate finance. Why you going out with a trader?"

Alison sees nothing of her father in Charlie and the implied comparison is beyond asinine. She feels blood rush up the front of her neck and into her face. The knowledge of the flushing makes the flushing worse and so now she is enraged at the question, but also enraged by the fact that it has now made her flushed. And enraged and embarrassed by the flushing itself which leads to more flushing. Negative feedback loop.

"Dude you have no fucking clue about my father. Who he is or what he is. Jack the Ripper and the local butcher are the same thing because they both use knives? Charlie knows what is what and my father is a lunatic psychotard asshole. Shut your fucking mouth about things you know nothing... about."

Her tirade loses its force with the terminal syntactic error but the earlier momentum was enough to knock Jax off guard and he feels bad. He didn't mean to set her off and knows it was wrong to bring up her dad. His jaw is visibly clenched.

"Shit Al. I'm really sorry. I'm so fucking high I wasn't thinking OK? Honestly. I am literally beside myself I am so sorry."

Jax knows it peeves Alison when people misuse "literally". He notices a full-length mirror at the side of the room and points to his own reflection.

"See? I am literally beside myself."

Alison forces a smile. She does find the turn in the conversation theoretically humorous but the reference to her dad was the worst kind of buzzkill and the black mindclouds roll in and she knows no amount of booze or drugs will help now. In fact, contrary to how things worked when she was 14 or 15, alcohol and pills make the storms more awful now. She puts her half-finished glass down on a rumpled copy of *Flash Art* magazine and walks away. Jax makes a half-assed effort to go after her but doesn't *actually* care. She leaves.

Outside, the New York air is warm, humid and smells faintly of fish, like a frog's vagina. It is only 10:45 PM and she has nowhere to go and nothing to do so she heads south on Columbus. Her mood is half sad / half rage. A low boil. She sits on a bench outside of a bodega, popping gummi bears.

She pulls out a fresh pack of Marlboros and taps it three times on the bench between her legs. She pulls out a matte black Stussy Zippo and flicks it. In one smooth motion her cigarette is lit. She notices and enjoys the three-way flavor combination of butane from the Zippo, the first inhalation of smoke and the sweet gummi bears swirling around in her mouth. Then she remembers reading once that gelatin for gummi bears comes from partial hydrolysis of the skin, bones and connective tissue of cows, chicken, pigs and fish. She flashes to an image of a cow rolling up a slaughterhouse conveyor. A captive bolt pistol strikes its forehead, knocking it unconscious. Its heart continues to beat as it moves toward the exsanguination stage.

She wants to spit the gummi bears out but there are people around so she gulps them down and full body shivers in disgust. She takes another drag on the Marlboro, exhales smoke through both nostrils and then tilts her head back and blows three perfect smoke rings. They swim slowly upward, like unhurried jellyfish.

■ ■ ■

I'm out for a walk, trying to clear my head. I see a girl up ahead, sitting on a bench. Skinny. She flicks a cigarette butt and it arcs over the curb and down through a sewer grate. Why is littering not accepted but flicking cigarette butts on the ground or into sewers is fine? Wait. Is that Alison? I think? Yep it's her for sure.

"Hey! Alison."

"Hey baby!" she responds with a smile. There's something orange stuck in her front tooth.

Her smile fades a bit too fast. I sit down beside her and she hands me her entire bag of gummi bears in silence. I can see in her eyes that something is not right. She is off.

"I thought you were at a party tonight?"

"Yeah it sucked. So I left."

"Is everything OK?" I ask.

"Yeah. I'm fine. Everything's fine."

Everything is not fine.

"You want to go for a walk?"

We walk. The humid air is heavy and not filled with a lot of chit chat. There is a weird vibe that makes me feel insecure so I don't say anything. Five minutes pass in silence. Not awkward silence, more like serene. Finally, Alison says:

"My father is a terrible person."

This assertion takes the evening in a different direction, ripping away the mask of Alison's transparently fake good mood. Underneath the neon yellow paint, she reveals layers of dark green and black.

"I don't know why I'm telling you all this," Alison admits, after almost 90 minutes of history and fairly but not overly detailed stories of childhood sexual abuse. "You have no use for any of this information. Someone brought up my dad at the party and this wave of shit and memories washed over me and I have no explanation whatsoever for why the hell I just subjected to you all of this. I am so, so sorry."

She straddles the crying / not crying border. I guess she had not meant to share but somehow her state of mind and her level of comfort around me came together and in a fit of verbal projectile vomiting she has spewed the most terrible and unhappy and disturbing and heinous moments of her childhood.

Heaviness.

I take her hand.

"It's not your fault. Don't feel bad for telling me. It's part of who you are. It's not your fault," I say.

She is tired now and wants to go home. I feel helpless and sad.

I am hopelessly crazy in love with this girl.

■ ■ ■

7 YEARS BEFORE THE RESET

I expected that in college I would find something I never found in high school: literate, intelligent peers that I could philosophize /

shoot the shit with on a higher level. Like the unrealistically erudite kids in a witty coming-of-age movie. But no such luck.

Instead, my peers were as dumb or dumber than those in high school, a group of hairless apes that taught me nothing about philosophy but plenty about Pig Night and how to funnel and different ways to roll joints, skip class, pickup girls and catch scurvy. The scurvy thing is no joke. We ran an experiment, eating only Kraft (NASDAQ: KHC) Macaroni & Cheese and drinking only beer (NYSE: BUD) for a month and ended up as the first three cases of scurvy recorded in Ann Arbor in over 50 years.

We talked farts, not Descartes. Coin slots and brown stars and NCAA. Poker and cornhole and dirty hot dog water. I could have risen above but I sunk to the lowest common denominator as my need to be liked / cool trumped my desire to not get dumber. I learned to smoke and vape and steal other kids' mattresses using a precisely tied black t-shirt as a ninja mask. We set off fireworks (and the fire alarm) in the stairwell and pissed on cafeteria trays angled under enemies' dorm room doors (a trick I learned from Scott Mitchell in high school). My first year was financed with poker winnings; I played with a crew of freshman who had zero knowledge of pot odds or expected value.

Random Thursday night, junior year: seven of us gathered, as usual, in Jack and CJ's dorm room. Cheap green carpeting under our feet absorbs fallen beer. Topics of conversation run a limited range from sports to music to girls to cafeteria food to girls to music to sports to questions of manliness or lack thereof and back to sports and girls.

"Do a funnel, Charlie," one kid says to me (I forget who).

"Fuck that man. I'm chilling tonight. I have my ECO 20 final tomorrow."

In my zeal to capture the hearts of my new brothers I have learned in recent weeks to funnel like a master, downing as many as five beers at once via funnel and rubber tubing. The key is to manage your breath and ignore the pain in the throat. The cold temperature of the liquid and the carbonation burn the throat but the peak discomfort is reached early on and then it stops getting worse so if you can just manage to keep gulping through the pain, you can then drink until you are out of breath. For me, that means five beers at once and the next best funneler can do barely three.

"Charlie, you are such a wilt."

"Dude, I'm not a wilt, I just need to wake up tomorrow. I got an exam."

They start a chant.

"Wilt! Wilt! Wilt!"

Hairless apes, as mentioned. I am so, so bad under peer pressure. But I'm not going to cave this time. I have an exam, after all.

"WILT! WILT! WILT!"

No chance I cave in.

"WILT! WILT—"

"Alright I'll do three beers."

Crowd goes wild. Eddie gets up on a chair and holds the funnel up high while CJ (the pourer) gets onto a desk. I kneel down on the floor and prepare for the rite. Timing of the breath is key. The funnel is full and I pinch it closed, preparing myself. I begin. 1,2,3, and... Release.

"Go! Go! Go!"

The liquid pours straight through my throat and splashes into my stomach. But there is a surprise here as CJ pours the next beer—and eight ounces of discount vodka—down the tube. I can see him out of the corner of my eye but I'm not really sure what he's doing. I finish the funnel and see the empty fifth of Luksusowa on the desk. I put two and two together. The boys all look at each other and stare. They wait for my reaction. Fucking CJ, you asshole. You fucking idiot douchebag asshole. But I need to be cool. These are my friends, right? I throw my arms in the air, like a champion.

"YEAHHHHHHHHH!!!!!"

I give them what they want. They respond:

"YEAHHHHHHHH!!!!"

"Give me a fucking cigarette. A real one."

Two of my friends pull out packs at the same time and I take a cigarette from each pack and place both in my mouth. CJ rushes to wet a towel and block the slit under the door so that the smell of the smoke doesn't go into the dormitory hallway. No smoking in the dorms. I light both cigarettes and smoke them.

"CJ you are such... SUCH a cock. Agree or disagree?"

"Agree."

The buzz hits me like a switch flicked and I'm humming now and the music is good. The decision is taken that we will go to The War Hall, a local club / pool hall / hangout. A regular haunt. The key selling feature of The War Hall is that they provide pick-up and drop off via the famed and infamous "War Hall Bus", a party bus that makes the circuit from the University of Michigan dorms to The War Hall and back, all night. Our residence is big; 750 co-eds. It's the first stop on The War Hall Bus route.

The bus picks us up at 8:30 PM. We get on and go to the back. 20 passengers or so are already on board as we pull away. The seemingly senile driver of the bus dances to the beat of the cheesy vocal dance music blaring from cheap, tinny speakers mounted around the bus.

We pull around a circular driveway and in front of an all-girls dorm. There is nobody there waiting but it's freezing cold outside so the driver gets off and goes inside to check for pickups.

I think back to all those times riding the city bus as a kid. The driver would get off and go into 7-11 to get a coffee and I would see him through the window, going into the store and I would imagine in great detail what would happen if I walked up to the front, sat in the driver's seat, dropped the bus into D and drove away. It was a fun thing to dream about.

"$1,000 to anyone that drives the bus," CJ yells. His parents are loaded, so it's credible.

I don't think, I just move. I stand up and stumble a bit toward the front of the bus. A few murmurs.

"Dude."

"Oh shit."

I sit down in the driver's seat, drop the thing into D and drive away. The bus lurches forward and a few rowdies in the back cheer. I pull the heavy mechanical lever to close the front door and we're off.

I have no clue where to go and while my friends are screaming and hollering "GO BUS DRIVER, GO BUS DRIVER, GO!", others are worried. Legitimately fearful for their lives. I drive off campus and onto West Huron Street. I figure the rational thing here would be to drive to The War Hall and deliver the students safely to their destination. Maybe I can hurry out of the bus before the cops know who drove it and disappear into the crowd on the dance floor. A girl taps me on the shoulder.

"I want to get off. Please let me off."

There is real fear in her look. I feel bad. I pull over, open the front door and yell back:

"Anyone that wants off, this is your chance!"

I figure a few people will bail. Maybe five or six, max. But soon everybody is hurrying off the bus except my four friends. I watch the nervous students push and hurriedly step down off the bus and into the freezing cold darkness. I look in the rearview mirror, close the door and crank the music. My boys in the back whoop. We barrel down the street and I steer and dance. We almost clip a parked car on the right, but I jerk the bus back into the middle of the street.

"Fuck."

"Dude! Slow down!"

"Don't listen to him! Pedal to the metal. To The War Hall!"

"Go bus driver, go bus driver, go!"

I remark that the road is surprisingly void of traffic for 9:00 PM on a Thursday. Odd. We barrel on for another few minutes, adrenaline pumping, tinny house beats doing their best to go Oontz Oontz Oontz.

"Shit. Goose, we got company."

I flick a glance at the side mirror. Flashing police lights.

For the first time, thoughts of consequences reach my left brain and I don't want to get into some sort of crazy crash / accident / disaster. I slow down and turn right at the first side street. Two paddy wagons come out of an alley on each side of the road and block our forward progress. As I slow the bus, three or four cop cars roar up behind and block us in. I throw the bus into P, run to the back, and think a stupid drunk brain thought: Maybe they won't know which one of us was driving.

A cop, very agitated, pushes the door open and storms onto the bus. He comes straight at me and grabs a fist full of my plaid button down. He pulls me up and drags me off the bus.

"I'll cooperate. I'm not going to resist," I assure him pathetically as there seems a non-zero chance I'm going to get my skull cracked here.

He throws me over the hood of a cop car.

"Spread your legs. Put your hands on the car. Shut the fuck up. Don't move."

I glance over and my buddies are all spread eagled against the side of the bus, getting patted down. I wish I could take a picture of them, instant classic on Insta. 15 or more cops scurry around. One cuffs me and Mirandizes me and pushes me into the back of his cruiser. Takes me downtown.

I spend five hours or so in jail. Finally, after no sleep in the cold cell, I return to a hero's welcome at the dorm just after 4:00 AM. Everyone is still awake and immersed in an epic game of Asshole. I fill them in on the details of my night; but I need to get to bed. I have an exam in the morning.

I sleep for three hours; a short, adrenaline-addled sleep. I drag myself to campus and write my Economics 020 exam. When the Scantron torture is over, I return to my room and go back to bed. Head in severe pain from alcoholic dehydration.

I slip into a bad sleep for maybe 30 minutes. Then: KNOCK KNOCK. It's a woman at my door, maybe 28. Bookish and cute. Small eyes, small mouth, small nose. Mousy.

"Are you Charlie Bloom?"

"Yes. I am," I mutter. This doesn't seem good.

"Your actions last night put a great number of students in harm's way and put the reputation of our school at risk. This is your notice we have recommended your expulsion for multiple violations of the law and the University Student Conduct Code. You may appeal to the ombudsman if you do not believe the expulsion is warranted. Thank you."

She hands me an envelope. I believe the expulsion was warranted, so I do not appeal.

The charges are dropped from reckless driving to "Driving Vehicle Without Owner's Consent" (legalese for joyriding). And so ends my time at college. I never belonged in college anyway. Typical of my life, this is another case of bad decision / good outcome.

PS: CJ checked my grade after they posted the ECO 020 results. A+ 98/100.

■ ■ ■

1 YEAR AND 79 DAYS BEFORE THE RESET

After a few dates with Alison, things move fast. We both see there is something huge happening. Now Alison has moved off the couch at her friend's place and she's in theory crashing on my couch though obviously this means she has de facto moved in with me and it is all happening superfast and she shares my bed every night and my lingual frenulum is persistently sore.

We are both fine to not overthink it and anyway it makes no sense for her to look for an apartment when she doesn't have a ton of cash and I have plenty of room at my place and besides I like seeing her pink electric toothbrush in my bathroom and her girl stuff strewn around my place. It feels good.

I have not had a serious girlfriend since high school and that adolescent experience really cannot compare to this situation since I'm much older now and less needy and (slightly) less insecure and: this is fucking awesome. I have never met anyone so smart and with so much depth and light and darkness and fun and sadness all wrapped up into one crazy incredible high-speed little package.

We are each other's bad influence. Random Tuesdays become 15-hour drinking and drug-filled events. Nights where maybe I don't feel like getting messed up, Alison will, and so we do it together and vice versa. On the other hand, we also have long periods (three or four days in a row sometimes) where we encourage each other to stay clean and sober and get our brains functioning properly again. We'll go for a run here and there and play a ton of Scrabble and my kitchen has been used a few times for cooking food (!) which is something new.

The recreational activity of choice is to drop a few mills of Sight and watch a movie or two and then once the waves of synesthetic insanity normalize we rail a gram or two of coke and then smooth it out with a couple of crushed up Adderall. Then smoke Marlboro Golds and play Scrabble until sunrise while pontificating oh so smartly about life and our amazing new relationship and how one day we will find a more productive and mature future but not right now.

It's easy to quit. But it's hard not to start again.

It's only been a few weeks but I am 99% sure this is the person I will marry. Uncharted territory for me emotionally, but I have almost zero doubt. There is only one tiny little bit of nagging doubt that I have and it relates to the fact I feel a bit like I am not just falling in love with a girl but also rescuing a broken puppy from the SPCA. This puffs my ego because I add nothing of value to the world right now and so wouldn't it be wonderful if I could outdo all of the king's horses and all of the king's men, and slowly put her heart back together again?

In a weird way my want to be with her seems to emanate from a selfish desire to do something useful by fixing this broken woman. But is that bad? Anyway, best not to idle too long on that topic. Better to focus on the insane / amazeballs chemistry and the instant and hardwired connection we have formed. Soulmates type of thing.

flatland's reaction to this turn of events is typical: logical and measured. She communicates to me with empathy that I am moving way too fast and all that stuff a friend is supposed to say but of course I am having none of it because she doesn't really get it. What we have is something that is hard to explain and does not fit in any normal box. The word destiny comes to mind but is too cheesy to utter. Anyway, that's the drift of the feeling. That this was meant to be / decided before it started.

This time is different.

I see that Alison and flatland don't get along too well though neither one is willing to admit it. I sense a certain frostiness between them that one might call jealousy. In the past, flatland has always been on the lookout for periods when I got over my skis on the recreational snow and she will say something / intervene without condescension. But she is smart and strategic enough to know this is a freight train that is not to be stepped in front of right now and so she hangs on the periphery tossing out the occasional "be careful" or "just make sure you know what you are doing".

Other friends have been more judgmental and territorial in evaluating my disappearance into the love bubble, asking whether or not she is paying for her own drugs or her part of the rent and similarly-offensive Q's. Honestly, I have been weeding out most of my second and third tier friends over the past few years anyway. I don't have a lot of time for lower-tier friend maintenance. If they don't like how much time I'm spending with Alison or the way I am spending it, that's cool with me. In fact, it simplifies things.

■ ■ ■

@realdemocracy tweeted
"if the american people ever allow private banks to control
the issuance of their currency, first by inflation and then by
deflation, the banks and corporations that will grow up
around them will deprive the people of all their property until
their children will wake up homeless on the continent their
fathers conquered."
thomas jefferson

■ ■ ■

1 YEAR AND 73 DAYS BEFORE THE RESET

Sun slices through a tiny opening between the curtains and my eyes have decided to pop open without my consent so there will be no more sleep for now. My body and eyelids are tired but my brain is wide awake and seems to have plans for today which it has not yet shared with me. I get out of bed as nimbly and quietly as possible, so as not to disturb Alison, who lies on her stomach in full starfish. Her white panties reveal a small slice of firm, pale white butt cheek and the sight makes my grapes tingle. I climb out the window onto the fire escape and Strike a Lucky.

9:00 AM and already protesters are out. *We want our money back. Where's my bonus? Where's my Gary?* Things are getting worse as the protests take on a darker, more aggressive tone. Homeless and outside for the better part of the past three years, many of the protesters now have that sketchy, vagrant vibe that is 65 percent human and 35 percent animal. They scavenge for food. They huddle for warmth. They struggle to stay alive.

These are not the animal spirits of which John Maynard Keynes wrote.

About 250 protesters march on the street below and a copswarm follows on each end. The NYPD has encouraged cops to stay in groups of ten or more now for their own safety and often the copswarms number 20 to 50 officers, even when there is no protest nearby. It is not unusual to see a group of 15 or 20 cops standing around, smoking, swearing, spitting and texting, completely blocking the sidewalk like a group of punks in front of a high school. The cops have much more of a "fuck it" attitude as their job becomes increasingly difficult.

Alison crawls outside with me. She rubs sand from her sleepy red eyes and I pass her my lit cigarette and light another for myself. She tells me she had a bad dream last night about a kid named Tyler.

"Who's Tyler?" I ask.

■ ■ ■

Alison was in between eighth and ninth grade but hung out with a bunch of sophomores from Staples High School in Westport. She met them through tennis because the U14s sometimes practiced with the U18s and she kind of came across as 17 years old or so that summer before her 14th birthday. She was pretty and edgy and projected confidence.

There was this kid Tyler who she always noticed looking at her but she didn't feel worthy so never reciprocated plus she had a hard time telling if it was an attraction kind of look he was giving her or more of a pervy vibe.

Tyler was tall and sinewy. Red hair. Long on the top, short on the sides. Half child, half man. His voice was unpredictable and his feet were disproportionately large despite his nearly six-foot frame. He wore a 75-dollar haircut and got pissed off if the help didn't have his favorite Villebrequin shorts clean when he needed them. Raised mostly by nannies and sometimes by a mom in leggy striped dresses who occasionally returned from the gym or a Brazilian to take him to Kumon or piano or mathematics or parkour. She sometimes tucked him in before she tucked into a 60-dollar bottle of Pinot, a pint of Ben and Jerry's and a few hours of HGTV. Sometimes she would be too drunk and the help would tuck him in.

"Mommy went to sleep already, chiquito. Sweet dreams, OK?"

She was a loyal soldier in the PTA, Botoxed to the gills and mired deep in the existential doo-doo. Doing the best she could with no help from family back in Illinois. She kind of drifted apart from everyone since the divorce. Got her lips done and looks a bit like a cartoon duck. Power through the days. Drink away the nights.

Tyler's dad moved on and married the nanny in the classic Fairfield County move. Marry hot—then when your wife hits 40: fuck the nanny. If you're lucky, you marry the nanny and do it all again when she turns 40. Why wives sign off on the model-hot nanny hire instead of insisting on a qualified but big boned and buck-toothed Eastern European nanny is beyond comprehension—but strangely commonplace.

It was 3:45 PM on one of those thick sweaty July days where an adult might say "it's not the heat, it's the humidity". As Alison stood outside the tennis club waiting for her Lyft, Tyler strutted over, full of that unique brand of dumb overconfidence found only in high school seniors. He smelled like a faint mixture of fabric softener and onion-vinegar boy stank and spoke through a mouthful of Skittles. His left shoe was untied. Cute but dumb, he was not a beneficiary of the Flynn effect.

"My parents are away this weekend. I'm having a party Saturday. You wanna drop by?" he said.

His eyes flicked to the road as a black Porsche Cayenne with tinted windows came into view.

"Sure. Text me your address. Can I bring a friend or two?" she replied.

"Yep. Sure."

His dad rolled up in the gleaming black vehicle and the conversation was over. Tyler stepped in and the SUV growled off. Alison was stoked at the invite; she texted her best friend Winnie right away.

■ ■ ■

36 HOURS LATER

Alison and Winnie shared a fifth of raspberry Schnapps in the car on the way to Tyler's earlier and she has been swilling piss-warm keg beer from a red solo cup all night. Now she's stumbling around the downstairs of a poorly lit McMansion, looking for someone, anyone she knows. Drunk kids are sprawled everywhere and smears and greebles of coke stain a glass coffee table and a heavy weed smell hangs thick over everything. She accidentally bumps an empty bottle of Grey Goose with her leg. It was way too close to the edge of the coffee table so it teeters then tips and falls off. She stops and stares for a bit; watches it clunk onto the floor and roll away over the hardwood. She is glad it didn't break.

The beer in Alison's stomach fills her right up to the top and she can feel the liquid sloshing inside, undigested, threatening to tickle her uvula and send streams of foaming gold spray outward across the expensive and beautifully distressed, wide-plank reclaimed hardwood maple floor.

She is wasted, but the non-wasted part of her brain is still just barely in touch with central processing and so a couple of coherent thoughts find their way through the mindsmoke, out into consciousness:

I need to find Winnie and go home. Mom is going to kill me.

Alert for a moment, she racks her brain, trying to remember if Dad's around this weekend and then she remembers he's in Japan.

Thank you, God.

She is sloppy drunk, asking randoms if they've seen Winnie and everyone is like: "Who's Winnie?" or mostly just yelling: "What?" Their drug and boozefucked brains can no longer compute. Plus the music is crazy loud, and it's not good music; it's those pale, whiny thin-faced guys from Santa Monica that she can't stand. She stumbles over to the kid on the electronic decks and yells: "You got any Nirvana?"

She is instantly mortified by this poseury move and turns away before the kid can answer.

Where the hell are you Winnie? I gotta go.

The house is like 10,000 square feet or something stupid and she wants out. Alison fumbles her smartphone out of a tight front pocket, taps Lyft and orders a car. Heads for the front door to wait outside then feels a searing pang of guilt and thoughts like: "What if Winnie gets raped or something?" ping around in her head and so she hits cancel on the Lyft and stuffs the phone back in her jeans. A brief jolt of panic: will that hurt my rating on Lyft? I really have to be careful—

But before she completes the thought there is a big shock of reddish hair bobbing in front of her and Tyler has appeared out of nowhere yelling:

"Alison! There you are!"

He's slurring. Wrecked. There are big drops of wet on his Vineyard Vines pink gingham button down.

"Come with me!"

He says it with such confidence! As if it were the only logical thing in the world to do right at that moment and so Alison grabs the back of his shirt and follows him through various rooms and to a stairway that goes up. It is dark upstairs but she follows without fear, just dumb drunken childish curiosity like: Oooh, I wonder where we're going!

He opens the door to his room and shuts it behind her and suddenly his shirt is off. He pulls her in and they kiss, but it's awkward. She is really hammered and so is he and their teeth clonk at one point and then he whispers deep into her ear:

"Take off your clothes."

Her nether regions tingle at the whisper and the touch of his moist, cold lip against her ear. She is undecided for a moment. Aroused, but way too drunk. And also, what about Winnie? But before she can think or act or answer either way, Tyler jams his hand into the front of her pants. Now he's fingering around like someone who lost a ring down a kitchen sinkdrain.

She says: "I don't want to do this. Stop it Tyler."

He pushes his hand harder into her pants and finds her manicured patch and then forces his fingers down over her arid labia majora. It hurts. He uses his other hand to undo her fly and he is really strong, much stronger than the resistance she starts putting up. Alison feels a wave of nausea and thinks: *Where's Winnie? Where's my mom? Somebody help me.*

"Stop it Tyler."

He hears her but doesn't stop.

"C'mon. Be cool, bitch."

He takes his hand out of her crotch and gets a grip on each side of the waistline of her pants. He has a handful of jean waistline and panty on both sides and is about to pull everything down when three things happen, pretty much all at once:

Her phone rings. Buzz buzzzz.

Winnie pushes open the bedroom door and flicks on the light.

Alison projectile vomits two liters of undigested beer onto Tyler's bare chest.

As soon as the firehose of foaming liquid stops erupting from her mouth, Alison wipes her lips with her shirt sleeve and pulls out her still buzzing phone. Turns out she screwed up when she tried to cancel the Lyft and now the driver's texting:

Are you coming?

I'm outside

Winnie stares, one third horrified, one third confused and one third LOL. She immediately knows this story will go down as an all-time classic and is already wondering who to tell first, Morgan or Allanah?

Tyler stands there with a wet chest and soaked pants that reveal a smallish diamond hard erection curving severely to the left. He runs his hands down his chest over and over in a futile attempt to squeegee some of the exhaled beer that still trickles down his chest. He kind of realizes he is guilty of attempted date rape or something similar and this guilt exactly offsets the anger at having been puked all over, so he is silent and dumb.

"I guess that's my ride Tyler. Thanks for the party. It was really fun."

For weeks afterward, she replayed that moment.

I can't believe I fucking said that!

"Thanks for the party? It was fun?" WHAT THE ACTUAL FUCK, AL? She wished she had said a hundred other things like maybe:

"Make sure your ringer's on because you'll be getting a call from my dad's lawyer about this."

Or: "We're leaving now. And no, I'm not sorry for puking on you, you fucking white trash rapist."

Or whatever. But as much as she boiled about the incident for more than a year afterwards, there were no repercussions. No consequences. Her mom was asleep (passed out, drooling on the sofa) when she got home that night and she never went after Tyler and he never spoke to her or texted. Four weeks of self-conscious glances at tennis camp and then they never saw each other again.

■ ■ ■

@realdemocracy tweeted
"the 8 richest people in the world are worth more than the
bottom 4 billion."
source: oxfam

■ ■ ■

1 YEAR AND 55 DAYS BEFORE THE RESET

ENVY

Mike and The Wife roll silently in a gleaming black 7 Series BMW. Heavy snowflakes waft down in slow motion, visible in dual cones of light projecting from twin xenon headlights. The Wife looks in the vanity mirror of the passenger side and wonders if her lipstick is right. If her lips are right. The lips are gorgeous one day, malformed the next, depending on her brain chemistry. She has spent so much time looking at them, obsessing over them, crying, that the cosmetic surgery she had six years ago could be perfect or disastrous. She can no longer tell. Are they too close to the color of the skin on her face? Too puffy? Too flat? They look too flat. *I need to get another treatment. They definitely look too flat now.*

"Your lips look fine."

"Thanks. I know. Just checking."

"They look fine."

The Wife fought tooth and nail, refusing to let her body undergo the natural aging process. Ricotta cheese piled up on her haunches and countless surgeries have left her a weird, distorted, macabre, time lapse anti-aging experiment gone awry. She often sits in the giant California Closet and stares at (actual printed) photos of herself in a bathing suit at age 18. She just wants to be that girl again. Just for one day. Please God. Now her heart is scaly, cracked like dishwater hands. She is out of love with everyone. Her husband, her family, her former friends. She can no longer recall what love feels like.

Last week she stood in that same closet naked in front of a full-length mirror, staring at the cuts from her latest surgery. The augmentation procedure had gone well and she looked forward to healing so she could share with Mike. She never showed him until it was all healed. Before that, disgusting. *When Mike sees these, he will love me again.* But maybe they never were in love with each other. They fell in love with avatars. Symbols and illusions. But illusions never changed into something real. Now there is only decay, and insane efforts to staunch it.

She was desired, like a child's red balloon once. But now she found herself snagged high in a tree, faded, deflated and sad. In the middle of winter. Reeking of old lady perfume from Nordstrom's. You can't really blame The Wife for her body image issues. Her father told her at age 15:

"Make hay while the sun shines, girl. You won't be hot forever."

And such. She wasn't exactly encouraged to dig deep and unleash those latent STEM talents.

"You look fine," Mike says again.

He tries to hide the frustration in his voice and is really, honestly trying to make her feel better or okay or something. Not because he cares about her but just because he wants her on an even keel tonight, not drinking too much. This is one of those parties he just needs to survive. Eric Eastman, Senior Managing Director, Global Head of Capital Markets, is the host. Eastman is Mike's boss. He occupies the job Mike thinks he deserves but "the rumors" have hurt Mike's chances at promotion in the last couple of years. Anyway, Eric is good, he's a good manager, good boss, good trader and all that. No hard feelings.

Eastman's wife is fucking hot, like naturally hot. Not one of those cyborg plastic surgery freak ass things like The Wife. Mike wants Eastman's wife so, so bad. He wants to press himself against her naked body. No. He wants to control her. Own her. Oh, the things I would do to you if I was Eastman. His grapes swell. As he walks, they swing back and forth, pendulum-style.

Eastman's wife slides across the room in a beautiful dress that drops perfectly, like a waterfall. The Wife intercepts her and they talk a bit. Next to this perfection, The Wife feels insecure. Mike looks over at The Wife just as her God-forsaken fake lips contort into a fake laugh. The laugh is empty and canned. The Wife tips back a bit too much as she guffaws and a splash of red wine spills out of her glass and dots the Safavid rug. She is already drunk. Fucking disaster. Eastman's wife politely moves along. Mike's guts churn. He needs a divorce, really fucking bad. But he has no time for that right now.

■ ■ ■

TWO HOURS LATER

If scientists set out to purposely design a genre of music which would clash the most with a cocaine high, they would create jazz.

Mike's mind races and he has the impossibly fast heartbeat of an Etruscan shrew. He stands in the bustling, luxurious living room as a three-piece jazz band belts out Christmas carols and Hanukkah songs via trumpet, saxophone and a ridiculously small drum set. The party is in full swing. Mike is wired as fuck. Loud voices are like plates clanking in sinks all around him. Mike is trapped; one of the new managing directors talks his ear off about some bullshit trade idea for next year.

"...Can't lose, boss! Can't lose!"

The guy's voice is loud and Jewish, like a pack-a-day crow from Tel Aviv. Mike pretends to listen as he checks the market on his phone. Then his eyes dart randomly around the room and he spots the Jeroboam of Cristal on the bar and a hot VP from investment banking (*a VP? What the fuck is a VP doing here?*) and the goddamn three-piece band. Clanging brass musical notes fly like sharpened sonic darts across the room and into Mike's ears. They rattle around his skull and spiral down through his bloodstream, into his speed-racing heart. He wishes he could take a 28-inch hunting crossbow and fire a carbon arrow into each band member's left eye socket from close range. Thwack! Thwack! Thwack! The music stops, one instrument at a time.

Mike harbored a special hot hate for jazz since his 20s. Ever since that upstuck cunt at the Village Vanguard kept shining a flashlight in his face because apparently he was "talking too much during the set". What-fucking-ever, beyotch.

Mike had planned to ration the eight ball of coke he brought to the party but he's already managed to snort about 2.5g out of 3.5g and it's only 9:30 PM. He knows from past experience that snorting so much so early is good for his ability to go to sleep later on but bad for his ability to keep his shit together right now. He ponders whether the correct strategy at this point is to just rail the remaining blow or slow down and save some for later. If he saves some for later, he might extend the enjoyableness of the night and avoid that crashing "I have no coke left" feeling that will otherwise hit around 11:00 PM. But on the other hand, if he finishes the powder now, he'll be drunk and exhausted and asleep by midnight instead of lying in bed awake all night listening to his heart pound behind his ears and wondering just how much of this shit do you have to snort before you have a heart attack or heart explosion, anyway?

There are two types of women at the party. In the world. There are those girls as yet unweathered by life's various cumulative torments. Lithe skin that fits well over healthy muscle. The glow of hope and unshattered dreams. Bright eyes that suggest smart playfulness and secrets of the highest value. And there are the mothers. Skin now creped, with reduced elasticity. A quarter or a half size too large for its host. Wrinkles and ass bulges. Crow's feet and subtly sunken eyes that betray the sadness of all the girlish dreams never realized. Or worse: every dream WAS realized. Then what? Big house, pretty garden, rich husband, empty void. Joyless wardens of a hellish 6,000 square foot penitentiary where the inmates run screaming at random, incessantly demand food, argue compulsively, fight and frequently piss on the floor and in bed. Dreams replaced by black empty and white wine. Totally confused with no idea what even went wrong. Fat asses Spanxed into too-tight yoga pants. Namaste away from me.

The trumpet rapes his ears and this fucking twat in the Men's Wearhouse suit is rattling Mike's psyche with sophomoric trade ideas and so Mike finally just bolts away from the kid in mid-sentence and heads into the small vanity bathroom off the side of the living room of this massive Connecticut mansion. To be clear, this is a true mansion, not some rinky dink McMansion. It is an estate. Three professionally decorated Christmas trees. Fully functioning apple orchard yielding more than 10,000 apples/year. Two Rothkos and a Richter before you get past the main foyer. Caterers buzz around guests in a ratio of 1:3.

Mike pulls the sliding pocket door shut behind him and turns the flimsy lock. He tips the remainder of the cocaine onto the back of the toilet. It's good shit so it's mostly rock not powder, and so he pulls out a fifty-dollar bill and covers the pile of rocks then takes out a credit card and crushes the rocks under the bill, using it to keep the rocks and crumbs from flying everywhere. He drags the edge of the card back and forth along the bill feeling the rocks and crumbs crack, crush and crumble under the pressure until he can feel as he drags the edge of the card back and forth along the bill that there is no more resistance or cracking or crumbling and therefore underneath the bill is now a perfect, flattened pile of fine white powder.

He lifts the bill and admires his handiwork then uses the edge of the credit card again, this time to chop the pile even more finely. Chop, chop, chop he could do this all night he just fucking loves the ritual. Chop, chop, chop. He strokes out six huge lines of powder on the back of the toilet and admires them for a second. He is about to roll up the fifty-dollar bill to snort the lines one by one.

Are you sure you wanna snort all six all at once?

Well yeah, what else am I going to do at this point, scrape them back into the bag?

He snorts the lines and rubs the remaining powder on his gums and then wets a few squares of toilet paper and wipes the back of the cistern to erase any evidence and then he feels a cramp or something in his stomach and then...

He realizes that he has to take a shit. A violent, emergency shit.

Good cocaine is a fierce laxative and his guts were already burbling for the last half-hour as he's been scarfing down bacon-wrapped scallops and snapper crudo with chilies and blue crab beignets and some steaky cheese things on crostini and even though coke fucks up his appetite by numbing and partially closing his throat this isn't his first rodeo and he knew if he didn't force himself to eat something he'd be borderline incoherent by midnight.

There are nine bathrooms in this house and of all of them this was by far the worst one to pick if one were to take a shit. Partygoers mingle just meters away. But at this point he has no choice as no amount of clenching or sphincter squeezing will stop this imminent dam burst. No one saw him go in so he figures he can take his shit and sneak out all stealthy and hopefully blame for the stench won't be assigned to him.

He sits down and SPLASH. He forcefully vomits out of his ass, instantaneously splattering the bowl with brownish green and filling the small bathroom with a stench so hideous he gags, then gags again and vomits slightly in his mouth. He tastes bacon fat and acid and wine. The thing is over as quickly as it started and so he wipes his ass with a few squares of the softest toilet paper in the world. *How do we not have toilet paper this soft? What am I, fucking poor?* He plans to talk to The Wife about this later.

The door rattles a bit. Someone else wants to use the bathroom.

Fuck.

"Just a minute."

His heart jackhammers now (from the gear, not from nerves) and he insurance wipes his ass one more time and then flushes the toilet and one could imagine some sort of epic toilet travelling, shit tunnel scene here like in *Gravity's Rainbow* (or the *Trainspotting* scene that plagiarizes *Gravity's Rainbow*) but Mike's imagination is not vivid and he's too focused on the tamburo grosso going boom boom boom behind his rib cage. There are five or six *TIME* magazines in a rack beside the toilet and he zones in on the face of some politician who stares back at him and they remain locked in a staring contest for six or maybe 90 seconds and then a gentle knock on the door again snaps him back to reality.

"Just a minute," Mike utters, jaw clenched.

He catches a whiff of the army green smell blanketing the bathroom and looks around frantically for some spray to mask the stench or at least a fan to turn on or a match to light but: none of the above. Washes his hands. Fixes his hair. Straightens himself up, shoulders back. Looks in the mirror.

You look pretty fucking good for fifty, man.

There is an extra layer of puff to his skin and a slightly unhealthy sheen maybe but nothing too dramatic. He smiles at himself then quickly runs through a few possibilities of who might be waiting outside the bathroom. Mostly just hopes it's not a chick. He checks the market on his phone.

He slides open the door and walks out with his head down but glances up to see that Anna, the eminently fuckable 20-year-old daughter of the owner of the house was the one waiting. Complete and utter mortification. Earlier thoughts of fucking her upstairs in her childhood bedroom were unrealistic but now the odds of riding this fantasy to fruition are absolute zero. The bathroom door closes and Mike swears he hears Anna gag.

The intolerable clanging racket of the fucking Christmas jazz band still pollutes the main room and there is now a goddamned labradoodle walking around in case this wasn't the gayest fucking party ever already so he decides to locomote. He sees The Wife going upstairs. She is leading one of the caterers by the hand: a boy, maybe 22 max. Hipster beard, pants a bit too short. This is a common trick The Wife pulls when hammered. It doesn't bother Mike (much). It further motivates him to find something to fuck, ASAP.

His nuts are sore from lack of use and full from the cocaine high. There are plenty of easy targets around including a few of his direct reports who have given him signals in the past. He chats up one of the personal assistants from credit. She is absolutely gorgeous but offputtingly dumb. Talks in sentences that all end in a question mark?

As she goes on about some vapid foodtech start up idea, he sees that she has stepped straight out of a magazine ad. Unrealistically perfect photoshopped supernormal gorgeous unblemished weightless uncontrolling wanting nothing offering everything loves to give head and never complains. He feels aroused but repelled by her perfection. He wants equally to fuck her and to spit on her, though he does not get why. And the overthinking stops and he decides to get some.

Now she is naked except for a pair of pink, orange and white striped Paul Smith socks and he has her bent over a king size bed upstairs and there is a slappy clapping noise as he drives himself up into her. He is almost positive he can hear The Wife groaning in the next room and this kind of turns him on and pisses him off and he takes all the energy from the blow and from his contempt for The Wife and the multiple clusterfucks at work and he channels it all down. Down. Down. Down through his dick and up into the girl. Slamming her / banging her / in the literal sense. His mind is off the rails. Eyes shut hard and every muscle taut and tensed. BANG BANG BANG BANG BANG...

He wears no condom. He has never once worn a condom. *Fuck that shit. I'm a legit risk taker.*

BANG BANG BANG—

His pumping goes too deep and the dick bends a bit as it crashes into cervix. Her groans turn to yelps of pain then quick pleas.

"Ow. Ow! That hurts... Ow. It hurts."

Mike stays inside her but slows down and apologizes not because he is sorry but because he doesn't want her to get up and leave before he's finished. The ecstasy is lost now, obviously, and the excitement / energy is sucked out of the exchange and so he finishes the transaction and pulls out and wipes his own translucent residue and drops of her blood onto the incredibly soft white comforter. Mike gets dressed in the silence and heads for the bedroom door to leave without a word. The girl scrambles and hops around as she tries to get her clothes on in a hurry. She's drunk and disoriented by the abruptness of the whole thing.

Mike walks out of the bedroom and nearly bumps into someone —*fucking hilarious*—it's The Wife who just walked out of the adjacent bedroom. Mike laughs pretty much right in The Wife's face but her face is stone. Not angry or shocked, more like just further beaten down emotionally. New lows.

"You ready to go home?"

"Yes. I'm exhausted."

"Me too, let's go."

"You alright to drive?" she asks.

"Yeah I'm fine. Let me take a piss. Here's the valet ticket. Give it to the guy out front and I'll meet you in five."

Mike hands The Wife the valet ticket and a five-dollar bill and heads for the can. The live music in the living room has finally stopped. Mike pictures the three band members dead on the floor, each with an arrow sticking out of a bleeding eye socket. He chuckles at the visual.

■ ■ ■

1 YEAR AND 51 DAYS BEFORE THE RESET

7six7 have incorporated this new light show where various lasers shoot out over the dance floor into a cloud of evaporating dry ice and create hyper-realistic holograms in 3D. Lions copulating. Armadillos sword fighting. Robots doing the robot. It's a cliptastic series of mindfucks as I burn 500 calories an hour pulsating to the audio buzzsaw slicing down my spine. There is a sauce of tequila and shoe dirt and sweat and water on the dancefloor. Images above are partially reflected in puddlettes on the ground. A distorted face of a cackling clown appears at my feet and then vaporizes.

Drunk Ghettopunk Barbie falls into me and I guide her at arm's length toward the bar. She stinks of perfume and I don't want it on or near me so I lean her up against a pole and walk away praying she doesn't timber. Vape on a cig-o. Exhale. I watch the girl out of curiosity. Will she fall over, or won't she?

Picture Barbie drawn in anime with double the makeup and some punk rock accessories and you get the gist. Grotesquely over-primped. Hair dry like hay. Not sexy. But sexy isn't the point. It's more about who can do it craziest and to the max and really go full retard and be so extreme it totally proves, like, zero fucks given, ya know?

The blowback to this Barbie Harujuku Chic is a contingent of girls that have just decided like basically "screw this, I can't keep up so I'm not even going to try" and so there is this aggressively-disin-terested-in-fashion thing where girls wear zero makeup and just random baggy pants and whatever shirt but the thing is: it isn't random. It's intentional. Calculated. "I'm too cool to try so I'll not try on purpose so that you will know for sure that I'm not trying" type of thing.

Some girls can pull it off and look good. Like Alison. She walks up and leans on me in a way that says she's really tired from dancing but also super comfortable with me and with being in my space. She smells hot.

"Having fun?"

"Yep. You?"

"Yep. Want a drink?"

"How about some orange juice?"

"Yes please."

I am a little bit wired but mostly lucid as I haven't dropped anything into my bloodstream in about three hours and I've been drinking a lot of water and not much booze tonight because it's Sunday and I plan on trading tomorrow. I'm in the trough of the biochemical sine wave and the peaks are getting lower, but I still feel good.

Alison leans against a slightly humid metal pillar; she is mellow, buzzing like neon yellow. Green, pink and orange lasers flash over the dance floor in front of her and light up and color her pale face. She looks beautiful and exhausted. I want to pick her up and carry her out of here and outside to safety and we can both lay down and sleep for weeks and weeks and weeks and then wake up on a remote island beach off Thailand and live a simple life together in a straw hut. Eat pineapples and magic mushrooms every day.

I walk over to the bar and get myself a pineapple juice and Alison her OJ. I think about how I really want to get out of the city / out of this life. Trading is awesome. It's super fun. But it's nothing. Meaningless. Like dealing blackjack all day. Exciting for a while. Fun, but empty. I wonder if this is how my dad felt. Trapped in a shopping mall with an infinite credit limit. You can buy anything you want but eventually you don't want to buy anything. You just want out. I want to ask him but I can't, obviously. We never really had a real conversation. And then he stepped off the curb. And that was it.

I miss you, Dad.

There's something wet on my face. Alison touches her fingertip to my cheek and catches a tear as it rolls down.

"Dude. Are you crying?"

"What? No. Probably sweat."

"You're sweating out of your eyes?"

I fake a smile at Alison.

"You wanna go?" she asks.

"Yeah, I'm done."

We walk outside the warm, beating cocoon of the club. The city is gaudy and clanky and awful. We walk home in silence, shower together and go to bed.

■ ■ ■

@realdemocracy tweeted
"in the absence of the gold standard, there is no way to
protect savings from confiscation through inflation. there is no
safe store of value."
alan greenspan

■ ■ ■

1 YEAR AND 46 DAYS BEFORE THE RESET

The death of the euro was not the flashy apocalyptic event speculators were cheering for in 2010/2011. Instead, it was a slow and tedious disintegration as populace and politicians stopped believing one by one and the project cracked slowly. And then suddenly.

Italy left and faith evaporated and a final fragmentation and redenomination plan was agreed upon. The mirror image of the 1999 process was negotiated over several years and most of the original currencies were reborn with Germany updating to the neuemark while Spain, Malta, Greece and Estonia agreed to keep the old (and massively devalued) euro. The euro went from a symbol of unity to a symbol of global fragmentation and failure.

With the fractured euro, the devalued renminbi and the always-maligned dollar competing in an epic ugly contest, the neuemark and gold should, in theory, be the only respected currencies for those interested in long-term wealth preservation in a world where fiat currencies may or may not have a realistic future. Don't even get me started on crypto.

The dollar is ripping higher today even as more bad news comes out. CPI broke into double digits for the first time since the 1980s this year and CPI ex-food and power is pushing 30% now. Global battery shortages and lithium hoarding have driven power costs through the roof and food is doing this weird barbell thing where cheap stuff (flour, bananas) is just completely unavailable and luxury food (sushi-grade tuna, artisanal bacon, mozzarella di bufala) has tripled or quadrupled in price. Meanwhile middle of the road groceries (granola, pasta sauce) have barely gone up in price and are still regularly available.

The market seems to think the Fed will respond to rising inflation with rate hikes at some point but it's not gonna happen. As long as real GDP is below zero, I just don't see it. Policy makers have completely abandoned the nominal GDP targeting approach launched by the last Fed Chair and have now moved to Real GDP targeting. Experimental monetary policy continues to evolve as each successive Fed Chair finds new and creative ways to keep rates too low for too long. Inflation in 2022 was the appetizer and here comes the main course.

Negative interest rates: completely and utterly absurd. You lend me $1,000 and in one year I will pay you back $980. It makes no sense. They have sodomized common sense and inverted capitalism with futile efforts to resuscitate a corpse. Let the patient die. But they will never, ever do that. And so the zombie economy lumbers on, undead.

They can't raise rates with Real GDP down here and some members of the FOMC are now calling for another joint FOMC/Treasury Outright Monetary Financing (OMF) package to boost output. Recent Fed research suggests that the inflation targeting approach used by the Fed in the 90s and early 2000s was highly suboptimal and a new framework emphasizing employment, fiscal coordination and Real GDP targeting has gained acceptance among most policymakers and Nobel Prize winners. Krugman was too hawkish. He just didn't get it. The mantra since 2009 remains: if it doesn't work, do more. MMT was too conservative. Neoliberal extraction economics does not function sans unlimited free money.

I scan the market for dislocations. FoneApp rings and Alison's voice is in my ears.

"Hey. It's me."

Her voice is salty caramel. A quick shot of adrenaline to the heart; a splash of dopamine on the brain.

"Hey baby. Where are you?"

"Watertown."

"What? What's a Watertown?"

I walk into the kitchen and 3D print a cig-o. Drag. Inhale. Exhale.

"Watertown. New York. On the Canadian border. Don't worry about it. I'm just calling to say.............. :]"

The emoticon flies at me in 3D via goggware and I duck. I hate those things but I like her, so I smile.

"Thanks. You going to be home anytime soon? I haven't seen you in almost a week."

"Yea, I'm getting on the bus in twenty minutes. How about dinner tomorrow night?"

"Bus? You are so ghetto; I love it. How about you come straight to my place and we get naked?"

"OK, deal. I smell like armpits though."

"I am simultaneously aroused and grossed out."

"You should be."

The USD has rallied 70 basis points in the time it has taken to have this conversation.

"I need to take profit on a trade. Shoot me your ETA when you can."

"OK, will do," she says.

"Bye… I love you," I say.

Click. Whoa, did I just tell Alison I love her? I don't think she heard me. I just kind of blurted it out last second. I just want to see her. Smell her. Did she hear me? If she did, she'll definitely call back. So if she doesn't call back, she didn't hear me. Fine? Got it.

Do I love her? I do love her. I do! I totally do. I know it 100 percent for sure. But I just can't tell her yet. In case I'm wrong.

■ ■ ■

Alison heard something just before she hung up but didn't catch it and she figures if it's important Charlie will call back. She's had a great day and now everything she needed to get over the border is over the border. A few adventurous snowflakes fall from way high in the sky and one lands on her top lip and she licks it and feels its coolness on the tip of her tongue before it melts away in a few microseconds. She feels small electrical jolts in her chest as she pictures Charlie. She is possessed by the thought of him.

She is also afraid she might be crazy / retarded in love with him beyond anything she's ever felt for any guy before and she is telling herself to not screw this one up and then telling herself to relax because you screw it up by trying not to screw it up and then she starts thinking for a second about the only other man she ever loved and that ever truly loved her and she can feel his rough face for a second and smell the whisky then she does the trick where she can empty her entire mind for very long periods and her mind is now an unconscious void—completely empty but clear and empty and then the bus pulls up and she gets on.

■ ■ ■

1 YEAR AND 41 DAYS BEFORE THE RESET

In high school I was insecure because I was afraid that I was smarter than everyone else and I didn't want anyone to know, lest they might think less of me. I would go on in transparently overdramatic fashion about messing up on exams and then hide my A+ test results when I got them back from the teacher. The roots of my insecurity lay not just in being smarter than everyone else but also thinking I was paler and ganglier than everyone else though in retrospect I was pretty normal-looking and not any nerdier or skinnier or uglier than any other boys my age.

In those days when I looked in the mirror I saw spaghetti arms and translucent skin blotted with too many freckles. I saw a pale face pocked with throbbing blackheads and pickle warts and patches of eczema that glowed and flashed like Fremont Street neon whenever girls approached. Kids that were different or weird or unique in any way petrified me and I avoided them for fear that some of their weirdness might rub off on me and render me less popular.

High school: on a class trip to see Shakespeare somewhere by a river. I can't remember where. It's around 9:00 PM and four of us go sit under a play structure in a schoolyard near the motel where we were staying. Sean brought some contraband from his parent's liquor cabinet and so we sit on the cold sand and laugh nervously and drink peppermint Schnapps. Syrupy peppermint alcohol lights our brains and after an hour of laughing and feeling dizzy and all that, Sean gets up, stumbles away and starts puking and Jessica leaves to help him and so it's just Carrie and me. We sit under the playset talking and looking at the impossible number of stars in the cloudless sky.

"There's so many more stars here than in the city," I say.

There *are* so many more stars here. Did I fumble the syntax of that sentence? *Syntax? What kind of word is that for a 14-year-old?* I silently reprimand myself and briefly am unsure if I said the word "syntax" out loud or something but I didn't. I take a nervous sip from the Schnapps bottle and pass it to Carrie. I am lit, like Times Square.

By 10:30 there is a night chill even though it's summer and I can feel the cold sand through my rugby pants. Sweet, cute Carrie is shivering. She slides over and pushes against me, trying to get warm. I tense up and go full rigid as I'm not used to being pressed against by anyone, other than maybe Mom saying goodbye before school when I was a kid or whatever. It isn't that I'm not into girls, I just have no idea what to do around them, or how to talk to them, and now I have one pressing against the side of me and I'm not sure what should be done about that. I feel inferior to this girl in the pretty blue dress. I'm not sure why. I am not stupid or ugly or hideous or whatever but anyways for some reason I am just generally terrified of pretty girls and find it hard to breathe or construct full sentences around them. My tongue gets puffy.

We keep each other warm. Carrie holds my hand and I like how it feels. 5 or 50 minutes pass. Then Carrie takes my hand and puts it up under her shirt. It is warm and soft under there. A good soft, not the soft of a chubby fat person but the soft of young and healthy female skin. My head swims soaked in a supernova cocktail of adrenaline and hormones plus six or maybe eight ounces of peppermint schnapps and so I just go with it.

She moves my hand up onto a nipple (rubbery / surprisingly like the tied end of a balloon!) and makes a few circles and back down to the belly button. My brain completely void, I try for her panty line and get a quick fingertip feel of some sort of lacey margin of underpants but she pulls my hand gently back up away from the forbidden zone.

A few more laps of her perfect, tiny breasts and my hand is pulled again by the gravity of my curiosity and down it goes again. This time as I move a little faster, the tips of my fingers feel a few bristly hairs. What mysteries lie beneath? She less gently moves my hand away again but I am overwhelmed with curiosity and not really thinking all that straight and so I push a bit harder to get down into her pants. Innocent and curious with no ill intent.

Carrie drops her elbow hard, squarely cracking my right gonad with pinpoint accuracy. I have been hit in the junk before, by a tennis ball, a foot, the corner of a wooden coffee table and a perfectly executed no look pass in a game of pickup basketball, but never before or after in my life was one of my testicles ever hit with so much force and accuracy. Carrie scrambles up out of the sand and I scramble to get up too and then I fall in the sand and now I am by myself, covered in sand, drunk under a playset in a town I cannot name. Carrie disappears back towards the motel.

The crappy thing is, I kind of like Carrie; she's cool and fun to be around. Eventually I stumble through the night and find my motel room and crawl into bed, finding my way by the thin ambient light of a dollar store LED-clock. The next morning, dehydrated and with marinated head, pasty mouth and tenderized ego, I make my way to the free hotel breakfast. I pass Carrie in the hall.

"I'm not a slut you know," she blurts.

"I know. Carrie, I'm really sorry—"

Gone. She was never outright hostile towards me back at school but we never said another word to each other. Actually, that's not quite true.

Two years later, Carrie's mom, who apparently is the most awesome mom in the world or something decides she's going to have a surprise party for Carrie's 16th birthday. She contacts everyone in our grade and invites us all to the party. The invite says "It's a surprise! Please come at 7:00 PM and not after 7:30 PM because that is when Carrie will arrive!"

Due to some complications, I am running late.

"Come on Dad. Hurry up. I got to get there before she does or this is going to be a disaster."

It's impossible to find the house plus all the lights are out because of the surprise party but eventually we find it and roll up in front. The green digital clock on the dashboard of Dad's Audi A4 reads 7:31 but I can tell by the way the house is completely dark that Carrie hasn't arrived yet. I see a few shadows move around inside the house. I grab the present and quickly get out of the car.

I walk the flagstones from the sidewalk to the front of her house. The damp air smells sweet and earthy from the carpeting of dead leaves. At about flagstone number ten my stomach drops. A Jeep Wrangler turns into the driveway with Carrie in the front seat. I need to make myself invisible but I can't as the headlights sweep across the lawn and spotlight me. Here I am, fully lit and frozen in place. Carrie gets out of the car and stares at me like I am a piece of gum stuck to her left shoe. I look sheepishly at the birthday card in my hand. It reads "Carrie" in 30-point Black Sharpie. My eyes meet hers. Her face is 50/50 confusion / repugnance.

"What are YOU doing here?" she blurts out in that perfect teenaged girl tone of total disgust. YOU is audibly all caps.

Whatever scraps of self-confidence I have painstakingly built up over the last few years all come rushing out of me. My fragile teen ego is an untied helium balloon, released. It lands flaccid and empty on the flagstones. 35 classmates look on from inside the house, all thanking sweet Jesus it's me, not them out here in the wet fall air. Not only have I ruined the surprise but I have ruined it in grand style and full view.

Mortification.

■ ■ ■

1 YEAR AND 40 DAYS BEFORE THE RESET

Alison wakes up in a great mood for no reason and doesn't want to waste it. Maybe because she is falling in like / love with Charlie or something but anyway the fat ass of darkness that often sits on the face of her psyche right from the moment her eyes open in the AM is absent today and so she gets up and gets dressed in something soft and comfy and grabs some cigarettes and heads out for a walk.

She strolls through SoHo where the stores are as crowded as ever and she sits down on some stairs that go up to a shuttered store and puffs on a Lucky Strike and peoplewatches. No homeless here, private street security patrols. Beautiful shoppers. Who are these gorgeous cyborgs with their ceramic doll faces and factory-ripped G-Stars? Blonde Asian chicks with too much lipstick. Ugly bridge and tunnel girls made up to look pretty. Upper East Side women with too-plump lips and stupid yappy dogs. Facial features augmented with so much surgery they walk with one foot in the uncanny valley.

Alison challenges herself to smell the waft left in the wake of people passing and finds the older they are, the stronger they smell. Not necessarily in a good or bad way.

Am I falling in love with this Charlie guy?

Fond, but not in love. Nothing so idiotically teenage and desperate.

The idea that she might feel something more for Charlie is fine, not too scary but just kind of like: *nothing to worry about because I'm sure it won't work out anyway* type of thing.

Enough cigarettes smoked and butt now sore from the coldish stone steps, she wanders more, making love to the City of New York on this rare day she can appreciate it. She looks at a puddle of dog urine on the sidewalk and sees in it the heavenly reflection of a church across the street. Yesterday it would have just been a disgusting puddle of dog piss.

After thirty or forty blocks, Alison's feeling a bit drained so she hops on a subway headed back uptown. She sits and sips her coffee and drinks in the collection of New York stereotypes and weirdos. Two black girls, 18 or so, argue in way too loud / nearly lyrical ebonic histrionics. A Staten Island union guy on his way to the jobsite, jonesing for the cigarette he flips between thick yellowed fingers; he's tired, wired on coffee and still can't believe the end of the Giants game last Sunday. *Can't wait to talk to the guys about it. 51-yarder!!*

Sad souls stand with shoulders slumped. Vacant eyes. Skin too loose.

A marginally employed woman with three kids in moon boots is overstressed. The kids share a huge bag of Swedish Fish and pass around a bottle of Poland Spring while she tells them to shut up. She yells at the youngest boy who keeps passing the water to his sister:

"Stop giving her all that water she have to go to the bathroom don't give her no more..."

The boy responds by randomizing who will get the bottle next: "Eenie meanie miney moe catch a tiger by the toe if he hollers then he know eenie meanie miney moe."

He lands on himself and chugs. His mom chastises:

"Nova! Stop it! Don't finish it you moron!"

This is... 23rd Street.

A red-faced pockmarked teen wears fake Nikes and grey track pants, a dirty blue hoodie and a scowl. A square-jawed lax bro in a Brooks Brothers checked slimfit button down under a fleece vest avec broker logo and slightly slicked haircut from one of those hipster haircut clubs where you have a scotch while you wait. He's wearing $440

Allen Edmonds monk straps. A cute, fit Latina with edgy haircut who is totally gonna make it on Broadway, she knows it for sure. A ten-year-old in preppie clothes speaks French with his friend.

A completely hairless man.

The smell of subway brakes and discount perfume bought in Queens compete for nostrilian airspace. Ads for skin peels stare down. A Tourette's patient rocks like a hobby horse as eyes all face down at handheld rectangular super computers linked to satellites via subterranean broadband. More blind people per capita on the subway than one might expect given the obvious safety hazard presented by gaping rat-filled litter trenches lined with electrified rails frequented at somewhat regular intervals by hurtling multi-ton wheeled metal locomotives.

This is 34th Street. Penn Station.

A 6-year-old girl in a tutu eats an ice cream cone. Three twenty-somethings in a row (all with ponytails) tippy tap on phones. Black / white / black like an Oreo.

A smell wafts. It is reminiscent of cooked cauliflower but probably from a less edible provenance. Formerly trickling rivers of brownish sugarliquid are dry on the black spackled subway floor, collecting light dust. Two respectably dressed ladies with fistfuls of shopping bags eye Alison with disapproval. Yoga pants in public? My Gawd.

Photoshopped six-packs and jaw lines decorate wide rectangular advertisements curled into concave recess above the seats. Breast augmentation! Two kids with feet that don't reach the floor swing their legs and sing "Monday. Monday. I hate Monday" in unison. A 20-something girl in a rhinestone-festooned baseball cap, faux fur jacket and big freckled nose reads a miniature Thora.

This is 42nd Street. Times Square.

By 2:00 PM she has her first thought of the drink and this is a victory in itself as she sometimes has her first thoughts of drinking before breakfast these days. *A vodka soda would go great with these Cheerios* type of thing. Tired of thinking about drinking and thinking about thinking about drinking. She flushes her mind. Clear and empty. Clear and empty. Her mind, usually a packed car full of arguing passengers, is better today. But the thought of getting high will be a mental hangnail now. Persistent and annoying, it emits a touch of pain. Annoying as fuck.

Alison gets off the subway in midtown and does the zig zag thing where you let the traffic lights determine your path. Whenever a light turns red, she turns and keeps doing this to follow a crazy huge real-life Monte Carlo simulation that has 2^50 branches or whatever.

An endless stream of buses, taxis and black cars flows by. She stops to smell the fabric softener (Bounce) coming out of a brownstone on the Upper West Side and as she weaves up Columbus Ave. wonders if there were ever any independently owned stores around here? Or was it always just Starbucks and Bed Bath and lululemon and Nike? Alison thinks she probably knows the answer but she, like all the other post-gentrification New Yorkers, really has no idea what the city looked like 30 years ago. There were probably independent clothing stores and bookstores and internet cafes and all sorts of cool shit.

Internet cafes!

By 6:00 PM it's getting colder and she has legs that are tired like when she used to go Christmas shopping with Dad at the Danbury Mall back in the day and now she's pissed off that this memory of Dad has entered her skull. She banishes it for a few seconds but the thoughts of Dad are here now. The darkness crawling over the city now makes its way inside her; it rolls into her mind and fills her brain with black and grey matters and she is too tired to find the energy to fight the impending doom-mood and so she thanks the world for a good day and surrenders to the mental storms and Lyfts home.

In the Lyft, she has this random memory of free time during a class trip in high school. They were four BFF's (Alison, Andrea, Claire and Meghan) walking around downtown Montreal around 8:00 PM. Andrea said:

"Fifty bucks to anyone that blows a random stranger," as they walked up Saint Catherine Street.

They all laughed and carried on with other conversation but then a few blocks later, Alison sees this slick-looking, clean enough kid, maybe 16 (and she was 17 at the time) and she goes straight up to him and makes the offer. Cut to: she's blowing him in a side alley. Notable memory: his dick / balls smelled good and bad at the same time—exactly like Funyuns.

Afterwards, Andrea gave her the fifty bucks and everyone acted like it was all pretty funny but then later, back at school, Andrea and Claire made Alison out to be this huge slut. But, like, it wasn't even her idea and what the fuck? Are these my real friends or what?

Now she emerges from the memory and her thoughts jump to freezing cold vodka. Her mind is suddenly full of hexbugs. Her limbic system itches. She texts her dealer.

You around?

■ ■ ■

1 YEAR AND 38 DAYS BEFORE THE RESET

flatland. Number 57 DJ in the world but she does not consider herself a DJ at all. She's an artist. One who makes a lot of music. But she also makes walls of sound, freaky video collages and tripnotic soundscapes. If you think it sounds cheesy, you're wrong. flatland is to EDM as {insert name of your favorite band here} is to music. Pioneer in the sense that she constantly goes somewhere new but nobody has the stones or the skills to follow. Also notable: vegan, Berklee dropout and extremely spiritual. Spiritual but not religious. She understands that the bible is a metaphor. There is no actual subterranean region occupied by a red-skinned horned master / soul thief. God is in your head. He's not a guy with a beard. Do wrong, you feel wrong. Simple.

flatland is remixing a collection of noise that she's once again bottled fresh around the city for tonight's show. Straight from the street to your ears. Car horns. PS 191 kids laughing and playing ball. A siren on West Broadway. Kick boxers at a boxing club downtown. She's got more than 600 sounds, all ready to combine or play acapella in various bursts and patterns. No beat or melody joins them; it's about as unmusical as music can get. You probably wouldn't like it. But pack 500 steaming Sight droppers into a gutted building in Hell's Kitchen and let this stuff loose and it unleashes all sorts of synesthetic sensations and gets up under the listeners' prefrontal cortex and tickles their ventral tegmental area until dopamine is delivered like magical elixir.

And then the beat drops. DJ as puppet master, she brings the kids in and out of the trancelike vortex over and over again.

Now it's 1:30 AM and flatland fully controls the crowd with sonic stimulation so overwhelming there have been rumors of actual physical ejaculation in the crowd. flatland does not participate in the recreational stimulant festivities. She needs to be sharp. On. Clean. In control. She bears zero grudge against those that ingest these unapproved chemicals and understands that the trips she Sherpas are made possible for many by the GHB, Sight, MDMA, coke, ketamine, tequila, Red Bull, Adderall, Percocet, Xanax and so on. She is clean and sober by choice in a world full of degenerate drug users and this does not bother her one bit. She does her thing and lets everyone else do theirs. Judge not lest ye be judged.

It's Saturday. Kids peel out of the main room and head for The Box. This is a popular club gimmick these days. A cool one. A perfectly soundproof room that holds 10 to 15 people. You go in and close the door and it seals shut and you hear nothing. The effect is dramatic as you come out of a raging soundstorm into a sonic vacuum. The walls are white and the room is brightly lit. Close your eyes and try to see the nth color.

The Box blows minds.

I sit cross-legged with my eyes closed in the corner of the box, riding another high speed rush. The skin on my face pushes back as I accelerate up to full speed. I'm underwater. Water pushes past and I desperately try to keep my eyes closed so they will not be stung by the salt. Things slow down and I reopen my eyes. The totally white room is completely empty. Just me inside a white cube. Total silence.

"Echo."

There is no echo.

The room is soundproofed, man.

"Oh yeah. Duh."

I pull out my Electric Blu cigarette and vape a few puffs then tilt my head back and lean back against the wall. My hair is sweaty and I can feel the back of my head, wet and cool against the white wall. Blue sine waves squiggle past. Chasing each other. Then purple ones tag behind. They skitter across my field of vision—pastel-colored ghostly tracer vision snakes. 30 or 40 at a time now. Green. Purple again. I hear children laughing on a playground, a hearlucinated echo of a sample flatland dropped over and over a few hours ago. Blue. Yellow. Cyan. Then 200 of these imagined digital squiggle-snakes come in fast from the left and fly off the right edge of my peripheral vision / mindscreen before I can really absorb what I've seen. That was no color I recognize.

The nth color. I just saw it.

Holy shitballs.

I'm 100% sure. It's one of those things where when you haven't seen it you think you might be seeing it but you're not sure but the second you actually see it there is no doubt in your mind. I just saw the nth color! Fucking A.

I look around for someone to share my excitement but there's no one here. I guess I already told you that. Such a tease though, as it came and went so fast I barely knew what I was seeing. I am lucid enough to try to conjure it back. But it's just a plain white cube now. All the snakes are gone. The harder I try to think about the snakes, the more lucid I become and I've lost the state of mind completely now and I am weirdly sober. Thoughts of foreign exchange and currency values and the price of gold briefly pop into my head but they are a tremendous buzzkill right now and so I banish them. I need a drink. Tequila shot and a mini Red Bull to chase it. As I go to leave The Box, Alison walks in. She's sweaty. Hot.

She says nothing. Grabs the top of my pants and pulls me close. Slight head tilt and her mouth comes towards mine. I feel heat from her face and her breath. Smell of candy, maybe strawberry lollipops? She slowly puts her bottom lip against my top lip and kisses. Frisson. I feel the warmth of her lip, a slight stickiness. Her lip is dry, as yet unmoistened by my saliva. Then her tongue goes into my mouth and her pelvis presses against mine and for a second I worry that someone might come in because I'm instantly hard.

I am tripping again but this is all real—her mouth is full of pop rocks and so my tongue feels the release of tiny carbon dioxide bubbles and it sizzles and fizzles and pops. My eyes are closed and we grind a bit more. We disconnect and stand face to face, an inch apart. We stare deep into each other. She smiles and I whisper in her ear:

"You are the most beautiful thing in the world."

She is a hologram. Thin fragile and pale. Like the ghost of Kurt Cobain. Blonde hair a bit sweaty and falling naturally down to her shoulders. Cut abruptly by an underpaid stylist and it looks fucking great. I love her.

"I love you."

"Don't let the drugs talk."

"It's not the drugs. I love you."

"You're rolling. Tell me tomorrow."

"I want to tell you now."

"Tell me tomorrow. I might believe you."

Two kids, probably 17, fall into the box and the moment breaks.

"Let's go," Alison says.

"Home?"

"No."

"Where?" I ask.

"Outside. A walk or something."

"Out into the real world? You sure? Can we get back in?" I am messed up; scared of the real world right now.

"I don't want to come back in," Alison says.

"OK. Just let me say bye to flatland."

"Sure. I will too."

Even in my messed up state I already regret it. What a waste of the first (time she hears me say) "I love you". She is so right; what kind of idiot am I? FUCK. Also noticeable was the fact that she did not say "I love you too" and I don't want this to be a repeat of the situation with my dad.

I'm sure she just didn't feel like the moment was right and would have certainly requited had we been in a more sober state. Anyway, too late, it was a heavy moment and I got caught up in it and she is so beautiful and I do love her so I'll tell her again tomorrow and the day after that and the day after that. And the day after that.

I'm still craving a shot of tequila but given the quantity of chemicals and booze I have ingested tonight it seems unnecessary plus it seems kind of rude at this point as Alison and I are holding hands and she clearly wants to bolt. We sit off to the side, waiting for a break in the show to say goodbye to flatland. Alison draws circles on my back and I see neon tracers in mid-air that mimic the circles on my back. The circles form and disappear in synch with her finger. She reverses direction and the circles form counterclockwise. Trippy.

There is a gap in time and now she is half dragging me out of here so we wave past flatland and she waves back and the last thing I hear before the warehouse door closes is a mix that flatland ran by me last week: a baby crying (pitch shifted down four octaves) with snippet samples of a Gospel Choir and long, autotuned roosters crowing—all layered over and under and over and under. The strands of sound spiral and weave together like a DNA helix.

Outside, the cold air grabs my face with two hands and fills my ears and my nose and lungs with ice. The cold burns my nostrils like wasabi, snorted. Traffic lights starburst as my visual system cannot fully compute. The hot box of the warehouse disappears behind us and we walk slowly towards nowhere.

"Are you tired?" I ask her.

"I'm not sure. I don't think so."

"Let's get a shawarma."

"OK."

It's 5:22 AM. Imminent dawn. Manhattan looks dirtier than usual and 10th Avenue is full of litter. Protest signs and leaflets and flyers swirl, some from recent days, but others have collected along the curbs with paper bags and beer cans and blackening banana peels. The streets around here are starting to look like whoever is in charge of the place gave up. Park Avenue and Tribeca and the residential zones of the 1% still get the cleanup crews at night but even affluent areas like the Upper West Side north of 90th and Gramercy Park are starting to look a bit like NYC c.1983.

"You like the music?" She's making small talk.

"Yes, I loved it."

"Charlie... I love you too... I think."

"You think?"

"Well I'm sure. But I'm scared."

"Scared? Why are you scared?"

"Because I don't want you to hurt me."

"I'm never going to hurt you."

"That's what every guy says. Even the ones that hurt me."

"So, what am I supposed to say to that?"

"Nothing. It's not about words, it's about actions. Just don't hurt me."

I am not sober enough for this conversation. My thoughts scatter. An ambulance flies past us up Broadway, screaming. Then two more. Three police cars and then a fire truck. I am beyond fucked up. Thoughts overlap. We walk aimlessly—

■   ■   ■

1 YEAR AND 37 DAYS BEFORE THE RESET

Two drills bore down, screaming through my temples and into the backs of my eyeballs. Atmospheric pressure crushes my forehead and the fluid reservoir that usually lets my brain float safely inside my head has dried up and now my cerebellum rests deflated and raw, on dry bone. The slightest tilt or movement of the head and my frontal cortex bumps painfully against skull. Dopamine tanks: Empty. Cigarettes smoked by the pack leave black circular burns all over the inside of my lungs and thoughts spin and I wonder how sick you must have to be to be dead but I'm not dead.

My tongue might have died; it is toasted, taste buds broiled and frayed, burnt by incoming wave after wave of smoke leaving a dusty feel and a white layer of gunk that cannot be removed by any amount of toothbrushing. Clipped, distorted memories of last night flicker in my mind like poorly rendered digital ghosts and where did I sleep and what is this shit on my pants (mayo) and where's my phone and ouch, the grinding of the teeth (!) has left my jaw sore with pulsing electric jolts of pain at random intervals and my parched throat tries to scream "Fire!" but cannot. I wince as rays of sunlight hit the back of my eyes like blinding torture. The blast of a car horn outside rips like an explosion through my mind.

Too many drinks. Too many drugs. This is an absolute nightmare.

Sight and Molly and Red Bull and Coke and booze last night and really, it's Alison's fault because around 2AM I was like:

"Let's bail, we gotta get up tomorrow!" and she was like (yelling over the music and dancing all around me like a sprite):

"C'mon! No way! This is fucking amazing!"

And my rubber arm was twisted and so we went back onto the dance floor and flatland *was* amazing and so were the drugs and the trip and there was a point where three different songs we both know and both love all merged into one beautiful, crazy, hypnotic track and as the music throbbed to pre-climax she primal screamed and when the song ended it was like she had come and she kind of went limp and just fell into me and the smell of her neck was like heaven and sweat and lemon Starburst and the world spun around us while we stood still and everything was perfect for just one second which is all anyone can ever ask for out of life. Just one perfect second.

But our proverbial credit cards were maxed last night and now it's time to pay up in the form of what is without any doubt the worst hangover in the history of the developed world. Also: in less than one hour I am scheduled to meet the father of the girl I am in love with.

I "fell asleep" at 6:20 AM but it was more like I slid from one form of lucid semi-conscious dream-state to a different, less lucid state of dreaming and then the alarm just went off at 8:30 AM and now it's 8:38 AM and shit what the hell am I going to do? I cannot go golfing like this; are you serious? With Alison's dad? He's a big swinging dick on Wall Street and I love his daughter. I cannot do this. This is a major problem.

Get your shit together.

I scan the room and look into my bedroom for Alison and she isn't here (???). I hear groaning from the bedroom and I walk in there and she's curled up on the floor in the corner, wrapped up full burrito-style in my comforter. There is an empty bottle of vodka on the ground and I specifically remember it was ½ full when we left the apartment to go see flatland. She summons enough energy to mutter a few words:

"I think I died. Like... Seriously. I am actually dead."

She is to "sounds" as I am to "feel".

"I can't meet your dad like this, Al. What are we going to do?"

"Dude. We can't bail. He's halfway from Connecticut to New York City by now. I haven't seen him since I left home. It's too late to cancel."

"This is not good."

"No. This is bad. This is really fucking bad."

For the last few months Alison's dad has been in touch with her and she had sworn she will never go back there and never talk to him again but it's messed up because she really loves him a lot despite everything that happened all those years. I cannot get my head around it, but it is not the type of thing you argue with someone about.

She has all kinds of crazy cognitive dissonance about her dad. She loves him and she hates him. He is the source of many of her good childhood memories and most of her bad ones. As a kid, she went to Stew Leonard's Supermarket with Dad on Saturday and watched the (creepy yet captivating) animatronic farm animals and Chiquita Banana dancers and he would pick a few grapes and slide them to her underhanded for her to sample like it was their little secret. The night was a parallel universe out of a horror movie.

Alison told me one time, when she was 15, she caught her dad in a spare room, having sex with one of the cleaning ladies. The first emotion she felt was jealousy.

Dissonance.

So finally, last week she agreed to meet up with her dad but wants me to come with as a buffer, and also even though he is a monster he is still her dad and so she wants us to meet. A few weeks ago, we picked today for him to come to the city and take us to breakfast and then the three of us would go back out to Fairfield County and golf together and it would be nice or something. Despite her urban and edgy exterior, Alison still grew up in Westport and spent enough time at country clubs to know her away around a golf course.

We have 45 minutes to get ready so I undress and get in the shower and then Alison is in with me. I notice there is a new text tattoo on her lower back. It reads:

If you die first, can I come with?

I'm still riding the last waves of the Molly and so we fuck that deep, true, I really love you right here, right now type of sex that is only possible under the influence of MDMA. I go down on her and she tastes umami, like warm McDonald's ketchup. The sex clears my mind a bit; I feel slightly better.

I brush my teeth ferociously to rid my mouth of the gunky layer of white fungus on my tongue. One hour later we're dressed pretty nice and sitting at Felix on West Broadway eating Eggs Benedict and drinking Bloody Marys with Mike Leary at a corner table for three. My mental eggs are scrambled but I don't think Mike suspects anything. I have insane tunnel vision and try to minimize interaction without seeming weird, leaving most of the talking to Alison.

She is incredibly composed but maybe a bit too much like a person trying to act normal instead of a person actually acting normal, but then I look around at the rest of the people in the restaurant and realize they all seem like they too are ACTING NORMAL instead of actually normal and this is a weird loop and I cannot figure out what all this means and then—

"How's the videogame, slash, day trading world treating you these days, Charlie?"

There is clear condescension in his voice but I don't linger on it.

"No complaints, sir. Pays the rent and I'm learning a lot so really cannot complain. No complaints."

Mike laughs way too loud at the idiot he is speaking to. It is a pre-recorded laugh, staccato and fake.

"So, no complaints then? Good stuff."

The day is a series of jump cuts. Felix to a black car to a short, sweet nap and then we're on a golf course in Connecticut. By the 7th hole, Mike clearly has a buzz on (via the cart girl who seems to have prior experience serving him and knows his drink of choice is Dewar's on the rocks) and this makes me feel way less self-conscious with regard to my still completely pickled mind. Alison is a decent golfer. She grew up doing the country club thing but her mind and body are out of synch today and she just hit one in the rough then two in the water. But whatever, she birdied 11. Overall, I am impressed.

I'm shooting pretty good for someone who cannot really tell whether or not his feet are touching the ground most of the time. I shoot 95, Mike shoots 83. The last 6 or 7 holes are absolute torture as my body no longer wants to participate in this charade and my mind is off working on side projects, but we manage to skate through without any major incident and by 10:00 PM Alison and I are both fast asleep in the back of a Lyft on the way back to Manhattan. We did it! We did not die. Duty fulfilled.

Alison threw up three times today—once at home, once into a sand trap on 14 and once back at The Club. We cannot continue at this pace. We cannot keep getting wrecked like this. I don't want to do this anymore. Dark thoughts invade: I want to kill Mike. I want to actually murder him. Shoot him in the face with a gun. I hate him so much. He has wrecked this beautiful girl. He deserves to die.

As we get out of the Lyft, Alison has a terrible idea:

"Let's go out. Let's find some Molly or something and keep going."

In the apartment, I dig around in a drawer and find a 2-gram bag of coke and some Sight. I drop them onto the counter with a bit of drunken flair.

"How about this?"

We go out and it's fun, I guess. We get to bed around 6:45 AM.

■　■　■

I dream distorted dreams of zigzags and apparitions. I float in the netherworld between asleep and awake. Spliced electronic sound-scapes reverberate in my semi-consciousness. I hear pops and beats. I hear snaps and a distant child's voice. I hear knocks. I hear more knocks. The knocks finally penetrate deep enough into my dream-state and I realize they are real. What the—

Who is knocking on my door?

I climb out of bed and move to respond to two more heavy knocks. KNOCK KNOCK…

I open the apartment door. In front of me stands a fattish lady with skin that is too white and too translucent. She is stuffed into a baked bean brown pantsuit with gold buttons. Her feet pour out of the tops of her shoes. *She needs to be Photoshopped.* She holds a manila file folder with maybe 20 pages of documents inside. She stares at me and without subtlety looks past me, checking out the interior of my apartment.

"Charlie Bloom? Are you Charlie Bloom?" Her voice is like that of a cartoon bird.

"Yes, I am."

"May I come in?" she asks.

"What is this about?"

"Let me come in and explain."

"Umm. OK."

She walks in, scans my place. Evaluates. Judges. She sits down and I bring her some water. I quickly remove two overflowing ashtrays and I'm thankful I didn't leave any party favors lying around. The place is messy but could be worse.

The woman pulls a glossy 8X10" photograph from the folder and plops it on my coffee table. The picture is a kid, maybe 8 or so. Pale face, messy blonde hair. Some freckles. It looks like he is standing outside a rent-controlled brick apartment building. His Kermit green winter coat is too small and worn out, like, from Goodwill.

"This is your son, Seven."

"Umm. What do you mean?"

"This is your son, Seven."

I don't want to be rude.

"I'm sorry. What are you talking about? Can you explain, please?"

My brain bricks. I have no frame of reference here. I am frozen and trembling; a hare in the headlights. I search for an explanation and come up empty. My brain is especially ill-equipped to handle the situation given its current exhausted and marinated state. And while part of me wants to call bullshit, the kid looks exactly like me. Exactly. Fucking. Like me.

The explanation for the arrival of this child is as follows: nine years ago, I met this girl from Strong Island at a party. She was 16. Friend of a friend of a friend. Lots of tattoos. (Apparently, I like the edgy ones.) Things got sexy in a huge walk-in closet off the master bedroom. An ovular membrane was breached. We texted a few times after but then I never saw her again. She never contacted me. I forgot about her.

Two years after this boy named Seven was born, the girl was sentenced to 10 years in prison under the RICO act for her role in making cash payments to a low-budget hit man who liquidated two enemies of the mail-order Fentalyn trafficking organization she co-founded with her brother Bill. Her parents then took custody of the boy. Three days ago, Grandma and Grandpa died in a fiery auto crash on I95. The next link in the chain of custody is me.

I cannot compute. The conversation continues but I have wicked tunnel vision and cannot concentrate or process what the woman is saying. Forms come out. I desperately need some adult supervision here.

"We will need to conduct a paternity test, but the birth documents include your name as father."

"OK."

"And if you are the father, are you able and willing to take custody of the child?"

"I don't know. Can I think about it?" Wrong answer, probably? Shit.

"Yes. This is an important decision. If you cannot or will not take custody, a foster home can be found but you may still be liable for support payments."

I'm not sending my own kid to a foster home. Support payments? This is absurd. This is not real. But it is real. I am not going to ditch my own kid.

Where am I? What the hell is going on?

"You know what? No. I don't need to think about it. I am absolutely able and willing to take custody. If this is my son, I will take care of him."

I just blurted it out. No analysis. No thoughts of ramifications or implications. A sense of duty just kind of came over me like a wave and there was no decision to make. I mean, it's my kid. He needs to be taken care of. There is nobody else. I guess that just leaves me. Things wrap up, some appointments are made, follow ups scheduled. Bird voice lady leaves.

Alison, who has been silently comatose in the bedroom all day, emerges for the first time around 2:30 PM. She pops her head out and asks:

"Hey. What's going on?" she asks.

"Oh, not much…"

PART TWO

QUIET DESPERATION OF TODD

INSIDE HIS RUMPLED OLD WALLET, Todd carries a tattered piece of hotel note paper folded precisely in four. He recovered the paper from Jessica's "Box of Special Things". That box which brought the most painful moments of the cleaning of the closets after she died. The box he could not bear to look at (or destroy) for so many years.

What was inside? Notes from the girls: "Thak U Momy for tacing ker of us", "I luve you dady! u ar osom". Every word, a knife jammed between his ribs. There was a clipping of hair, unrealistically blonde, from Charlie's first haircut. Some letters Todd sent to Jessica in those tricky long distance years, when she was doing her Master's at Stanford.

When he finally chose to dispose of the box, he first pulled the note out, folded it with meticulous care and placed it in his wallet. He never unfolded it again but he knew it was in there. Each time he saw it he felt various pangs. Guilt, loneliness, grief, anger. He could not bear to throw it away.

They were out on a date in Manhattan. Both 28 years old. Two years into the relationship. They finish an early dinner (he liked eating early; she didn't mind either way) and walked in happy silence past Penn Station. Jessica blurted:

"Let's go somewhere!" She, her usual spontaneous self.

"What do you mean?" He, conservative. Not boring, just conservative.

"Let's get on a train and go somewhere!" Her voice was sweet, smooth and intoxicating, like Chateau d'Yquem. It took away his inhibitions and so he agreed.

"Being with you is the best," she said to him and he thought *being with you is better*. They were high on each other. Floating in the love bubble, completely oblivious to external reality.

"I love you so much."

"I love you more."

"No, I love YOU more!"

etc.

They hopped the Amtrak Acela, First Class (he had plenty of cash by this point) and headed for Philadelphia. It was Saturday and their stated plan was to return Sunday but suddenly it was Monday and he called in sick to work and loved the feeling of playing hooky with his beautiful high-energy sprite.

He still could not really understand what she saw in him. He asked her directly a few times and she sounded convincing as she told him he was a likeable guy and not everyone needs to be loud and life of the party to be a good companion and she was yin and he was yang and that sort of thing.

"Can you imagine me with someone else like me? Total chaos! Opposites attract for a reason. You're salt; I'm vinegar. You're mac, I'm cheese. Think about it: cheese and *cheese*? Blech! Not good."

Todd laughed and said: "Good point. But if we're going to be a duo, how about something more romantic like... ummm... Romeo and Juliet. Ummm [remembers how the play ends]... Without the dying."

Jessica laughed. They loved each other. Like crazy.

They spent a lot of time in the hotel and wandered the city (Pat's and the Liberty Bell and the Rocky Steps and all that) and stayed again Monday night. Tuesday morning, Todd did one of the first really spontaneous things of his life: he woke up super early, called in sick to work (again) and snuck out of the hotel room while Jessica slept. She stirred as the door clicked shut, but did not wake.

Todd went downstairs and outside into the cold Philly morning. He went across the street to a bodega type of store and bought a single tulip, a plastic bottle of water and a glass bottle of Coke. He went outside, took one sip of the Coke and poured the rest into a sewer. He chugged half the water and poured a tiny bit into the Coke bottle. He swirled the water to clean out the Coke. He dumped the Coke / water solution into the sewer. Finally, he poured the remaining Poland Spring water into the clean Coke bottle and used the bottle as a vase to hold the single tulip.

Then, Todd went back into the hotel lobby, got a piece of hotel note paper and a pen from the front desk and sat down in a huge leather lobby chair. He leaned forward over the thick mid-century modern glass table and wrote:

MAY 17

Dearest Jessica:

First of all, good morning. I hope you had a great sleep. While I should probably say all this stuff to you face-to-face, we both know how that would go. A lot of nervous fumbling and stammers and all that and the message would get scrambled and you would giggle and probably poke me and I would get distracted and not tell you everything I want to say the right way. So here goes:

We have only been together a short time, but for me everything that came before you is a blur. My life with you now is my only reality. You are more than everything I dreamed I might find in a woman.

So… I want to ask you a question. I spent a long time thinking about this but the time was not right before; now it is. I want to spend every minute of the rest of my life with you. I want to have kids and buy a house and grow old with you. I want to fight and make up and cry and be madly happy and sometimes sad with you. Now and forever. So…

Will you marry me?

Todd

p.s., I'm in the stairwell.

Todd walked upstairs, placed the bottle and flower and note on the floor in front of their hotel room door, knocked three times and then bolted down the hall. He hid in the stairway for an eternity. The closing door and his thumping heart echoed through the freshly painted gray stairwell. The fire extinguisher was incredibly red. Tangy smell of fresh paint.

Finally, there was the noise of a woman skipping down the hall and the stairwell door flew open and tears flowed and she borrowed every particle of joyful energy in the universe for just one second to hug him and they both nearly exploded with joy. She stepped back away from Todd, a smile and tears on her face and hair still messy from bedhead and she handed him back the note and in huge happy capital letters she had written:

YES!

■　■　■

GLUTTONY

Gluttony was a standard part of trading floor life as might be expected from a large sedentary group of mostly white males with unlimited cash and paid assistants for fetching. This expensive caloric ostentatiousness followed an exponentially upward-sloping curve by day of the week. After a crazy weekend, someone might even order a salad on Monday. A salad with meat. But a salad at least.

Then how about a gooey rigatoni Bolognese covered in melted parm, served piping hot in a foil takeaway container on Tuesday? Wednesday, the desk might dig into chicken burritos of a diameter to challenge the largest male mouth (+ chips + extra guac) and then Thursday a full steak sando with extra sauce and onion rings. Friday, how about pizza? Shake Shack? Bibimbap?

Mornings, a full brekky or two featuring bacon, egg and cheese + side bacon + Nova Scotia smoked salmon + freshly squozen OJ + giant fruit smoothies at ten bucks a pop. Shopping bags overflowing with bagels brought in at least once per week by management. Plain, blueberry, onion, cinnamon raisin, everything bagels. Multiple 1L tubs of cream cheese. Nobu platters of tuna and salmon sushi, rare grilled Toro with yuzu miso and black cod and yellowtail sashimi with jalapeño.

"Who's celebrating?"

"Who fucking cares? Dig in before it runs out."

"Agreedination."

Half of the food is paid for by unknown benefactors. Management. Brokers. Someone who lost a bet. Someone recently promoted to MD. Someone who won a bet. A trader celebrating a P&L streak. A vendor.

Random scene Todd witnessed around 9:50 AM one day:

Trader 1: "Dude, what do you wanna get for lunch?"

A piece of egg falls out of Trader 1's mouth and he flicks it. It sticks to his monitor, just below a 10-minute tick chart of NASDAQ futures. He flicks it again and it arcs up and into the nothingness behind the screens. A moth flutters out from under the computers.

"Are you literally asking me about lunch with your mouth still full of breakfast?"

"Yes, guy. Fucking starving. I was complete and utter lampshades last night. Saint Venus and Dolls double play. Wiped."

"OK. Furry muff. Steak sandos?"

"Done."

"Wait. Isn't Todd buying us Chinese today?"

"Dude. I literally forgot. Chinese. Donezo!"

TO: *ALL SALES AND TRADING
TIME: 9:52AM
FROM: JANET ELLIOTT ON BEHALF OF TODD BLOOM
RE: LUNCH

To celebrate my recent promotion to MD, I would like to buy lunch for everyone in sales and trading today. Mr. Chow will arrive at noon sharp.

Best,
Todd

Massive tin trays of beef and broccoli and General Tsao's Chicken and fried rice and so on are laid out in the open spaces at the end of the rows (near the color printers). Those who receive the email first (RE: Chinese food is here!) rush to get the fresh food before the hordes invade. Only sales and trading receive the email but soon randos from middle office and then back office hover nearby, like vultures waiting for lions to chew off all the good parts of a just-killed antelope. Like gulls circling above Wrigley in the top of the

9th. Smart ass traders shout seagull noises or play .wav files of seagull squawks on their computer speakers.

The food is consumed in hierarchical order. MDs converge, then directors and VPs. Associates and analysts follow. The shoeshine guy or someone from another floor might be spotted 40 minutes later, scooping scattered protein bits from large pools of orange or brown sauce in mid-congeal. Finally, by 1:30 PM or so it's just a wasteland of dirty, empty containers, disgusting remnants, scattered rice particulate, sticky gloopsauce and 30%-full soy packets slowly oozing brown-black rivers of salty aftermath. Bloated traders burp and fart at their desks for a while then hurry to the bathroom to vacate the blowback before the stalls fill up with slower metabolizers.

It took Todd a while to figure it out but eventually he knew the schedule. The stalls were always full at 8:45 AM (traders have by this time felt the laxative impact of their morning coffee and had enough time to react to the US economic data which comes out at 8:30 AM) and 1:30 PM (post-lunch). Early morning was safest. If he was desperate and it was 8:45, he hit the gleaming management bathrooms upstairs.

Meals not free were paid for with debits on an .xls maintained by the desk analyst. The kid carefully collected everyone's requests and then transmitted the full order via internet or phone and then paid with his own credit card (accumulating large loyalty points, btw). He collected balances owing each Friday afternoon. Traders questioned his math skills and his honesty. Throughout the week they questioned his ability to do the most basic tasks.

Analyst returns with food. Traders begin to ravenously unwrap subs and rip open bags of chips.

"I didn't order mustard on my sub! What are you, a fucking retard?"

"Well. Umm. Let me check. Nope. Right here on the receipt see. I said 'No Mustard' but—"

"Fuck. Just go get me another sub with no mustard on it. Fucking disgusting." Shakes head. "Mustard. Fuck. Idiot."

Finished lunch now? Taken a nice afternoon shit? Ready for more food? The afternoon was all random desserts brought daily by visiting vendors. Ice cream on a stick. Apple, cherry and chocolate pie on a stick (!). Donuts, Cronuts(TM) and Magnolia Cupcakes. Deep fried Oreos. Green Tea Kit Kats brought back by Japanese salesman and Bamba snacks brought back by that weird Israeli guy on the derivatives desk. And the eating went on and on. All washed down with full fat lattes and Diet Cokes and Root Beer and Cream Soda and Monster Beverages and such.

Yogurt, lettuce and apples are foreign. Exotic like starfruit.

After work: client and broker dinners. Duck spaghetti and caramelized bananes and Hudson Valley foie gras and sashimi of geoduck and shaved white truffle risotto and so on. Minimum one Michelin star, prix fixe, omakase, Yakatori. Eat and eat and eat. More, more, more, more, more, more, MOAR.

Todd opted out of the lunch routine at some point and got himself a salad most days and while it was tough at first, he soon transitioned to a point where the wafting odors of fried greasiness and blackened animal carcass and boiled vegetables no longer made him hungry but instead made him nauseous. In fact, everything made him nauseous in those days as if something was wrong in his inner ear or something. Out of balance. Forget riding roller coasters, even reading on the subway or looking quickly to one side. Probably somehow related to the ocular migraines. Or riding the market roller coaster. Or c.

■ ■ ■

EARLY 2008 – WESTPORT, CONNECTICUT

Todd slept a grand total of 120 minutes last night. Tokyo called him three separate times. Twice for call levels in US 10s and once about some $20,000 booking error. He had that edgy, sleep deprived feeling that hums in the background and scratches like a tiny, sharp-clawed rodent trapped inside your brain. *Today is going to be a crappy day.*

He walked into the bathroom and smiled a huge fake smile. An attempt to improve his mood as suggested by various self-help books. The causation between happiness and smiling can be reversed as the act of smiling releases endorphins and elevates one's mood. If you are smiling, you must be happy, right? Todd felt the distinct loneliness of a single father whose son was losing interest in hanging out. Charlie had his own friends now and Todd had never felt less useful.

Todd swung out the 8-inch, 2-sided, wall mounted swivel mirror with 7x magnification and checked the dark lines under his eyes. No better, no worse. *I need sleep. I need effing sleep.* He eyed the growing percentage of white and gray hairs infiltrating his goatee. His Blackberry buzzed. London calling. The two words "London Calling" flipped a memory switch.

■ ■ ■

WINTER, 18 YEARS EARLIER — ANN ARBOR, MICHIGAN

It is 1:20 AM on a random Wednesday. There has been another false fire alarm in the student dormitory and everyone has been forced outside into the freezing cold. Todd is a freshman and so he hangs with a few other freshmen.

"Stone Temple Pilots are so fucking derivative man. The guy sounds exactly like Eddie Vedder."

"You're totally wrong. STP came out before Pearl Jam. Scott Weiland is the shit."

"Alice in Chains is the shit."

General nods of agreement.

A somewhat overweight but potentially cute Junior walks by, notices Todd and stops. Todd knows her, but barely. They were both in the student lounge a few weeks ago and the TV was busted so they played some ping pong together. She won 21-19 / 17-21 / 22-20. Todd is a decent player so this, he thought, was an interesting result. *The pudgy but cute junior is good at table tennis.* She plays that loopy type of spin game that's hard to counter if you haven't run into it before. And she seems smart and kind of fun to be around. Hmm.

"Todd. You have no jacket? You must be freezing."

He is freezing underneath his plaid button down. Visibly shivering.

"Nah, I'm not cold!"

He is kind of surprised and happy that she knows his name.

"You sure?" she continues. "Come and sit in my car. We can stay warm."

There seems to be subtext to the comment and the other boys ooh and ahh like high school. Todd heads with the girl. Her car is a silver 1988 Toyota Tercel, leprous with rust. She creaks the driver's side door open and gets in as he sits down on the freezing cold plastic passenger seat.

"My ass is frozen!" he blurts. He gets dorky when he's nervous.

She laughs and turns the key. The car spends ten or twelve seconds audibly deciding whether or not to start before the engine turns over and coughs to life.

"It'll warm up. This thing is a total shitbox but the heat works."

She pulls out a joint the size of a small carrot and fires it up without comment. Todd is kind of nerdy but not bothered or anything and willing to submit to pretty much whatever peer pressure is dealt out even though he doesn't love the paranoia from smoking weed. She pushes "London Calling" by The Clash into the front-loading cassette player and soon they are floating in a heavenly hotbox.

Warm and high and surrounded by this amazing music they talk / sit in silence / talk for an unknown amount of time. They rewind "Train in Vain" to listen to it on repeat maybe four or five times and then it's total silence for ages. The other students have long since gone back into the dorm but the kind of overweight girl and Todd are feeling dreamy. Even though the heat is pumping, the windows are fogged over completely and the effect (THC-enhanced) is cool. Delta-9-tetrahydrocannabinol activates reward centers.

Todd thinks he hears his friends' voices outside the car. *Are they laughing at me?* He rubs a circle in the window frost and peeks outside. Nobody around. Total darkness. Everyone's gone.

The plump girls asks: "Whatcha doin'?"

Todd looks over at her and smiles and he smiles back. A dumb, glazed smile. They share a moment. She leans, puts her right hand on the back of Todd's head and pulls him closer and Todd thinks many simultaneous thoughts:

She's really nice.

She'd be cute if she lost a bit of weight.

I am such an asshole for thinking that.

She is two years older than me: Bonus points! But—

Body by Doritos.

And then concludes:

If I make out with a fat chick, I'll never hear the end of it.

Todd regretted these thoughts quite a few times in the years that followed. But at the time he just pulled his head away and said:

"No thanks."

An awkward and unfriendly choice of words and he did not mean to be a dick but sure came across as one. As with most college boys, he sorted women by body fat, facial symmetry and fun factor. Not intelligence, maturity or kindness. Like Jessica always said back in the college days: boys are assholes / Chicks are crazy.

■ ■ ■

I was such a dick back then. Todd looked at the clock. It was 5:33 AM and his mind had been wandering too long. He was running way late.

Hurry up man. Hurry up. Check the voicemail from London later.

There is nothing more annoying than missing the 6:14 Express and then having to take the God-forsaken 6:22 Local. 71 minutes instead of 53. Brutal. His mind flicked one last time to that girl and how nice she was and how he would love to apologize to her and see if she ever lost the weight—scratch that—see if she's happy and doing well or what. He thought briefly about how shallow he was in those days. Good looking and fun were the only two criteria. Life was so simple and stupid back then. So easy.

5:39 now. Gah!

OCTOBER 1994 – MANHATTAN

LUST

Todd was into bubbles before bubbles were cool. He majored in Finance with a specialization in the History of Capital Markets and a special focus on speculative manias and panics. He knew the history of speculation better than most academics in the field. He was endlessly fascinated by how humans made the same mistakes, again and again. And again. The Dutch Tulip Bubble was the cliché example, but there were hundreds of speculative bubbles over many centuries and they always look pretty much the same.

A revolutionary idea appears and some smart and open-minded people identify it and buy in. The price of assets linked to the narrative rally a bit then rally some more. Wealthy investors with experience identify an opportunity and get involved. Then, the fascination moves from the story / technology / idea itself to the move in the price of the asset. Like the British railway bubble in the 1840s:

"You see how much those railroad stocks have gone up, Thomas? My brother in Sheffield has made a pretty penny!"

"Don't sell me a dog, here, William."

"Not a word of a lie."

"Then so it shall be. Let me call my broker forthwith!"

Or the sports card bubble in the late 1980s:

"Dude, you see that Griffey Junior rookie doubled again?"

"Really? I was going to buy one but it had already gone up too much."

"Yeah I got the new Beckett. It, like, doubled again."

"Crap. I'm going downtown right now. I'm gonna buy two. Then I'll sell the other one after it doubles again and the first one will be free."

"Sweet."

In a reversal of how supply and demand normally interact with price, the higher price attracts more buyers and the new buyers drive the price even higher, attracting more buyers.

Then the media gets hold of it and things ramp up some more.

Then the general public starts to panic. FOMO. People who have never invested hear tales of instant riches and cannot resist the lure. Wave 5. Euphoria. Prices extend higher at unimaginable speed. The story dominates the public imagination. Greed completely eclipses fear and measures of valuation become meaningless. A Dutch tulip sold for the price of 12 acres of land at the peak of Tulipmania in the 1630s. Pets.com went from $10 to $90. Long Island Ice Tea gained 500% in one day in 2017 when it changed its name to Long Blockchain.

Then, once there are no buyers left to buy... The first wobble. A scary sell-off. But then there is always one last sucker rally and then fear, capitulation, crash and despair. Hearts and bank accounts are broken. Fortunes and lives are lost.

Todd loved to regale Jessica about bubbles and she was a patient listener. This night, they shared a $24 bottle of Australian Shiraz and watched *Melrose Place*. Typical Thursday. During the ads, Todd rambled on in his lovable way and Jessica accepted this and enjoyed a warm buzz from the wine. She put in some microwave popcorn as Todd talked.

"You know, true love is a bull market, and lust is a bubble. They both start out the same. You hit on a new idea, you invest in it, carefully at first, with great fear of loss, of getting hurt. Then you start to let your guard down more and more. You suspend your disbelief. *This can't be true! But it IS true! No way! Way!*

Eventually you go all in. You feel euphoric. It's a new paradigm; nobody, anywhere has ever felt like this before. Your heart goes boom boom. Momentum builds feverishly and feedback loops kick in. The more you love her the more she loves you back. Total mania. You pour all your time and all your money into this fantastic, shiny new asset. You ignore warnings from friends. They know you've been hurt in past love bubbles. 'This time is different!' you scream from the rooftops. 'There has never been anything like this before!'

You take excessive risks and extrapolate your current situation into the future. *We're going to get married! We're going to have five kids!* You are temporarily insane. This period of euphoria usually lasts 12 to 24 months.

And then reality hits. You realize that yes, this woman farts and yes it smells bad when she does. And she makes this really annoying sound with her ankle. Crick. Crack. And her breath in the morning. *God.* And so on. *Why does she have to stay at my apartment six nights a week? I mean, I still like her a lot and all that but maybe I should have paid more attention to the warnings.* You think maybe you should hit a bid but you've invested so much. You need to stick with it and so you buy the dip. If it is real love, things rally. These sorts of bull markets can last for years. Forever, pretty much. There are the inevitable pullbacks along the way but you always make new highs. That's true love, the bull market scenario.

But maybe she gets a little psycho. You catch her reading your e-mail one time. She gets mad at you for wearing your shoes in your own apartment. NEW TEXT MESSAGE: *Why you never text me nomo?* 20 minutes later: *Are you ghosting me?* (sad face emoji). Then she demands to know your bank password, ya know, just in case. This is the beginning of the fear stage. Things reprice rapidly. *Thank god I didn't buy her that $1,200 necklace.* You want out but everything's happening so fast now it's like you are falling. Spinning downward. 'Let me out!' you scream. But nobody hears.

The relationship is a total bust. You panic and stop calling her back. You send her a terse e-mail and drop her stuff with her doorman one day when you know she's not home. Then total despair. You have no idea what happened. You cut your losses and move on."

Jessica smirks at the supreme nerdiness of all this.

"But we're a bull market, not a bubble, right?"

"Bull market, all the way."

"Booyah!"

They clink glasses. Jessica flashes a deliberately cheesy grin. The ads are over; *Melrose* comes back on. Todd thinks that life would not be worth living without Jessica.

"Life would not be worth living without you, Jess."

"Thanks babe. Let's watch the show."

■ ■ ■

@realdemocracy tweeted
"all money is a matter of belief."
adam smith

■ ■ ■

NOVEMBER 2007 – MANHATTAN

When markets start to move quickly, the energy on a trading floor picks up. The faster the market, the greater the electricity. Energy builds and builds to an electric fever as stocks fall but then—abruptly—there is a point where the fall turns from exciting to scary. At this point the energy is sucked out of the room like the conversational buzz at a party after someone says "cunt" just a little bit too loud. There is a pall as traders think more about keeping cool. They mentally calculate losses on their personal holdings.

If it's the first drop in a while, it's no big deal. But when it's another fall in a long bear market, the vibe turns dour pretty quick. When financial stocks are at the epicenter of the crash, traders start to wonder first about their bonus, then their jobs, then their industry and at the worst point, the very logic or validity of democratic capitalism. Two percent drops are fun to trade but falls of more than five percent lead not to fun but to visceral fear and liquid shits. The smell of dread wafts over crumb-filled keyboards and the 4:00 PM closing bell cannot come soon enough. This was one of those days. The Fed had cut rates and stocks were lower. Again.

Don't fight the Fed, my ass.

Harry Osler, the head of trading, did not have the EQ or common sense market awareness to feel the tension on the floor as he strutted out of his ivory tower office. He walked up to Todd and sucker punched him on the shoulder, way too hard.

"Having fun?" Osler asked.

Todd grokked more and more over the years that smart people do stupid things and the link between Ivy League education and functional, real world intelligence was surprisingly weak.

The behavior of his boss, Harry Osler, confirmed to Todd that even a math PhD from MIT could have the decision-making skills of a pregnant 17-year-old. That the same mind could be genius and idiot all at once. Meanwhile, Osler had latent insecurity issues and was unconsciously using his current position of power in senior management to act out revenge fantasies as retribution for humiliation like middle school swirlies and wedgies.

Osler left Todd alone most of the time but loved to bully Todd's direct reports. The Boss Man, as he called himself, would walk the trading floor and "joke" about firing traders, point out when a trader had put on weight ("Hey fatty, nice trading this week") or combine a threat and an insult into one like when he muttered to a trader of Indian descent "Don't think I won't fire you just because you're from Calcutta!"

"I'm from Long Island. I was born and raised there."

"Well don't think I can't fire you just because you're brown, then!"

Uncomfortable laughter. The recipients of these threats took them as 85% joke and 15% serious but when things were going badly (as they were in 2007) the comedy was not evident or appropriate. Traders were being replaced like typos at the time so the ribbing was not well received. When Osler left the row and returned to the comfort of his ivory tower, Todd was left to deal with a row full of pissed off, disrespected traders. Todd reported to Osler and so he was meant to be the buffer / voice of reason.

Osler's series of bang-bang promotions in recent years was textbook Peter Principle. Analogous to promoting Jose Canseco from right field to coach to general manager of the Oakland A's on the back of his steroid-fueled 37 and 44 home run seasons in 1990/91. But in 2007, Wall Street was shockingly bad at understanding how the money got made. It didn't matter how you made it, as long as you didn't get arrested. And nobody ever got arrested in those days.

Osler advanced through the ranks mostly on the back of a few well-timed one-off trades. He had a suspicious, uncanny ability to get ahead of huge client flows. The other traders derisively called him: Shoe Phone. His book would be flat, running zero risk for weeks on end and then suddenly Osler would have a huge position out of nowhere. Nobody on the desk would know why. Then, within a few days, some epic flow would appear (in the same direction as Osler's position, of course) and then Osler would square his position, taking the other side at the tail end of the customer flow. Instead of dicking around in $150,000 DV01 of risk, in and out, in and out, all year he would just strap on a $2,500,000 DV01 position once or twice a year and pump out $30 to $50 million bucks of P&L in a few days. Then he'd humblebrag a bit:

"Musta got lucky on that one. Good thing I had huge size!" and then go back to insulting other traders, talking fantasy football or name dropping after conference calls with Roubini or Soros or JC Trichet or Dr. Doom or whoever.

His Bloomberg header was: it's not gambling if you know you're going to win.

Osler would make vapid suggestions like "take smart risk" and "if you just eliminated your ten worst days, you would have made a lot more money last year!" Umm, yes. Because... Math. He was the kind of guy that would see the VIX go from 10 to 14 and scream:

"VIX is up 40%!"

A rebuttal sentence would form in Todd's mind but he could not muster the energy required to say it:

"Umm. No. VIX is already a percentage. It's up 4%. You are a numbnut."

Osler once announced to everyone on the desk that he had just posted a fake senior trading job with a headhunter so that he could get every trader from every major competitor in for an interview. He explained:

"You gotta keep in touch with what's going on in the industry. These people are so desperate for a Gary they'll tell you anything. Client names, revenue numbers, trading strategies. It's part of my job to mindrape these idiots!"

The clients Osler ran in front of and pillaged could not prove wrongdoing but they were sophisticated and so once bitten, they became twice shy and refused to trade with Organ Manley again.

Osler's short-term greedy trading style killed off the firm's golden geese one by one. These sweet, fat, golden geese had taken years to bring in and were groomed and entertained religiously by huge teams of salespeople.

Then Osler slaughtered them, one by one.

Meanwhile Osler's sub-zero EQ pushed out the best traders one by one, too. So, while he slowly and simultaneously destroyed the business from the inside out and the outside in, Osler played master politician and also dropped a big P&L number beside his name most years. He took in three to five million dollars of total comp, year after year. A walking Harvard Business School case study in bad management.

Ironically, while his entire career was built on the abuse of customer flow, the misuse of proprietary client information and the dropping of client names to produce the impression of in-group status in the world of high finance, Osler generally had no patience at all for the actual clients.

"Tell those fucking whiners to shut up or find another bank to trade with," was a standard response when he was politely approached by a senior salesman with a customer-related issue.

"This client is a huge pimple on my ass. You deal with him."

God forbid the client was female.

"Tell her I'll see her next Tuesday."

Same went for employees, natch. When Todd went to Osler saying a senior trader felt he was underpaid relative to his market value, Osler's reply was like:

"Tell him to go work at another fucking bank, then."

And one after the other, that's exactly what most of them did. They liked working at Organ Manly and found Todd a reasonable person and good leader but they eventually found the push of Osler's douchebag ego and the pull of a 30% pay bump from the competition irresistible. It was nearly impossible for Todd to run a business under Osler. He longed for the days when he was just a trader.

Wall Street senior management was filled with many of the particular sort of blinkered, self-centered shitface sociopath typified by Osler. Most decent folk in finance, like our man Todd, face someone like Osler at some point. The probability of encountering a highly intelligent lunatic as a manager rises exponentially with each rung risen on the Wall Street ladder. The better you are at gaming a system, stepping over others and remaining single-minded and self-centered, the more likely your business card will eventually read "Senior Managing Director".

Todd dealt each day with his various personal hells, the continual market turmoil of the period leading up to the Global Financial Crisis, the massive crater in his P&L and all shit Osler. And he had to try to be a better father for Charlie.

I don't think I can do this.

Todd pulled his Blackberry out of the top drawer, got up from his desk and found an empty stall in the gleaming management bathroom upstairs. He sat there and played Brickbreaker for so long his legs fell asleep. Level 11. 5640. New record high score. Hard to stand up. Pins and needles in his legs and feet.

■ ■ ■

34 YEARS BEFORE THE RESET

At the age of nine, Todd was allowed to walk home and this was a great convenience for his single mother Catherine who usually didn't get home until at least six or six-thirty each night. This allowed Todd, the prototypical latchkey kid, to make his way home, watch *Inspector Gadget*, do his homework, play outside for a bit and still have the table set and dinner on the table by the time Mom got home. He got plenty of help with dinner from the likes of Chef Boyardee, Hamburger Helper, and Sloppy Joe.

The route home was the same every day: out the side door of the school, across the basketball courts, over the baseball diamond, cross Meyer Street at the crosswalk, walk down the hill, down Ledgemont, left on Northview, past the Dead End sign, into Northview Suites, the townhouse development where they lived, past the two-story outdoor garages and up to Apartment 2J.

To pass the time on the walk, he'd kick a tennis ball all the way home (which was tricky on the downhill part of Ledgemont) or hold his portable radio with the accordion buttons (blasting Hits FM or an Iron Maiden cassette) or jump and hop in an attempt to avoid all lines and cracks in the sidewalk. In winter he'd kick a gradually shrinking chunk of white and gray snow-ice. He wore Kangaroos on his feet and kept his house key in the small zippered pocket on the side of his right shoe.

Honestly, he was never a huge Iron Maiden fan but he liked how whenever he played heavy metal on his ghetto blaster, adults gave him a bit more respect—they appeared to take a slightly wider berth as they passed him on the sidewalk. He imagined they looked at him as if he might pose some sort of risk. He liked the feeling of being treated as potentially volatile or dangerous. His favorite letter was X. He grew his hair down to shoulder length and wore black concert shirts with Motley Crue or Quiet Riot or Twisted Sister printed in red on white three-quarter-length sleeves.

This carefully crafted danger boy image had no effect on the two 14-year-old boys who often turned up on his route home from school. They knew he walked the same steps every day and so he frequently found them sitting on their BMX bikes in plain view as he shuffled home. They showed up maybe once every two weeks. One had a bitchin' rat tail and the other always wore the exact same blue and white JIMMY'Z pants. They hustled him for baseball cards or lunch leftovers or spare change, occasionally pushing him into the ditch or spitting in his face to send a message of like, "Don't fuck with us."

He wasn't especially afraid of them but he also knew two against one they could easily kick his ass if he fought back so he simply went limp emotionally and physically whenever he ran into them. He also realized over time that his refusal to fight back majorly annoyed them as the main entertainment value of bullying is the fun of it and what fun is it giving a kid a face wash when he just goes limp like a fag and never fights back?

There wasn't much Todd could do about the two bullies since there was only one path from school to home and Todd definitely wasn't a tattletale so no chance he'd rat. He used the limp strategy as his go to and was careful to hide any valuable baseball cards, money or other items of value in his sock or shoe pocket or deep enough in his backpack that they would not be easily discovered.

It looked like rain as he walked home after one particularly bad school day. He replayed a memory over and over. Lunchtime: he bet his entire Pringles can full of marbles against another kid in a game of Black Snake (marbles) and beat the kid fair and square. Then the kid refuses to give up the Super Giant Root Beer Beauty Bonk marble on the other side of the bet. Todd was so frustrated by this blatant welch that he decided to go to Mrs. Bess, the only great teacher he ever had, and tell her what happened. He was sure that Mrs. Bess would take care of it in an expeditious but confidential way. Instead she condescended to him about "gambling" on school property. No way should he be gambling and no way would he get that sweet Root Beer Beauty Bonk. This betrayal left him rattled and confused.

Having already been taken advantage of once by a bully at school he was in no mood to run into the pair of dickhead BMX riders today and so he went off the normal script and decided to pray. Todd had thought a fair bit about God for a 9-year-old with an agnostic mom and found himself caught in the conundrum where you understand the whole God thing fails every possible logical test and so you believe there is probably no God but yet you find yourself appealing to one at specific times when the upside of the existence of God would be most convenient. A part-time subscriber to Pascal's Wager. Todd pleaded to whatever powers might probably not be.

Please don't let them bother me today please don't let them bother me today please don't let them bother me today please don't let them bother me today—

But he only had time to say that fourth cantation before the pair of dreaded dickheads appeared up ahead. The smaller one with the bowl cut and rat tail looked especially happy to see Todd. Almost as if he sensed Todd was already upset and was pleased by this. Like: this numbnut is finally showing a little emotion.

"What do you have for us today little boy?"

"Nothing. Sorry. Can you guys just let me go? I don't have anything, OK? C'mon."

"Bullshit. Let me see in your bag."

Todd felt his face get hot and he was about to go limp but then instead a weird dark energy erupted inside him and he lunged at Bowl Cut. Todd rained a frenzy of furious, uncoordinated punches into the kid's face and stomach. *Today is the day I get my revenge on these guys! Enough is enough. Game on, dickheads!*

CUT TO: Both boys on top of Todd punching him in the ribs and face with extreme gusto. Todd rolls onto his stomach and goes full turtle, still wearing his backpack. Blood flows dark hot red from behind his ear and out of his left nostril. One of the boys gets up and zips open the backpack and fills it with maybe 15 hork lougies then they see a car coming and so they hop their BMXs and bolt.

Todd got back up and assessed the scrapes on his knees and the taste of blood in the back of his throat. The worst thing of all, he learned, was that they had taken his Duran Duran tape ("Seven and the Ragged Tiger") out of the ghetto blaster and crushed it on the ground. He had barely even listened to that cassette! Three weeks of Pennysaver delivery, wasted.

The brown magnetic tape laid strewn, partly unspooled and mangled around broken bits of plastic. Sad, humiliated and incredibly pissed, Todd thought for a second how hard would it be to get a gun but he didn't have it in him to follow through with the thought of what he might do with a gun if he got one.

Dejected, he walked. Mind hot. He walked for a while and slowly his mind settled and went kind of numb. Generally sad but not really angry anymore. Void. A few feet ahead of him a small bird, maybe a sparrow, stood innocently on the curb. It faced away from Todd.

BKAH!

Todd made a loud noise and flung his arms in the direction of the bird, releasing a burst of anger towards the tiny, feathered bystander. The timing of this normally harmless gesture could not have been worse as a pickup truck came down the road, fast. Just as the startled bird flew off the curb, it was hit and crushed under the wheel of the pickup.

Oh Shit. No. Oh shit!

The truck drove on, unaware of the double-crunched bird.

Todd hadn't meant to hurt the bird (obviously) but now it was absolutely dead. He felt a deep and real guilt. Such real guilt that he would occasionally think back to killing that bird even 10 and 20 years later and feel really bad about it. The worst part was that he continued to walk this route home for the next few years, and so he saw a daily slow-motion time lapse of how a bird crushed on the street slowly decomposes and eventually becomes a bird skeleton.

He never felt sorry for himself with regard to the bullying that day or any other day but he felt extremely sorry for the bird and would've done anything to be able to undo that stupid spontaneous action that led to its death.

He never felt bad for blaming God at the time because the timing of the BMX boys' arrival right while he was praying either proved there is no God or implied some sort of Asshole God who sends you the exact opposite of what you pray for just to be a dick. The cocktail of guilt, sadness and humiliation was complicated and made him believe more than ever that God does not exist. A Venn diagram where A = "People that don't believe in God" and B = "People that are angry at God" and in the intersection of the two circles (A ∩ B) is "Todd".

■ ■ ■

OCTOBER 1998

Yellow hyphens flew by at ground level and the dark air of rural NY enveloped the car completely. Todd's brain was numb from the same Disneyfied ClearChannel DJ radio bullshit buzzing like a fridge from every frequency on the FM band and so the radio was off and the weak purr of the Jetta's engine was the only noise. He pinched his leg. *Stay awake.* The battle was lost and his eyes closed for a moment. Rocks crackled underneath tires and the car went off the road but on a slight enough angle that he was able to jerk the wheel and weave back into the right lane. He was going 37mph on the interstate.

He pulled over, under a bridge and fell asleep.

Tap tap tap. On the window. *What the? Where am I?* Sunlight. Dashboard clock read 6:22. Freezing. Freezing. The window was too fogged to see through. Todd fumbled. Tried to put down the window but it was electric and the car was off.

Tap tap tap. On the window. A bit more urgent or peeved or something.

He started the car and "rolled" the window down.

"Hello officer."

"Hello. Everything OK?"

"Yes, I was just tired."

He sat there for maybe 45 more minutes after the cop left. Mind full of confusion. All his dreams from college had come true. Top of his class in b-school and big Wall Street trading job plus a big house, sweet car and now here he was. Heavy. Once the American dream comes true there is nothing. A fullness worse than hunger.

The pursuit of the thing has utility, the thing itself does not.

2007

Todd had commuted for too long. When Jessica died, Todd thought since it was just him and Charlie left maybe they should move to New York City but the therapist said it was best to stay out in Connecticut for Charlie's sake. For continuity and stability. Out in Westport, land of the manicured and medicated melancholy MILFs. They are blonde, wear yoga pants, volunteer at the kids' school, and have had some work done (but it's subtle; looks natural).

Jessica was different. Gentle and delicate but not weak. Feminine and confident, usually in a simple but cute cotton dress. Granola but not condescending. Attractive enough that Todd's friends would tease him:

"You're doing a lot better than she is."

And he would laugh and think: *it's funny because it's true.*

He could no longer listen to the radio. AM radio, 1010 WINS,

WFAN (The Fan Sports Radio) or FM radio, WEBE 108 and STAR 99 or WNPR or whatever it all sounded the same, like the same scrambled fucked up script being read over and over and over. Meaningless noise like the adults in Charlie Brown. Mwah, mwah, mwah, mwah...

Ira, from Staten Island, you're on the air / The Jets QB situation has not improved / ... fighting broke out after weeks of calm in the disputed region / Lebron is the greatest of all time! No Michael Jordan is... / an IED killed four soldiers in Afghanistan and critically injured two others / the Knicks need to rebuild but they just don't have patience / the struggle for women's rights in Saudi Arabia continues... Same bullshit day after day, so the radio was off limits.

Audiobooks were better but had their own particular droning monotone.

He learned not to hate all the other drivers on the road. Their stupid "Proud Parent of an Honor Student" and 26.0 stickers and how they talked on their phones while they drove in the left lane and hit the brakes for no reason and all that. He would rage here and there but was pretty good about controlling it.

Whenever he saw roadkill, he yelled "Hamburger Helper!" just like his dad used to. And he would laugh but it was kind of a sad laugh. Also like his dad, he derived more than the expected pleasure from the act of throwing apple cores out the window. He watched them disappear into the roadside foliage then imagined complex scenarios of biodegradation involving ants and sometimes deer or even wild turkeys.

He saw various types of carnage over the years, mostly twisted metal but sometimes prone bodies on stretchers lifted into emergency vehicles. One brain would feel jealous of the victim. *Good for him, he can finally rest. I would love to be in a hospital right now with nothing to do. Unlimited guilt-free sleep.* The other brain would tell the first brain not to be so stupid. *You really wanna be paralyzed on a stretcher, man? Get your shit together.*

He longed for the days when he had to deal with crying babies and stepping on Legos—he wanted those days back. But the thing is, he never appreciated those days at the time, so that made him double sad when he waxed nostalgic. Sad times one, for the times gone by, and sad times two for having failed to appreciate life as it unfolded back then.

Occasional violently swerving skid marks on the road and median piqued his imagination.

One morning the traffic was slowed way down which was unusual for 5:30 AM. As he inched forward, he came upon a police cruiser at the side of the road. The cop was standing on the shoulder by a dented Honda Civic and a writhing deer. Just as Todd pulled even with the deer, the cop pulled out his service revolver and shot the deer in the head. BLAM! Probably twelve feet away from Todd. A jarring and macabre way start to the day.

It was hard to stay awake, especially on the drive home in winter darkness. Ptosis. Vision discontinuous as he tried to stay awake. He would flick to partial dream state and back out before anything bad ever happened. The red brake lights in front flickered like lit parentheses. *Must stay awake. Must keep a minimum two chevrons apart at all times.* Gravity exerted undue force on his upper eyelids and his awareness blinked. He pinched his leg and slapped his own face to break the tired. Gravity pulled unevenly sometimes; his right eye drooped as the left eye remained mostly open. Rumble strips buzzed. *Damn it.*

Seventy percent of single car crash fatalities involve run-off-road crashes. In that few hundred milliseconds of unconsciousness he saw that the cars moved significantly in absolute space but not much relative to one another. He would crank some pop music and activate his levator palpebrae superioris, pulling the eyelids up and back with the mental effort of a 25th push up. Lights starred and swirled as if he saw the world through an out-of-date eyeglass prescription. He saw himself smashed against the console inside twisted wreckage and was unsure how this made him feel. Relieved? Sad? Then he felt disgusted with himself for feeling the wrong feelings about this imagined calamity. *Get your shit together.*

Todd played the license plate game, a game Charlie invented. Take the three letters from a license plate you see and add whatever letters you want to make a word, but keep the original three letters in the same order as they appear on the plate. 1 point per word. First one to 21 wins.

Example: 332 FLR. You can make: flyer, fuller, cauliflower, fluorescent, muffler, etc. Some Connecticut plates had four letters so if you could make a word using all four letters that was a 3-pointer. Todd became an expert at the game, trouncing Charlie whenever they played on long trips because he had so much practice.

Hour after hour he played the license plate game alone in the car on the Merritt Parkway. GGB 426: gigabyte. 971 DRV: drive (that's an easy one) 4ABCD21: abracadabra (nice!) CKE: pickle. RCE: barbecue. MBT: emblematic. RTP: roadtrip (wait, is that two words?) and so on.

Most of his drives home were silent and he sometimes liked the meditative aspect of this but at the same time it was so fucking boring; so mind-numbingly boring that the top of his mind would throb behind his eyes. Not a headache or pain exactly, just a throb throb throb throb throbbing.

He learned long ago how to shut off thoughts completely so that the throbbing space was empty instead of filled with thousands of words and thoughts and ideas rebounding around inside like cacophonous rebounding subatomic ping pong balls. He could empty it out and leave it devoid of ricocheting thoughts but it was never light in there. Always dark, always full of psychic batshadows flapping and flopping around all confused, knocking against the backs of his eyes and the front of his brain.

He played the same games that you played as a kid, watching raindrops race down the windshield. In control of the wipers, if the drop he didn't want to win was winning he could simply wipe it away. Scrub the track clean. New race.

More than once he thought: *I would love to just pull the steering wheel hard to the right and drive full speed into the ditch.* Not necessarily to kill himself but more like: *I could just sit there, stuck in the crashed car in the ditch and sleep until the fire trucks and ambulance showed up.* And if he died, he died. He knew that life had only a brief moment between unripe and rotting and he was well past that momentary apex of ripeness. The most fun day of Todd's life was already in the past. But he did not have the courage to drive into the ditch.

The level of boredom sometimes increased to the point where Todd felt physical pain>>>>>>>>>>>>> tightness just behind his eyes where the optic nerve joins the brain. He imagined the feeling he had on his commute must be what caged animals like cheetahs in zoos or pigs in crates feel as they pass countless empty days imprisoned. Joyless, unfillable nil. Like the zoochosis of the caged wildcat that paces a worn track around and around and around and around his cage forever. Knausgårdian monotony; worse than sadness because at least sadness is something. This is more like void. Throbbing. Throbbing. He is a pig in a crate waiting for the nail to be shot through the front of his skull and into the brain and then the boredom and the pain will cease and he will finally be bacon.

Todd's black void was non-standard, not the vanilla sadness everyone feels as they become a grown up. This was supernormal oblivion. The wounds left by what happened to the girls and to Jessica were still gaping.

What do you mean, "What happened to the girls?" It didn't happen to them. You did it to them. You drank, you drove, you killed them. You crushed them against that—

He cuts off the memory; abruptly changes mental channels. He has to.

Annual 18-hour drives to Myrtle Beach as a kid were painfully boring too and it was a similar brand of boredom but different. Punctuated by rest stop Frisbee and a bit of reading until he got carsick and at least at the end of the painful drive to Myrtle Beach there was "South of the Border"... And then ecstasy: video games (Asteroids and Berzerk) and that Williams baseball pinball game where the steel ball rolls out and you press a button and a small bat hits the steel ball up over jumps for singles, doubles, triples and home runs and outs.

And then they'd run out of quarters (Todd and his kid brothers) and so they would make up games on the pool table using just the cue ball because it always came back out even if you hadn't put any quarters in. Cotton candy and Skee-Ball and collecting hundreds of tickets to buy plastic frogs for 20 and a stuffed penguin for 175. Save 10 for a Lik-M-Aid. Dinosaur Adventure Mini-Golf and cans of Mr.

Pibb and clackety clacking rides and all that beautiful, beautiful American bullshit.

The end of the commute held no such jackpot: a bowl of cereal and a few hours in front of the TV and then take out the garbage and then to bed and hope for seven hours sleep at best but usually more like six. Interrupted by that super annoying 4:00 AM piss before the alarm goes off at 5:00 AM and then you do it all again.

There didn't seem to be any reasonable way off the hamster wheel. Wake, drive drive, watch numbers jump around on a screen for twelve hours, drive drive drive drive, watch TV, dream of numbers jumping around, wake, drive drive drive... He sometimes floated pointless fantasies of quitting his job, moving away, but to where, to do what? He had no clue, there was no way to get quiet or peace.

Fantasies of walking into a freezing cold lake. The water moves up slowly, soaking his pants and when it touches his balls he flinches and he remembers this feeling from Myrtle Beach as a kid. It was easy to get into the cold ocean water once you were in past the chilling of the balls.

Mind empty, he keeps walking into the lake. His torso is soaked and then his face goes underwater slowly. Cold water touches his earlobes and the coldness moves up his auricle over his antihelix and then cold liquid fills his ear canals. Beautiful black silence and he smiles as the water fills his nose and mouth and lungs and then the peace finally comes. But he did not have the courage to walk into a freezing cold lake.

The commuting infrastructure was hypersensitive to any sort of anomaly. A few drops of rain or some light snow and: complete grid-lock. Nighttime driving was worse than day so the winter was absolutely heinous. In summer it was light in the morning and still light at night so the drive was bearable. The fall also had the occasional moment. Todd often remembered early on, one of the first fall evenings that he commuted. The changing leaves in rolling waves of red and orange and yellow out over the horizon. The words "beautiful commute" popped into his mind. Almost an oxymoron but not quite.

One fall morning, around 5:45 AM, he drove south on the Merritt and saw the soul-racking beauty of a gigantic sunrise straight ahead. A few seconds later, as he checked the rearview, he saw the moon hanging there in the dark blue morning sky. As he drove he managed to fix his sight in a way he could see both the rising sun ahead and the setting moon behind, at the same time. *Beautiful commute.*

Todd never complained. A proponent of the fake it 'til you make it school, he looked at himself in the rearview and made himself smile before getting out of the car each morning. This smile stayed on his face all day long at work and all night long at home, for the most part, and everyone thought he was pretty happy and he even convinced himself a lot of the time. Maybe everyone else was more worried about maintaining the believability of their own smilemask and so didn't have time to question the authenticity of his. Todd wasn't even totally sure anymore if he was unhappy or just numbbbbbbb or what the—

There was no obvious remedy. He had enough experience with drug experimentation just after college to know there were no answers there; so he stayed away. There was really nothing he could confidently identify that he truly enjoyed doing anymore so he repeated his mantra. Fake it 'til you make it. For Charlie. But the frightening and depressing accuracy of the Hasbro Game of Life hung over him. College | Marriage | Kids | House | Retire. That's all there was. With unspeakable tragedy interspersed.

His life was like the lobby bar at a Marriott in Wisconsin. There was just no way to make it fun.

The license plate in front of him read BND 653. Rebound, abound, bend, bond, bind, binder, binding, bound, blend, blending, blended, bland, blind, blinded, blinding, blinders, blinder, band, banding, bender, benders... PNF 744: panfried. Is that two words? YGT 221: zygote. 443 GEV: grieve.

Once a week he would be in so much psychic pain from the boredom that he would try the radio again but the nattering nonsense was always too much so after less than five minutes it was back to the license plate game over and over. ASZ: fantasize. CSH: crash. BAK: black. END: end.

■ ■ ■

SLOTH

Sloth is a thing on Wall Street, which Todd found surprising at first since the finance gene pool was stocked mostly with Type As and ENTJs. If you enter an investment bank lobby and the trading floor is on 2, you might be surprised to see 95% of the workforce take the elevator. Todd noticed even the Big Swinging Dicks keen on loudly advertising their 4AM workout or weekend Ironman were just as likely to take the elevator up one floor as the perennially dieting single moms in middle office.

Paunchy traders sent still-lean 22-year-old analysts for lunchtime pizza or steak sandwiches saying "I gotta watch the market" and such, even when things were completely dead and they (the traders) could really use the fresh air.

But the worst sloths on Wall Street, by a mile-wide margin, were the people Todd hated most in the entire world. The goddamn, lazy, selfish, leaving-the-seat-down, small-dicked, girly-man, sprinkler-spraying, motherflicking stall pissers.

Trading floor bathrooms were bad enough with all the unflushed shits and newspapers and internal research and Gartman letters strewn all over the floor but these stall-pissing whoresons walked into cubicles (even when every single urinal was free) and went for long, Austin Powers unfreezing style pisses without flipping up the seat lid. The piss sprinkled outward from their tiny, limp, impotent dicks and splashed up out of the bowl and so the toilet seat was decorated with huge dribbled drops of yellow piss and toilet water. Dried piss globules, sticky like melted banana popsicle.

Todd walked into the bathroom in a hurry. His internal seismometers had sent an emergency shit warning just before the economic data came out at 8:30 AM but he held back because despite tremors registering around 6.2 on his intestinal Richter, there was a fast market in bonds post-data. By 9:45 AM he felt it was safe to get up and go.

He crossed the trading floor and walked into the bathroom. Nine of ten stalls were locked. They echoed with the tortured intestinal gurgling and audible vibrating anus lips of nine fecal hotboxers discarding last night's meats and carbs. Sounds of splashing and pages turning. Fat white asses suctioned against whiter plastic seats. Brown semi-solid partially digested proteins discharged. Hypersensitive autoflush delivers spontaneous, unwanted bidet action. Overpaid overweight white men wheezed, groaned and grunted like nine sows jammed in nine gestation crates on a factory farm. Todd felt his guts churn and he saw Trap 5, open.

A free stall. Thank you, God.

Todd walked into the cubicle and directly into the stale stank cloud of the last shit recently taken therein. He started the unconscious process: check floor for puddles / spin around / drop pants. But he stopped midway when he saw it. The last one in here was a stall pisser. The toilet seat was completely covered in wet drops of piss and toilet splash from the Son of Satan who was too arfing lazy to just kick the plastic seat up with his foot before he took a slash. The droplets clung thick and liquid like globs of mercury, surface tension resisting the gravitational pull of the slightly inward-sloping toilet seat.

Todd saw this moist mess and clenched his sphincter as he contemplated the idea of traversing the entire trading floor, legs crossed. That option was not on the table. So he grabbed a bundle of toilet paper and balled it up into huge a mound. The ball was large enough to provide a buffer so his hand would not come in direct contact with urine. He carefully wiped off the coworker's piss. The smell of Sugar Crisp or some similar wheat-based cereal wafted, filling his nostrils. And two ass pubes that clung to the back of the toilet seat were scooped up in the process. Disgusting. There is no shortage of urinals in this place. DO NOT PISS IN THE STALLS. Simple. DO NOT PISS IN THE STALLS.

Gah, stall pissers.

■ ■ ■

OCTOBER 30, 1997

Todd got home on October 30th and could not shake the dread. The bottom was falling out and there was nothing he could do to stem the losses at this point. To exit the positions completely was out of the question as liquidity was severely compromised already despite it being only the early stages of what came to be known as The Asian Financial Crisis. With no bids to hit, all he could do was watch the stream of red numbers line up on the daily P&L .xls like a roulette wheel that doesn't understand the concept of mutually exclusive events. Fact was, his daily P&L was autocorrelated big time and so each day he lost meant an even higher probability of losing again tomorrow. His only hope was some sort of IMF intervention on an unprecedented scale.

This was the first P&L downdraft in Todd's career and it caused him serious vertigo. He had only been in the biz for four years but had raced up the org chart as employee turnover was constant and he knew how to trade EM bonds better than most people with twice the experience.

He walked into the mud room of their upscale but modest Connecticut home and kicked off his $95 Kenneth Coles and thought something like:

I should probably get a new pair of shoes; these things are looking a little homeless. But then again, I guess it's probably 30-delta I have a job in 6 months so maybe better to hold off for now. Something smells good. Chicken fingers? I'm starving; I hope it's chicken fingers.

The sea of red in the P&L spreadsheet .xls appeared in his mind and his YTD, now minus $6,000,000 flashed. Normally he maintained a chart of his YTD P&L at work and he loved updating it and lingering on it each time he was on a hot streak. But this year he had deleted the worksheet 'YTD chart' out of his Excel workbook completely so that he didn't have to look at it. It looked like the DJIA in 1987... Up, up, up and... Crash.

He visualized a terrifying extrapolation: -$10m, $-20m, $30m, -

$50m, -$500m, -$1 billion and the chart could barely rescale as the P&L crashed like a downward-plunging roller coaster after the rack-ety-tack-tack-tack-tack upward-sloping starting part. He felt like when you take that last step down the stairs in the dark but there are two stairs left, not one. As if *he* was falling, not his P&L. He had not eaten since 11:30AM and his stomach was folding in on itself.

"Hi Daddy!"

Allie and Jane both appeared at the bottom of the steps in their matching pajamas and they were so happy to see him and he was startled and he loved them and hugged them and felt better for a sec. They didn't really want to be hugged so they giggled and squirmed away and then escaped back to the playroom to resume their game of restaurant. As per routine he changed into civilian clothes and helped the girls get their teeth brushed which can be extremely annoying when the kids are giddy and uncooperative and you really just want to eat some chicken fingers and rice and sit in front of the TV and watch football or whatever.

He became very gradually more annoyed as the evening dragged on. Jessica was busy with the dishes downstairs and the kids were disobliging. Finally, the kids were in bed—but Jane asked a few questions and Allie asked a few more and Todd went back and forth to each of their rooms, closing the door gently each time even though he kinda wanted to slam a door just because. He was ready to finally go downstairs and say "Hi" to his wife when one of them would call "DAAAADDYY!" before he could even get to the top of the stairs.

He popped his head into Jane's room and said:

"Sorry, but that's it. Daddy has to go eat, OK? Time for sleep. I love you so much but no more questions OK?'

And Daddy closed the door to Jane's room and just as it clicked shut Allie called him again.

"DAAAADDYY!"

He pushed her door open, not too aggressively (but getting really annoyed) and asked:

"What? What is it?"

"Sorry, Daddy. I just had one more question."

"OK, hurry up. What is it?"

"What does perpendicular mean?"

"Do you know what parallel means?"

"Yep like two lines beside each other?"

"Right. It's the opposite of that."

"I don't get it."

"Like two lines that cross at right angles instead of running beside each other."

"What's right angles?"

Gah!

"OK, umm, Allie. I can't do this anymore, OK? Time for me to eat. I gotta go."

"OK, but I don't get it Daddy."

"Listen," his voice was louder, "I gotta go. I have to eat."

"OK Daddy. I love you."

Annoyed, he let the words hang in the air and closed the door. He felt guilty for being such a shitty Dad and thought he should go back and at least say "I love you too" but it had been such a long and shitty day and then the P&L number "minus $6 million" popped into his head and he was stressing about the risk meeting tomorrow and he caught a whiff of the chicken fingers in the microwave and went downstairs.

■ ■ ■

THE NEXT DAY – OCTOBER 31, 1997

A customer lunch turns more liquid than originally planned and suddenly it's 3:30 PM and Todd is sporting a solid buzz. He is supposed to be home by 6:00 PM. It has been ages since he had a drink; he is a family man and today is an outlier. It started with a beer and followed with maybe three glasses of wine and now time has flown. At least he has stopped thinking about his P&L (minus $6.2 million at last report). He needs to get moving. The traffic is always scary on Halloween as everyone drives to work in order to get home early—of course this exponential increase in vehicular traffic leads everyone to get home late no matter how early they leave.

An alcoholic hummmmmmmmm fills his mind as he runs to the parking garage and hands over his ticket. He waits almost fifteen freaking minutes for the valet to bring around his black Volvo S90.

The drive home is in fits and stops and starts. Bumper to bumper. He tries to drown out thoughts by cycling through WEBE108 and NPR and 1010WINS but to no avail. The radio stokes his angst so he shuts it off. He is going to be late. The girls are going to be so disappointed. He really does not want them to go trick or treating without him. GAH! He is stressing out. He bangs the steering wheel repeatedly with his right palm until searing pain runs up his wrist bone and through his arm.

Tick tick tick tick. Minutes race by on the dashboard's digital display as his car creeps forward at a glacial place. It's getting dark and he still has over twenty miles to travel. He wants to be home with his wife and kids. Out of the gray city and into the green / yellow / orange / red / brown of NY. Laughing. Tricking. Treating.

He loves his twin girls and Charlie like good fathers do; he loves his wife too. He wants to be with them on Halloween. He simply messed up and lost track of time. A cop sits perpendicular to the highway, on a flip phone, arguing with his girlfriend. The buzz from the 1994 Cakebread Cabernet still swirls in Todd's cerebrum but he's not drunk. *I am definitely not drunk*; he thinks to himself (as drunk people often do).

The invisible bottleneck unplugs and the traffic starts to move. *Hallelujah.* He hits the gas and gets up to full speed. *I might be able to get home before the kids go out. They'll take forever to get their costumes on.* There would be unplanned undressing for initially denied pees. There would be arguing over where to go first or whether jackets are necessary. *If I drive quick, I can still make it.* Smooth sailing off I-95 and onto the side roads. He drives over winding, dark country roads and into the hills where mostly one-acre lots sit in gaps in the forest. There are no streetlights or traffic or light pollution.

Jessica pulls the three costumed kids down the lane in the big, green plastic wagon. Charlie is dressed up as a UPS guy. Allie and Jane, both princesses in pink. The crunching gravel pops underneath the wagon's wheels as Charlie explains to his sisters some of the intricacies of trick or treating understood by a 7-year-old but not by children of just three. Distracted by thoughts of her perpetually regenerating TO DO LIST, Jessica fails to observe that she is trudging through almost complete blackness. She forgot the flashlight. She parks the wagon to the side of the private, gravel lane and tells the kids to wait.

Todd races the black Volvo at somewhat unsafe speeds through the black night. Up, over, around. Down the last country road and then he turns left onto the long, private lane where they live. 7:05 PM. He remembers they didn't get outside until after 7:15 PM last year. He can hear Charlie's voice last year, repeating over and over. *Dad, it's 7:15 c'mon! It's 7:15, Dad, c'mon!*

He drives down the very dark, very long private gravel lane towards his home. Gravel pops beneath the tires—the comforting sound of arriving home. He reaches up to press the garage door opener from long range but it's missing. The girls love to climb around inside the car when it's parked in the garage and obviously they've been playing with the remote opener again. He takes his eyes off the lane for a moment, flicks on the interior light and paws around on the passenger seat. No garage door opener. He leans over and reaches into the side pocket of the passenger door. Maybe it's hiding in there.

Charlie is bored of waiting for Mom. He gets out of the wagon and starts poking around. Feels at the ground for cool rocks in the dark. He sees headlights coming down the lane.

Daddy!

Todd's fingertips find the plastic garage door opener. He picks it out of the passenger door side pocket but fumbles it onto the floor of the car on the passenger side. He stretches further to get the garage door opener and now inadvertently pushes his foot down (hard) on the gas pedal. The car tires spin a bit and the car lurches forward.

A series of quick bangs and then a loud crunch as he drives the black Volvo full speed into an oak at the side of the lane. The wagon and both girls are crushed squarely between the car and the tree.

Screams, yelling. Horror. The girls are dead before Jessica gets back with the flashlight.

■   ■   ■

JANUARY 2008

Todd could not just sit there and stare at the screens anymore so he went for walks. Initially these were brisk 5 or 10-minute strolls. Years of sitting on a trading desk meant he felt weird spending anything more than a few intraday minutes off the desk. Traders were known to hold in their piss for hours, waiting for a market lull. Nobody wants to miss a gravy trade. Jokes about catheters and all that. So, the idea of walking out midday for a saunter and some Vitamin D was not something a normal trader would even consider.

Over time, though, Todd got used to leaving the desk. 15 minutes turned into 30, then 60. Soon he found himself walking and walking and walking and walking. Mind a void as he wandered, strolling through Riverside Park or Murray Hill, 30 or 40 blocks from work. His mind was mostly blank during these walks, as was the case more and more throughout the endless days and nights of the Global Financial Crisis. Not a zen state of empty clarity—just numb.

When someone eats a death angel mushroom (*amanita ocreata*), they get sick for a day or two. Then, the symptoms pass and they enter what is known as the "walking ghost" phase. A two-day period when they can no longer be treated and thus are destined for certain death but have 48 hours of feeling pretty much normal before they die. For the past many years, Todd has been in the walking ghost phase. Still alive but already dead. Like a cat in a bag. Waiting to drown.

His days blurred together.

Todd hit F9 and PandL2008.xls displayed a large red loss. The worst so far. Minus $44,500,000 year-to-date P&L already, less than one month into the year. And so Todd stood up from his desk. The guys rolled their eyes like "here we go again" as they knew he was about to go off on another one of his lengthy walkabouts. He looked at his feet and for the first time today noticed that he was wearing two different shoes. Both black dress shoes and not dramatically different, so nobody had noticed, but clearly two different shoes.

Get your shit together.

Todd exited the bright and shiny corporate lobby, past the perfectly crisp American flags and the two huge dumb security guards. He headed out into a sunny winter day and headed north on 7th Avenue, past a street meat vendor blasting Amy Winehouse, "Rehab". *I said, no, no, no...*

He walked north until he hit Central Park and went in past Hecksher Playground where he once took all three kids in happier times. The thought of the girls hit him in the face like a pillowcase full of quarters and he tried to let the bad thoughts through. They went through but they ripped him to shreds on both entry and exit. His knees wobbled.

The weight of everything that was and that would never be pressed down on him and his walk slowed. He turned left towards Central Park West and emerged around 63rd Street. He headed west and stopped near the corner of Broadway and 63rd. A huge intersection, right across from the Lincoln Center. Especially bustling that day because there was a small farmer's market set up and as he passed it he smelled dirt and cilantro specifically and he saw a handwritten sign advertising Local Honey.

This triggered the memory of a recent conversation where George the Intern told him all excitedly that honey never spoils and "Wow! You can eat 3,000-year-old honey!!" This annoyed Todd because everyone knows honey doesn't spoil (don't they?) and how young are these interns anyway? Or how old am I? Like when someone says "The book was better than the movie." Yeah, thanks. Everyone knows that. Not interesting.

Then he got even more annoyed with himself for being so annoyed at the intern who was just being nice and was not an idiot by the way so there was no need for Todd to feel so annoyed in the first place but now he wore two overlapping layers of annoyed.

There was zero spring in his step as the replay of this memory brought his mind back to the trading floor and then to a flash of the big red number. -$44,500,000. It flashed up on his mindscreen like a $1,000 CASH BACK DISCOUNT graphic in a low-budget car ad. Gravity suddenly tripled and he thought he might fall down and so he looked around for a park bench or something to lie down on but found nothing appropriate. He could have probably kept walking if he really pushed but he was too tired to even try and so he just laid down right there in the middle of the freezing cold sidewalk. An unknown amount of time passed. Passersby passed by.

"Sir, are you okay?" a man asked.

"I'm fine. Thank you."

Todd lay there motionless / emotionless, his Brooks Brothers BrooksCool® Double Stripe Suit collecting fine dust.

"Are you okay man? You want me to call a doctor?"

"No, I'm fine. Just leave me alone, please. I'm fine."

A few minutes passed. Todd closed his eyes for a bit then reopened them. He saw legs scissor by. The cool of the sidewalk felt good on his right shoulder. The ground smelled like cold dust. A black circle the size of a silver dollar (made from a few sticks of chewed, then expectorated Juicy Fruit in 2002) created an interesting focal point on the sidewalk about eight inches from Todd's eyes. He focused on the gum splat. It went blurry then clear. Blurry then clear. Like the tunnel vision he would get in the principal's office as a kid.

"Hey! You can't just lie there. Get up. What are you doing?"

It was unarmed private neighborhood security. Gentrification enforcement. Todd tried to ignore the guy but he stood there, impatient. Hands on hips pose.

"I'm just tired. I'll get up soon," Todd muttered.

"No can do, amigo. Up you go. C'mon. Let's go!"

Please leave me alone. Why do you have to bother me?

Todd rose like Colm Toibin's Lazarus, barely conscious. The sun ripped through his pupils, stabbing the back of his eyes. Shooting pain. He crumpled and grabbed at his eyes. The rent-a-cop touched Todd's shoulder in a helping gesture but he pulled away. Passersby detoured. Eventually he found bearings and headed, slowly, slowly back to the office. The security guy's voice faded in the background.

"You need help man... Get some help..."

Wandering slowly back to the office, he eventually got his mental shit together, entered the building and walked through the sparkling lobby. He went up the elevator, onto the trading floor and sat back down at his desk. He had been gone for almost two hours.

"Where you been?"

They asked but knew to expect no straight answer.

"Ran a few errands. Anything going on?"

They snicker on the inside but still respect Todd enough to not laugh outright. They message each other on Bloomberg and he notes the clickety typing as they chat behind his back.

MATT MACLEAN: Looks worse than usual.

BRAD MULLIN: Dude

BRAD MULLIN: sooper bad

MATT MACLEAN: what do we do?

BRAD MULLIN: he;ll figure something out

MATT MACLEAN: Or b

BRAD MULLIN: Yea.. Or b.

■　■　■

FEBRUARY 2008 – WESTPORT, CONNECTICUT

Todd woke to his 5:02 AM alarm and dropped out of bed. Literally. The world was so dark and heavy he could not stand up and so he rolled out of bed and onto the carpet below. Thud. *I can't wait for this day to be over.*

Smoky black dread filled every crack in his mind. Complete anhedonia. He was afraid to check his Blackberry as the news from the markets was almost certain to be bad again. He had a quick thought: *I should quit and move to California. Charlie and I can just go. There's nothing left for us here.*

But he was too chicken to do something radical like that. Too tenderized by years of punishment to crawl up off the mat and fight on. He dragged his way through the morning monotony. Showered, dressed, teeth etc. ready to go with just enough time to make the 5:46.

Charlie slept behind a closed door, down the hall. Still more than 90 minutes before he would wake up for school.

Later buddy. I love you.

It took great physical effort to lift his feet and locomote and he tried so hard to think positive thoughts but no matter how hard you look around in an empty garbage can, there are no gold coins. Outside, invisible black rain stormed down through an ink black sky. The sun was busy lighting another hemisphere.

Todd pictured taking a Big Sleep in the garage. A hose running from his A4 tailpipe through a small opening in the driver's side window.

Recently or maybe a lifetime ago, he used to be one of the cool kids. Fun loving. Young and free and handsome. The kind of boy your mom would like. Captain of the high school baseball team. A shiny happy kid. But now he buckled under the unbearable sadness of adulthood.

He caught sight of a photo of his ex-wife on the mantle. The mother of Charlie and the girls. The girls who it hurt too much to think about. There was not much light in the room but Todd knew every detail of the picture. The exact peak of their lives, captured.

I miss you so much, Jess. I miss you so so much.

He told her once that life would not be worth living without her; and he was right. It isn't. The crushing weight of everything that was and would never be nearly knocked Todd over. He stumbled sideways and caught himself on a wall. *I need to keep going. I need to go to work.*

Todd climbed in his Audi A4 and pulled out of the garage. The rain pattered like impatient fingers on the top of his car. In the light of the moon he saw two crows fly by like a warning. *Birds fly in the rain?* He had never noticed that before but maybe he wouldn't have. Not sure. In his 20s he would have seen the birds as some sort of sign but now he understands there are no signs. It is all just randomness without meaning. He envied his younger self and the kid's ability to spot meaning in every coincidence. *How quaint I was.*

He slid the audiobook CD into the stereo's slot.

"...And once we realize that all is meaningless, we can proceed to the next phase: acceptance. The moment you stop asking why and realize that there are no answers, you are free. The existential angst you feel is not a necessary part of the human experience but rather the curse cast upon those who ask too much and live and love too little. Be here now."

The self-help CD made Todd feel better. His mind relaxed to the point where there was some risk he might fall asleep. He pinched his leg to avoid this. He drove on through abject darkness.

"...now your mind is a passive observer. Mute the voices that ask too many questions. Mute the voices that doubt. In front of you there is a beautiful painting. Mute the voices that must know every detail about the types of paint used by the painter and the price he paid for the canvas and just look at the painting. Appreciate its beauty and its—

BAMM!!

Todd ducked reflexively and nearly hit his head on the steering wheel as a crow slammed into his windshield, deflecting up and over then disappearing into the dark wet nothingness behind the car.

What the?

Todd shook, rattled. He made it safely to the train station. He parked, quickly got out of the car then hurried for the train.

There was a small black feather wedged under one of his windshield wipers.

On the train. Fat guy, smells kinda bad, wearing a Hermes tie and an expensive but ill-fitting (too tight) suit. Beads of sweat dotted his forehead and he was out of breath as he boarded the train. He walked past Todd and dropped down onto the seat behind him.

Vague sour waft of B.O. Then a wave of bad breath that smelled like hot throat or fried plaque.

5:46 AM train: Westport to Grand Central. Full of men 42 to 52 just past the best days of their lives. Faces puffy, the hot red skin of too much drinking and too much disappointment. Life is good but just not great. They wear the same suit a few days in a row because what does it really matter. Who's going to notice? Nobody. Unless someone catches the whiffy odor of sweaty wool and aging balls. Someone a few rows back was clipping their nails.

Click...

Click...

Todd played a few games of Brickbreaker then cursed himself for wasting valuable commute time.

Sleep or read?

Sleep or read?

Sleep.

The train was painfully bright (and rattly as fuck) but he was out in two minutes. He disappeared into a black, dreamless sleep. Peaceful.

Then: a strange, loud noise, like from an animal (?)

Todd was jolted awake by something like a yelp or a short, girlish scream from the seat behind. The fat guy in the suit—he had a nightmare and called out. It should have been funny but was not. The terrified yelp made Todd sad. It echoed in his mind for hours afterward.

The train arrived and Todd got off and he walked slowly through Grand Central Terminal. He walked very slowly as others hurried past on all sides. He felt the opposite of rushed. He noted the perfect line formed by the small and big hand on the iconic four-faced clock at the center of the famous concourse. You might guess it was 6:00 AM, and you would be right, though hands of a clock make a straight line 22 separate times per day so it could have been 4:54, 7:05, 8:10 or 9:16. He stood in the center of the concourse and looked up. *I can't believe humans built this.*

As was often the case recently, Todd could feel the inordinate weight of his $340 Clark wingtips as he pulled them across the buffed, reflective floor. As he walked past the entrance to Track 24, he tasted the burnt smell of brake pads and diesel. That hot, metallic smell pumped into Grand Central by incoming trains as they pushed giant tubes of dusty displaced air from the tunnels into the main terminal. He passed two of those terrifying post-9/11 military police officers clutching AR-15s.

A homeless man held open the heavy brass and glass door.

"Spare a little change for the homeless?"

Todd dropped a twenty-dollar bill into the man's rumpled Anthora™ cup (WΣ ARΣ HAPPY TO SΣRVΣ YOU) and walked out of Grand Central Terminal.

The New York air smelled sweet but also bad, like the shit of someone who eats exclusively lollipops, or the exhaust from a Dunkin' Donuts franchise. Todd walked down Vanderbilt, the small avenue that went from 42nd to 47th Street right along the west edge of Grand Central. One of the rare named streets inside the grid system dominated by numerical nomenclature. Todd liked Vanderbilt Avenue for this reason, like it was ballsy enough to show some independence and not just be another number like all the others. Not as cool as 6½ Avenue, but still. He grabbed a bagel and a Grande SBUX dark roast and shuffled his still-heavy loafers toward the office.

The walk to work was normally 15 minutes but today it took more than 25.

Todd kicked a plastic cup for almost two blocks. It reminded him of the walk home when he was 9. The bird. Still sorry about the bird. He stopped for a few minutes to study a bus sign. M104. M20. He took an unusual interest in the schedule noting the nice regular pattern. Steady 11-minute intervals between buses. 8:11, 8:22, 8:33, 8:44...

It was still dark out. Freezing cold but no snow. Gusty. This relentless winter drones on, pounding New York City, endless like a war. *It feels like it has been winter forever.* His right eardrum throbbed and ached from the wind. Two feet jammed inside leather dress shoes, unfeeling like frozen steaks.

Near Times Square, he stopped to take in the flashing neon lights marking a C MERA ST RE and noticed the slight difference in timing between the flashing of C MERA ST RE and the flashing neon above the shop next door that read SOUVENIRS. It reminded him of the windshield wipers on the city bus as a kid. How the slightly different speed of each wiper blade across the windshield created a strange arrhythmia that was both fascinating and slightly vertigo-inducing as the brain desperately wanted the wipers to line up, timing-wise.

They would come into synch for one fleeting moment, then fall out of synch again.

He remembered the time, taking the city bus when he was 13. A kid in a Black Sabbath t-shirt and a gelled mullet walked onto the bus and spat a huge loogie right into Todd's face, for no reason. Todd felt so violated, so gross and angry and weak and unsure what to do.

He looked back up at the uneven rhythm of the signs:

\ C MERA ST RE /SOUVENIRS \ C MERA ST RE /SOUVENIRS \ C MERA ST RE /SOUVENIRS /SOUVENIRS / C MERA ST RE /SOUVENIRS

He berated himself out loud:

"Stop feeling sorry for yourself. Go to work... Go to work. Go to work."

He hurried a bit as you would hurry when pretending to hurry despite having no desire to hurry. He approached his place of business. As he neared the revolving doors, he realized his coffee cup was empty. This had never happened before (finishing the coffee before arriving at work) and it alerted him to just how slow he had been walking. Some subconscious part of his mind might have been convinced that if he just walked slowly enough, he might somehow never get to work.

"I need another coffee."

Jean-Baptiste drove the taxi with one hand and held a Nokia flip phone in the other. He chattered in a patois of Haitian Creole and French to his sister Flore in Cite Soleil. Rihanna's "Umbrella" was on the radio, but not very loud. The minimum possible number of snowflakes started to fall outside.

"The cold man. The cold! I been here five years and it still make me skin turn white... What you laughing for? Pale white skin I'm swearing to God. Like snow. A black African man with white skin. Anyways, how's mama?"

...

Todd pulled out his buzzing Blackberry as he walked over the subway grates toward the edge of the sidewalk. The boss was calling. Unusual for this time of day but Todd was unusually late. Yesterday's P&L (minus $12 million) and then the YTD (minus $130 million) flashed in his mind and he felt gravity double then triple then milluple. As if he might be sucked through the subway grate into subterranean NY—sliced into little rectangular cuboids on the way through.

Realistically, if one were sucked down through a subway grate, there would be a lot of tearing of fabric and ripping of flesh and cracking of bone and so forth but Todd imagined being sucked down and sliced into perfect rectangular cuboids as though he were a humanoid figure made of high-viscosity gelatin.

Todd hit ignore on his Blackberry and stuffed it into a pocket. His mind was completely blank. Numb. He stood at the edge of the curb.

...

Jean-Baptiste drove the taxi at 50 mph, south down 7th Avenue. He laughed, revealing perfect teeth. God's gift.

"You are so funny, Flore! You are such a clown!"

Jean-Baptiste's head tilted back as he guffawed.

...

Todd's mind flashed like the last flash of a bulb before it burns out. A memory:

...

Charlie is five years old. Todd and Charlie, both in rubber boots, stumble down the leafy embankment toward the frozen stream in the ravine down behind the house. There is barely any snow on the ground but it is cold cold cold and when they walk down there, they find the stream frozen solid. They can see the water running beneath the perfectly clear ice. It is beautiful.

"Daddy, can we break it?"

"Of course we can, kiddo."

The ice is solid and their repeated efforts to crack it with smallish rocks and branches fail.

Charlie points out a pumpkin-sized boulder, partially stuck in the snow. Todd pushes and pulls at it. The thing wobbles enough and comes out. Probably 45 pounds. Todd lifts it, Incredible Hulk style, and does the head gesture to say "move out of the way / go over there". Then he drops the rock with full force on the middle of the frozen stream icetop and the boulder slams through the ice and kerplunks onto the muddy bottom of the stream in one perfect motion. A perfect circle in the ice. Muddy water splashes straight up out of the hole and all over Todd's face. Charlie is hysterical. Todd is hysterical. Rolling on ground laughing.

...

The huge red negative number strobed in Todd's mind. The wind whipped a bright orange unpaid parking ticket up into the air. In 50 microseconds, Todd scrolled backwards through time and saw his life as six distinct characters: BANKER, FATHER, HUSBAND, UNDERGRAD, STUDENT, CHILD.

And then, without looking, he stepped out onto 7th Avenue…

BAM! THUD. SLIDE. CRUNCH.

The taxi, still doing 50 miles an hour, drove straight into, then straight over the man in the $340 Clark brand wingtips. Jean-Baptiste slammed on the brakes, but much too late.

Victim died instantly.

PART THREE

PARABOLIC ACCELERATION TOWARD THE RESET

BEN BERNANKE ON *60 MINUTES*

PRIDE

Q: Can you act quickly enough to prevent inflation from getting out of control?

A: We could raise interest rates in 15 minutes if we have to. So, there really is no problem with raising rates, tightening monetary policy, slowing the economy, reducing inflation, at the appropriate time...

Q: You have what degree of confidence in your ability to control this?

A: One hundred percent.

■ ■ ■

1 YEAR AND 16 DAYS BEFORE THE RESET

I am deep in REM sleep when my new son, Seven, gently stirs me.

"Can I have some breakfast please? I'm really hungry."

It's 9:00 AM.

"How long have you been up?"

"6:30. I get up at 6:30 every day."

Oh boy. This is Day 2 of me as a dad. I am not good at it.

"What have you been doing?"

"I was looking out the window. I didn't want to wake you up. I counted 88 birds and 11 airplanes."

The kid is still badly disoriented, afraid and pale. His eyelids are red. He weighs about 60 pounds. Soaking wet. He looks exactly like a miniature version of me.

Over the last few weeks, there was a paternity test, then forms were signed. Handshakes. The kid was dropped off last night with just a small suitcase and a backpack. Alison was shocked, obviously, but there was not much for her to say. My decision was made. All instinct and no logic so there was no input from her. She was just kinda like "whoa". I had no time to figure out how she would fit in. We will see what happens, I guess.

In less than 90 minutes start to finish, Chubby Pantsuit Lady was here again, then gone. My apartment door clicked shut and now here is this thing that has just awoken in my apartment for the first time. This alive thing. A small human. I stand silent, facing the boy. Eternal seconds tick.

"I would like something to eat if you would, please sir," Seven says.

Oh man. Sir?

"Sure pal. I can do that."

I walk into the kitchen and look around. I am still not a "go get groceries" type of guy. All bodegas and takeout. I offer Seven half a blue Gatorade and a banana.

"Thank you, sir."

"Call me Charlie."

I should have told him to call me "Dad" I guess? I don't know.

"Not to be weird, but is Seven your real name?"

"Yep. Mom says number seven is lucky."

"Do you ever get to see her?"

"No, Grandma and Grandpa said it was a bad idea."

"I'm sorry about your Grandma and Grandpa. Do you want to talk about that at all?"

"I'm good."

"Let me know if you change your mind, OK?"

"OK."

"You sure you're OK?"

"Yep. I'm good."

His voice is so little.

Did I just give my kid a half a blue Gatorade and a banana for breakfast? I suck.

"You know what, pal? Let's go get some real breakfast."

We step outside into pupil-constricting sunshine and freezing cold wind. We hustle, hunched, to a diner. Seven orders waffles, bacon and an over hard egg and I have a dry bagel with jam and a coffee. The waitress smells like she just had a cigarette outside. That triggers me and now I feel like a cigarette but that seems inappropriate with a kid in tow. The appearance of this kid is still messing with my head. I do not dislike him or his presence but I don't see how he can really fit in the context of my current existence. Can I leave him alone at times? What do I feed him? Can he live in my 600-square-foot apartment? What kind of name is Seven?

I feel connected to him in a way that probably relates to biology but then I feel hopelessly disconnected from him given his sudden appearance, totally out of context and without history. One of my first tasks will be to learn more about his past.

There is no question in my mind about responsibility. I am now responsible for this kid and there is no liking it or not liking it. It just is. There is a simplicity to duty. You have no choice. You just do. I have never felt this before and I kind of like the lack of optionality. My life has just changed in a massive way and I am not in denial of that fact.

The partying will stop immediately, as will the smoking. The recreational stimulants. I've been wanting to focus more on trading anyway. I'm trading better and better but still nowhere near potential. Too many distractions. Lack of true commitment. Poor work ethic typical of those in a semi-permanent hungover state. All play and no work make Chuck a dumb boy.

In college you learn to mix partying with performance as you go out two or three nights a week and still perform at a high level academically. In the real world, you can stretch the binge nights to 4 or 5 per week and still function pretty normally but after five straight years of five nights a week I can feel that my mind is not quite the perfectly-tuned Les Paul it once was. My thoughts are sometimes scrambled. Willpower is poor. Memories are fuzzy. I've been working to get my brain back into shape, without much luck. Seven's arrival is perfectly timed.

The kid is completely mute as he shovels his breakfast down in a manner that screams lower middle class. I feel bad for thinking that about my own son, but yeah.

Diners' heads swivel to look out to the street as chants and shouts increase in volume. Echoes from a few blocks away. Another anti-inflation march. As the price of everything continues to rise, these marches have become more common. With interest rates absurdly low for so many years, the inflationary pressure has been building and building and now it feels like the lid is finally about to blow off.

I pay the bill: $51.27 plus tip for a two-person diner breakfast. Totally outrageous. The protesters are right. The Federal Reserve is asleep at the wheel. Interest rates should be way higher by now but no one has the cojones to hike. Stocks keep going up but unlike the halcyon days (when the hopium flowed, stocks ripped and consumer prices went up slowly), now stocks are going up slowly and consumer prices are ripping. Wealth disparity hits another all-time high. Get long GINI coefficient futures. Low rates push stock prices and gold higher higher higher. The wealth effect benefits the rich and super rich. Low rates push food and gasoline prices higher higher higher. The poverty effect hits the ever-growing lower middle class. Central banker's bad deeds go unpunished.

Seven and I walk along for a few blocks, exchanging mostly silent glances. I try to ask him some ice breaking type questions.

"You like sports?"

"A few."

"Which ones?"

"Just baseball actually."

"Me too."

Long pause. I don't think Seven senses the awkwardness.

"What's your favorite team?"

"Yankees."

Ugh.

"Do you like school?"

"Some parts. Math mostly. And music."

"Those were my favorites too; when I was a kid."

"OK." A three-minute pause in the conversation then he asks:

"If you're my dad, why did I never meet you before? Like, are you my REAL dad?"

A lie crawls up my throat and onto my tongue but I swallow it down. I am not going to lie to my son. No way.

"I never knew about you, Seven. Your mom never told me about you. If I had known I would have been around for sure."

"Oh. That's weird. Why would she not tell you."

"Well she didn't really know me. Maybe she was scared."

Seven's face goes white.

"Why is she scared of you?"

Poor choice of words.

"No no. Not of me. Just of the idea of bringing me into your life. There is nothing scary about me, I just mean..."

Blank stare still from Seven but the blood slowly returns to his face.

"Anyway, here I am. I am not going anywhere now. I am going to take care of you from now on, okay. You and I are a team. I'll help you and you help me and we'll figure this out together. I'm sure you feel super weird and uncomfortable and scared about everything but that's ok. I feel pretty weird too. Today is only my second day as a dad. So let me know if I'm doing okay and if there's anything I can do better, alright?"

"You're doing a good job so far. Can you carry me, please? My legs hurt."

"Sure. And how about you call me 'Dad' from now on, OK?"

"Ok, Dad."

He puts a weird emphasis on the word dad; like it sticks in his throat for a half second. I pick him up and he puts his arms around my neck. I carry my 60-pound parcel back towards the apartment. The moment is disorienting and awkward and beautiful.

Later, after a few hours of video games and TV, I Google "tips for new dads" as Seven takes a shower. I need to take a parenting course or something; I have no clue what I am doing. School starts in three weeks so first up I need to register him. He's been going to school on Long Island, where the grandparents lived. Entering fourth grade.

I have a son. Repeat after me. I. Have. A. Son. This is supremely messed up, like alternate universe kind of messed. We order some pizza and play vids for a few more hours. After a while, Seven puts down his controller and curls up at the other end of the couch. Then he's asleep. I take the comforter off my bed and cover him. My first thought once he's asleep is that I'm dying for a cigarette. But I can't smoke with a kid in here.

■ ■ ■

@realdemocracy tweeted
"by this means (fractional reserve banking) government may secretly and unobserved, confiscate the wealth of the people, and not one man in a million will detect the theft."
john maynard keynes

■ ■ ■

1 YEAR AND 7 DAYS BEFORE THE RESET

An interesting reaction to Seven's arrival has been the varying feedback from friends. Most still implore me to come out partying with them all the time despite my obvious, sudden and colossal change in circumstances. Motivated purely by their own self-interest.

"C'mon dude, get a babysitter!"

"Bring back Fun Charlie!"

"You are such a pussy now, man."

And so on. It seems many are much less interested in my legitimate well-being than I might have previously thought and are more interested in what I bring to the table. To the glass coffee table in my living room, specifically. The drug-fueled nights have petered out and my "friends" are not happy about it. Fact is I don't really need too many friends. I could make do just with flatland, tbh. Most people kind of enter stage left and exit right without leaving much impact. I get along with everyone but hardly anybody really matters all that much. People come, people go.

Life is much simpler now. More purpose; less aimless drift. I drop Seven off at school and watch as he takes my heart with him and disappears inside. I go jogging around the reservoir in the morning after drop off. I was spending $2k/week on myself (mostly takeout, booze, blow and Sight) now I spend $300/week on myself + Seven combined. Seven eats toaster waffles with syrup 17 out of 20 meals and the other three require intense negotiation and sometimes actual begging on my part.

I truly have no clue how to be a dad.

Seven is asleep on the couch and I am not sure what to do tonight. I feel like firing up the TV but I don't want to wake him. I am, however, insanely bored and dying for a cigarette and maybe a beer. I have decided not to smoke around Seven as it just seems rude and wrong and bad parenting so maybe just a beer. But a beer will make me want to smoke. Blurg. I am bored.

I could place him in my bed and sleep out here on the couch tonight but to be perfectly honest I much prefer my own bed whereas a nine-year-old doesn't really care where he sleeps, right? I walk over and as I am about to pick him up, I stop. I stand and watch him breathe for a bit. His chest rises and falls under a blue blanket. Who is this strange child that looks so much like me? What is he doing here? Is any of this real?

Then I see a flash of my mom in Seven's face.

...

I am 10. I run up the hill as fast as I can but the snow falls harder and gets deeper as the day nears expiry. My boots are heavy. The sun is thinking about setting (*Already? It's only four o'clock!*) and Mom is already at the top of the hill.

"Wait up, Mommy!"

She's got the Red Rocket plastic sled ready and there is that faint taste of blood in my throat as the cold air hurts my lungs and I struggle to catch my breath. Finally, I reach the top of the hill and drop back into the V of my mom's legs in the sled and we're ready to go back down the hill. There's nobody else here, just me and Mom.

One, two, three!

Perfect exhilaration as we tear down the hill like Olympic lugers. Snow flies up and falls down. Snowflakes melt on my face and the odd trickster comes to rest on one of my eyelashes. It is hard to see and as we reach terminal velocity, we careen over the side of a mogul and flip sideways. I am tossed from the sled and so is Mom and we tumble a few times and then come to a stop halfway down the hill. Mom is out of control laughing like I have only ever seen maybe one or two other times.

"Race you the rest of the way down!" I yell.

I start to run, trip and run again, feet spinning like egg beaters, out of control as gravity pulls me downhill. I get to the bottom and collapse breathless in a heap of exhaustion. I lie starfish, and look up at the blackening sky and falling flakes. Total silence except for my heaving breath and blood pulsing behind my ears. I spread my arms out and turn my head to the side.

Then, a small miracle: a snowflake falls perfectly straight down into my ear and onto my eardrum and I hear the softest imaginable tinkle of breaking glass deep in my ear. *I just heard a snowflake break.* Mom always told me to be on the lookout for miracles and finally! Here's one. So cool! Speaking of Mom, what is she doing? Super quiet.

I stand up and look around. No sign of Mom. Wait, there she is, resting like I was, on her back.

"Mommy! That was so awesome! You're never gonna believe what just happened! A real miracle! An actual one!"

The day is dusk now and I'm thinking maybe McDonald's.

"Mommy, can we go to McDonald's for dinner?"

No answer.

I walk closer and it is immediately clear that something is not right. Snow is piling up on her face and her eyes are open. A snowflake hits her open eyeball and melts, and she doesn't react.

"Mommy?"

This doesn't make sense. It's not that cold out. Why isn't she moving?

"Mommy? Mommy!?!"

...

"Dad?"

Seven snaps me out of the memory. He is groggy.

"What are you doing?" he asks.

"Nothing, kid. Just thinking. Let's get you to bed."

I am gradually more comfortable with the fact that this child residing in my apartment is my actual son. When I'm not sure how to act, I think to myself: pretend you're his dad.

I put my arms out like a forklift, make an exaggerated forklift engine noise, scoop the boy up like a floppy pallet and place him in my bed.

'Goodnight, kid, I love you."

"Goodnight, Dad."

I watch him for a bit. He looks at me for a second with heavy eyelids. He tries to stay awake and maybe say something to me but then his eyes roll back and close and he is asleep again.

■ ■ ■

"It would be a great mistake to suppose that the statesmen of France, or the French people, were ignorant of the dangers in issuing irredeemable paper money. No matter how skillfully the bright side of such a currency was exhibited, all thoughtful men in France remembered its dark side. They knew too well, from that ruinous experience, seventy years before, in John Law's time, the difficulties and dangers of a currency not well based and controlled. They had then learned how easy it is to issue it; how difficult it is to check its overissue; how seductively it leads to the absorption of the means of the workingmen and men of small fortunes; how heavily it falls on all those living on fixed incomes, salaries, or wages; how securely it creates on the ruins of the prosperity of all men of meager means a class of debauched speculators, the most injurious class that a nation can harbor—more injurious, indeed, than professional criminals whom the law recognizes and can throttle; how it stimulates overproduction at first and leaves every industry flaccid afterward; how it breaks down thrift and develops political and social immorality.

There is a lesson in all this which it behooves all thinking men to ponder."

Fiat Money in France, Andrew Dickson Smith, 1896

1 YEAR AND 6 DAYS BEFORE THE RESET

It feels like it has been snowing forever but a few hours ago it finally stopped. Three or four straight days of eff-you blizzard has stopped NYC in its tracks and now I look outside and see New Yorkers emerging like post-hibernation bears. Stretching and yawning. Walking around, dazed by blinding sunlight reflected off still-fresh snow. It will be gray slush soon enough and so Alison took Seven out to play in Central Park while I take care of covering some currency and equity trades predicated on weaker US growth.

The economists can never get the weather adjustment right and so when you get a world-stopping snowstorm like this in the Northeast, markets take the conservative view and mark down forecasts for the economy until they can figure out what's what. I have been selling dollars and short retail stocks since the blizzard was first forecast about a week ago and now it's time to take profit. Liquidity is a joke as it seems like fewer people are playing these days and it feels like it's just me and a billion robots left trading this market.

Alison seems to have her shit a bit more together these days which is a relief and there is this weird "I have a family again" feeling that pops into my mind here and there and today is a good example as it felt like a real Mom and Dad situation as we all had homemade breakfast together then Alison took it upon herself to go play with Seven. I tell her directly that this makes me happy.

I am doing my best to be straightforward and ask for help when I need it and ditch the passive-aggressive approach; speak directly instead of burying truths in sarcastic one-liners. If there is one thing cocaine has given me, it's the ability to take feelings as they form in my head and keep them intact through verbal delivery instead of pushing them back down or obfuscating via sarcasm or flippant redirection.

Five years ago, it would have been almost impossible for me to straight up say "I really care about you" to a friend (especially male) without giving it some sort of fake, jokey-ironic "I love you man" cloak to offset the real emotion or meaning of what I was saying. Now I have the tools to come straight out and say directly: "I am really glad we're friends" and such without couching with a series of disclaimers like "I don't mean to be cheesy" or "Not to be all gay and stuff but…". Apparently, nobody really minds if I come straight out and say something honest and positive instead of beating around twenty bushes beforehand.

I take profit on my trades and just mindlessly watch the market go nowhere. Eventually, Alison and Seven return. They are laughing and freezing wet with melting snow and reveling in some sort of post-Winter Wonderland euphoria. They bought a cheap blue plastic sled for $26 at Duane Reade and this is the first time Seven has ever gone sledding and for a second I'm smalls jealous I couldn't go and that I missed the whole thing but mostly I'm glad that Alison and Seven got to share something and have a real connection / experience together, with or without me.

Alison hangs the wet clothes in the bathroom just like my mom used to way back in the day and I feel the sadness of that memory and then just let it through because I don't feel like feeling sad right now and Alison puts the wet mitts on the vent so they can dry off. We all sit down and I make instant hot chocolate with mini fake marshmallows and this is now some sort of 1950's Norman Rockwell moment.

Then after about 10 minutes of old-fashioned family fun, Seven just starts bawling.

"What's the matter buddy?" I slide closer to him on the couch and he jumps away.

"Nothing," he mutters through sobs.

"Well it can't be—"

"Nothing I said!" he shouts, cheeks wet with tears.

I am confused, obviously, and Alison has no answers and so I press Seven more but he just won't come clean.

"Dude. You have to tell us what's wrong."

Eventually it comes out that Seven had secretly made a snowball and put it in his jacket pocket and his plan was to hide it in the freezer and save it to throw at me in the summer. We check the pocket of his jacket and they've been home for more than 15 minutes and so the snowball is fully liquefied and the inside of the jacket pocket is soaked. Alison and I find it cute and we laugh a little and our laughter sets Seven off again and now he's wailing and red-faced. Inconsolable. He runs into the bathroom and slams the door. Locks it.

"Holy moly. What was that all about?" I ask Alison.

"I don't know. Maybe he's embarrassed? Like he feels stupid or something?"

"What should we do?" I ask. "Umm. When's the last time he ate?"

"I don't know. Breakfast, I guess?" she responds.

"It's 2:45," I tell her.

"Oh shit. Oops."

"It's OK. Parenting is hard."

"Yeah. I'd be the worst mom in the world. I should never be allowed to be a mother."

I smile at her but she doesn't smile back and I cannot tell if she's joking. For a second I'm annoyed she didn't think to feed him at some point but on the other hand they left around noon so really it's my bad and let's not forget I'm the parent and she is just my girl-friend and she is freaking 19 years old so actually... This is 100% on me.

I don't know if I should go in there and console Seven or just let him cry it out or what but after about ten minutes the crying dies down and he comes out and then next thing he's asleep on top of our bed. There's a huge wet circle of tears on the comforter by his head. I close the door quietly and go back into the living room.

"Thanks for taking Seven out today. It means a lot to me." There I go again: openly communicating my emotions without disclaimer or obfuscation!

"Sure. We had a lot of fun."

"How are you doing?"

"Fine thanks! And you?"

Fucking sarcasm. Sometimes I hate it so much. She knows I'm asking about the drinking.

"Ha. I mean with the drinking. Are things getting any easier?"

There is a pause long enough to indicate to me her answer will be strategic, not genuine.

"Oh yeah, totally. Way better... Seriously."

She is very unconvincing and she knows this. She turns away from me, lies down on the couch and flips on the TV.

■ ■ ■

I have realized that I can now (kind of) get the high without the drugs. My neural pathways are carved by all those nights out and now all I need is the right music or just the right trigger thoughts and I can fly through those same tunnels again, sober. When I run around the reservoir in Central Park, I run as far as I can, and a bit more, and then stop. Exhausted. I experience something. Fleeting. A flash. The clarity. *What is life? It is the flash of a firefly in the night. It is the breath of a buffalo in the wintertime.*

I have realized that those chemical higher highs brought lower lows and it is absolutely imperative in the long run that I smash this need for constant exogenous stimulation. This is made easier because going out mostly stopped being fun a while ago. My overused pre-frontal reward circuitry is burnt out. Besides, I have other responsibilities and any fleeting thoughts of getting rekt now come with a heaping side of guilt and paranoia. "Woohoo", etc. is at least half replaced by nattering voices chirping "What about Seven?", "Where's Alison right now? You can't fix her until you fix yo'self" and such. Annoying but helpful voices as risk / reward around nights out has completely inverted.

Also, I've noticed that all those years of hard-partying and self-destruction have slowly merged into one giant composite memory blob. And that memory blob is no longer altered by new nights out. In other words, there are no new experiences left to add to the composite memory built over all these years. One can only stay up until 10AM snorting powders and dropping chemicals into one's eyes before the pattern becomes familiar and the desperate groping around the apartment for one last cigarette or milligram of stimulant is completely pathetic and not edgy or cool.

7:10AM, about a year ago. I am alone in my apartment. Every baggie has been licked clean and there is no chemical left to ingest. My heart races at what must be near lethal speeds. My e-cig won't satisfy at this stage of the night / morning and so I shake empty Marlboro packs hoping for a rattle but find nada. Polar vortex outside so the idea of going to the bodega is not fathomable and my pupils are black saucers so I'd rather not interact with normal humans at this point anyway as commuters are out getting their coffees, and kids roam the streets and I feel like a pale and stumbling, Sight-addled mole rat. But there is no hope of sleep for at least another 5 or 6 hours and so I need cigarettes. Real, tobacco-filled darts.

Kids down the hall sneak a smoke in the stairwells sometimes so I skitter down the hall and take a look. A few flights down, three butts, squashed but smokable on the floor. I pick them up and roll them in my fingers to try to get them back to ~ cylindrical—they were stomped upon completion. Two of my fingertips are black and I give them a sniff. Gag. The smell is deep, deep burntness of a sort that would bring back memories of a house fire or forest fire if I had ever experienced either. Pure post-inferno carbon.

Drips of drugs snorted hours ago drip drop down the back of my throat and I gag again. I hold the three cigarette butts in my open palm so as not to further stink up my fingertips and walk back to my apartment. The clinical white fluorescence of the hallway reveals a boot mark on the wall. I catch a tart vinegar whiff of garbage as I pass the closed door marked "TRASH ROOM".

Back in my apartment: I light one of the butts, the longest, the loveliest. It's got maybe three uncooked puffs of tobacco left and the first inhale is sickly throat-coating blackness of burnt charcoal but then it evens out and I get three or four good drags off it before it burns to the filter and I don't realize it's at the filter so I take one last horrid inhalation of burnt filter and then jam it out in the filthy, overflowing ashtray.

My mouth is pasty and white but tastes like the color black. I need something to wash down this dryness but the fridge, once opened, is nothing but a rectangular cuboid full of exploding light shards, shooting into and through my stretched pupils. I fumble around in a few cupboards where a gifted bottle of wine, forgotten, might serendipitously appear. No dice. I need something to slow my heart. My benzodiazepine script ran out last week and this is really not ideal. I'm too sketched out to trade and the TV hurts my mind. Its blaring makes me skeevy and there are too many thoughts at once and I just need some sort of downer.

That girl Kelly I dated last year that worked at the walk-in clinic gave me a box of random samples of various first aid and medicines they hand out and wasn't there some cough syrup in there? I go into the bathroom and dig deep under the counter past the bags of Epsom salt and the Wahl hair trimming kit and the boxes of contact lenses and some dust and a few coppery bits of goatee stubble and in the back is the shoe box she gave me, full of samples.

I pull off the lid and throw it behind me and feel around in the shoebox for the mini bottles of cough syrup then realize it's so dark because I'm half in the cupboard under the counter and so I pull myself back out and into the bathroom and—wait—blood is dripping really slowly onto the white tiles in the bathroom floor. I put the shoebox down and stand up and look in the mirror and, yep, my nose is bleeding and so I wipe it off with a Kleenex which I drop in the toilet. The Kleenex makes a beautiful floating, sinewy white and red blob in the water of the toilet bowl.

I open one convenient sample size bottle of cough syrup and drink it and then another and another and a fourth. Belatedly, I notice there is an expiry date on the bottles. More than two years ago. Shit.

I stand up and sway a bit and here come the spins and I sit down and then crawl over to the toilet. I stare into the bowl. Spinning. Gut tremors. Pressure builds. Gushing fluid stream from the depth of my body's center, out of my mouth, into the bowl, smothering the bloody Kleenex, filling the water. Splashing all over the bowl and back into and onto my face. I timber sideways then feel a nanosecond of coldness then impact on my left temple as my head hits the side of the toilet bowl and then

CUT TO: BLACK.

■ ■ ■

Major internet and cell phone blackouts have become a problem. At first, they lasted a few minutes here and there but lately they last as long as a few hours. Hackers have moved on from DoS attacks and data farming to intentionally manufactured brownouts of the entire web. No internet = frustrating and scary.

Alison and Seven are at home and there is nothing to be ordered online because of the blackout, plus Polar Vortex Brianna has hit the city and so there is no chance of going outside. Apparently they are calling this storm a combination polar megavortex / bomb cyclone / thundersnow, though someone from the 1980s or the 1990s might call it a "blizzard" or a "really bad snowstorm". The media have always loved weather events but the bar for what qualifies as newsworthy has dropped steadily over the past twenty years.

Weather drama. Get excited.

Charlie is out, taking a guitar lesson. He and Alison agreed recently that they each need to find things to do that don't involve drinking or drugs and so she is at home taking care of Seven. She acts like a babysitter but obviously there's more to it than that and there is this weird possibility that she could be the kid's mother one day, in theory.

They play Monopoly. Seven knows the real rules and so they auction off the properties that are not bought and Seven has all sorts of strategies to pretend he doesn't want a property and then get it for less than half the value which is technically an arbitrage since if you buy Boardwalk for less than $200, for example, you can just instantly mortgage it for $200.

Alison barely pays attention because she has a terrible hankering for a cigarette and a drink. She is jonesing like a motherfucker right now, but also trying to be a good babysitter / potential future mom and play along. Her mind is dark but she fights it to be here now with the kid as best she can. She catches a glimpse of the white daisies Charlie bought her last week, still fresh, sticking out of three Coke bottles lined up on the bookshelf. He is a good person. She loves him so much. Why is she making it so hard? She has to do this.

I have to do this. I can't not do this. There is no alternative. This is the best life I will ever get.

She wonders if there is beer in the fridge. Vodka in the freezer? This need for a drink is like a really bad itchy eye. Just a tickle at first. Then it gets niggly in the corner. Then the center gets dry and hot. The whole thing gets hotter and more insistent until you finally rub it. Don't rub your eye. Don't rub your eye. You rub it. Ahhhhhh. That's better. But the next day your eye is all red and you wish you had just had the discipline not to rub it because now it's itchy again. So itchy. Itchy itchy.

Seven wins at Monopoly and they switch to Risk. Alison played a lot of Risk as a kid and now she's passed the worst part of the jonesing and is quite a bit more focused now and kind of wants to beat Seven because she just now realizes how badly he smoked her in Monopoly. She was elsewhere, lost in her hankering for a drink but she has returned to reality for now. She builds a beachhead on the purple territories in Australasia and then steamrolls Asia bit by bit. Her mental cloud cover has broken and she is having fun.

"You totally don't suck at this," Seven says as Alison wipes him off the face of Kamchatka.

"I don't mean to get all mommy on you buddy, but the word 'suck' doesn't sound very nice, OK?"

He feels bad for being rude.

"Sorry."

"It's cool, don't worry. You're fine."

She rolls three fives. He rolls a one and a two.

"Ouch," she feels bad but also good as she picks his two armies off Irkutsk and puts them back in the clear plastic bin. Alison has an insurmountable lead and she can see it is getting under Seven's skin. He sounds frustrated. "Hey, it's 8:05. I gotta get you to bed. You wanna just call this a tie?"

He likes that idea.

"OK," he responds. He picks up the dice and starts to clean up, good little guy that he is. He drops the five dice in the clear acrylic storage box and they all randomly land on ONE.

"Wow, five ones. What are the odds of that!" Alison says to Seven.

"Hmm. I don't know."

"What's one sixth to the fifth power?"

"I don't know," he responds. Because he's 9.

"So it's one sixth times one sixth times one sixth, five times. So that's…"

Alison does math in head.

"One in 7776."

"That's neat."

"Yeah. You know what else is neat? 1111 times 1111 is 1234321."

"Whoa." Seven is genuinely impressed.

"Yeah it works with longer strings of 1 too."

She writes down 11111 X 11111 = 123454321.

"You just put the number of ones in the middle and count outwards. Pretty sweet, right?"

She could get the hang of this 'being a mother' thing.

"Uh. I really like this. But I'm supposed to go to bed at 8 on school nights and it's 8:07."

"Oh. My bad, kid. Do you know how to do everything? To get yourself ready for bed and all that?"

He does and so he gets himself ready and a few minutes later Alison stands by the side of the tiny, tiny bed Charlie got for Seven and tucks him in. She remembers Dad tucking her in as a kid back in Westport and the huge four-poster bed with the fluffy pink cloud-like comforter and Seven's single bed looks crazy tiny in the corner of the room. Flashes of her dad on top of her. Various positions.

Fucking asshole. She imagines him crashing the Imperial Blue 7-Series BMW at high speed into a wall. KABOOM. Her mind has gone from placid lake to fiery explosion.

"What should I dream about?" Seven asks.

"Hmm. Great question! How about you dream that you are wearing one of those hats with a propeller on top and an elastic that goes under your chin and whenever you want you can make the propeller spin just by thinking about it and when the propeller spins it makes you fly?"

"OK." Seven smiles. He likes the visual. "Can you sing to me? My dad usually sings to me at bedtime."

She feels uncomfortable for a second and then realizes it's just her and a nine-year-old kid and what is there to be embarrassed or insecure about? Her voice isn't half bad as she quietly sings Pearl Jam's "Daughter" to him.

Seven is asleep impossibly fast. As someone who lies in bed flipping and flopping for ages battling voices and thoughts and unwanted adrenaline spikes before finally slowly drifting down through incremental phases of hypnagogia, Alison is envious of his ability to cut straight to black without fadeout.

She steps out of the room and gently clicks the door shut. Before her ass hits the couch, she is thinking about drugs and then she mentally crosses them off one by one and then moves on to how she would love just a single drink right now. Just one.

It's not really her that wants the drugs or to have a drink more like some really loud subsection of her mind that the rest of her brain would rather ignore but cannot. No drug or drink is an option here and now which makes life easier because if drinking were an option that option would certainly be exercised right after the obligatory internal struggle which always ends with the same conclusion.

She knows there is no beer in the fridge, but she checks, just in case.

She knows there is no vodka in the cupboards, but she checks, just in case.

She knows there is no wine under the sink, but she checks, just in case.

There is nothing obvious to do, no good TV to binge watch and she doesn't want to start a new series because she feels these days like once she watches the first episode of a series the rest of the series becomes this mountain that needs to be climbed, this task to be completed, an unclosed Zeigarnik Loop. It doesn't matter if it's a great show or a terrible one. So she's trying to stay away. Can't drink, can't watch TV, can't do drugs. What else is there? The whole concept of boredom is pretty much alien to her as any boredom in the past would simply be washed away by chemicals or TV.

She flits around the internet for a while but finds nothing satisfying. What else is there to do? Is there anything? She's just finished the third of the three books she recently took out of the New York Public Library. There is a *TIME* magazine on the coffee table: "The American Favelas"; but she's read it like twenty times. Her thoughts turn from reading to writing. *I will do some writing! Yes, finally.* But first, she procrastinates, wanders over to the window to see what the weather's like outside.

Heavy wet snowflakes fill the sky, falling slowly, swirling. The huge LED NYC info screen at street level flashes the usual stream of propaganda: Report broken windows; Help is Available: Suicide Prevention. Call 988; Sex without affirmative consent is RAPE!; Si ve algo, diga algo. And so on. Alison looks down through the snow, counting homeless people: 1... 2... 3... 4... 5... 6... 7... 8... BANG!

A white-throated sparrow slams into the window glass, leaving an oily mark before disappearing below. It leaves Alison rattled and she takes a few slow breaths to regain composure. *What the fuck was that about?*

She thinks back to the bird that hit the train window the day she left home and cannot believe how long ago that feels.

Everything has happened since then.

Her breath fogs up the window a bit and she draws a happy face in the fog with her finger then pulls her sleeve over her hand and wipes the window clean so she can see out properly again. She should have left the happy face there but it felt wrong somehow. There are a pair of binoculars by the window and she looks through them, down at the city.

The homeless population is growing and has a different look lately. They have spilled out of Riverside Park and into the streets of the Upper West Side. Not just the regular down and outs of old but other categories. Entire families, newly homeless for example. There is a Mom and Dad with two kids all huddled together on the subway grate. The mom has two broken fingers tied together with duct tape. Crusty, purple / black dried blood and crystallizing yellow pus oozes out and hardens at the tape's edges.

A guy, maybe 30, truly starving, brittle wrist bones exposed to the freezing cold by a size small jacket on his medium / large frame. He is missing teeth. He lies against a brick facade. The snow slowly covers him in a crystalline shawl. Alison feels sad for the guy and briefly thinks she should bring him some food or something but then realizes obviously she can't leave Seven alone here and anyway it was just a thought it's not like she was actually going to do anything.

She goes back to thinking about writing. Like every half-decent writer, Alison is insecure. She worries most that everything good has already been written. How many metaphors could be left to describe a sunrise, for example? Surely all the good ones must be taken by now with English getting on for 1,400 years old? But at the same time, she knows this cannot be true. People have been saying that everything good has already been written since forever. She walks into the kitchen, makes a coffee, sits down and writes this:

■ ■ ■

A curious sun peeps over the horizon, like Tom, and lights the unremarkable city of Norwalk, Connecticut. A five-minute drive from the main building of the unremarkable Norwalk Children's Hospital is an equally unremarkable 4-story, windowless brick brown building with a small sign planted in the front grass that reads "Norwalk Children's Hospital: Ward 6". High metal fencing surrounds the small property. It is more prison than hospital, a psych ward of sorts, officially named: "The Center for the Long-Term Care of Criminally Insane Children".

The building houses the most egregious mentally incompetent

child criminals from the Northeastern United States. 7-year-old murders both parents, 12-year-old child executes baby brother, six kids poisoned at Farber Elementary in Massachusetts. That sort of thing. Staff turnover is high and the rehabilitation rate is close to, but not quite zero. Extreme powers of empathy and/or complete ability to detach and avoid judgment are key job requirements for those employed at what's generally referred to as CIC.

Audrey Emma Pickering lives in room 208. She's 15 years old, soft black hair. Awake already though it is only 5:48 AM. Fit but extremely pale. A white t-shirt and baggy pajama bottoms with an elastic waist hang loosely on her thin frame. She's whistling Top 40 and reading something not dystopian. Seems completely sane. Supposedly killed both her parents and her baby sister in three separate incidents in the past few years before she was finally put away. The evidence was sparse on the first killing (Dad) and still mostly circumstantial on the second (baby sister Anabel) but she was alone with her mom when the third poisoning happened and the cumulative evidence was too much to ignore. She always claimed (and still claims) she had no role in any of the killings but the evidence is strong. Same MO all three times. Bedtime, she kissed the victim goodnight. The victim went to sleep and never woke up.

Doctor Francois Dupechier walks into Audrey's room. His hospital shoes are padded, noiseless on the rubber tile floor. He stares at Audrey the way a very close uncle might. Caring. He sees her past and future and feels sad. *Ne garde pas la tristesse.* He clears his throat to get Audrey's attention without a startle.

"Ahem. Time for our daily chat, Madame." He's got a thick French accent. Quebecois but educated. Dupechier was chosen as top five most influential doctors by *Pediatric Criminology Magazine* last year and it would be hard to argue otherwise. Bedside manner plus intellectual chops and a true, deep interest in finding ways to get the few salvageable cases out of CIC and back into productive society. Rehabilitation is just one tiny part of the process. Societal re-entry is hideously complicated by stigma. There is also the somewhat recursive fact that the crimes committed often involve elimination of the parents and therefore leave no obvious source of support for those very few who exit. '

Francois sees Audrey as the best rehab candidate among his current stable of 33. They are called patients but it is well known that most are essentially incarcerated at CIC until they reach the age of majority then transferred to lifetime stints in adult institutions to die cross-eyed and emaciated in a pool of their own bodily fluids at, let's say... 48?

"How are you feeling today?"

"Fine. Bored."

"I see."

"I miss my dad."

"I see."

Francois has a strong suspicion that Audrey speaks the truth.

Things would all be a lot simpler for all concerned if they knew that Audrey suffers from an as yet undiscovered genetic mutation whereupon her saliva became fatally toxic to humans when she reached puberty. Her mouth is the murder weapon but all three killings were accidental.

The only other legit sane kid in the CIC is Eric Plinth. His lawyer made a solid defense based on the merciless abuse Eric took from his dad but the mother was not involved in this abuse, except by her refusal to get involved, and thus the double murder was ruled to be more than self-defense. A momentary act of madness in response to years of abuse would normally be treated differently with the youth violator going through all sorts of rehab and halfway houses and eventually foster care and such but this case got diverted as the judge in the case had a bee in his proverbial bonnet and was determined to keep Plinth out of society for the duration.

The judge, also abused by his dad, was subconsciously jealous at not having meted similar Plinthian justice upon his own parents and so he punished Eric to the extreme, going as far as to falsify some documents and exaggerate statements to make the kid look more screwloose than a wholly unbiased assessment would have suggested.

16 years old and stable, he is allowed a computer (no internet

access) which he uses to create amazing music, aka sonic landscapes. He is a musical Vivian Maier, creating a prolific body of world class music but sharing it with no one.

Dupechier believes that social interaction by patients within the CIC carries tremendous risk and prefers the strategy of full rehabilitation and then reintegration with the outside world as opposed to any attempt to resocialize internally before going external. He believes, however, that an exception might sensibly be made in the case of Eric Plinth and Audrey Emma Pickering given their elevated stability scores and similarity of age. Neither has met a peer in more than two years and both spend more than 22 hours/day inside their mostly white rooms. She reading, he tippy-tapping on his tablet.

Before their first meeting, Francois meets with Audrey and Eric separately to go over the ground rules. They will meet on neutral ground, outside in the garden courtyard. No discussion of each other's crimes. No physical contact. No exchange of items. They will meet on February 14th which Francois, unmarried and not super romantic, fails to realize is Valentine's Day.

Eric arrives a few minutes before Audrey. He sits on a bench, kicking at loose stones that make up a path. It's cold, maybe 50 F. Warm for February. He's loving the white hoodie and black toque they lent him for the trip outside. The sun peeks out from behind clouds that motor across the sky on their way to urgent meetings. Continents of shadow slide across the ground and make Eric mildly seasick as they pass. His skin is freckly and pale. He's excited to meet Audrey but nervous. No idea what to talk about. He's been at CIC for almost three years and the real world has mostly faded from memory.

"Hey. I'm Audrey," she floats over pebbles towards Eric. Same standard issue hoodie and toque. She must weigh like 50 pounds. Her skin is alabaster with dark brown freckles. She's not ugly but looks a bit like a junkie or a waif or something.

"Hey," Eric tries to deepen his voice a bit but it cracks in the cold, "I'm Eric." He comes across as mildly dumb but it's more socioeconomic rough edges, not low IQ.

He shakes her hand. It is oddly soft and very cold, like a glove

THE RESET

filled with spray cheese. She likes how his face is probably paler than
hers. She plops down on the bench as the last cloud in the sky zooms
away. Audrey can barely open her eyes. It's too sunny. She chews at
a split pinkie nail.

"Sorry. The sun is killing my eyes. Vampire style. Can we move
somewhere else?"

They walk down the path until they are in the shade of a large,
weeping willow. A security guard watches from across the courtyard. He is nervous as they walk to a point where they are somewhat
obscured. The guard turns to Francois for guidance.

"It's fine. Let them be," he says quietly.

Eric and Audrey stand underneath the tree. A garbage truck
backs up two blocks away. BEEP. BEEP. BEEP.

Leafless branches hang and bob around them. Someone has
carved EJ + FM in the bark, near the ground.

"I like it out here. It smells like cold," Eric breaks the increasingly
awkward silence.

"I didn't kill anyone, you know. It's all bullshit. Don't listen to
anything they tell you."

"Doctor Dupechier said we shouldn't—"

"I don't really care. I think it makes this whole conversation
impossible unless I tell you. I didn't kill my parents or my sister."

"OK."

As Francois would have surmised, if one broke the prohibition,
the other was put in a very uncomfortable spot as now Eric kind of
needs to explain himself or say something about the unseen fingers
pointed in his direction.

"I'm sorry. I killed my parents. I did. But they deserved it. I
wouldn't hurt anyone else. I won't hurt you. I promise."

"I'm not worried. I'm not scared of you. I mean, don't take that
the wrong way. I'm sure you could kick my ass. I just mean in the
context you're describing. I'm not scared."

She is telling the truth. You can tell just from Eric's manner that
he is not the killing type.

Extenuating circumstances and all that.

"OK, so now we can proceed. Air cleared. Elephant slain."

They discuss and observe themselves and each other. Her: pretty normal childhood in Minnesota. Intimidating taste in books and movies but surprisingly conventional / mainstream taste in music. Fairly upbeat state of mind considering the circumstances. Strong believer in a person's ability to control their own mental weather regardless of exogenous storms. High level of baseline happiness. Is bothered by the fact that "baseline" does not rhyme with "Vaseline".

Him: strong upper body from doing 100 pushups twice / day since being institutionalized. Thick, coppery hair. Pale skin with patches of big, interconnected freckles. Hates TV. Stiff demeanor which may or may not be a shield.

"You wanna climb the tree?" she asks. She generally feels invincible or at least doesn't fear death. The idea scares him but he kind of likes this chick and doesn't wanna be a pussy.

"Yeah," Eric answers, a tad unconvincing.

She disappears up the tree like a sprite and now she's cackling 15 feet above him. Eric makes his way slowly up one of the branches but it sags under his weight and he loses his nerve.

"I'm too heavy," He looks up but can't see her. "Come back down."

Skitter, swing, hop. She's down. There is a huge smile on her face.

And an equally huge beetle in her hair.

"Holy shit."

"Yeah not bad, right?" She's beaming. Excited to be outside, excited to maybe have a friend or something.

"No. No. Like. Holy shit. There's a huge bug in your hair. Don't move."

Her skin goes from pale to milk. She is frozen. Not even a tremble. Truth be told Eric is kind of scared of the thing too, it's one of those huge kick ass intensely black Coleopterans with the sheeny shiny back and weird long proboscis. Eric leans forward and slowly moves to catch the beast. He snatches at it and pulls but it has attached itself to Audrey's hair Velcro-style and so he pulls a clump of hair with it and now he pulls harder and now she can't take it anymore and so the levee breaks and she starts screaming hair-raising screams of absolute terror like a fleeing rape victim or a winner on Oprah's favorite things.

Security Guy moves in and runs toward Eric as Francois follows a few steps behind. The security guard sees Eric ripping at Audrey's hair and saliva stranding her lips as she's still screaming and so he tackles Eric, taking him to the ground with utmost purpose. Thud. Wind, knocked out. Francois is mostly worried about Audrey and possible ramifications and future implications of this small experiment gone wrong. The beetle is free; it shuttles away.

"Stop it," Audrey weeps, "He was trying to help me."

Security Guy quickly senses that he's overplayed it. He awkwardly dismounts Eric and apologizes profusely now and it's only his first week on the job and he just got engaged and maybe he had too many 5-hour Energy drinks and he's really, really sorry and Eric is like:

"It's fine. It's fine. Audrey, you alright?"

But Francois ushers her away, afraid of what damage may have been caused to her and/or to his reputation. He needs to separate the two kids and reassess. But he's wrong to be concerned. Audrey is ecstatic. Recently she was more and more frustrated with the lack of meaningful experiences at her disposal. Trapped in that stupid white room, reading books. She was desperately parched for something real.

The last forty minutes: All these tiny experiences, meaningless in any broader context, were one million times more intense than the most epic adventure she could read about. A beetle in her hair, the screaming, pebbles stuck in her skin where she fell, friendship(?), white skin, fat lip, sunshine. A drip of blood from a scratch sustained descending the tree. Red beautiful dark half-dried blood on her calf.

Back in her room, Audrey goes straight to the bathroom mirror and surveys her reflected image. One word comes to mind. Ratty. Or is it natty? Ratty. Her heart races like that of a rabbit, chased. *Will I be allowed to see him again? I need to. I need a friend.* This is more than that. Maybe. *I think?* She sits down to write him a note and half an hour later a handwritten sonnet stares up from the page:

There was a girl who once penned a sonnet
And she met a boy, outside in the sun
Warning! There's a beetle in your bonnet
Security came and ended the fun
We should hang out again sometime, OK?
Even if you don't like me: Fresh air... Nice!
Would you share your music with me one day?
Dupechier can sign us out a device
I'll tell you two more things about myself
One day I will be a famous writer
I know I look pale but I'm in good helf
I don't smoke smokes so I need no lighter
I get it if I make you feel unease
I know this poem is totally cheese

Audrey reads the sonnet back and knows it's great but also knows it's full retard to communicate with this kid via iambic pentameter. But she likes the note and stops the insecure thoughts (she's good at that) and puts the scrawled message in an envelope and seals it with her venomous spit.

Eric gets the note from Dupechier the next day and he has to say it's a bold play though (as expected) he doesn't really appreciate the rigorous formatting requirements of the Shakespearean sonnet. He tells Dupechier to tell Audrey he would like to see her again and it has the feel of that grade 5 chestnut scribbled on a scrap of paper and passed in class: Tell Jenny to tell Ella that I like her.

■ ■ ■

Dupechier thinks it is a great idea to let the pair interact on a supervised basis and the one-hour sessions quickly become the light at the end of each week's tunnel. They talk with remarkable lightness for a couple of teenaged killers.

Audrey sips from a plastic cup of water through a thin red straw.
"You want some?"

He's thirsty and he thinks about it but then says:

"Nah, I'm good thanks,"

She puts her mouth around the top of the straw and talks to Eric.

"You want to see which letters of the alphabet make bubbles when you say them through a straw?"

Eric smiles but says nothing. He just looks at her dark brown eyes. She exudes a particular and intense energy. He likes it. She puts lips to straw and makes bubbles as she says the word "bubbles". Then she speaks the letters one by one with her mouth on the straw:

A: No bubbles.

B: YES!

C: No.

D: No.

E: No.

FFFFFFFFF: YES!

Eric laughs. He thinks it might be the first time he has laughed since arriving at CIC. Like, seriously. The first time.

G: No.

H: No.

I: No.

J: No.

K: No.

L: No.

M: YES!

N: No.

O: No.

P: BIG TIME!

Q: No.

R: No.

S: A little bit. Small bubbles.

T: No.

U: No.

V: Yes. A bit.

W: No.

X: No.

Y: No.

Z: Yes, but only when she pushes the Z out really loud.

"Bubbles are so much fun," she says.

It is the first warm day of April. 96% of the snow has melted away and the air smells beautiful and fresh and earthy and warm, like the top of a baby's head. She can taste thawing loam in her nasopharynx. The sun ever so gradually defrosts the brown lawn. Eric reaches out, takes Audrey's hand and holds it. She allows this for a moment then pulls away, more aggressively than intended.

"They told us no physical contact," says Audrey.

"They did. I'm sorry."

"Don't take it the wrong way. I just don't want to get banned. I really, really like you, Eric. If we were in the RW, I would *definitely* go on a date with you."

Eric smiles but feels mildly dissed. The Black starts to roll in and he wants to bolt and just run back to his room but he can't and he doesn't want to go into the Black especially not around Audrey and he knows the trick is to get some new thoughts before the Black takes over and paints his brain inky / dark.

"You wanna hear my latest?"

Latest music he means. He's been working like mad on his music trying to impress her but also as part of just getting through. Passing the time. So bored, all the time. And angry. Devil makes Black work for idle minds. She pops in his earbuds. He waits, anticipating her reaction, watching her face.

His latest piece is just unfuckingbelievable, like a thunderstorm of drums and piano. She looks at Eric and smiles a huge ecstatic smile that says "OMFG!". An electronic manifesto, Beethoven's "Rage Over a Lost Penny" meets Deadmau5's "Ghosts 'n Stuff". The audio tsunami crashes over Audrey's psyche and makes her want him in a different way than before. The music is a window into his mind.

She takes his hand and continues to listen and her hand is less cold than before. The piece, the song, whatever, it goes on for about seven minutes and she is never once bored or impatient and she is truly Listening the whole time to every little bit. No one has ever listened to his music like this before. To him like this before.

When it finishes, Audrey is spent. She makes bug eyes.

"Wow. Incredible. Shit."

Eric is kind of embarrassed now. He doesn't' really know how to take a compliment, having received very few.

"Ah, whatever. It's not that great."

"Dude, your music is so good. There are no words for this."

Eric shifts uncomfortably and looks down at his right shoe.

"OK. Anyway. You were saying you have something for me to read?"

She has been sharing short stories and poems with Eric. He likes them. Doesn't really always truly get them every time but he tries and it's fine. He is her muse. She unrolls a few pieces of paper jammed in her back pocket.

"Here. The latest and greatest."

He kind of doesn't want to use up all their time just sitting there reading but he's not sure if it would be insulting not to read it right away and so he rolls open the sheets and reads what she has hand-written in black scratchy pen:

■   ■   ■

Anabel is 7 years old, she wears a white cheap summer dress with a patterned print of orange daisies. It's a bit too big and not properly washed and there are fresh stains of orange popsicle on the front.

Anabel is running through a forest.

She has been running for as long as she can remember. Or, she can't remember anything before right now, as if she's entered a dream half-way through. The smell of Pop Tarts toasting flashes in her mind for a nanosecond (was I having breakfast with Dad?) then she hears branches crack behind her and leaves moving. There are footsteps coming towards her fast. Animal footsteps. Something is chasing her and so she keeps running. Keeps running.

The forest is mostly dead leaves and branchrot and plenty of open space. She jumps over a stream. She races over cracking twigs and mossy logs and a fairy circle of mushrooms. She keeps running. After a while the running is more like floating or going downhill; effortless.

Anabel comes to a small river and there is nowhere left to run and so she just goes full speed over the bank and dives in. Underwater. Silence. Effortless breaststrokes underwater; her dress is light and she is a good swimmer.

The river has barely any current and it's a 90 second swim across. The water is cold, like almost freezing. The arch of her left foot cramps up badly but she keeps swimming. Halfway across, something grabs at her from below. Slippery fingers, an unknown number of strong hands covered in algae, grab at her legs and feet, trying to pull her underwater.

She is strong enough to shake the hands loose at first and they can barely reach her as they extend up from the very bottom of the river. Anabel swims hard and nears the far bank when a hand finally gets a good grip on her right ankle. It pulls her under water a bit and she gasps for air and goes below the waterline and back above but her arms keep swimming and now she's very close to shore. What is this pulling at her? There are many hands grabbing at her, maybe five or six. She doesn't dare look.

There is a small tree at the edge of the muddy bank and Anabel lunges for it and wraps her freezing white hand around it with a firm grip. The fingers around her ankles are slippery and so she pulls herself free and up onto the shore and gets up. Without looking back, she starts to run again. She hears the chasing thing splash into the water at the far bank.

She runs and runs for like, ever.

Sun cuts in through gaps in the canopy, flickering as she runs, alternating with shadow. She remembers when her and Dad used to drive past the vineyards. How the rows of grape vines would flick by, one by one: flick, flick, flick, as if the world was spinning. The memory makes her dizzy and now it's less easy, then much less easy to run and she slows down. Her legs morph from flesh to stone. She collapses onto a bed of young ferns and blooming frost asters.

Anabel closes her eyes, knowing that whatever was chasing her will catch up soon and pounce and most definitely rip her into a thousand pieces. She goes fetal and closes her eyes tighter and tighter and tighter and tighter until the sides of her eyeballs hurt. She hears footsteps coming slowly, padding through the leaves.

The footsteps come closer. Closer and closer. But then she realizes they don't sound heavy or menacing. These are not monster footsteps. Anabel opens her eyes and there's a girl, maybe four years old, walking towards her. The girl is wearing a wet, dark red dress. She holds out a handful of orange daisies.

"Look. I picked these for you."

She holds out the flowers and Anabel takes them and hugs the girl, really tight. She looks down and sees the girl's bare feet and ankles are covered in dirt and bloody scratches. The small girl's hands are covered in blood. Anabel realizes the girl's dress is not red and wet but white and soaked in blood.

Behind the girls, a huge, dead tiger lays motionless by the riverbank. Its eyes have been removed and blackening blood flows from two empty eye sockets.

"I killed the tiger for you," she says.

"Are you sure it's dead?"

"Yes."

Anabel is confused. She should be happy that the tiger is dead but she is not. She feels glad and sad in exactly equal quantities which sum up to: Nothing.

But I loved the tiger.

Anabel finally mutters, through tears: "Thank you. Thank you for killing the tiger."

"Alison, why are you crying?" the girl asks Anabel.

"My name is Anabel, not Alison."

"Are you sure?"

■　■　■

Eric likes the story and asks: "Who is Alison?"

Audrey says: "I don't know."

■　■　■

Alison stops typing. Her mind floods, then breaks. She weeps. Uncontrollable sobs, like a 7-year-old girl.

■ ■ ■

"the money power preys upon the nation in times of peace and conspires against it in times of adversity. it is more despotic than monarchy, more insolent than autocracy, more selfish than bureaucracy."
abraham lincoln

■ ■ ■

1 YEAR BEFORE THE RESET

GREED

The point is, Mike realized early in his days on Wall Street, is that greed (and there is no better word for it) is good. Greed is fun. Greed works. It cuts through moral ambiguity and allows the speculator to pursue a sociopathic and single-minded self-interest. Greed, in all its forms—greed for excess, for profits, for snatch, for inside information—has marked the upward surge of Wall Street and American capitalism since those early days under the Buttonwood Tree.

But what Mike willfully ignores is that greed also breeds corruption and waste and accrues benefits only to those at the top. There is no such thing as trickle down. Greed has failed to save that malfunctioning corporation called the USA while enriching the corporations that make decisions based only on dollars and cents.

Let's say engineers at Profit Maximizing Car Corporation (PMCC) come up with a new safety latch that will help keep seatbelts in place in case of an accident. Comprehensive simulations show this innovation will save 14 lives per year. PMCC then simply multiplies the cost of the latch times the number of cars to get an incremental cost number. Let's say 10 million cars X $5 per latch = $50,000,000. So it costs $50 million to install the latch.

It then estimates, if the latch is not installed, how many out of the 14 customers killed will sue. PMCC then multiplies this projected number of lawsuits by the estimated payout per lawsuit. So say half the victims will sue and win an average of $3 million per settlement. 7 victims X $3,000,000 = $21,000,000. Whichever number is lower, that's the right decision. So PMCC is better off by a wide margin if they DO NOT install the safety latch. The correct decision is clearly not to install the latch and so they do not.

The decision is obvious. Right for the shareholders, and thus right for the corporation which is bound by duty to maximize shareholder value. Perhaps not right for the single mother of two who was launched through her windshield and into a lamppost head first when the seat belt failed. But hey, that one's a win. She's poor (and a bit of an idiot, honestly) and the corporation's lawyers bully her legal aid counsel into a $240,000 settlement.

*PMCC STOCK RALLIES AS Q3 EARNINGS BEAT ESTIMATES BY 4 CENTS.

Mike licks his upper lip then smells it. A vaguely vinegar smell. He smells it again. *Buzz. Buzz.* It's the burner phone he uses to communicate with the gnomes. These gnomes, which he calls "information consultants", are loosely scattered across the financial system, inside various corporations and in the big governmental statistical agencies. The moles are paid serious scratch to feed Mike actionable info. As a senior manager he's off the desk too much to come up with legit trading ideas anymore, so now his edge comes from his network of gnomes.

"Mike here."

"Friday payrolls. The number's gonna be strong. Headline, and details."

Click.

This is the kind of inside info that gets Mike hard. Literally. He texts one of his girls. The NYU art student who likes her hair pulled.

This dick ain't gonna suck itself, right?

She shows up in under half an hour and proceeds to give him a $350 celebratory blowjob in his wood-paneled office upstairs on 12.

Mike Leary: winning.

■ ■ ■

GRAND RAPIDS, MICHIGAN, WINTER, 1984

Mike Leary (age 13) stood outside, bouncing a tennis ball off the garage. The ball was defuzzed by age and hardened by the cold Michigan air. It made tiny dints in the garage. The dints were too small for Mike to notice from 20 feet away but his dad would notice them a few days later and there would be consequences.

Mike liked how the ball took weird bounces off the frozen strips of the DIY tar job that patched the driveway. It was getting hard to see the ball as the sun was mid-set but he was too lazy to go inside and work on his middle school Geography project. *Maps are so pointless, who cares about stupid Europe!* He heard a squeaking sound coming up the road. Evan's bike.

"Hey Evan."

"Hey."

"Wanna go for a ride?"

"Yeah, sure. Gotta be home by 8 though. Haven't done my homework."

"OK."

They rode off and out of the row house development with no destination and nothing in mind. Evan jumped a few curbs. They cut through the woods. Mike ducked under branches and sticks riffled and slapped at his pants. He saw something out the corner of his eye.

"Porcupine!"

"Cool."

A dead porcupine. Mike plucked a few quills from its cold, dead body and analyzed them. Stripey. With extreme caution, he tested their sharpness against the pad of his left index finger.

"Oww! Yep, they're sharp," he informed Evan.

"Awesome!" enthused Evan.

Mike put two quills in his winter jacket pocket, zipped the pocket and made a mental note not to put his hand in there later. Evan watched and commented:

246

"You sure that's a good idea?"

"I need them for my nature collection. You know the big mason jar?"

"Yeah I know. OK. Cool. Don't forget they're there though."

"They're there. That sounded funny."

"You're a retard."

Mike tried to roll the porcupine over with his foot a couple of times but the quills poked through the top of his shoe so he gave up. He picked up a crushed, rusty Fresca can and dropped it on the porcupine's head. It bounced off the dead animal and fell to the ground.

"Plonk," he said.

Mike looked around for something with more girth. He found a big rock and raised it up over the porcupine's head. Evan objected:

"Leave it. Let's go."

"Yeah, fine. You're so boring."

As Evan got on his bike and pedaled off, Mike dropped the rock onto the dead porcupine's head with a dull thump. The rock rolled aside and thick and dark red blood trickled out of the animal's mouth and eye sockets and collected on a curled-up leaf. Mike chuckled and hopped on his BMX.

They rode around but nothing much was going on. Nobody around. Nothing to do. Most people still probably finishing up dinner. They got to the hockey rink. Nobody was around but the lights were still on. Weird. The nets were put away so maybe someone just forgot to turn off the lights? They dropped their bikes and ran around on the ice for a bit. Sliding, slipping. The bum and knees of Evan's jeans were soon soaked from falling and then those wet patches started to freeze. *Crunchy*, he noted. Evan found a puck sitting on the boards.

"You think I can hit one of the lights with this?"

The lights were high above the ice. Standard height. 18 feet.

"Nah, way too high."

"Five bucks. Whoever hits one first."

Evan wasn't a bad kid. Just bored.

"Deal."

They attempted a few chucks but it was hard to brace on the slippery ice and they didn't come close to hitting the rink lights. Evan made another lame attempt and Mike slid in and caught the puck in the air as it came down. He walked off the ice, onto the frozen grass and fired a line drive that just missed the metal frame around the light.

"Cheater! You can't go on the grass!"

"Who said?"

Evan picked up the puck and went on the grass. He fired and put one off the metal frame. CLANK! Missed the bulb by maybe 5 inches. They looked around and obviously nobody heard so they started laughing like kids do. Mike ran and picked up the puck.

Two sharp blasts of a car horn cut the cold air.

"Hey! What are you kids doing? Get the fuck out of there!"

Grumpy old man in a family truckster station wagon. Wood paneling and a crooked rusty bumper. Not super threatening since he was on the other side of the road. The boys' heart rates went up but there was no need to flee.

"Yes, sir," said Evan.

"Yes, sir," said Mike.

Evan and Mike pretended to walk away and the man drove off, shaking his head. *Fucking kids.* Once the car disappeared around the corner, Evan and Mike turned around and headed back towards the rink.

Mike threw the puck up and missed short. Evan missed wide right. Mike ran onto the ice to grab the rolling puck.

"My turn."

Mike went back onto the grass. He eyed a specific light and started his windup like total Jack Morris style. The windup and... the pitch... STEE-RIKE! The puck crashed straight into the large halide bulb and the thing exploded like something out of a Robert Redford baseball movie. Sparks flew and glass rained down onto the ice. Mike took in all the information. The fizzing, smoking light above. The glass tinkling down onto the ice. He noticed it was pretty much dark outside now. There was a poorly lit, shadowy patch on the rink where the light should have been shining.

"Holy shit! Jackpot!!!"

Evan was gone, he bolted seconds earlier. Mike turned and ran for it, heading back towards his bike. Evan bounced along the frozen grass on his BMX and disappeared into the darkness but when Mike got to where his bike was supposed to be: no bike. He was sure this is where he left it. He looked around and soon saw the station wagon from before. Headlights off. The old man had turned around, come back, pulled over and put Mike's bike in the back.

"I told you kids to get the fuck out of here."

"I'm sorry sir. I'm really sorry. Can I please have my bike back?"

The man reached backwards and flipped open the back door, passenger side. Mike was close enough to see him now. Grey stubble on his face. Muscular like a guy that knows how to use a chainsaw. Ripped plaid shirt. The car smelled like wine.

"Get in the car."

Mike knew it was stupid to get into the car but he also knew if he went home with no bike there were going to be a lot of questions. Hard to answer ones. He looked around to see if anyone could help. Nobody. Just dark, empty night. In hindsight, he obviously should have got the license plate.

He got in the car and closed the door.

The car pulled away slowly. Country and Western was on the radio, barely audible, and Mike recognized Anne Murray but didn't know the song. The man flipped on the headlights and sped up. There was an open newspaper on the other back seat, open to the Classifieds Section. A few of the ads were circled. A can of Raid rolled back and forth on the floor in the back. The inside of the car smelled old, like damp fabric and sweaty McDonald's containers. Mike was kind of scared but weirdly he was mostly just thinking about how he needed to get home to get his geography homework done.

"Where are we going, sir? I just wanted my bike back. Please. I didn't mean anything back there. We were just goofing. I'll pay to fix the light. *Please*."

Mike and Evan never talked about that night. Mike never mentioned it to anyone. He figured he got his bike back and that was all that really mattered. He managed to black it out for most of his 20s. Later on, in his early 30s he flashed a few times to what happened that night in the man's dusty, cat-shit polluted basement. He could see the fossilized cat feces, small dried pools of hairball cat vomit on the floor. The disorganized piles of wrenches, pliers and screwdrivers on the guy's workbench. A Chock Full 'O Nuts brand coffee can full of unmatching screws. He could hear the ancient clothes dryer in the corner spinning with great effort. Thump thump, thump thump, thump thump. The musty tang of an unclean litter box. The man's smell, all damp hair and sweat.

It crossed his mind to go back to Michigan and find the guy and give him an amateur vasectomy and then kill him with a dull fishing knife or something like that. But Mike had moved to NYC by that time and if he did go back to Grand Rapids to disembowel the guy he'd have to at least stop by and see his mom after (she got super pissed if he came back to Michigan and didn't at least say hello) and that was too much hassle.

And the whole thing didn't matter anyway. No sense living in the past. *I'm a big swinging dick on Wall Street now. I got everything.* Better to just man up and move on. Plus, he kind of got even with the universe not too long after that when he lured that non-verbal retarded girl behind the 7-11 with banana popsicles then gave her a little bit of the old in out, in out.

She wouldn't stop crying the whole time.

"Before the end of the year 1795 the paper money was almost exclusively in the hands of the working classes, employees and men of small means, whose property was not large enough to invest in stores of goods or national lands. Financiers and men of large means were shrewd enough to put as much of their property as possible into objects of permanent value. The working classes had no such foresight or skill or means. On them finally came the great crushing weight of the loss. After the first collapse came up the cries of the starving."

Fiat Money in France, Andrew Dickson Smith, 1896

337 DAYS BEFORE THE RESET

I haven't dropped a drip of Sight in six weeks now and no coke and maybe three or four beers and 6 or 7 cigarettes max. Doing a decent job overall. I'm trying to be a normal person. Be a dad. But the temptation to go out tonight is just incredibly strong. flatland is playing her biggest gig yet and it's invite-only and all kinds of minor celebrities and most of my friends and Alison and basically everybody is going to be there. 7six7 is spinning in the other room so this is going to be a mofo of a show and I've got FOMO and I'm really capital J Jonesing to get out and get on it. One last time.

Change the subject.

"Seven, you wanna go play catch?"

We play catch in Central Park. The American cliché father and son thing to do and I love it. We grab an ice cream and Seven notices my wallet is full of fifties and hundreds.

"Hey Dad. Why do you have so much money? Mom and I never had money."

"Oh man. That's a tough one. Let's just say... I'm really good at playing this video game called 'the stock market'. And the way capitalism works is that if you are good at something that hardly anyone else is good at, you get paid a lot. Regardless of whether you are adding anything to the real world or not."

"Like baseball players?"

"Yeah. I guess. But baseball players entertain people. They make people happy or distract them from the hard parts of real life. I just play a video game. So for me, it is a really good deal because I get to make a lot of money and that helps me take care of myself and take care of you. Some people think that the market helps the economy grow and that used to be true. But now the market is just kind of a separate thing from the real economy. It has nothing to do with the real world anymore."

Seven stopped listening, but that's fine. He doesn't need to hear the cynic's take anyway. It takes more courage to be optimistic than it does to be cynical. I hate when I'm cynical. It's so easy. So lazy. Dad used to say: "Don't mistake cynicism for intellect".

I pay my taxes; I try to be a good person. Not everyone can be a teacher or a doctor or obvious contributor. The world needs people to grease the machine too. Garbage men, baristas, traders. Tiny cogs that may or not play a role in the giant machine that grinds us ever forward. There is no need to brand myself morally inferior. Kings are not inherently worth more than serfs. Emperors are not worth more than salarymen.

I have firmly realized as my life evens out and I become less degenerate daily that Seven is my savior. He is my ticket out, my reason to stop acting like a sketchpad and get my life together and monetize the trading opportunities and choose life and all that.

And anyway, I noticed over the past year (pre-Seven) that each night out gets a little darker. The specter of addiction lurks, subtle but clearly there. I'm drinking because I'm bored. Because there's beer in the fridge. Snorting Sunday because I have two grams left from Saturday and I can't control myself and can't bring myself to flush the shit down the toilet where it belongs.

So instead of raging nights out with groups of friends making new highs, the last few years have been a lot more just me or maybe me and one other friend cutting lines until the birds tweet outside and then sleeping in until 4:00 PM. Less fun. More dark. I barely go out anymore for obvious reasons but I have done the babysitter thing a few times and gone out to party. It is not fun anymore. I need to make a firm stop. Draw a red line. I am a dad. I have responsibilities.

Just one more night. Please? Go see flatland one more time?

Maybe I'll do just one last hurrah. And then I'll go cold turkey. Completely. That's a fair trade off.

One more night and then never again. I promise.

Not one more drop. Not one more line. Not one more drink. Not even another smoke. Deal?

OK, deal.

You've made this deal many times before and reneged.

Yeah, I know. But this time it's for reals.

But dude, what about Seven?

We can get a babysitter.

OK fine but you promise this is really and truly the final big one and then we completely shut it down?

Yes.

OK.

OK?

OK.

The decision has been made and the voices quiet down and there is no more debate. Adrenaline pumps and endorphins release in Pavlovian fashion as I anticipate the Drop. Railing the coke. Sucking a Cig-O without having to peek around the corner to see if my son is watching. My son? What the? How did that happen? I am way, way too immature to have a son.

I text flatland and she's all: "ok great but no pressure man. i know you have responsibilities now." And I'm all: "Dude, don't make me sound like a grandpa." And she's all typical flatland: "just saying. there are more important things than uncle robo." She will be a better parent than me. Way more level-headed and responsible. She is a better person than me.

I text Danny but hear nothing back after half an hour. Usually his response time is sub 60 seconds. I go off the matrix for three weeks and already the guy's forsaken me? Call me back, dude! I text Alison. She's excited; glad to hear from me. I have no idea where she is right now. She's been jonesing to get messed up too but has been polite enough to keep it to herself.

"Any suggestions on a babysitter?"

"Yeah, sure." Alison's on the ball. "My friend Ella. She's got a little sister. 17. She's perfect."

"What about reservations? I can't get in touch with Danny."

Reservations = code for drugs. Can't be too careful with the NSA and others listening.

"I'll take care of it."

She texts me the dets on the babysitter and 45 minutes later I'm showered and smelling soapy clean. Intercom buzzes. 17-year-old child woman walks into my apartment (the babysitter) and I'm Gonzo. I give her the instructions. Not overly complicated. And my phone number.

"We booked a hotel for tonight. See you around noon tomorrow, OK?"

"OK. Sounds good. I'll put him to bed around eight for sure."

The apartment door closes and I am insanely pumped. The guilty voices are quiet now. Let's get this shit started! Heartbeat accelerates. My mind tries to tell me that the anticipation of the event is often more enjoyable than the event itself these days. I tell my mind to please be quiet.

■ ■ ■

3:10 AM

I am a dark, heavy sort of fucked up. Wired as hell but tired and pangs of guilt buzz like noisy, invisible black flies I cannot swat away. THC gummies make me paranoid. A guy with the eyes of the devil passes in a shirt that reads: *Imma bang your girlfriend*. Sweat pours down the walls and wet drops shimmer on dark paint. Sweat pours down my face. Beads of liquid trickle down the black painted and repainted walls of the club and are cut by laser light and tremble from the buzzing bass vibrations as flatland flattens the heaving mass. Drops of water fall or don't fall on my head.

My vision is composed of partial and badly rendered 3D images. A full-on Robo moment as 1,100 souls march in synch like old North Korean military footage. My eyes knock around like marbles in their sockets and my hair may or may not be crawling off the top of my head and down my back.

For some reason I cannot get the bartender's attention as she darts around serving everyone but me.

I just want a water. Please.

She passes me again. I am actually invisible.

Alison is manic. Hyperactive. Overhappy. She screams way too loud:

"This is so amazing!"

"Yeah."

"It's nice to see the real you again! Out having fun!"

This is not the real me. Alison dumps a wildly inappropriate amount of Special K onto the back of her hand and while I have zero interest and I just want the night to be over, I snort it. Because that's what you do. And then very soon after—

Dropping. Dropping. The combination of horse tranquilizer, THC, cocaine and Sight give me a bad feeling of unexpected downward acceleration. I don't like it. I need to go sit down. I sit on a bench, alone at the edge of the club. Alison has rejoined the heaving throng. I fall through darkness. Urge to puke. Dark energy pulls me down through the floor and towards the center of the earth. Psychic blackout. My mind is a vacuum. Hours pass. Maybe seconds.

A fleeting thought enters my mind. One of those voices that is you but cannot be you. *I want to be free of this. I do not want a son.* Then I am truly sorry for thinking that. That is wrong. I don't wish that. I did not just wish that.

Too many bad thoughts.

One time I wished for something really bad to happen to Scott Mitchell after he used an angled cafeteria tray to piss into my locker through the bottom vents. Now the memory of what happened three months after I made the wish runs on the big screen in my head:

Scott Mitchell stands on the sidewalk, staring down the barrel of four lanes of traffic on Richmond Road. The traffic is heavy in both directions and it's going pretty fast, maybe 40mph. Rob Parsons puffs on a cigarette like he's too cool for school and waits for a gap in the traffic so he can cross along with Scott. They're going to buy comics. Scott looks to the right. Rob yells: GO! A terrible joke.

Scott goes.

There was no gap in the traffic. 30 or 40 kids are sitting on the grass hill, eating lunch, including me. A crunch sound that can never be unheard. Scott is a flying, bloody rag doll. DOA.

Be careful what you wish for.

My leg buzzes... I think? It buzzes again. The bass is so insane it's making my right leg buzz. I don't like the feeling the third time. I'm sketching out. The girl beside me laughs and I look and she is gone or was there ever a girl next to me or was it the music? My vision is discontinuous; everything unfolds in front of me like a flipbook.

Buzz. I tap around at my legs and arms to stop it and finally after maybe 10 seconds or 20 minutes I'm not sure but I realize that it is my phone buzzing. Nine new texts. I struggle to focus and read the texts:

Seven cut his arm.

It's bleeding really badly. call me?

I wrapped it up with a t-shirt. Can't find bandages.

Still bleeding. Seven crying a lot.

Going to the hospital.

At hospital waiting. Bleeding has stopped I think.

If you get any of these txts, call me or txt back. I need your help.

Doctor came. Finally.

Bleeding stopped. Do you have health insurance? Please call me.

Alison finds me standing there mute. No idea what to do. She's got her shit together still but I'm completely convoluted. Twenty minutes ago, I was in The Box with my eyes closed, standing on a circular carpet and flying 100 mph about 10 feet above sea level over some sort of entirely blue planet with little islands in the shape of the word "island" spelled out in flashing neon letters. Real life has poked its freaky albino head through the inter-dimensional curtain and into my distressed world and I do not know what to do. This is bad. I show her the texts.

"We need to get to the hospital," she says.

"I can't go into the real world. I can't function. I can barely talk, Alison."

"You have to. We have to go."

"OK."

I send specific commands to my feet, asking them please to take me where I need to go. I go into the bathroom to see if I can find a window through which I might peak into reality. I look into the scratched mirror. Green toilet stalls behind me scream "Flush!". The words "ASS FUCK THE RICH" scribbled in Sharpie on the mirror. Kids pass. Water running. PSSHHHHHH. PSHSHSHHHHHH.

OK. You're at a club. In New York. *Charlie? You with me?* You're at a club in New York. Seven is hurt but he's going to be fine. BANG! WSHSHHHHHHHHHHHH! A hand dryer turns on, shattering the first attempt to defrag my thoughts. I look in the mirror at my face. It is white, completely blank. I am lost.

I force a smile in the mirror. Smiling makes me feel better. Trust your instincts. Don't talk unless you need to. One foot in front of the other. The next few hours are going to be absolute hell and there is no way to change that fact at this point. Thoughts of backward time travel. Decisions altered. *Stop it.* How long have I been in this bathroom? It's empty now. I can hear flatland's work flowing out of the speakers still. I don't want to leave. I have to leave. I said I don't want to. *You have to.* I walk out of the bathroom and Alison is standing there, smiling. Patient. Angel.

"You are the most beautiful thing in the world."

She tries to smile, then shuttles me along like the loving mother of a severely retarded teen.

The Lyft ride is mental torment as raging self-hatred has gripped me completely. What kind of sad idiot leaves a kid at home with a 17-year-old babysitter and then tells her: back at noon, see you tomorrow! Ass. Idiot. Degenerate. Addict. Actual worst human being in the world. Alison is holding my hand but I pull it away. *I am not worthy of love.* Electric ants crawl up my arms. Every turn in the Lyft brings hellish centrifugal nausea.

The hospital is impossibly bright. White and bustling with clangy, acrid smells. Vinegar, Purell, pus, fresh paint. Computers on wheely stands everywhere. Bags of Ringer's Lactate hang from dangly metal ceiling hooks. Everything is bathed in impossibly harsh light. *You are inside a UFO and they are conducting experiments on humans.*

No no no no. Not true.

Seven is in side room B3 with the doctor, getting fixed up. Eight stitches. I am ashamed to see him. I let him down massively, whether or not he realizes it. He probably won't. Kids are really bad at noticing things that are super obvious to adults but then they are amazing at observing things that adults totally miss.

There are tubes and machinery. The machine that goes beep beeps at perfect intervals. Beep..............Beep...............Beep...............

A lavender latex glove sticks out of a box of lavender latex gloves like a pastel tongue. Philips monitors draw green lines that move in a smooth and oddly satisfying way from left to right. So much beige. A woman behind a pale blue curtain in B2 cries from the pain and between sobs she begs:

"I need some OxyContin. Please."

The big fat nurse is talking to Alison. There is a chocolate milk stain right by her belly button area. Her name tag is blue and rectangular with a surprisingly modern recessed white font with black edging. It says Cheyenne. Shy Anne. I mouth it; maybe say it out loud? Dying for a vending machine treat. Twizzlers maybe. Shy Anne. Shy Anne. *Can I smoke in here?*

"He's the dad. Sorry, he's just really drunk," Alison says.

"It's OK. I'm not drunk. Just had a few beers," I slur.

A PA announcement blares. I flinch, visibly. I may have just ducked.

"Let's sit you down, sir."

I sit down over in the corner and just veg / trip out for a while. Women's magazines scattered. TV news squawking about a horrific stretch limousine crash. A nerdy little 14-year-old with a peach fuzz moustache and a black Donkey Kong t-shirt cries in the corner. Hit his head or something. I can't fall asleep here, it's too uncomfor—

I fall asleep.

...

A long dream. It's winter. My dad and I are walking through a forest of pines but he's way up ahead and yelling for me to hurry up. I'm going as fast as I can but I can only see glimpses of him up ahead. I keep up by following his footsteps in the snow. First a drizzle then torrential rain falls and the snow melts and Dad gets further and further ahead. The footprints disappear and I cannot follow. Bats, or maybe holes in the sky shaped like bats, circle. One dives at me.

...

I wake up, horizontal across three chairs. Seven is tapping me on the shoulder.

"Dad. You OK? Wake up."

I love it when he calls me Dad. My eyes open and meet his and he's confused and tired and I am ashamed to say he is a lot more mature and stronger than I am right now. The Sight has worn off a bit thank God but I'm still all sketched out from the coke and the Special K and this is the last time this will ever happen again. The. Last. Fucking. Time.

"Yeah, I'm fine bud. We're going to be fine."

I look over and see Alison, the trooper. She has weathered the last two hours alone like a hero while I slept like a complete loser as my son was treated for profuse bleeding caused by a wayward paring knife. A cutting board with pieces of drying apple splattered in blood sits on my counter at home. I hug Seven way too hard and while I know this night has been a complete disaster from a parenting point of view it will be a win in the long run because I am never going to touch another chemical again in my life. This is not a bullshit promise. This is it.

Thank you, God, that the consequences of my terrible decision making were not more severe.

This is the last night of this bullshit. Ever.

■ ■ ■

After the incident with the knife and the hospital, a switch flipped inside my mind. An addiction is never truly gone in theory so perhaps the correct phrasing would be that my addictions suddenly became wholly manageable. The voices still call for me to do coke and drink and drop Sight but I own the voices now; they do not own me. The voices are more like what you hear when you have that urge to push someone off the subway platform or punch someone in the face. Urges easily suppressed. They simply bubble up and disappear before my mind can consider acting on them. Bubble. Pop.

Alison was also deeply disturbed by that evening but the impact on her addictions was nil. She is dying to go out and chase the night still and she knows, even consciously, it isn't so much that she wants to see her friends or have a good time or enjoy music. She simply wants to fill her skull with chemicals. All the time. It is the chemicals that she really misses. The way all the anger and fear and tension in her mind just fall away when she is high. Almost like the actual high isn't the thing but more the absence of low.

Post-hospital, I am super serious about protecting Seven and keeping the drugs and alcohol thing away. I barely see any of my friends at all since almost every engagement or encounter with a friend necessarily involves drinking or snorting some sort of powder. Getting blitzed is the common thread in every single one of my friendships and so I have no place for that type of friendship anymore. I guess I need some new friends.

Alison and I wrote up a contract, printed it out and signed it.

I, Charlie Bloom and I, Alison Leary, hereby declare that we will not consume any illicit recreational drugs ever again, from this point forward. As adults with responsibilities we do make this declaration. Signed,
　　Charlie and Alison

Alison has been kind of uncomfortable throughout the process of drawing up and signing the contract as it just seems like an incredible buzzkill to her but it is non-negotiable for me and she gets it. A big part of her knows that it is boring but also necessary. She asked for a few exceptions. What about birthdays? No. What about New Year's? No.

It was easier for me. After that night at the hospital, drugs are simply no longer an option. There was no thought process or debate necessary. Like killing a cat with my bare hands is not an option. It is unambiguous.

While the contract has turned me into a somewhat reclusive but very engaged father, Alison still goes out here and there with her friends.

■ ■ ■

330 DAYS BEFORE THE RESET

Alison has stuck to the no drugs contract, drinking only alcohol for the past seven days despite the raging, throbbing psychic pain and screaming desire. Has it only been seven days? *This is going to be impossible.* She wants to do just one more line of blow or one more drop of Sight. *Please, God.*

It might seem odd to pray to God for drugs but Alison sees God not as benevolent ruler, nor as indifferent observer… She sees God as a mentally ill prankster. It is the only theory of God consistent with the data she has collected over many years. So, yeah, praying for drugs is perfectly consistent with her concept of God.

Please. God. Give me drugs.

In the old days a normal night out might end at 3:30 AM or maybe even 9:00 AM but without chemical enhancement Alison now finds herself squishy and exhausted by 10:30 PM or 11:00 PM, her brain screaming and scheming for chemicals. Going from turbo coked up nights to just drinking reveals what a depressing and dumb drug alcohol actually is. Sloppy. She can barely hold a conversation past 10:00 PM as she is too drunk and the inside voices scream for drugs so loudly that outside voices barely register.

As Charlie puts Seven to bed, Alison takes out a Mead notebook (Alison's Funderland #41) and starts to write. She finds romance and tragedy too simplistic. Unrealistic. She favors ironic stuff like Richard Cory or *Fight Club* or Romeo and Juliet. She's never been suicidal but absolutely loves the fact that Richard Cory (spoiler alert!) kills himself—genius. She tries to write as much as possible but finds it comes in bursts and mostly when she's high.

Bursts of material that seem thematically related but a little too incoherent to work as a manuscript. She collects reams and reams of handwritten paragraphs in Mead notebooks with green covers. Much of the writing features recurring characters and recurring themes and so someday she might stitch them all together into some sort of megaquilt patchwork novel thingamajig that might work for some reader somewhere.

In the margins and interspersed within the stories and half stories and ramblings are skilled, hyperrealistic line drawings done in Bic fine point black. Dragons and sick kids with giant heads and giant feral bananas eating dead monkeys. A homeless man with a huge snake bite on his leg. A big dog fucking a small cat. When alone on random weeknights, she used to like to drip 15 mills of Sight and do a few lines of coke or meth and fill page after page with words and images. Uncurated collections of high and low quality mental ejaculation.

Alison sits uninspired on the couch, waiting for Charlie to come back. He disappeared half an hour ago. Went to brush Seven's teeth and tuck him into bed. Tired of waiting, she sticks her head through the doorway and sees Charlie asleep next to Seven; they're snuggled in the bed with Charlie on top of the sheets and Seven underneath. Alison hates herself for the flash of a thought of her dad and all the bad things.

She knows Charlie is good and she knows he loves Seven and she knows she loves Charlie and Charlie is nothing like her fucking piece of shit Dad. Charlie is the opposite. She sees him in a moment of clarity. All the good he represents; her future. *You are good, Charlie.* Maybe too good, though? *Do I deserve someone like you?* She kisses him on the cheek and goes back to watch TV.

Flips on CNN to see what's what. Financial turmoil continues. Civil unrest in China spreads. Japanese economy records ninth straight quarter of negative growth. Blurgity blah blurg. Business news. So crazy boring. New channel. News again. A homeless man is smothered to death by construction workers after he is caught shoplifting bottles of water. Local children's librarian fired after child sex scandal. All bad news, all the time.

She despises the mainstream media. How it makes scary, ultra-rare events seem highly probable and encourages an elevated national fear of extremely unlikely modes of death. 110 people died in terrorist attacks last year (which is like 3.666667×10^{-5} percent of the population which is ~0) and yet heavy coverage. Where are the news features about the victims of big pharma? Hundreds of thousands of them. There isn't enough airtime on every news channel combined for a postmortem fluff piece on each modern pharmacology victim yet two worthless Midwesterners are shot in the face by a radicalized teen and we get a 20-minute commemoration of their so-called lives.

Why did no one else see this? Fiery car crashes, shooting rampages and freak accidents pepper viewers who should be more worried about death from a sugar-filled processed food diet than from suicidal airplane pilots or explosive vests. Who watches this shit and believes it to be the reality we inhabit? Plot a chart of probable causes of death and you have to go way way out to find anything newsworthy, so why are we so obsessed with hearing on-location recaps of these low-probability events and interviews with the families of the victims thereof?

She turns off the TV and writes a quick note to Charlie. "Went for a walk. Back around 11."

As she prepares to leave, Alison checks herself in the mirror and thinks "a little too upper-middle-class". Street crime is a real risk these days so best not to exude any hint of wealth. She changes into a white t-shirt and a slightly discolored green vintage cardigan with two exterior pockets. She puts her hair up. That's better.

Alison gets on the elevator and half-smiles at a Mexican line cook (from a Greek deli) on the ride down; he just delivered two pastramis on light rye with extra pickles to 27J. A streak of dried mustard stains his apron like splattered ochre paint. The line cook has that dank mungy smell of someone who spends a lot of time near the dishwasher, at the back of the restaurant. He stares down through the hole in his worn-out New Balance sneaks and through the smaller hole in the top of his greasy sock and wiggles his partially visible big toe.

Alison pops out of the elevator, crosses the lobby, 180s the revolving door and heads out into 10:07 PM NYC. The New York air is cold, pungent and sour, redolent of burnt hair and parmesan. She pops in her earbuds and hits play on Bill Withers: "Lovely Day". Catches her reflection in a store window and thinks: *looking pretty cool*. Fit, maybe not model hot but skinny and cute at least (maybe)? Dying for a cigarette but trying to hold off so as not to disappoint Charlie or herself.

The Upper West Side homeless have multiplied; they slump in shadows, asleep against boarded storefronts. Soggy blankets and cardboard windstops and licked-clean takeout containers and hand-drawn signs that read simply: Help me. The wind whips up wrappers and garbage out of drifts that line curbs all the way up and down Broadway. A thin light brown wax paper wrapper from the bottom of a Reese's Peanut Butter Cup floats up on a light gust and presses flat against the front of Alison's leg. It sticks there for a few seconds as if to say "hello".

"Hello," Alison says to the wrapper. It flutters on its way. It feels to her like a cryptic message from The Universe or something.

"You are weird," she says out loud to herself (and agrees silently).

She passes one particularly savage casualty of the US health care system. He is surrounded by a wide whiff circle of heavy piss and sweat. Like urine to the 5th power, he emanates a thick bleach-like stench that triggers Alison's gag reflex as she passes. She hurries off, breath held.

The decline of New York City has been slow and gradual. Hard to notice. At first just the black gum spots and the familiar shitsmears of mostly-picked-up dog poo and then more garbage then entire garbage bags and then everyone stopped picking up their dogshit altogether. Windswept garbage swirls even in upscale gentrified areas and cigarette butts and crushed water bottles and empty ketchup and soy sauce packets and miscellaneous and crumpled bits of paper float above the dark brown shit stains that spread across sidewalk squares like Nutella on concrete toast.

Up and down Broadway, more and more stores are closing. Darkened sections of the bisecting diagonal avenue provide proof of the irreversible irrelevance of retail. The cheap stores and restaurants are still packed. 80 people in line at Gray's Papaya. And the high end booms. "That new French-Korean place! Three month waiting list! But it's sooo worth it! Ohmigod the dumplings!" There is only high-end and low-end now. Nothing in the middle because there is nobody in the middle.

The only other growth segment in Manhattan retail is gold shops. Everyone wants physical gold. Hard assets trade at a huge premium to paper assets with the basis between physical gold and futures almost $100 these days. Diamonds, silver, gold... The people want hard assets.

Alison walks for about five minutes but feels uncomfortable because there's barely anyone out tonight and it's not really a good idea for a single girl to be walking alone on the Upper West these days. Plus, with half the stores dark, there isn't enough light to feel safe. Her Spidey Senses tingle and she thinks "better go home".

Spray painted in massive army green letters on a brick wall: *"Where are the cops?"* and echoed in neon orange spray paint, much smaller underneath: *"Donde esta la policia?"*

Alison picks up the pace as she enters a 50-foot long dark patch cast by four straight vacant stores. Halfway through the darkness, three skinny wiggers on skateboards roll out of nowhere.

"Give us your phone, betch."

"It's biometric guys. Come on. You won't even be able to turn it on."

"You heard the kid. He said give us your fucking phone, bitch."

She hears a faint ripple of nervous insecurity behind the punk's swagger.

Alison reaches around with her right hand, into the back of her pants. She holds her hand behind her back and hears herself say:

"Do you fucking idiots know what a Glock looks like?" Her eyes dart, casting a bit of crazy at each of the three kids. "You want to see one?"

There is also a bit of crazy in her voice and this isn't an unrealistic bluff as NYC gun ownership has skyrocketed in the past few years.

"If you bluffin' you got balls, betch."

The three boys are unarmed and nervous. Two of them are 15. The 14-year-old twitches. They wanna stay cool but they also don't want to get shot in the face. They look at each other and Alison pulls a heavy steel pistol out of the back of her pants. She holds it up sideways like a bad ass movie G, closes her left eye and aims at one of the kids. The three kids spin, hop on their boards and roll off into the darkness. They disappear. Alison puts the gun back in her pants.

She walks on, shaken. Trembling. She can feel the cold metal of the movie prop gun she bought a few months ago against the small of her back and she thinks for a second how if those kids had real guns she would probably be lying in a puddle of blood back there right now. *You are so stupid.* She feels like an idiot for having bought the fake pistol and so she pulls it back out and drops it into a garbage can. She takes a detour on the way home to buy a pack of cigarettes. To calm the nerves.

Should I tell Charlie what happened? Probably not. Another case of bad judgment. She feels really self-conscious about her bad judgment these days as it pertains to how Charlie sees her even though he has never mentioned anything of the sort even once. She feels like a child and Charlie is an adult and it is way too obvious for him not to notice it. He is not judgmental but she constantly feels judged. She enters the bodega. Cigarettes are not getting any cheaper.

"Forty-five dollars please."

Alison touches her phone to the scanner and the payment drops electronically from her account. *Charlie knows my password; he might see I bought cigarettes. What are we, married now? I can't buy a pack of cigarettes without feeling bad? He's just trying to do the right thing, take care of his son. It's not his fault you're thinking all these crazy fucking thoughts. They're gonna add a chapter about you to the DSM-V. Just chill the fuck out.* And so on.

Alison unwraps the pack, tosses the foil as she exits and pops the filtered end of the cigarette in her mouth. She opens the book of matches, rips off a match and drags the potassium chlorate, sulfur, red phosphorous and powdered glass of its head against the sand, powdered glass and red phosphorous of the striking surface on the matchbook. This friction causes heat which turns the red phosphorous to white phosphorous. The resulting flame burns slowly down the coated paper match until she puts the tip of her cigarette to it. She inhales, pulling air through the delicious tubular treat. The tobacco burns and the cigarette is lit.

The first inhale is delicious and tastes faintly of caramel. She flashes back to Guverment 2.0 in Toronto and a particularly pleasant cigarette she smoked that night. A few happy brain circuits crackle and flip to the on position and dopamine fires. She tilts her head back and watches dual streams of smoke exit her nostrils and rise up into the moist air.

She's barely done the first exhale when a homeless kid appears out of nowhere and asks to bum a smoke. She pulls out three and hands them off and he trudges away without saying thank you.

A properly enjoyed actual tobacco-filled cigarette takes about five minutes to smoke and in the four minutes that it takes her to smoke 80 percent of this one she is approached by four different people asking for cigarettes and/or money. Finally, she flicks the mostly smoked butt onto the ground and it emits a quick hiss as it expires in a tiny puddle. The puddle reflects the lights of the building behind her.

She reflects for a flash on the alarming pace at which the city is circling down, down, down into the toilet. Little does she know, the smear of dog shit she just stepped over was in fact human shit. Broken Windows theory has been revealed as a sham. Republicans love to give Giuliani credit for his Broken Windows theory and how it saved New York but every other city in the USA saw a massive drop in crime at the same time. Correlation and causation confusion. Now the cops have given up on the theory. Not enough cops to enforce every tiny infraction anyway. Vandalism and graffiti and aggressive begging go on pretty much unchecked now. Foodswiping is a scourge.

*NYPD LAYS OFF 1,400 OFFICERS AFTER NEW ROUND OF BUDGET CUTS

Alison thinks about how Charlie does not really need her the way she needs him. Especially now that Seven is here and has "saved" him from his demons. *Who's going to save me, then?* When the three of them are together she often feels redundant, like a totally completely useless adverb. Like Hoboken feels when it hangs out with New York and Brooklyn. Unnecessary.

I am unnecessary.

Her heart rate is not yet back to normal from the skater incident and she has that nervous tweaky feeling she used to get for days after a major coke binge. Well-trafficked neural pathways fire. Her thoughts are like hikers, always trying to get back to the worn pathways in her mind. Those pathways all lead to the same place. Her mind gaps past justification, skips internal dialogue and now she is texting her dealer:

You around?

Distant, barely discernible flickers of conscience attempt to intervene: *Charlie's gonna kill you*, etc. but those thoughts are like piccolos played by children behind a booming adult marching band. Addiction: tubas and bass drums. Logic: piccolo. The heart pounds and dopamine fires again now in anticipation of the drug and probably drugs and now she is just thinking: Where should I go? Who should I call? And a brief thought enters: *I really just want to get high with Charlie.* And knowing the extreme disappointment and disgust that will be showered upon her tomorrow she feels like the convict doing one more huge night out before heading to prison.

The night lasts 7 hours but it feels like 7 minutes. The last thing she remembers is asking someone she doesn't recognize to help her call a Lyft because: "My fingers are not too accurate, sorry".

■ ■ ■

"Dad! Dad! Wake up!"

It's Seven calling me from the bathroom. I climb out of bed and throw on a pair of underwear and a T-shirt. It's 6:50 AM. I notice right away that Alison is not in bed which is weird. I walk into the bathroom, and into a complete disaster.

There is orange puke splattered on the inside of the toilet bowl and all over the toilet seat. There is dried orange hurl in splotchy patches on the floor. Bits of ziti from our dinner last night are still clearly identifiable inside the drying splattered puddles of orange and red that have been orally broadcast onto bathroom tile. Alison is fully dressed, asleep in the bathtub.

I cannot deal with this. This is not fucking cool.

"Alison has the flu, Seven. Go play some vids."

Seven exits. Alison stirs. Her left eye flips open. She gives me the guilty look of a puppy that just ate through an entire bag of cookies. I won't fall for it.

"Listen Alison. I know this is not much fun but I have responsibility here. I'm sorry. Please get out of here okay?"

"What? What do you mean get out?"

Her breath is ghoulish like acid, hell and plague.

"I'm asking you to leave Alison. This isn't working. This is not cool. It's not what we agreed."

I try not to get angry but I want to physically drag her out of here and throw her into the hallway. Does she not realize I have a kid to take care of here? What the actual fuck.

"It was just booze Charlie. I just got too drunk that's all. I didn't touch any drugs. I promise. I know we have an agreement."

"But that's not the point. That's not the spirit of it. You getting hammered and coming back in the middle of night and puking and then falling asleep in the bathtub. Do you think that's the spirit of what we agreed? Please Alison. I can't do this okay? I just can't manage all this. I need you to act like an adult."

"I don't want to be an adult!"

Now Alison is crying and stuffing shit into her backpack and she looks like absolute hell and I feel sorry for her and I feel happy that I'm not jealous that she went out and got wasted last night. In fact, I feel vaguely superior at the knowledge that I'm glad I stayed in last night. That old feeling of missing out is gone. I don't really want her to go but I already said so and she's already going, going and now she's gone. She's hysterical as she leaves but she holds it inside because Seven is standing there watching.

"Is she okay?"

"I'm not sure buddy. I'm not totally sure."

There is no time to contemplate or brood because I have to get Seven ready for school. He brushes his teeth and all that and picks out an orange long-sleeve T and a pair of maroon pants. And blue socks. I throw together his lunch and grab his homework and books and load his backpack. It dawns on me that I don't even know where Alison would go right now. I text her an apology:

I overreacted

Come back when you're ready

We can figure it out

I imagine myself in Alison's shoes and how shitty she must feel and I feel super shitty for making her feel so shitty. I fight off the urge to cry. This is not the only incident. Things have been hard between us lately. There is no rock bottom, only lower lows.

A few nights ago, we were having sex with the lights on and Alison looked at me and I saw something really strange in her eyes. A sudden look of fear, out of nowhere. I am positive she saw me as her father for a second. A brutal flash in her mind that I could see and it made us both recoil. We slipped apart and never got back together. Something between us broke at that moment.

But I still love her. I feel responsible for her. As I go to text her that I love her, she texts me first.

Okay I'm not ready right now

I need to think about what I want

What I'm doing

I don't know if I'm ready to be what you need me to be.

I need to let her sort her own shit out so I just text back:

OK.

My phone sends me a ↑Marketz!↓ update. Japan down 3%. DAX down 4%. Palladium is up 40 bucks which is completely bizarre, especially with oil and gold both lower.

"Dad! Let's go. We're gonna miss the bus!"

■ ■ ■

328 DAYS BEFORE THE RESET

I am starting to be okay with the whole "I'm a dad" thing. Seven is an amazing little human and we are developing some sort of real relationship. I don't know where I fit in as far as he is concerned. He doesn't really require any discipline so I am somewhere between big brother and father in his mind, I guess. I've quit smoking and zeroed the drinking. Life is clean and sober and good. The saying is true: drinking is just borrowing happiness from tomorrow.

Seven's cool to go to school by himself now; if I take him, I miss the equity open and while I realize that sounds terrible, I do have bills to pay. Including $100k+ for Seven's tuition. He seems to be some sort of dual math / piano prodigy so I've got him at NYSMM, the New York School for Music and Mathematics (pronounced nism). He's robotic about his schoolwork and piano; I never have to ask him about it or tell him to do his homework, he just does it. He's pounding out some kind of new age electronic pianochord song in the background right now. Amazing shit.

The piano stops.

"Dad, I need fifty bucks for tomorrow, please."

"What? What for?"

"A field trip. With school"

"OK, sounds good. Where you going?"

"We're going to go see some show. It's called the Mathemagician."

"And is fifty dollars enough? You know how it is with prices these days."

"Well it's 5.50 for bus fare, plus I'm allowing 35 dollars for lunch. That leaves a 9.50 buffer for miscellaneous."

"Miscellaneous?"

Ha, nice word. He catches something in my tone but not the correct something.

"Yes. What? You don't think that's enough of a buffer?"

I don't want to betray that I am cackling on the inside so I just shut down the conversation before I make him feel bad.

"Fifty. No problem. It's in your jacket pocket."

"Thanks a lot, Dad."

I pull out seventy dollars, fold it in half and put it in the red fall jacket hanging by the front door. The piano starts back up and I sit down to just listen.

I close my eyes and mentally summon the dopamine rush of a 4:00 AM dancefloor. This is a skill any clubber can master after a few years. It's like your brain has been charged up so many times via chemical enhancement that you reach a point where you can just put yourself in the altered state without pharmaceutical assistance. The piano's notes pour into my ears like butter over popcorn and splash my brain. This kid is absolutely amazing. I used to scoff at the cheese of those "Who Rescued Who?" SPCA bumper stickers but now I kind of grudgingly get it.

The day after that night from hell, when Seven got cut, there was a moment he looked right up into my eyes, which was rare. And granted I was still tripping smalls from the night before but I looked into his eyes and saw the me I once was. I teleported back and I was him and he was me and it was all a flash and from then on I just suddenly had this Understanding. Play time is over. A crackling, electric connection was made between my past and Seven's future in that moment and now everything has changed. Real life has begun. My behavioral code has been altered.

Addictive impulses are not completely gone but they hold no clout. The voices in my head are babbling idiots now, not the superior hypnotists who once dictated an unreasonable percentage of my nights and days. The insatiable fire-breathing dragons in my mind are now sparrows.

The thought of a 4:00 AM dancefloor fires a nicotine signal in my brain but to smoke is no longer an option. Only by completely ruling it out at all times can I stop the pathways of addiction from staying lit. Of course they light up. They probably will for the rest of my life. Every time I hear great music, play poker, go golfing, exit the subway, have a bad trading day, have a great trading day...

■ ■ ■

307 DAYS BEFORE THE RESET

A few weeks after the highly regrettable puking and sleeping in the bathtub incident, Alison returns to live with Seven and Charlie. It's hard. She is still dying to drink and do fun stuff and chase the night and all that but she loves Charlie. The thing is, she also loves drinking. And chopping and dropping and smoking and snorting. She loves all that. She tries as hard as humanly possible to go full wholesome and is doing an okay job of it. She filled a couple of prescriptions without telling Charlie but otherwise she's clean and sober. *A couple of pills here and there aren't going to bother anyone.* Without something to take the edge off, she's too sketched out all the time and that isn't good for anybody—not for Charlie, not for Seven and not for her.

She spends a lot of time online working on a nano degree in app building. She has Charlie's full support. He's got more money than he knows how to spend and given his views on fiat currency and The Reset and all that he doesn't care much about money. Alison has some cool ideas for apps and has no interest whatsoever in taking some fucking retail job at Trader Joe's or Old Navy or whatever. Not that she is above those jobs—*Gawd I am SO silver spoon Westpo sometimes! Don't be so Fairfield Cunty*—but Charlie is still printing money at a cartoonish pace so she is free to pursue something more interesting / fulfilling.

While openly acknowledging that it seems kind of parental on his part, Charlie insists that the contract be updated to reflect that neither of them will drink alcohol for the next six months. Alison is terrified that life going forward will now be hopelessly boring and stale but at the same time she knows she has to at least try. It's like: staying in is boring unless you get high (especially weeknights). Going out with friends and not drinking is absolutely zzz / out of the question. Can't drink. Can't do drugs. So Alison realizes she needs a totally new set of things to do. At first she watches a lot (a lot) of TV and pulls out a cigarette or vape every time thoughts of drugs or alcohol enter her mind. She smokes 295 cigarettes the first week. Unsustainable.

Then she comes up with this visualization exercise: *My brain is a bowl. When it's empty, there are no thoughts of drugs or alcohol. When it's full I am completely saturated with thoughts of drugs and alcohol.* Every time the bowl gets more than a quarter full she mentally empties it and starts over. This trick works at first but her thought pattern is like: I feel like a cigarette. I would love a drink right now. Wine. Beer. Wine. Vodka. Empty the bowl. The bowl is empty. I feel like a cigarette. I feel like a drink. I'd love to do a line of coke (or ten) tonight. Oh the feeling of just one more line of crystal or white flying up my nostril and slamming against my mucous membranes! Dopamine jolt. Empty the bowl. The bowl is empty.

So she tries to choose education and buries her mind under code instead of circular thoughts of chemical self-annihilation. Charlie is great but also super fucking annoying because he seems to have just instantly forgotten that alcohol and drugs and fun ever existed. He's like this awesome adult human dad thing that she sometimes has trouble recognizing but also loves like crazy. She feels wicked insecure because he makes it all look so easy. *Why am I so weak? Why can't I just be an adult? Because I don't want to be an adult!* She thinks about rehab a few times but doesn't really think her situation quite warrants it. *I can do it. I can do it myself. Charlie can help me.* Dying for a cigarette. A beer. *Empty the bowl.*

■ ■ ■

Maximilian Bern, a writer, editor and scholar in Weimar Germany, "Withdrew all his savings—100,000 marks, formerly sufficient to support a modestly comfortable retirement—and purchased all it would buy by that time: a subway ticket. The old gentleman took a last ride around the city, then went back to his apartment and locked himself in.
There he died of hunger."

■ ■ ■

272 DAYS BEFORE THE RESET

No amount of P&L makes me feel better about what's going on these days. The market has stopped making sense. Gold is rocketing higher, up 3%, 4%, 5% just about every day and stocks are flying in tandem with overall price inflation but oil is freakishly heavy. Correlation breakdown.

Sirens wail outside; overworked police, fire and ambulance workers plead for some kind of respite. Dispatcher nervous breakdowns hit an all-time high. Even when bad news comes out and I make money on it, I don't feel good anymore.

As more and more bad outcomes show up in the real world, trading is less satisfying. Whether I'm making or losing money in the ↑Marketz!↓ and whether or not the stock market is going up or down or diagonal, the real world is getting noticeably and unmistakably worse every single day. I need to close my account and switch to gold while I still have real money. Then I need to figure out how to do something useful. Contribute. I don't want to facilitate this machine anymore and the longer I stay plugged into it, the harder it will be to cut the cord.

Every day I worry more about The Reset. The day when everyone will simultaneously realize that the entire capitalist and fiat money system is all based on a shared illusion. "These green, numbered slices of cotton and linen can be exchanged for goods and services at a rate universally agreed-upon by all citizens of the United States and the world!" It is collective madness. We are near a point where faith will disappear and illusions will crumble and only those holding hard assets will have anything left. Weimar Germany, but worse.

Google got hacked the other day. Search history for 23,000,000 people, Wikileaked for all to see. Fully searchable by name, mobile number and keyword. So much porn. So much fucked up shit. What is wrong with these people?

"Does every siren mean somebody got hurt somewhere?"

It's Seven. He was in the other room studying and has now appeared to my right. The top of his blonde head is approximately even with my armpits. We're both looking out the window at the squirming, unsettled map below. A screaming ambulance can barely get up Broadway. Too much traffic. Garbage bags flap. A homeless teen asleep on the median.

"Nah. Lots of false alarms. Maybe one in twenty sirens is for something real. The rest are meaningless. Just noise."

I flash back to flatland's last show where she intertwined two samples of NYFD sirens to create the most ridiculous, eurythmic soundscape. Flying through oceans of red and orange liquid.

"Can I have something to eat?"

"We don't have anything. You wanna go for a walk?"

He smiles, excited. He loves hanging out. I'm learning to love it. Lower highs and higher lows.

"You done your homework?"

The public school teachers have been on strike for almost two months now but Seven's private school is still running full time. The rich get richer. Half the time when I peek in to check that Seven's doing his homework I see he's playing some sort of video game but I'm not overly bothered. He's crazy smart. He does the work. Principal says they think he might be on the spectrum so he's going in for an eval next week. I am not worried about it. Everybody's on the spectrum.

"Yep. I'm almost a week ahead in my planner."

As far as I have seen he is incapable of lying so I take his word.

"Cool. Let's go. Wear a jacket."

I grab a jacket and pull on a blue Montreal Expos ski hat.

Outside it's cold, maybe 30F. Not much wind but dark gray skies, bulging heavy clouds. Hard to say if it will snow or rain. I reflexively reach to pull out a Cig-O but I threw that thing out ages ago. Garbage bags line 68th Street, two or three deep; there is barely room for cars to pass. The garbage strike is in its third week. It doesn't stink much yet but they better get things settled before spring. Seven ducks, pops back up and walks in and around the piles of trash. He crouches down in front of a particularly mountainous mound.

"What you up to, kid?"

"Taking pictures. For my art project."

"Cool."

We didn't eat much for breakfast. Two apples and a piece of toast. Such a colossal pain to get groceries these days. Starbucks and McDonald's are lined up down the street as usual but I don't touch those places anymore. They've gone hardcore down market to feed the masses on the cheap.

We go to one of the new high-priced fast joints, Bokks'z (pronounced, boxes). Bento boxes to go. Not just Japanese. Italian, salad, sandwich, whatever. 20 choices, all $30. And a 6-ounce drink for "free". Simple, easy. And a lot quicker than going to the grocery store and picking through the random dregs on the half-empty shelves these days. I line up early once a week to get rice and bananas and bread but otherwise it's Bokks'z most of the time and the cheap places if I'm desperate.

Seven and I sit down at the red, acrylic tables and eat. Seven has poor table manners; he scoops up cubes of chicken with his fingers and wolfs them down like it's a race. His table manners are vaguely animal and it makes me wonder about his prior life. I have been dodging the question of his backstory mostly as I am not sure either of us is ready to open those doors yet. I will get to it when the time is right.

"Can you use your fork please, bud."

My initial probes into more details of his history have been unsuccessful, met with flat answers completely devoid of information. He's got a 4-inch scar on the back of his neck that I would especially like to know about and there is another scar (burn mark?) on the back of his hand. Two cop cars and a fire truck scream by.

"Why is all this crazy stuff happening these days, Dad?"

"Well... Something's broken. And nobody knows how to fix it."

"What do you mean, though? What's broken?"

"I dunno. America, I guess."

"Why? Why is it broken?"

"There are no real leaders anymore. Just professional politicians. So we've been taking the easy way out for so long we don't know any other way."

"Can we learn another way?"

"Maybe at some point. But maybe things have to get worse first. Then they can get better."

"I don't really get it."

"Just don't worry about it, pal. Concentrate on your school work. Your vids. Don't worry about everything else. Everything's going to be fine. Do you know I love you, buddy? I've only known you for six months but I already love you. Pretty crazy. I'm going to take care of you and do whatever to keep you safe, OK? I promise. All we need is you and me and everything will be fine."

"OK."

"How's the chicken?"

"Good."

There is a quiet moment as we eat and process our thoughts.

"I love you too, Dad," Seven says, "I'm glad I get to see you now."

"Thanks, buddy. That means a lot."

He has no idea how much it means. The conversation I never once had with my Dad. Amazing.

See Dad, it's not so tough to say: I love you. There. Easy.

A dope black teen walks by outside wearing a t-shirt that reads "I Love You, Nork." Some garbage swirls up and blows toward the restaurant window. A yellow wrapper twists around, flips and passes across the window right at my eye level. Kind of trippy. I feel like a Cig-O. *It is not an option.* Quitting the nicotine has been hardest compared to the rest of the stuff. Like they say: it's easy to quit smoking; I do it all the time.

The first few weeks without Sight and coke were tough. The Voice entered my head every night, around 7:00 PM. *Psst. Charlie? You wanna come out and play?* No thanks. *You sure? It's really fun out there. Forget what's bugging you man. Listen to some great music. Good times. Forget what's going on and just glide, man.* Nah, I'm good. Thanks. *Dude, c'mon. Remember all the good times we had? You can't ignore me. I need you. You need me. I wanna roll between your fingers. Go up your nose. In your eyes. Inside your brain. I'll make you feel good man. Really good.* I got a son now. I can't. Remember what happened last time? Seven gouged his arm. Really bad. *Just a few lines. Nobody will notice. You can get away with it.* No.

The voice, which used to rule me, is now just this idiot who won't shut up or get the hint. But nicotine is always an option. No big deal, a few drags here and there. Keep the nicotine flowing. Keep the shakes and the headaches at bay; what's the downside? I want to be a good example for my son. *It makes no difference man. C'mon. Just a few drags.* Eff off, voice.

I need a smoke. I look at Seven and he's watching something online, laughing quietly, oblivious.

"I'm going to the bathroom. Don't go anywhere, OK?"

No reply.

"OK?"

Kids suck at multitasking. I put my face right in his.

"Dude. Back in a minute."

"OK! OK..."

He's mildly startled. Annoyed. I sneak outside for a few quick hauls on a Cig-O and try to come in via a circuitous route through the restaurant that could realistically suggest I actually just went to the bathroom, not outside. I sit back down at the table. Seven's eyes flick out of the goggosphere and lock onto mine.

"You smell like cold. Like outside air. Cig-O?"

"Yeah. You're too smart. Let's jet."

I suck.

Seven asks me to take him to Ground Zero because he is learning about 9/11 in history class. That part of Lower Manhattan is full sketch these days so I would rather not but Seven doesn't ask for much and so we hop on the 1 train and go. On the subway a teenager with the signature blank eyes of a Sight user sways like a straphanger, most certainly feeling the train ride in a way that I can remember feeling subway rides home from various big nights out. A quick flash of the nth color in my mind and then it's gone before I can focus on it. The smell of the subway car vibrates between expensive cheese and fresh vomit.

The teenager rocks back and forth not far from where we're sitting. Seven is a little scared; he takes my hand in a way that makes me feel important and powerful and gives me substantial gravity. Like with great power comes great responsibility sort of thing. But also scary / heavy. Like maybe how a superhero feels when he first gets the ramifications of being a superhero.

"I love you buddy," I tell him.

"Me too."

I do love him. Crazy amounts. Sometimes I have this irresistible urge to just squish him. Because that's how much I love him. Squish. Squish.

There are more protesters than tourists these days around the 9/11 memorial site with Zuccotti park nearby and lots of places for skaters and sketchpads to hang out. Two fire trucks and an ambulance scream by. We walk to the edge of the memorial fountains and look down 30 feet of black granite wall into the gigantic pool that fills the footprint of where the North Tower once stood. 26,000 gallons of water flow down the walls and disappear into an abyss below. The names of victims engraved on the walls remind me of all the ragged flapping "LOST" posters and teddy bears and pictures posted by relatives with unrealistic hope in the days after the planes hit.

"It smells like chlorine."

"Yeah."

The more years pass, the more 9/11 really becomes something where you had to be there. Watching a video clip or looking at an old newspaper or staring into the abyss of flowing water at the footprint of the old buildings doesn't really deliver a true understanding of the event. The footage just looks like something out of a movie now.

I want to explain to Seven how it felt to sit that morning and watch as the first plane hit and then the confusion about whether it was an accident and the tone of voice of the TV announcers as they, like the viewers, realized all at once as the South Tower was hit that this was not some random, unfortunate incident but something more terrible and historic. It is impossible for Seven to grasp or for me to explain the severity of the damage caused to the American psyche. With the benefit of hindsight, it is clear now that the government response to 9/11 was this hysterical overreaction and the cure was worse than the disease but hindsight is always 20/20, right?

"Okay I get it. Let's go," Seven says.

"Do you want to see the survivor tree? They pulled it from the wreckage and planted it and it grew back despite the fact that—"

"I'm kind of cold, Dad. I get it. I wanna go."

"OK."

On the way back to the subway we pass a huge open-pit construction site marked with a sign that reads:

"This site is the future home of The Google Tower. At 3141.592 feet, this will be the tallest building in the world upon completion. *Financial support from The Larry Page Moving Faster into the Future Fund.*"

Throughout economic history economists have noted that whenever a country builds the new tallest building in the world, that country soon experiences a major financial crisis. The Singer Building before the Crash of 1907. The Empire State Building then the Crash of 1929 and Great Depression. The World Trade Center and the oil crisis of 1973. The Petronas Tower and the Asian Crisis in 1997. Burj Khalifa and the collapse of the Dubai economy in 2010.

The reason this happens is very simple. The only time you can build a very large ego-driven project like the tallest building in the world is when credit is extremely plentiful, lending standards are lax and hubris is at an extreme. These are the same conditions necessary for financial calamity.

I've heard of Google Tower before but never walked past the site. The very existence of the Google Tower site is one more piece of evidence that The Reset is coming soon. 2008 was a walk in the park. A warm up act. The Reset is the main event. There will be no "Big Short". We need different strategies now. The final outcome this time will not just be a collapsing banking system and stock market but instead no stock market and no banking system at all. Not just the stock market will fall. The elite will fall. Buildings will fall. The whole world order will fall.

The authorities' desire, motivation and commitment to maintain a leveraged financial system producing 3% annual GDP growth regardless of demographics or pre-existing debt levels is nearly—but not quite—infinite.

I have two strategies running simultaneously. The first is to trade the ups and downs in the market and the dollar. Everything is going to zero but it won't happen in a straight line. Authorities will attempt to reinflate over and over creating massive updrafts like we saw, for example, in 2009, 2012 and 2016. These waves of reflationary euphoria will eventually become shorter in duration and weaker in magnitude. Reflation efforts will amount to pushing on a string and the big one will hit. The financial tsunami. I have surfed the waves up and down the past few years but it's almost time to head for higher ground.

The second strategy is to prepare for The Reset. Accumulate physical assets. Store canned food. Set up access to a survival cabin in Canada. Secure a means of escape from Manhattan for when all the bridges and tunnels are gone. And so on.

■   ■   ■

207 DAYS BEFORE THE RESET

flatland is often awake at 3:00am so a few months ago when she saw a new york city audubon 'project safe flight' flyer soliciting volunteers to help collect bird carcasses from the base of new york city office buildings in the early morning (4:00am to 6:00am) she thought "sure".

the point of the exercise is to collect information on the species and frequency of bird vs. building collisions in manhattan in an effort to convince developers to play their part in tagging large windows (or turning off lights) to reduce unnecessary bird deaths. around 600 million birds die this way each year as they mistake clean, backlit windows for open spaces and crash violently to an instant death leaving a ghostly imprint of oily bird dust behind.

flatland sees these pre-dawn walkabouts as an opportunity to see a different face of the city plus a chance to collect odd sonic loops for future musical concoction. she has no shortage of time or money anyway and she's not the kind of person who watches tv.

she steps out of her apartment building and the freezing air whips her face skin. she has done these bird collecting junkets for a few months now and today on her rounds she notices several new homeless men have turned up since last month. plus, a family of four: mom, dad, 8-year-old boy + 10-year-old girl curled up together, asleep on a subway vent like penguins huddling to share body heat. where do they go during the day? *i've never seen these people before. where do they all come from? i want to bring them all into my apartment but i know i can't.*

she pulls five twenties out of a money clip and slides them into the mother's grimy jean pocket without waking her. she puts the money clip away, then takes it back out and puts five twenties in the man's pocket too. the man stirs and a perfect bubble of snot forms and pops in his right nostril. he makes miscellaneous sleep disturbance noises but does not wake. the boy's big toe sticks out of a worn shoe two sizes too small. the toe is clearly frostbitten, a disturbing shade of purple. flatland meditates on the sad beauty of the scene for a few beats and then walks on.

the state of the city and the nation weigh on flatland and threaten her general state of unconditional optimism. charlie once joked that flatland is so optimistic she doesn't see the glass as half full or half empty but just as completely full—half with water / half with air. this optimism strikes some as naive but flatland has no major cares about how others see her or her perpetually sunny outlook. it works for her.

but as much as everything always works out for flatland and every bad moment opens some new door or offers a useful life lesson, she can see that the same no longer applies to broader society. a family of four curled up on a subway grate learns nothing of value from the experience. that eight-year-old boy isn't learning life lessons; his suffering is meaningless.

■ ■ ■

A TRANSPORT CLERK RECALLS THE HYPERINFLATION OF 1923

"I vividly remember paydays… I used to have to accompany the manager to the bank in an open six-seater Benz, which we filled to the brim with bundles and bundles of million and billion mark notes. We then drove back through the narrow streets, quite unmolested. And when the workmen got their wages, they did not even bother to count the notes in each bundle."

FRIEDRICH KRONER ON HYPERINFLATION — AUGUST 1923

"It pounds daily on the nerves: the insanity of numbers, the uncertain future… An epidemic of fear and naked need: lines of shoppers, long since a customary sight, once more form in front of shops, first in front of one, then in front of all… The lines always send the same signal: the city, the big stone city, will be shopped empty again. Rice, 80,000 marks a pound yesterday, costs 160,000 marks today, and tomorrow perhaps twice as much. The day after, the man behind the counter will shrug his shoulders:

'No more rice!'"

■ ■ ■

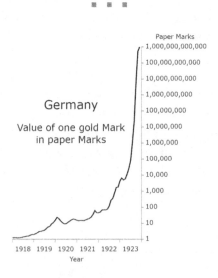

■ ■ ■

149 DAYS BEFORE THE RESET

Seven and I go on walks. I tell him about all kinds of random stuff and mostly he just listens. And just when you think he's not really paying attention he drops a comment that shows you he's been engaged the whole time.

Having a kid is the bomb.

We walk through Central Park, avoiding tent city and the larger packs of homeless. The Loeb boathouse area is protected by private security and this seems like a fun thing for a dad to do with his kid and so we wait behind a long line of mostly Chinese tourists and soon we are rowing slowly out on the lake in Central Park known simply as "The Lake". We drift in silence for a bit then I speak:

"Hey did you know that this boat is like a time machine?"

"What do you mean?"

"Well, we are moving physically across the water and forward in time all at once. Super slowly."

"That's dumb."

"Ok well what about a book? Is that a time machine? You can go back in time and read the thoughts of another person who might not even still be alive."

"Yeah I guess that's pretty cool. How about a machine that really moves through time like in that story? By that guy..."

"HG Wells?"

"Yeah that one. That story is good."

"Did you read that in school?"

"No, Mom read it to me once. During one of her good times."

"What do you mean 'her good times'?"

"Can we not talk about my mom? I like it better if we don't."

"OK. Sure pal."

This is still how the talks go whenever his mom comes up. I've had a few conversations with the woman from child protective services but they don't provide many details. I get the impression the mom was high most of the time and playing video games when not high so Seven was left to fend for himself a lot. He has above average microwaving skills for a ten-year-old.

My thoughts flick to Alison and I picture her strung out on the couch, binge watching Netflix and smoking cigarettes. Her hair is messy and she is wearing my Pokémon sweatshirt. She blows a purple-gray smoke ring and it pulsates up on wafts of stale air. I miss her, but now I see what she is and while I feel guilty for thinking this way, she is too broken for me to fix. I no longer feel like I am in a relationship but instead like I am riding the front edge of a wave in the last moments before it inevitably crashes to sand.

I know it's over but I haven't got the sack to break up with her yet even though it is clearly inevitable (to me). This feels like an arrogant thing to say, but I will break her heart. I will absolutely crush her. I don't want to crush her. I don't want to break up with her; I just want to be broken up.

It's tempting to be that dick that just treats his girlfriend like crap until she finally breaks up with him but I'm not going that route. For now, I'm giving myself one more week—just on that one percent chance I change my mind. A week to let it simmer. Today is Friday so next Friday is D-Day unless something massively changes.

Which it won't.

As we float in silence in the rowboat I am the opposite of jealous of Alison's state right now. I am glad that I stopped drinking and sniffing and dropping and I am glad that Seven showed up. I don't miss the nights out and the shitty sleep and raging hangovers and kitty litter mouth and brutally tenderized mind. I do miss flatland a bit since I don't see her as much, but we've been getting together here and there. She plays me new tracks that are work in progress and we talk books and life and I know now that she is a real friend, not just a person to get drunk or high with like most of the other people I have hung out with over the past five years.

Thinking back, I can remember nights where I would call someone up not because I had any real interest in them but only because I felt like getting high and it seemed bad to drink or do drugs alone. Eventually I got past that feeling and spent plenty of nights high, alone on my couch. Getting high by yourself is kind of like going to a movie by yourself: it feels really weird the first time but then you get used to it and then you can do it whenever you want.

"I'm getting hungry. Can we get something to eat?"

"Sure, as long as it's something super healthy like ice cream or a salted pretzel ok?"

Seven smiles. Having a kid is the best.

■ ■ ■

122 DAYS BEFORE THE RESET

They had an argument. It was more than 24 hours ago but it still echoes in Mike's mind. Clanging, reverberating. The replay of the argument and smart voices that whisper smart things that could've been said but were not. The argument (like many of their arguments) was about a purchase. Another piece for the library, another piece of furniture they did not need. Mike had no shortage of money but he hated how The Wife spent it on frivolous bullshit. The day she started calling furniture "pieces" was his first warning sign that he should've put a Wusthof through her throat like a Wolverine claw.

Snikt.

The second warning sign: Early in the marriage, she used words like staycation and mancave. Impactful and irregardless.

"I just want to be, like, a flexitarian?"

And so on. Sometimes trying to be clever, maybe, but other times just reflecting her place somewhere in the center of the idiot, imbecile, moron zone of the early 20th century IQ scale. Or like:

"I just need you to work on the 'honey-do' list before you golfing, Mike."

She was trying to be cute but it made Mike shiver with disgust. Like fingernails over Styrofoam. How could he not have seen how dumb she was? Not like Eastman's wife. She's hot *and* smart as fuck. Managing Director at Stanley. Wrote a kids' book that sold 22,000 copies apparently. The whole package. Probably awesome at breastfeeding. Mike should have cut the cord with The Wife years ago but what was the point now. The cost, man. The cost. He'd lose half his net worth. The house. He knows how the courts are biased against men. No fucking chance he'll give The Wife that satisfaction.

Another warning sign, in year three of their marriage:

"Mike, do you mind not standing up when you go pee in the main bathroom? Pretty please? That shaggy white throw I put in front of the toilet keeps getting little yellow splash dots of pee on it. Is that OK, sweetie?"

What are you talking about? Why do you put a fucking white shaggy throw in front of a toilet where you clearly know piss is going to be raining down nearby? What the fucking fuck?

"OK honey sure. No problem."

And The Wife loved to play the "What's wrong?" game. That was the worst. She would sit there pouting. Waiting for him to ask her what's wrong. Or to guess what was wrong. He fucking hated that game. If something's wrong, just tell me. I don't want to guess. Fucks sake.

Their arguments roll from one day to the next and today Mike has spent 12 hours at work battling reams of HR and compliance and IT bullshit so he will not go home until after The Wife is asleep. He cannot stomach it. He hits PJ Clarke's for three Dewar's and Cokes and this occupies him until almost 9:00 PM. He pings a black car, estimating an ETA home of between 10:00 PM and 10:30 PM, plenty of buffer past The Wife's normal 9:30 PM bedtime.

Mike walks out of the pub and smokes half a cigarette in the freezing cold winter air. Hard bundles of slush make piles against the curb. The car shows up and he flicks the half a cigarette up and over the small snowbank and straight into the sewer. *Nothing but net.* He lingers for a few seconds, staring at the black space through the sewer grates and admires the awesome accuracy of the flick. The black Mercedes he ordered rolls up and he climbs in.

As the car heads northbound past United Nations Headquarters, he drops into one of those perfect beautiful, deep black, half-drunk sleeps. The car rolls out of Manhattan, across the Henry Hudson bridge, up through Westchester and into Connecticut. It rolls up the lane in front of Mike's CT home, between rows of carefully pruned dogwood trees. A cloud of bats flies by.

Mike looks out through tinted windows and his heart sinks: the lights are still on in the kitchen. *She's still awake. Fucking fuck fuckity fuck fuck.* He briefly contemplates asking the driver to turn around but he has nowhere else to go. More bats fly by. A few fireflies flash in the hot August night. He thinks 'Maybe I'll get out and just walk into the forest and lay down in the carpet of leaves and sleep there all night'. Thing is, he doesn't want to get bitten by a tick—he's heard enough horror stories about the Lyme. Bull's eye rash around the bite. Headaches. Fatigue and joint pain. Cognitive decline, night sweats, insomnia. Fuck that shit.

The only reason she is still awake is to continue the argument from last night.

Mike opens the door and pulls his 16 ½" Armani Collezioni shirt untucked. The Wife is standing right there in the foyer.

"Hi honey," she says with fake sweetness.

"Hey."

Just as Mike is about to kick his shoes off, this:

"Don't forget to take your shoes off, OK? The cleaners came today."

"Sure."

He kicks off his Oxfords and places them neatly to the side, on the mat. Just like she's asked him to do a million times.

Avoid confrontation. Get to bed.

"Wow, I am really tired. Gotta get straight to bed, ok? Talk to you tomorrow."

"OK, honey. I just had one quick question."

"Sure."

Let me go to fucking bed. For the love of God. Don't bring up the fucking Eames chair. Just don't bring up the fucking Eames chair.

"I know it's late but I just wanted to finish our conversation about the Eames chair from last night. If I don't order it by midnight tonight I can't get the promotional discount and free shipping."

"The chair is $16,000. I don't think free shipping really makes a difference, does it?"

"Well, that doesn't make much sense. You said yesterday you didn't want to spend that much money on a chair. If you're worried about the money, then shouldn't we use the promotional codes? I mean to buy it next week is just a waste of money, right? When we can get it 10% cheaper today?"

Boiling blood enters the brain and thoughts blur. Flooding.

"Listen I can't fucking do this right now. I'm tired. Today has been a fucking shitshow. I need to get some sleep OK? Just buy the thing. I really don't care. Just buy it."

Defeated. Mike sees two more fireflies flash outside. He walks into the kitchen and The Wife follows.

"But are you sure you don't mind?"

He says nothing, but thinks: "Of course I mind, you small-minded, fake-titted, Botox-injected, plastic-faced, dead-behind-the-eyes freak!"

Hot blood fills his face; his brain boils. Waves of red heat drown all rational thought. Mike zooms in on the top kitchen drawer and walks with purpose past The Wife. He pulls open the drawer then fingers and fumbles through a selection of knives. His fingers come upon a small paring knife, not exactly the best tool for the job, but good enough. He pushes the drawer shut hard; he wants to slam it and scare The Wife. But the drawer betrays him as it closes silently thanks to Pillow-Touch™ soft-close drawer slide technology.

"What are you doing?" Her voice is unusually weak. He likes that. He likes to see her scared.

His answer comes with a flurry of strong, surgical stabs into the side of her neck. He jabs the paring knife into her throat and the sides of her neck, repeatedly from different angles. The knife plunges in and out cleanly on most stabs but hits the knuckles of her spine a few times. The knife tip bends and there is a crunching sound when he connects with bone. His mind pops a flashbulb memory of carving pumpkins as a child, outside with Mom, on the picnic table.

Bam bam bam bam bam bam. He stabs The Wife's trachea and neck and throat over and over and over until blood streams out of maybe thirty ¾-inch slits all around her neck.

The way the liquid pours out reminds him of the chocolate fountain at their wedding. That stupid chocolate fountain! He couldn't get The Wife and the wedding planner to give up on it.

"It's too expensive," he implored. "It's a disgusting health hazard."

"Two against one!" the planner and The Wife chirped in unison. Then high fived.

The Wife tries to scream but there is too much blood running down her throat. The liquid flows down and blocks the air from coming up and so this weird burbling sound comes out, like urgent gargling. As The Wife falls to the floor, all Mike can think about is how badly he wants to go to bed. He wonders whether he should brush his teeth before going to bed or not bother.

Blood trickles then streams across the bamboo kitchen floor towards an expensive area rug. His dumb brain says: "Shit, The Wife is going to be pissed if that thing gets blood on it!" and then his smart brain knows she is forever done getting pissed about anything and he starts to laugh this insane laugh that comes from some deeply fucked up and previously unknown part of his brain. The laugh gains momentum and becomes this weird, cartoon villain evil laugh that gets louder and louder and out of control.

"You OK sir?"

The driver looks back and Mike is awake from the dream / nightmare and they roll up the driveway in front of Mike's CT home and past the rows of carefully pruned dogwood trees. Snow crunches under tire. The house is completely dark and The Wife is in bed. It's winter. No bats. No fireflies.

■ ■ ■

117 DAYS BEFORE THE RESET

wristphone buzzes gently and then less gently and eventually starts to beep and flatland wakes up. 6:06 am. she is scheduled to work at the shelter today at 7:00 am but she likes to get outside for a walk before the protesters and the homeless start to crowd the sidewalks.

last night was super windy so the garbage situation is worse than usual on west 3rd. there is a light smell of fermenting trash in the air. it's cold. big fresh white snowflakes swirl on gusts of wind. food scraps and plastic bottles and plastic bags and bits of plastic this and plastic that ebb and flow in drifts against buildings and curbs. the garbage strike ended more than two weeks ago but the streets are still not back to normal. not enough manpower. budget cuts.

the situation at st. mike's is bad. more than 400 people are lined up outside and the shelter doesn't open for another hour. these are not stereotypical homeless wino / addict types. more like single moms and regular peeps that just ran out of cash one day and then ran out of food some days after that. they are mostly dressed in tattered lululemon and banana republic: a testament to past prosperity. the supplemental nutritional assistance program (aka snap, aka food stamps) has been spread too thin for too long and it's being cut back now big time as it expanded way beyond its original purpose. you can't have half of 300 million people on food stamps. just doesn't work. so pressure on the shelter system grows exponentially. flatland makes her way through the employee entrance, doing her best to ignore the desperate calls from the line. voices of the broken.

"help us."

"we need food bad man. we're starving."

"i need something for my kids. please."

gwenna jacobs runs the shelter. she's 42, looks 55. ex meth addict with greasy red hair, balding in the front. many years of hard yards but she's clean now and trying to do the right thing and give something back. make amends. you only keep what you give away and all that. she sits on a metal fold up chair with her arms crossed and face empty. her eyes are red from weeping.

"what's going on?" flatland asks.

"look in the main storage room."

flatland walks across the small room and opens the door to food storage. the shelves therein are usually loaded with three to five days' worth of donated or purchased food and supplies: noodles, peanut butter, canned vegetables, canned fruit, toilet paper and all that. but now the room is completely empty. shelves barren.

"last night. everything was stolen. every crumb. i don't know what to do."

"who did this? did you check the video?"

"what difference does it make?"

flatland can tell gwenna is too shattered to talk to the people outside.

"i'll go outside and tell everyone."

flatland delivers the news.

crying. desperation. questions.

"what should i do?"

"where do i go?"

"when can we come back?"

flatland has no answers.

■ ■ ■

116 DAYS BEFORE THE RESET

Seven saved my life. I think back to how things were a bit less than a year ago. Fully addled three nights per week minimum and sometimes five or six. Smoking four packs of cigarettes a week and vaping like mad. Tripping like a lab rat on Sight and MDMA and sometimes Special K and GHB. *Gah, GHB. Satan's semen.*

Not nice to say or think but I think before Seven I didn't truly care if I accidentally killed myself. Like, what difference would it really make? There'd be a few sad friends and my crazy, oxy-chomping aunt in Chappaqua would probably feel sad for a day or two. Almost zero real impact overall. The value of your life drops a lot when you have no real family. Now with Seven around, it would be a complete disaster if I died. I am needed. It feels good. Duty. Responsibility. It feels heavy. The way a soldier finds it heavy to carry a fallen brother. A burden I am glad to shoulder.

It's unfair to Alison because I got this "Get Out of Jail Free" card handed to me. One day, addicted and the next basically off the hook. I am Pablo and she is Ramon Gris. With the benefit of hindsight, I realize that the partying I did wasn't so much "for fun" but more like "for avoiding boredom" or for "filling holes". I had nothing better to do so the default pathways when my mind idled all led to Sight or beer or coke or vape.

I know that while I feel this incredible relief and freedom to be off the night train, Alison is still suffering big time these days. I "accidentally" read her notebook (Alison's Funderland #43) the other day and there's all kinds of dark scary shit in there. Poems and demons (literal demons, drawn on the page I mean) and poems about demons and recipes for optimal recreational psychopharmacology and self-medication and black clouds and there was also this scrawled across the middle of an otherwise empty page:

Those who don't have the patients for grammar make me sic

So, she's keeping her sense of humor at least. On the same page in messy cursive:

All the priests are rapists. The psychologists are nuts.
Fathers crowned as kings. Daughters, angry sluts.

A fake website design for crystalmath.com, a site for recreational users of mathematics. Some shiny happy stuff and then dark stuff mostly scrawled while clearly under some sort of influence. That's the paradox of Alison. She is funny and sad. An old soul and a child. Full of liquid joy one day and drowned by despair the next. Beautiful outside and ugly inside. Enormous confidence, terrified and insecure.

There is a saying in poker that weak is strong and strong is weak. It means that when a poker player is loud and acts confident, he has a bad hand. And when he is quiet or acts weak, he has a strong hand. The more time I spend around humans, I find this applies a lot, especially with those who represent strength. The more confident someone appears to be, the more likely they are insecure and over-compensating. The weak wear fearsome masks.

Thing is: I don't know what to do about Alison because on one hand she never asked for any of this. When we met we were both on the same page, all happy-go-lucky without a care in the world. Let's get messed up together on a regular basis and think nothing of it. She's 20 years old and has barely lived any life at all besides that overprivileged and sick existence she left in Westport and now I'm telling her "No drinking!" and "No drugs!" and essentially "No doing the shit I've been doing with complete freedom and without consequence for the past 10 years!" and it's not fair.

But then on the other hand first of all I love her and so I want her to be with me and there is only one way she can be with me and that is clean. And second of all I now understand that a life of randomly getting high all the time gets tired quick and I know she feels the same way like it's the big empty so why not help her get away from it and we can both live happily ever after together (or something)?

But her addiction is different from mine. Darker and more insistent. When I used to chop coke or drink or whatever it was all about the ritual and the high and there were some social aspects most of the time. At its worst I was just relieving boredom whereas Alison is just on a mission to get destroyed. She self-medicates in search of oblivion.

Another difference: she uses chemicals to silence or drown out voices in her head. Voices of anger and self-hatred and hatred for Mike and her mom for doing nothing and so it's a different kind of high. Intense but scary. Normally, her mind is a chalk board full of complex, unsolvable equations. If she drinks enough she can erase all those thoughts and leave just one word on the chalkboard: fun.

Fun but... Even when it's fun, it's too fun. Too hardcore.

I have had all these bad things happen around me like my sisters' and dad's accidents and my mom dying and I'm alone as far as family goes, basically, but I don't feel like she feels. It sucks to lose my family one then two then one at a time like that (obviously) and of course I get sad and sorry for myself and wish I could talk to my mom just one more time. And I miss my dad like crazy almost every day. But there is no raging black fire inside my mind. My brain is pretty settled. Fairly peaceful despite all the bad shit that's gone down.

There is no peace inside Alison, ever. Her mindscape is continuously hellish like the floor of a factory farm. When she does drugs, the best she can hope for is to get high enough to feel raging, crazy, ecstatic joy. Transit from one pole to another.

With all the anger and hate though, a little girl still lives inside Alison too. I see the girl all the time. She dances and laughs and comes home after a run all sweaty and smelling like cool air and girl sweat. She sings along with shitty pop songs in a way that may or may not be ironic. I love her so fucking much. She is one of those duck / bunny drawings where you can't tell which one it is because it is both and neither. I don't know if I love the real Alison or just that girl that shows up sometimes. Or is that girl Alison?

I don't know if I can do this.

Should I just let her be free to grow up normally without me and Seven? Let her find herself / figure her shit out and then maybe we can get back together in a few years? But I think I can help her get her shit together. And if I'm being honest right now: I doubt she'll get her shit together without me. Not trying to be arrogant or condescending but that's just the way it is. She'll spend her twenty grand in savings on Class I and Class II drugs and probably end up back home. And if that's her endgame I don't want to be responsible for that. But... She's not my responsibility. *She is not your problem.*

And on and on it goes around and around in my head like that.

I love her. I want to save her. I want to fix her. I cannot save her. I cannot fix her. I cannot be with her. But I cannot leave her. I am going to break up with her tonight. That's it. Decision made. I cannot keep doing this. She is the most beautiful thing in the world. She is broken. I am tired.

"What are you doing, Dad?"

Seven has emerged from his homework.

"Just thinking about the markets, kid. Same as always."

"I heard food prices are going up like crazy. Everyone's talking about it at school. And gas is over ten bucks a gallon now. They can't fit the price on the signs. And Everett's dad is filling up a spare room with canned food and rice and stuff like that because he says everything is going to run out soon."

I feign a laugh but my fakery sounds fake.

"That's silly, bud. Food doesn't just run out like that. If the stores sell out, they order more. It doesn't work like that."

"But why are all the prices going up so much?"

"People are scared, that's all. The media loves a good scare story."

"OK. Can we play Uno?"

"Sure."

Everett's Dad is right. Something is broken in the economy and there are shortages all over the place. The online grocery companies still seem to find supply so we get around 60% of the items we order on average these days. But I stopped in at Food Emporium last week and now more shelves in the store are empty than stocked. No fruit. Nothing fresh. Every greenhouse within 500 miles of NYC is bare. Plenty of canned food and dry stuff is still available but the bakery and produce and dairy sections are all plastered with "SOLD OUT" signs. Employees are demanding wage hikes to compensate and employers are starting to comply.

Meanwhile, the falling dollar is spooking the shit out of people. The *New York Post* has the daily closing rates for USD/NEM and USD/JPY on the front page in 24-point Gothic. Strangers talk about the falling dollar on the subway and think about what currency or crypto might be best to convert to instead.

The crisis has crawled out of the financial markets and into the real world.

Now Alison texts:

I'm pregnant. Call me.

■　■　■

99 DAYS BEFORE THE RESET

We have decided that we will not have the baby. The decision rests on two main pillars: one, Alison is not fit to be a mother right now. The demons are in control and neither of us is sure whether she can stay sober for seven months. I want her in rehab but she has no interest. She's got in under control, she says. Hard to manage demons and a pregnancy all at once. Plus, I am privately unsure she has the basic tools, impulse control, maturity and whatever to be a parent right now. She's barely twenty. This would rob her of the most fun years of life and she will resent the kid because she never planned for or wanted it.

Also, our relationship is over / broken beyond repair and this is no psychic environment into which a fledgling humanoid should be introduced.

Feeling confident in the logic supporting the decision and then making the decision to abort an unborn child, though, are two different things. I have always thought of myself as pro-choice and it was a pretty easy position for me because obviously a woman shouldn't be forced to have a baby she doesn't want, right?

But I wish that right now we did not have this choice. That a religious edict or authority forbade a decision because I don't want to have to make it. A pro-life view is absolute and gives perfect clarity because there is no choice to make. No ambiguity. You made a mistake and now you live with it. Action, meet consequence. Period. Full stop.

Alison is waffling and noncommittal and pouty and I am pretty sure also self-medicating.

How do we have the right to truncate this huge Monte Carlo simulation of possible futures? There is a tiny life form already formed and still forming in Alison's womb and that being will be a kid in seven months and that kid could end up a mother or father and maybe a scientist or spiritual leader or at least another crucible of random human experience and future ecstasy and failure and blood and skinned knees and saliva, bile, tears and laughter and how am I such a God that I might choose to end the story before it begins?

I just learned that the word fetus means "little one" in Latin; this knowledge fills me with bottomless grief.

But we have to decide and we have decided. We will not have the baby. And I apologize in advance to this beautiful most-likely freckled unborn thing for flushing it from its warm, safe amniotic paradise before it ever had a chance to cry or breathe or laugh or taste Alison's milk. I am sorry about this in a way that I have never felt sorry before. I am so sorry Little One. Please forgive me.

■　■　■

81 DAYS BEFORE THE RESET

Once we decided for sure not to have the baby, Alison responded with 10 straight nights of getting completely fucked up. I hate that this is how she is. I have decided that I am done. We are done. I have thought it many times but now I am ready to take action so my plan is to break up with her tonight when she comes over. I know it's going to be a complete shitshow so I arranged a playdate for Seven from 5:00 PM to 7:00 PM. Alison's coming over around 6.

She arrives around 6:30 PM which leaves an awkwardly short parcel of time but I have been thinking about and dreading this moment for too long to punt. *Maybe give it another day. She's really trying. She can't survive without me. She is going to kill herself.* It's not my responsibility. Seven is my responsibility. Alison is not. And so the circle goes but I know the decision is already made and so I dismiss the false arguments one-by-one as my dumb brain introduces them. My smart brain knows what is best.

"Alison, we have to talk."

This is highly serious and unusual syntax from me and so she freezes right away, sensing imminent danger. Piloerection.

"What do you mean? What's wrong?"

"Us. Everything," I say. Her limbic system kicks in. Blood drains from her face. I continue, monotone and scared. "Sit down for a sec."

"Sit down? What are you talking about? What's going on Charlie?"

I blurt it out in one clip: "I want to break up. This isn't working. I need to move on. You have to get your shit together on your own."

She says nothing but stands, building energy like a volcano in its final pre-eruption moments. Tick tick tick... And then she explodes.

■ ■ ■

WRATH

"You fucking asshole! You said you loved me! You said you fucking loved me! Just yesterday!"

Her hands sweep across a desk, launching electronics, books and an empty plate of toast crumbs overboard. She kicks wildly at the back of a desk chair and it slams forward, hits the desk, bounces and flips backwards, sliding across the floor.

"I can't fucking believe this! I'm fucking pregnant with your baby and you are breaking up with me? What the fuck is wrong with you?"

"Well we agreed to have an abortion—"

"You can't even fucking wait for me to go the clinic?"

"Well. I'll still go with—"

I am a rabbit gone tharn as she ransacks my apartment like a honey badger. She is unhinged; literally foaming at the mouth. I am momentarily intrigued by the pattern formed by spittle on her dry, trembling lips. An animal yells from inside her. A picture comes off the wall and she stomps on it madly. Glass shards crunch underfoot and the print inside is punctured. Her right fist punches through the drywall then comes back out, leaving a perfectly fist-shaped hole near the middle of the living room wall. She screams at the apartment above. I am scared. For me. For her. For my stuff. Mostly for her.

I say nothing and do nothing. She rages for a very long and scary five minutes. The hurricane slowly loses its energy and now she is crumpled on the bed, sobbing like a bad actor in a melodrama. Huge, uncontrolled sobs. Her tears soak the duvet which she punches with less and less strength until she is finally just a whimpering fetal ball in the middle of my bed. She is destroyed.

"I'm so sorry, Alison. I'm really sorry."

"Don't be sorry. It's my fault. I'm a fucking disaster. I need help but I can't go home. I can't stay here. I don't know what I'm supposed to do."

"I can still help you. Even if we're broken up, I still care about you. I still want to help you..."

Don't say it Charlie. Don't say it. Do. Not. Fucking. Say. It.

"... I still love you."

Gah.

"I don't want your pity, Charlie. I'm not your problem anymore. I'll figure it out. I always do."

Back and forth like that for a few minutes and then I have the shitty task of letting her know that she has to leave because I have to go pick up Seven from his playdate. More apologies, more crying. As we wait for the elevator, she asks me a second time:

"Are you sure this is what you want?"

No, I am not even close to sure.

"Yes. I'm 100% sure."

"I love you, Charlie."

"I love you too."

For the first time through this whole exchange, I start crying and Alison hugs me really hard. Her face is wet with tears against my neck. I put my lip right to her ear and whisper.

"I still love you. I'm really sorry. Maybe in another time. A different place—"

The elevator doors open and the moment breaks. A good-looking couple dressed for the theatre look up at us from their phones then back down. Expensive perfume swirls around expensive cologne in the elevator's airspace. Alison gets on without another word. She sniffles and wipes her eyes with her shirtsleeve, leaving streaks of mascara. She stares into me as the elevator doors close.

■ ■ ■

Alison walks home in the biting cold. She stops in the middle of the sidewalk and is hit with the wrecking ball realization that she is absolutely nothing. Not a girlfriend, not a mother, not a daughter. Not a student. Not an employee. Not a wife or a sister or a best friend. She is nobody, inhabiting the nowhere between everything. No past. No future. No present. Nothing. *I do not exist.* Her mind burns.

I hate myself and I want to die. She runs various suicide scenarios in her mind. *This is complete fucking bullshit. All of this. Complete fucking shit. Fuck. Fuck you, Charlie.* It's not his fault. It's my fault. *Fuck you, Dad. FUCK YOU, DAD. It's your fault. I hate you and I hate myself and I want to die.*

But she will not give Dad that much freedom or Charlie that much pain. Dad, she figures, would probably be relieved that with her tragic demise he would no longer have to worry about a belated child molestation or rape case or victim compensation or whatever. Mind numb now, she enters the apartment and scours for alcohol but knows she will find none as all booze and drugs were cleared ages ago for temptation control purposes.

If Seven didn't exist, we would still be together. Still having fun and drinking and getting high. Why did he have to appear out of fucking nowhere, anyway? Where the fuck did he even come from?

Alison's mind is a storm.

Around 9:00 PM she calls Charlie and begs him to try one more time and he says a firm "no" in this weird condescending tone and when she hangs up she deeply regrets calling him and it hits her that this is actually over. She feels like a tiny, pathetic child. She sits in the middle of the living room and cries for a while and her roommate's not coming home tonight so she just sits there for what feels like ever. Thoughts rage like a torrent for a while then slow and eventually trickle to a stream. Finally, she dams her stream of consciousness.

She spends almost two hours just sitting there on the floor, mind a completely numb piece of unthinking rubber flesh. Brainwaves monotone like a dial tone. Eventually, past midnight, after more than 100 minutes without a single thought, an idea finally materializes:

I should have the baby. That will change his mind.

■ ■ ■

@realdemocracy tweeted
"if money doesn't mean anything, then there is no
civilization."
shantaram

■ ■ ■

37 DAYS BEFORE THE RESET

Mike steps out of his house into the frigid Connecticut morning. The Connecticut air smells damp, metallic and cold, like the inside of a meat freezer. His breath is visible and this brings back a memory of 6-year-old Alison at the window watching a familial group of deer nosing for browse and forbs at the edge of the woods by their home.

"I can see its breathing, Daddy!"

Things were a lot fucking simpler then. Before the girl became a taker. He misses Alison's body. Mike wonders if he could adopt another 9-year-old. A replacement for Alison. *Mike, you sick fuck!* He laughs to himself.

Gravel pops and crunches as an SUV makes its way toward the circular driveway. Once upon a time it was a Black Mercedes that made this daily run from Westport to Manhattan but Black Mercedes are magnets for protestors now. Bulletproof SUV is the new Black Merc.

It is 5:02 AM.

"Sorry I'm late, sir."

The driver rushes out to open the back door and Mike gets in, annoyed. He clicks on the interior passenger light and opens his work e-mail. 382 unread messages and 6 new voicemails.

Normally Mike gets around 200 e-mails overnight and he has given strict instructions to Hong Kong and London: "Do not call me

303

unless it is a fucking emergency" so obviously something big is going on. A quick flick through the messages and he quickly sees that yes indeed, it is something very fucking major.

There was a liquidity black hole last night and oil dropped from $60 to $25 in about 10 seconds. It rebounded and is now trading back around $54. These liquidity black holes have become a daily occurrence now. One day it's oil. The next day AAPL. Then bonds. Or HYG. When the entire ecosystem is built from AI and machine learning algorithms, all coded using data collected over the past few years, there is too much similarity in the strategies and the crowd looks for the same exit all at once. The microstructure is unstable; the entire system is fragile and it is getting worse.

Capital markets no longer serve their original purpose. Once upon a time, for example, the stock market was a place where companies raised money to support investment, innovation and new ideas. Now it is an abstracted cartoon version of its original self. Companies issue stock so founders can cash out and then the company issues debt to buy its own stock back to push the stock price higher so that owner-management can double dip and get paid even more.

Investors do not invest in management or good ideas or great products. They invest in factors and baskets and indices.

Silicon Valley forms companies that have no intention of ever earning a profit. The model is to get exponential customer growth by selling your product below cost. Pay for it all with VC and stock option-based compensation and promise later stage investors you will be profitable once you hit scale. Then, do one last round of financing at a bloated valuation, IPO to the suckers in retail and move on to the next scheme. Ponzi finance has gone mainstream.

■ ■ ■

29 DAYS BEFORE THE RESET

I have known Seven for about 13 months now and can barely remember the days before. I get excited to see him when he returns home from school. The Charlie that used to get high all the time is another kid from another time. I broke up with Alison and I am getting on with my life now. The jonesing has subsided completely other than this one recurring dream:

I roam an alternate, even more-dilapidated Manhattan in the wee hours; somewhere in SoHo, it looks like. I climb up a fire escape and into a cluttered, candle-lit apartment. There is graffiti on the walls and very little furniture. Wiry shirtless dudes snort lines of gray / white powder off the bottom of a skateboard without wheels. Music pulses. I can't find my dealer anywhere. I ask everyone but nobody knows where he is. Nobody will sell me any powder.

I sense there is a shortage but nobody explicitly says so. The apartment is infinitely large, with infinite halls leading to infinite rooms. Nobody in any of the rooms knows where my dealer went. I feel more and more frustrated. I call out and my voice echoes.

"Danny? Where are you, Danny? Danny!!!"

I yell but nobody pays much attention to me. The dream goes on for hours.

I've been trying to focus on my trading but the market has become impossibly random. Algos feeding on other algos and liquidity has become impossible to access. It is like a house of mirrors where every price is just a reflection of every other price. You try to sell and the price moves lower. You try to buy and the price moves higher. Machine learning bots battle other neural network bots but 90% of the data in the world was collected in the past two years so they all have extreme recency bias. When everyone is running the same algorithm, nobody wins.

The market is more chaotic than ever. 7% daily moves in the stock market and 5% in commodities are commonplace. Single names move 10% or 15% for no reason. Liquidity black holes are increasingly common. Every day there is at least one stock that flashes 99% lower or else triples or quadruples on short covering. When volatility goes up like this, correlations used to go to one; but this time it is disordered. Currencies sell off when a central bank hikes rates. Crude and copper trade with equities but palladium, zinc and silver are inversely correlated. It is impossible to make sense of anything. Trading is always hard but it has officially become impossible. Random and intensely volatile.

"What should I dream about tonight, Dad?"

Seven asks me the same question every night right before I tuck him in.

"How about yellow dinosaurs with purple wings flying over a blue landscape filled with yellow cacti? And then they fly over water and pass six islands. Each island is in the shape of one letter of the word "island" so the islands spell "island". How's that?"

Seven smiles. I tuck him in. Life is not terrible. *I feel like a cigarette.* The thought enters my head like someone else's voice but fades quickly. I watch the thought form and dissipate like a drop of ink in water. The voices are still around but they are whispers, not shouts. Idiots dispensing transparently bad advice, not clever manipulators.

I tap into ↑Marketz!↓ and assess the landscape. Gold is up, copper is down, S&P futures are down 29 handles and oil is down almost 8%. It's 8:05 PM NYC time (8:05 AM in Tokyo). Some yelling in the streets outside. Another protest. It sounds pretty big. I'm dying for a banana but there have been no bananas in NYC for about two months now. Any shipment that comes in is scooped up right away.

People are severely freaking out about inflation now. Wages are exploding but prices are exploding more. It's not like before where it was just idiots on CNBC worrying about it. Now it's the main topic of conversation on the subway. In restaurants. Everywhere. The Fed can't keep up with the demand for paper money. Gold and diamonds are sold out.

Like internet stocks and Beanie Babies in 1999 or housing in 2005 or banks in 2008 or bitcoin in 2017, the Great Inflation has captured the imagination of the general public in a way that is not healthy. Inflation expectations, which ranged between 1% and 3% throughout most of US history, are now above 45%. Rescale that y-axis. When the Fed abandoned the 2% inflation target in favor of Real GDP and Price Level Targeting, the wheels came off and I don't think anything will get things back on track at this point. They need to hike rates, Volcker-style, but it's just not even in the Fed's vocabulary anymore.

For the millionth time in the past few weeks, I go back to thinking about this unborn baby. Thoughts race. I cannot let this decision go. It is not right. I cannot kill this tiny future human. I have no right. There is no good reason. I am being selfish. Seven saved me; I will save this baby. I have plenty of money. Plenty of time. This is an easy decision. I need to do what is right. I want to have the baby.

I text Alison:

We need to talk.

About what. I'm not ready.

About the baby.

There is a 30-second delay and then she texts back:

There is no baby.

I drop the phone on the table and it clunks. I run into the bedroom and bury my face in a pillow. Strange sounds come out of me as I lay face down on the bed and weep. Crazy, uncontrolled, guttural sobs. I cry like a young child for a long time. In a life with plenty of sad moments, I have never felt as sad as I do right now. I should never have let this happen. I have gone into the future and killed my own child. He will never go to school. Never get to fall in love. Never get to be cool.

I am so sorry Little One.

■ ■ ■

@realdemocracy tweeted
"capitalism without bankruptcy is like
christianity without hell."
frank borman

■ ■ ■

7 DAYS BEFORE THE RESET

Mark Guilford's wife has left. His hair is long, his beard is clumpy and he shakes when he discusses the day, three years ago, when four dump truck loads of documents dropped onto his driveway and front lawn in suburban Ridgewood, New Jersey. His co-writer on the expose about the Fed's secret stock market intervention program died in a car accident under suspicious circumstances last year.

His boss at Bloomberg, under pressure from his superiors and the Fed, fired Guilford more than six months ago. Now he devotes all his time to the most important project of his life. Unearthing the Black Room transcripts.

And he has finally done it.

First, he built a wood frame structure covering his entire half-acre backyard and then covered that structure with tarps to protect it from rain. He moved all the documents dumped by the trucks into this "temporary" structure.

His initial thought was to randomly sample the documents until he found something interesting but there were simply too many pages and too little context. So he devised another plan. He decided to scan everything straight onto the web and ask the Zeroheads to crowdsource the analysis. Zeroheads were urged to read a page or two whenever they had spare time and send a message to Guilford if they found anything interesting. He wasn't sure what kind of response he would get, but right away he was pleased to see the crowd was reading his scans faster than he could post them to the internet.

Using two hands to feed two high-speed scanners at once for an average of 14 hours/day, he uploaded thousands of page scans to the internet daily. It took less than a year for useful information and patterns to emerge.

He didn't need to write the story; it wrote itself.

First, documents established the existence of the Black Room Meetings, though the purpose of these meetings and the names of attendees were not clear for months. Then papers were scanned showing a trade confirmation. InfCap buys 25,000 ESU9 on the bid at

699.50. Bot another 25,000 at 699.00. Bot 100,000 ESU9 at 675.25. Some of the trade tickets were together in the huge pile of documents but some had become separated. Using the prices on the tickets and the contract dates, Guilford was slowly able to parse together a pattern. Each day the stock market fell aggressively 2008, Inflection Capital intervened. They bought S&P futures. In size. The Plunge Protection Team was real; the Federal Reserve illegally bought stocks to prop up the market.

Eventually, enough pages were scanned to put together a pretty clear picture of the Direct Equity Intervention Strategy. The Black Room attendees, who Guilford narrowed down to Bernanke, the Treasury Secretary and one other unknown member, sent their orders once per day, around 8AM to the execution trader in Grand Cayman. The instructions might give a limit to the amount of capital to spend or a specific level to defend in an index. The messages were short and cryptic on their own but as the context was more established, the missives were clear. "Reduce downside vol. 4B notional limit." "Defend 1000.00 SPX post TARP vote. 8B notional limit." "Engineer closing squeeze. 2B notional limit. Late headlines should help ;)." And so on.

The day after President Obama famously declared "What you're now seeing is profit-and-earning ratios are starting to get to the point where buying stocks is a potentially good deal if you've got a long-term perspective on it," the Black Room went on their biggest intervention spree ever, buying almost $50 billion of S&P futures in one day. As Guilford placed the messages in chronological order (as much as possible given the limited information available and lack of time stamps), it became clear that the Black Room's intent moved from a) limiting losses to b) stemming the fall in the stock market completely and finally to c) driving the market higher.

Communications in Q1 2009 gave the trader in the Caymans carte blanche for the first time, ordering for example: "Create upside momentum, no notional limit" as opposed to the prior directives which were focused on stemming losses. The execution trader obviously has a sense of humor as he finally floored the S&P at 666 on March 9th by bidding for infinity contracts via iceberg. His choice of levels for the absolute low in the S&P was probably an early sign that he wasn't 100% comfortable with the role he'd been asked to play in saving the financial system from its own suicide.

Guilford has irrefutable evidence and a tight story to tell. He finishes off his 1400-word bomb, addresses an e-mail to the head of editorial at Bloomberg and hits send. He screams the scream of a madman finally proven right. The scream of a madman who always knew he was not mad but was never quite sure either. *I am not insane. Thank you, God.*

■ ■ ■

4 DAYS BEFORE THE RESET

I wake up and flip on ↑Marketz!↓ Seventeen news alert e-mails. Something huge is going on. I secure my goggs and they scan my retinas. Log me in. My retina scans the first headline:

*FED INTERVENED IN US STOCK MARKETS IN 2008/2009.

Holy shit. The rumors were true.

S&P futures are down 45 handles as the market reads this as bearish. I look at a 5-minute chart and wish I had been awake because the initial knee-jerk reaction was to buy stocks on the headline. The rally lasted about 45 seconds and I would have known it was a screaming sell. This is extremely bad news for the stock market. Loss of confidence in policymakers; the end of central bank omnipotence. The Bernanke Put was real but now everyone knows why, so the trick can never work again. The illusion of strong markets was a lie. A hoax. The invisible fist of the authorities, right up the ass of capitalism.

*FED INTERVENED REGULARLY AFTER 2008 BUT RECENTLY HALTED INTERVENTIONS.

This would explain the wicked, high-velocity drops in the stock market recently. Traders couldn't understand why things had become so violent of late. Buy the fucking dip is still always the mantra but the buy-the-dippers' faith is being tested. Now we have learned that the only reason that BTFD was a viable strategy is because the Fed was always there, on the bid, even after the end of the crisis. With the Fed gonzo, the downside is the weak side. Massive.

The omnipotence of central banks is no longer a thing. The illusion of a system built on something real is breaking. Everyone is realizing, all at once, that this capitalist miracle was all just a Ponzi scheme. It only works as long as you pile more debt on top of the old debt and then lie and manipulate the markets if they fail to cooperate. But the whole edifice is based on faith. On illusion. Faith is gone.

The emperor's balls are showing.

45 handles is nothing; the market should be down at least 100. I go to spam the sell button and get short the stock market but then realize there is no point. It's over. Soon, there will be no stock market.

▦ ▦ ▦

2 DAYS BEFORE THE RESET

"Another long fucking week but the good guys win this battle."

Mike talks to himself as he stumbles up the driveway. It is after 2:00 AM. He stops and stares at the looming black shadow of his huge stone home. It is a source of outward pride for him but also a subconscious source of embarrassment. A grotesque temple to everything that has gone wrong with Mike Leary's life. With Mike Leary's mind. A total disconnect from anything he ever hoped for or aspired towards. He wanted a cool car and a fun life and instead he got this. A seven-point-nine-million-dollar prison and a batshit crazy, cracked polystyrene wife. He needs to get a divorce so bad but let me just wait until stocks bounce and I can think about something else. One shitshow at a time here.

The coke and Johnnie Walker thump through Mike's veins but it is not a fun buzz. It is a dark, paranoid vibration, pulsating in his mind. He is alert, but sad. Wired and anxious. Exhausted of body but stimulated of mind. He wants to go to sleep but he knows he'll be up until 3:00 AM buzzing on this speedy blow and then he will get two shitty hours of sleep before he has to get up and be out the door when Taj picks him up at 5:00 AM. There's almost a full gram of blow left in the baggie in his shirt pocket and it would be such a waste to toss it, so he rips the baggie open and dumps its contents onto the back of his hand. He snorts it all sloppy.

Half on my face, half up my nose and half on my hand.

He laughs out loud. His mind is not right. The powder burns a few new holes in his sinuses and he licks up the remaining crumbs. He is a righteous mess.

This afternoon's events flash through his head in random order. The protesting gunman outside the building. Mike ducks behind a parked Escalade. Shots ring out, six or seven. Yelling and cops rushing everywhere. The CEO of SquidCo is gunned down. Mike saw him take two quick bullets to the chest and one through the forehead. Cops fire back. Gunman dead. There will be a celebration at the #occupy encampments tonight. Mike's boss is gone. The big fish is dead.

He should have been on his way home after that but without a second thought he speed dials one of his old brokers.

"Yo. Bruceee. We're out."

"What are you talking about, mate? I've got two kids now. And a wife."

"Me too, man. I said we're out. Meet me at O'Reilly's in half an hour and bring some gear."

Bruce is not amused but Mike has done so much business with him over the years he feels kind of obliged. Mike has essentially put Bruce the Broker's kids through school, as he funneled an absolute cartload of business through Bruce back in his big swinging dick trader days—back when Bruce was just getting started. And Bruce is a loyal guy. He owes Mike.

The broker / trader relationship is full of co-dependence and Mike and Bruce are no exception. When they were younger and things were different, they had some amazing times. Ate at the best restaurants, watched the best live music, partied like rock stars and all that. Bruce used to say he liked to bend New York over and make her come. Bruce demurred to Mike without being Mike's bitch. He was a good wing man. He'd set up a joke:

312

"Hey Mike: What's your favorite animal?"

"Steak."

Or

"This hedge fund portfolio manager walks into a bar," Mike starts.

"The bartender says: What'll be?" Bruce continues then leaves the punchline for Mike.

"I'll have whatever everyone else is having!"

Laughter. *Silly hedge fund sheep.*

Bruce would let himself or his wife be the butt of a joke too, when necessary:

"Hey Bruce: What do your wife's mouth and a birdcage both have in common?"

"I dunno Mike. Tell me."

"They've both had a cockatoo in them!" Then Mike would turn to the assembled crowd of Wall Street douchenozzles and say, "Make me a market on how many dicks have been in his wife's mouth guys! I'm 10/15 on the open."

Markets would be made. Laughter and no hard feelings. Bruce was a good friend. Went to Mike's wedding. Played golf with him a lot. There was the time Mike needed a drinking buddy at the last minute after The Wife called him late one afternoon to report that Alison (age 7) had a tantrum earlier that day and broke a $600 vase.

"Bruce, I need to grab a few drinks tonight. Join me?"

"Sure, Mike-oh, what's the occasion?"

"Ah nothing really. I'm gonna slap my daughter in the face tonight and I need a few drinks to loosen up beforehand. Never done it before so you know. It'll make things easier I think."

Tonight Bruce and Mike do a few lines in the bathroom and try to bring back old times but old times are gone. Clocks rotate in only one direction. Bruce feels sad for Mike. He looks like shit. Slurring already at 9:15 PM. Drinking to get hammered. The night drags on late and soon Bruce struggles to keep up with Mike's drinking and to put up with his bullshit. Around midnight, he pulls out the last two g's of blow and hands them to Mike.

"Listen, Mike. Great to see you, man. Awesome to catch up. I'm glad to see you're doing well. Global Head of Trading. Fuck man. Who would have thought?"

Mike manages a weak smile then bangs back the rest of his Johnnie Walker.

"C'mon man. We're having fun. Like old times."

"Yeah, like old times. Later, Mike-oh."

Bruce walks out of the bar without looking back.

"Bruceeee! Bruce! C'mon man! Don't go!"

The bar door closes and Bruce is gone.

"Fucker."

Random conversations clatter around Mike like the sound of a hundred TVs. The room swirls a little bit and light from outside mixes with the darkness inside. The place smells of cologne and female sweat and pheromones. For the first time, it really sinks in that his boss has been murdered. Things are not getting better.

"I need to get home," Mike says to himself.

He pays the bill and walks outside.

He finds Taj waiting. New wheels, as per Mike's request. A modded cherry red Tesla SUV with gigantic, fuck-you rims. Gorgeous. It attracts longing male stares, like a cheerleader eating a banana.

He would love to grab a nap on the way home but of course his brain is firing like a mouth full of pop rocks. Annoying. The lit city floats by outside the SUV and Mike drifts around in and out of various states of consciousness. Wired. Tired. Lit. Awake. Yawning. Jittery. Exhausted.

And then he's home snorting the last g off the back of his hand.

If they ever legalize coke, I'm going to open a store called "Powder and Crumb".

He manages to deactivate the home alarm with minimal fanfare. He strips off his clothes and throws them on the bathroom floor. Exhausted, he doesn't bother to brush his teeth. He wants to see Alison. Feel her. But she's been gone for almost a year. He never bothered to cancel the credit cards. *I still love you, Alison. I really do.* He crawls into bed, making sure he doesn't touch The Wife or wake her. He checks the clock (3:08 AM) and miraculously falls asleep right away.

BEEP BEEP BEEP. Two seconds later, it's 5:01 AM. His head is a pillowcase full of tin cans but he has done this so many times before it's no big deal. Ignore the bad thoughts and go about your day. Ignore the bad thoughts and go about your day. That is the hungover mantra. He gropes his way downstairs and pours himself a huge glass of tomato juice. As one might use tomato juice to wash the smell of skunk off a dog, Mike uses it to mask the smell of stale booze and cigarette smoke inside his dirty mouthhole.

This is going to be one hell of a day, he guesses.

He has no fucking clue.

> @realdemocracy tweeted
> "stability leads to instability...
> the longer things are stable, the more unstable they will be
> when the crisis hits."
> *hyman minsky*

■ ■ ■

The protesters are no longer just disaffected geeks and faggots and weirdos and homeless guys. There is an intellectual firepower to the throng that was lacking even a few months ago. As financial markets convulse, foreign currencies sky, the dollar is vaporized and the Global Finance Ponzi unravels at a previously unthinkable and still accelerating pace, this penultimate Minsky Moment has brought young professionals, retirees, students and older intellectuals into the streets. The government's decision to cut off the internet has proven disastrous, though we have no counterfactual and it may well be the pace of the unraveling is now beyond anyone's control. Packs of angry, disturbed and confused individuals in the streets have no proper agenda or direction until the hive mind slowly makes the decision to parade downtown. Into Zucotti. They circle the statue of Ben Bernanke. They stare up at his bearded visage. One of them yells:

"Take down the statue!"

"Yeah!"

"Tear it down?"

"Tear it down!"

"TEAR IT DOWN! TEAR IT DOWN!"

8,000 chanting now. Mostly 17 to 40-year-olds. Dressed in lululemon (NASDAQ: LULU), Banana Republic and Old Navy (NYSE: GAP). Extremely pissed off, but kind of having fun. You know how it is with protesting. It's exciting. But goddammit, we're mad too. We assure you we are not having fun but since this Best Buy (NYSE: BBY) has no windows anyway, we might as well take a few smartphones, right (NASDAQ: AAPL)?

Police checkpoints are instantly overwhelmed. The cops have no desire to shoot or harm the protestors. Most of the cops are as pissed off as the throng. Four-day work weeks and part-time hours. Pay as you go medical. What is this, fucking Walmart (NYSE: WMT)? Officer McCarthy takes his uniform shirt off and joins the protesters now. He's still got his pants, belt, gun and policeman's hat on but a shirtless cop is instantly non-threatening and adds to the carnival atmosphere, Village People-style.

"This is the most fun I've had in years," says a washed-up munis trader just before he's pulled under the heaving crowd and trampled nearly to death.

"Fucking A."

"Let's pull down those video cranes."

"Fucking A."

The cranes come down. Falafel huts invert. Cop cars sway. General civic destruction. Fruit flies. A hungry teen miraculously spots an apple flying towards him and catches it like a foul ball at a Mets game. He bites through its taut flesh and really, really tastes it. Feels the skin snap in his teeth and the spray of juice on his gums and in the back of his throat. He briefly takes a moment to wonder why apple juice tastes so dramatically different from the juice of an apple—

There is a unisonic cheer from the crowd. They have managed to unmoor the Ben Bernanke statue and have started to rock it back and forth. Fifty or sixty on each side of the 7X7 granite cube now. Push-ing. Getting the rhythm so the thing starts to rock a bit. Then some more. Then a lot.

The pushers on the near side need to scatter but it's New Year's Eve crowded and a few can't get out of the way as the multiple tons of granite and bronze go from ninety degrees to zero degrees in about 3.2 seconds. Four or five people are pinned underneath and Samaritans gather. An ad exec got 99.5% out of the way but the very edge of his shoe is pinned under the thing. *OWW!* He screams in pain. He manages to rip his foot out, leaving his pinkie toe inside the shoe which remains pinned underneath the huge stone cube. He is surprised how much blood spurts from the hole of the missing toe but then again feels lucky compared to the lady with the crushed spine whose shoulders and head stick out from under the fallen statue.

There are no sirens. Help is not on the way.

■ ■ ■

Mike walks around the perimeter of his office with the demented zoochosis of a caged lynx. He looks out at Central Park and sees hundreds of cops lined up at every entrance. The park has become a magnet for the homeless and the mayor's strategy is to keep them out via NYPD force. The original Tarp City on Sheep Meadow became such a political and logistical nightmare that the mayor vowed there would be no repeat. The Attack on Sheep Meadow, as the police action a few months ago was labeled, had been trouble-some on many levels.

Mike is concerned about his division's ability to manage its risk. S&Ps are down 275 handles now and the Fed has admitted that the stock market intervention story is true. This is extremely bad news. No stress test could have accounted for these moves and there is a non-zero chance his firm is going down like Lehman Brothers. The vol market is shut and credit markets are a total abortion. The firm's stock is down 45% today. Mike flashes back to last night. The bullet rips through the CEO's forehead over and over in his mind. Limp body falls to ground. $7,000 suit, wrecked.

Mike observes there is a good 25 feet between him and the large glass window and this might allow him to run full speed and jump into and through it. The fantasy turns dour as he visualizes himself running full speed, jumping shoulder first, cannonballing into the window and bouncing off. His right temple hits the glass, hard, and he falls to the ground on the conference room floor. Coworkers surround his unconscious body and everyone points and laughs. If he knew the glass would break, he might try. But he doesn't.

The CNBC ticker scrolls across the bottom of the TV screen:

Oil futures down 30%.

XLF cut in half.

Mike eyes the window again and tries to calculate the probability he could run through it. 70%? 80%? Imagine trying and failing. The embarrassment. He gags, then rushes to a recycling bin and retches. Partially digested lunch exits his stomach and splashes the bottom of the blue bin. The burrito he ate for lunch, some stomach acid and plenty of bile.

He staggers, looking for a tissue to wipe the acidic mucus dripping from his nostrils. He could wipe his nose with his sleeve but even in crisis, he does not want to stain the Armani french cuff. Yells of panic from the trading floor. Every face in sales and trading is ghost white, frozen. Staring up at CNBC.

Mike's mind goes blank. He takes two steps back and then sprints towards the plate glass window. He leaps and turns into it, shoulder first. There is barely an impact as he flies clean through. There is just a soft thud as he makes a perfect Mike-shaped hole in the window and cascades toward the cement below. He falls down, down, down like an intraday S&P futures chart.

Splat.

■ ■ ■

@realdemocracy tweeted
"in economics, things take longer to happen then you think
they will and then they happen much faster than you thought
they could."
rudy dornbusch

■ ■ ■

THE RESET

The S&P 500 drops fiercely now, cascading lower at such a rate that I can hardly process what's happening. My eyes flick to some other markets, oil, palladium, the dollar, gold, bonds... Markets move nonsensically. My brain cannot make any connections; it is a storm of numbers raining up, down and sideways. Correlation is shattered and prices walk randomly then sprint arbitrarily in every direction. Non-normal distribution of data. Obese tails. My brain spins and I briefly lose my mind the way you do when you have a fever of 104 degrees or when you say the same word over and over and over until it no longer has meaning.

Say it out loud: Bubble bubble bubble bubble bubble bubble bubble........

My P&L should be skyrocketing as I am now short 35,000 S&P e-mini futures and stocks are crashing but the dollar is falling so fast my P&L vaporizes almost as fast as it accumulates. In dollar terms, I am up almost $70 million now but as gold breaks higher through $75,000 then $150,000 USD an ounce my P&L in gold terms is barely rising. Markets move faster and gap more than at any time in history. I knew a few days ago it was time to stop trading. I should have cashed out a week ago.

There are trading halts galore. MSFT halted. Bond trading is halted. Crude oil trading is halted on the NYMEX. Bond trading resumes. Gold trading halted. And so on. This is way bigger than 1929 or 1987 or 2008. It is all impossible to deal with rationally. Untradeable.

This is it. The Reset is here. I will square up and get out. I hear sounds like war from the streets below. FIRE IN THE DISCO. I need to cash out before it's too late, get as much physical gold as I can and get out of here. This is it. It is finally happening.

Tyler Durden, Nouriel Roubini, Jim Rogers, Marc Faber, Martin Armstrong, Zeroheads, Myron Minsky, Kondratieff... Your day has finally come. The system is finally toast.

The President and The Chairman speak at a podium on TV but I have it on mute and besides, I know exactly what they're gonna say. The same thing the Bernank said in 2007. *It is contained. Nothing to worry about. Nothing to see here. Move along now.* The great irony of policymakers on TV telling you everything is fine is that the only time policymakers come on TV to tell you everything is fine is when you are totally fucked.

I send an order to cover my short and buy 35,000 S&P e-mini futures at market. The market gaps in 10% increments. Bid/offer is 5% wide. I await my fill. There is a time and a place for limit orders and a time and a place for market orders. When your mind is screaming GET ME OUUUUTTT!! at 145 decibels, it is time for a market order. When S&P futures are approaching the zero bound, it is time for a market order. When there are rocks flying through windows and elderly are trampled underfoot in the streets, it is time for a market order. I buy 35,000 S&P futures at the absolutely insane price of 52.25. The VIX breaks 1,000. S&P futures keep falling.

50.

40.

30.

20.

10...

S&P 500 futures oscillate between 10 and 20 now. Suspended like when a movie director drops the hero from the top floor of a skyscraper and then does the multicamera bullet time, freeze frame spin around move. There is a clear theoretical lower limit to stock prices and equity futures because common stock liability is limited to the price you pay for the stock. All the systems in place for individual stocks prohibit a price below zero. But what about the systems related to equity index futures? We are about to find out. It is a complete AI clusterfuck as the algos cannot identify or adapt to this regime. Most of them hit the autokill switch and turn off.

I want to cash out. This has been an amazing ride but I want to get off. Three years on the most awesomely ridiculous roller coaster in the world is bound to leave you feeling a tad nauseous and I am fully ready to hurl. I toggle to the cashier area and hit RELEASE FUNDS. I order my entire equity (now over $200 million, or 1200 ounces of gold) delivered in full. In physical gold via FedEx. I click SAME DAY RUSH DELIVERY, which costs about 20 ounces of gold extra but assures delivery of all my metal within two hours.

S&P futures break below 10.00. Every point is ten percent now so the moves are massive in percentage terms but also utterly meaning-less. We were above 800.00 less than three months ago. Near 3,000 less than two years ago.

FRA/OIS breaks 15,000.

This is the day I knew would come. I am fully prepared; I just need to act. The checkout procedure is taking forever, and it usually takes less than a second. Spinny wheels. Spinny wheels. Oh no. Do not DO NOT tell me ....

WITHDRAWALS HAVE BEEN TEMPORARILY SUSPENDED BY ORDER OF THE PRESIDENT AND THE CHAIRMAN. WE APOLO-GIZE FOR ANY INCONVENIENCE! THANKS FOR PLAYING ↑Marketz!↓

There is zero chance this suspension of withdrawals is temporary. Plate glass smashes outside. A woman screams. Horns, sirens and mayhem. I use the zoom feature on my goggs to get a closer look at the scene below. Sketchy dudes are everywhere, skittering like silver-fish. Looters emerge from bodegas with random handfuls of crap and I can tell from what people are carrying (pork rinds, Visine, pears) that all the good stuff is already gone. I text Alison.

The Reset is happening. Execute the plan.

She responds: *I know. Saw it on the news. Already picked up Seven from school.*

Even after we broke up, we agreed that if The Reset hit, we would still execute our "get out of NYC" plan together. Neither of us can do it alone. I have the transportation and she owns the cottage in

Canada. I am really glad to do this with Alison. I still love her. I just can't be with her.

Is Seven OK?

He's gogged in. Playing vids. He's fine.

See you at the boat.

My gold withdrawal from ↑Marketz!↓ will never get paid but at least I've stashed 1600 ounces in physical gold over the past couple of years; all is not lost. Only those who have collected ample physical or stashed wealth in non-extradition countries will prosper as the host organism perishes. Now I just need to travel 20 blocks north, on foot, through a riot. With 100 pounds of gold in a duffel bag. I remain stubbornly optimistic.

I text flatland:

"The Reset is on. Meet us at the boat."

"changed my mind, bro. got responsibilities here"

"You sure?"

"yeah positive"

"OK, text if you need. See you on the other side I guess."

"peace"

I'm still gogged into ↑Marketz!↓ and I watch as S&P futures hit 5, 4, 3, 2, and finally 0. They briefly flick into negative territory. Impossible. Surreal. CNBC headline:

*S&P FUTURES BREAK THE ZERO BOUND, HIT A LOW OF MINUS 4.

Then suddenly, every price feed in every market freezes. Nothing changes for about 10 seconds then every price is replaced with one word in big, red block letters ::::::::::: HALTED. Stocks, bonds, gold, oil, palladium. Everything. HALTED. The Fed's multi-decade Ponzi scheme finally bites the deflationary dust.

I scan the room for anything that might be missing from my go-bag. I grab a framed picture of Seven that Alison did up for my 27th birthday. I pull off my ↑Marketz!↓ goggs (cool souvenir / relic potentially?) and that's it. There's a picture of my dad. I will leave that behind. I need to move on.

I stand still for a few seconds.

I miss you, Dad.

I grab the picture, grab the go bag and drop in the three extra items. As I zip up the army green duffel bag, I catch a glimpse of the gold inside. It is full of power and potential energy, like a brand-new chainsaw or a matte black BMW M5. It is beautiful.

Chaos is come again.

I drag the duffel bag into the hallway and take one last look back at my apartment as the door hinges slowly shut. I have that feeling you get only as you take one final look back into an apartment you are about to leave for the very last time. A rapid-fire slideshow of memories as I turn and walk away.

The door clicks shut. Time folds back on itself and I feel future nostalgia for the current moment. I have a flash realization of how far I have come since I moved into this place. From degenerate coke addict to life-choosing dad in 24 months. Not too shabby. I feel an emotion I don't remember ever really feeling before: pride.

Two people wait for the elevator. A 60-ish woman with two gray cats in her arms and a teenager playing a video game. The woman's body language betrays impatience.

"Have you been waiting long?"

"Ten minutes. At least," she replies.

Shit. I'll have to take the stairs, not an easy task with this gold-filled duffel.

"Hey kid," I try to get the kid's attention but he's gogged-in. Doesn't seem to hear.

"You want to earn a quick ounce of gold?"

This snaps him out of his vidtrance. The power of gold. Dollar bills are a disposable commodity now, like toilet paper. They represent the failure of the system. The teetering edifice of electronic promises is crashing down. The shared illusion is shattered and what was once a store of value and means of exchange around the world has magically transformed, almost overnight, into meaningless scraps of paper. Gold represents truth, permanence, respect, integrity. A possible way forward. Half my bag is filled with bricks of $100 bills but the gold is on top and it's too much aggro and risk to toss the bills now. They might be cool souvenirs one day for Seven.

"Do I want to earn some gold? Fucking A, dude. I loves me some gold. What do you want? A blowjob or something?"

"No! Dude."

Jesus.

The woman pretends not to hear.

"Just help me carry this bag downstairs."

Together we lug the gold down one flight at a time, pausing on each landing for breath. My thoughts flick to the people trying to escape the North Tower in 2001. We finally make it to the bottom of the stairs and I zip open the bag and pull out an ounce of gold. As I give it to the kid, his pupils saucer.

"Dude, is that whole thing full of gold?"

I realize how stupidly careless I've just been. If this kid has a gun, I am screwed.

"No, no, it's bottles of water and shit."

"Right," he replies, totally unconvinced.

I hand the kid his payment and hurry out the back door of the stairwell and into the street. I look back and thank the kid and as the door shuts, I see him pull out his phone. But there is no service. No internet. No phone calls. No landlines. Everything has gone black.

The situation on 60th Street is worse than I expected. No sign of any police. The bodega is completely trashed. lulu has been looted; its front windows are smashed. Four armed guards stand in front, protecting The Gap and I notice that a few of the other big-name stores (AAPL, SBUX, BBBY) are still intact, guarded by private security. The only order is in the massive lineups outside the BofA and Chase branches. *Your money's gone, people. It's gone.* People run in all directions with random belongings, suitcases, plastic bags full of water bottles.

It's a warm day. No clouds. I smell the ripening of spring dirt.

I need to get to 80th Street. There are and will be no Lyfts and no taxis. Most streets are no longer passable as overturned newsstands and street meat carts block, along with the occasional flipped car or gushing fire hydrant. I smell grilled onions and chicken.

The duffel bag is so heavy I can barely move. I stop to rest my arms every 20 steps or so and worry about getting robbed. Nobody cares about me and my bag, though; I have nothing to worry about. A Latino nanny runs with a screaming white kid in her arms. I drag myself and the bag north through the madding chaos. Security outside the Ferrari dealership has trouble keeping its windows unshattered.

Blackhawk helicopters storm in at low altitude. They drop cubes of uncirculated $100 bills wrapped in plastic, attached to yellow parachutes. Dozens of these bricks of cash float slowly down toward desperate, outstretched arms. The Fed executes the final, desperate trick in its playbook. Money Drops in every major city, a last desperate move to get the economy back up and running. Greedy, desperate throngs rip packages open but the cash drops accomplish nothing. They can burn the money to keep warm, but otherwise it has no value.

■ ■ ■

@realdemocracy tweeted
"there is no means of avoiding the final collapse of a boom brought about by credit expansion. the alternative is only whether the crisis should come sooner as the result of a voluntary abandonment of further credit expansion, or later as a final and total catastrophe of the currency system involved."
ludwig von mises

■ ■ ■

Lines continue to build outside every major bank now and the panic on Wall Street has now spread to Main. As prices of goods continue to skyrocket and financial assets collapse, the US government assures stunned citizens that their dollars and bank deposits are perfectly safe and there is nothing to fear. 'This is a routine stock market correction', the Treasury Secretary assured worried investors just a few hours ago but now the Dow is halted, down 99.8% on the day. Bond trading has been halted. Currency markets are closed. The last trades in the currency market are said to have failed as the US dollar went into vertical decline. Clearing systems cannot not handle the extra digits. The final panic trades in the currency market were at rates of over sixty thousand US dollars for one Japanese yen and six million US dollars for one German neuemark."

Stock markets fall hard across the world but social order has not yet collapsed outside the USA.

■ ■ ■

@realdemocracy tweeted
"at the end fiat money returns to its inner value—zero."
voltaire

■ ■ ■

The crowds thin as I move west towards the Hudson. Duffel straps dig into my fingers. My legs and shoulders are numb but I make it. I arrive at the pier and it is oddly quiet. Some honking from multiple accidents on the West Side Highway and distant yelling but barely anyone is here. The air is filled with smoke from nearby building fires. A few men ready boats for travel. I walk up the pier and see the boat and then I see Alison and Seven standing there, waiting for me. Seven runs to me and hugs my legs. I rub his impossibly soft hair.

It is strange to see Alison here, like this. We officially broke up about a month ago and I have not seen her since. She stands totally motionless, except for her heart. She looks thinner and whiter than I remember. There is a big scratch on her arm. Dark eye circles. Her pupils look abnormally wide for a sunny day.

Her face is still beautiful, but sad and barren now, like a beach in winter. Then I notice it.

A small belly bump. Alison is barely but visibly pregnant. She reluctantly smiles and I smile and then tears gush from four eyes and we hug, hard. Her shoulder is soaked as I pull away and she apologizes:

"I'm sorry I lied about the baby. That was stupid and mean."

"I'm glad it was a lie."

She is the most beautiful thing in the world.

I hesitate for a sec. Then I tell her.

"You are the most beautiful thing in the world."

More hugging. Crying. Seven slips in between us, turns his head sideways and gently presses his right ear against Alison's belly; he knows what the bump represents.

Eight months ago, I put down $140,000 for a CoastRise 35 and a spot in the marina. The small houseboat has been sitting here at the pier, waiting for us. For this possible moment. Now we need to execute the plan. Get North to Ontario until the dust settles. 1010 news radio drones from inside the boat:

"The Canadian government has issued a statement welcoming American refugees but implores everyone to be patient and please use only legal border crossings. Those crossing illegally will be arrested, logged and deported and will permanently forfeit their opportunity to immigrate..."

"Let's go," I say.

We board the boat. Seven is excited. Alison is nervous. I am oddly calm.

■ ■ ■

flatland sits and listens to wnyc.com recap the shocking events of the day. national state of emergency declared by the federal government. nyse closed indefinitely. the external value of the us dollar uncertain with only thin black-market trading. gold skyrockets. the s&p breaks the zero bound. all trading halted. congress has authorized a temporary curfew from 8pm to 5am in an effort to maintain control. she turns off the radio.

it's 9:15 pm. flatland sits cross-legged on the floor. her index fingers make closed circles with her thumbs.

om.

she is completely numb but her mind will not stay quiet. she gets up and walks around. tries to quiet the thoughts. looks outside. small groups of cops huddled here and there, talking. nobody else. martial law.

"this is bullshit."

■ ■ ■

@realdemocracy tweeted
the time is now. real democracy begins tonight. everybody in the streets. don't let anybody stop you. step outside at exactly 10pm and walk to washington square park.

@flatland tweeted
surprise! free set, tonight. dress for fun. dress for a revolution. bring food and water. don't let anybody stop you. step outside at exactly 10pm and walk to washington square park.

■ ■ ■

at 9:59 pm, flatland walks out of her apartment with a backpack full of computer and sound equipment and a small, framed picture of mom and dad. she pulls two high-powered marshall amps behind her, stacked on a dolly. she says goodbye to her apartment and closes the door without locking it. she walks out into the warm spring night, puts on oversized headphones and keeps her head down.

she heads down macdougal street, toward washington square. cops at the end of the block turn to look. they approach.

"hey kid. what are you doing? get back inside."

flatland keeps her head down and keeps walking. the cops follow beside her.

"bitch. off the street. go home."

flatland keeps walking. she looks back and then ahead and sees a few, then several, then many people coming out of buildings up and down the street. not just kids. grey-haired intellectuals. moms. hipster neckbeards. jews, catholics, agnostics. kids in hoodies and jeans and girls in gas masks and all sorts of civilian and wild costumes. blacks, whites, latinos. there's a woman wearing multiple feather boas and a kid with a flashing led headband and pink adidas. the cops see the population streaming onto the street and back off flatland who still has not acknowledged them. she rolls on, past the empty speed chess tables and into the middle of the park. she quickly pulls out her gear and sets up an impromptu dj booth and speakers in the middle of the fountain that has been dry for months (to discourage homeless bathers).

by 10:20 the crowd is big but not massive, maybe 500 people. then it goes exponential, fast. the internet is spotty but not totally black. social media lights up with all sorts of cool pics and pretty soon it's viral and there is happy chaos—a full on rave / burning man event in the middle of the village. two sikorsky UH-60 black hawk helicopters rattle across the sky. 120 bpm happy house blares from flatland's amps and she lectures / raps like a preacher / emcee on the mic:

"peaceful revolution is here. the oligarchs are done. dance tonight and a new america will rise with the sun."

"lift your head up high! you are american!"

"the money illusion is shattered. welcome to the real world. welcome to real democracy"

"everyone who loves america: we will make america good again!"

and such. the crowd cheers. it is a beautiful thing. the first warm night in forever. the loamy smell of spring and warm air and hot dust and sweaty hope. beats echo around the square and soon attract thousands. some dance. others are just curious and worried and everyone wants to be part of this moment, whatever it is. nobody understands what is happening but everyone feels the gravity. all the wealth inequality and tech oligopoly and financial engineering and experimental monetary policy has created more and more pressure and now: kaboom!

there is a lot of unusual air traffic. not just choppers but f-16s and other warplanes, mobilized for reasons that are not yet clear.

washington square is the epicenter of the peaceful reset festivities. the gun shots here are celebratory. but in the rest of the city, chaos reigns. in the next 48 hours, looters and self-centered animals circle. they rape times square and remove every item of value in the rectangle drawn by 20th street, 3rd avenue, 50th street and 7th avenue. picture katrina, without the water. cops defect. every man for himself. the president has no good options and remains paralyzed by indecision until it's way too late. army is mobilized here and there to minimal effect. government authority is openly questioned. anarchy and chaos. guns and gold are currency.

■ ■ ■

@realdemocracy tweeted
wall street was a bug, not a feature of capitalism.
bug: meet windshield.
flatland

■ ■ ■

11 DAYS AFTER THE RESET — NORTHERN ONTARIO

The night air is damp and cold. Zero light pollution. I sit in silence with Alison by a fire outside a small, isolated cottage on a lake near Huntsville, Ontario. The fire burns hot and orange. It crackles. Alison curls into herself, shivering as I grab another brick of neatly bundled US $100 bills and place it in the glowing oven of embers. I stare at an image of Ben Franklin and watch as it slowly curls, blackens and disappears. We are burning money to stay warm.

"This is fucking insane, Charlie."

I'm too tired to respond verbally so I half smile and drop back into the janky lawn chair; it sags under my weight. Heat turns a tiny pocket of sap inside a log into vapor and an ember pops. Sparks firework. Alison turns and vomits into the grass beside her chair. I see ribs through her thin sweater as she buckles forward.

"Sorry," she spits.

"Don't be sorry."

Things have stopped getting worse; but it will be a long time before they get better.

Another pop from the fire. A meteoroid falls into the earth's atmosphere and streaks the black sky. I look at Alison to see if she saw but her eyes are fixed on the blaze. The light of the flame dances on her pale face.

"Do you think we're going to be OK? The four of us?" Alison asks. It seems like a thought, out loud, more than a question directed at me. The sentence drips with implications I am not yet ready to address.

I look at her calm face but then flash back to when she ransacked my apartment. Smashing glass. The spittle on her lips. Complete madness. She unconsciously puts both hands to her belly and I see another her: calm and crazy perfect beautiful. I have a vision of our newborn baby curled up naked on her bare milkwhite chest.

I don't know if we're going to be OK.

What do I say… Maybe? I can't tell the truth but I don't want to lie so I just say:

"I hope so."

THE END

Made in United States
Orlando, FL
10 February 2024

43409724R10200